AF560353

From Autocracy to Integration

Political Developments in Hyderabad State (1938–1948)

Lucien D Benichou

Orient Longman

ORIENT LONGMAN LIMITED

Registered Office
3-6-272 Himayatnagar, Hyderabad 500 029 (A.P.), India

Other Offices
Bangalore / Bhopal / Bhubaneshwar / Calcutta / Chandigarh
Chennai / Ernakulam / Guwahati / Hyderabad / Jaipur
Lucknow / Mumbai / New Delhi / Patna

ISBN 81 250 1847 6

Typeset in Aldine by
OSDATA
Himayatnagar, Hyderabad 500 029

Printed in India at
Novena Offset Printing Co.
Chennai 600 005

Published by
Orient Longman Limited
160 Anna Salai, Chennai 600 002

Contents

It is by now a familiar story that there exist personal and impersonal theories of history. On the one hand, theories according to which the lives of entire people and societies have been decisively influenced by exceptional individuals, or, alternatively, doctrines according to which what happens occurs as a result not of the wishes and numbers of unspecified persons, with the qualification that these collective wishes and goals are not solely or even largely determined by impersonal factors, and are themselves not wholly or even largely deducible from knowledge of natural forces alone, such as environment, or climate, or physical, physiological and psychological processes.

On either view, it becomes the business of historians to investigate who wanted what, and when, and where, in what way; how many men avoided or pursued this or that goal and with what intensity; and further to ask under what circumstances such wants or fears have proved effective, and to what extent, and with what consequences.

Sir Isaiah Berlin,
Historical Inevitability

Abbreviations

AICC	All India Congress Committee
AIML	All India Muslim League
APSC	Andhra Pradesh State Committee
AISPC	All India States' People's Conference
APSA	Andhra Pradesh State Archives
CPI	Communist Party of India
Dn	Deccan
FR	Fortnightly Report
HEH	His Exalted Highness, the Nizam
HSC	Hyderabad State Congress
HSNC	Hyderabad State National Conference
HSRA	Hyderabad State Reforms Association
INC	Indian National Congress
IOL	India Office Library
IRH	Interim Repository, Hyderabad Archives
NAI	National Archives of India
NMML	Nehru Memorial Museum and Library
PCC	Provincial Congress Committee
RHA	*Review of the Hyderabad Agitation*

Note: When more than one spelling exists, words transliterated from Urdu or Hindi and Indian names have been used in the rendering in which they are most commonly found in official records. Non-English words used are italicised only at first occurrence and appear in roman thereafter.

Preface and Acknowledgements

I first became interested in Hyderabad State when, during a trip to India in the late 1970s, I felt there were some parallels between what had happened in the former Portuguese colony of Goa in 1961 and the events which had taken place in Hyderabad in 1948: in both instances, the Indians had forcibly taken over an area which they regarded as an integral part of the nation.

In Goa, local acquaintances had explained to me that a certain amount of resistance to Indian intentions did exist at the time, but the might of the Indian Army had overwhelmed the Portuguese and pro-Portuguese forces. Besides, the Portuguese colony was a speck on the country's map, and it was generally agreed that, sooner or later, Goa would merge with India.

However, Hyderabad State was not the colony of a foreign power but an Indian princely State. It was not a tiny territory but was as large as England and Scotland together, with over 16 million inhabitants (in 1948). And yet, Hyderabad had been 'integrated' through army action and I wondered whether there had been any local opposition to this intervention. At that time I could not locate any independent study describing political developments in Hyderabad. The official version of the Government of India, not unexpectedly, made no mention of any popular resistance to its 'liberating' army. Various writings, ranging from general accounts regarding the integration of princely States to memoirs by local participants in the 'freedom struggle', generally tended to assert that the entry of the Indian Army in 1948 had been welcomed by all but a handful of 'fanatics', who had been easily defeated in a mere five days. Casualties as a result of the so-called 'police action' were reported as minimal. The overall picture was one of democracy and integration smoothly replacing autocracy and isolation.

But some nagging questions persisted in my mind. Had there been absolutely no popular resistance to the marching Indian army? If, as asserted in most Indian historical writings, there really had been no resistance, what was the reason? Was it merely democratic aspirations among the people of the State, in the context of Indian independence? Or had there been broader events at the social, economic and political levels which had resulted in disaffection with the Nizam's regime?

But, before I could attempt to find any answers, I had to obtain a clear idea of what exactly had been happening in Hyderabad during the years before the Indian Government's intervention. And it seemed to me that 1938, the date of the first serious instance of popular agitation against the Nizam's regime, would be an appropriate starting point.

One of my main concerns, at first, was whether I would be hampered in my goal by the fact that I did not know Urdu, the official language of Hyderabad State. However, preliminary inquiries with scholars familiar with the Andhra Pradesh State Archives at Hyderabad—Professor J.F. Richards (Duke University), Professor I. Leonard (University of California, Irvine), Professor H. Gray (School of Asian Studies), Dr V.K. Bawa (Hyderabad)—and a rapid assessment of archival material at Hyderabad, Delhi and London, reassured me of the viability of the project as there was ample material available in English, both published and unpublished.

Senior officials, who had headed the Revenue, Finance and Police departments throughout the period I proposed to study, had been British, and all their departmental correspondence had been issued in English. Further, there had been, since 1853, a permanent British Resident in Hyderabad whose duties included the dispatch of a Fortnightly Report to the Political Department of the Government of India in Delhi, describing all political, social and newsworthy events occurring in the State.

With internal tension in the country increasing from the late 1930s onwards, the Political Department had also compiled ongoing files from Residency reports on most of the important political developments in Hyderabad State.

A great deal of this material is available at the India Office Library in London. Of course, some caution had to be exercised in studying it, as any account given by the Resident and the Political Department would obviously represent British opinion. Nevertheless, I felt that the British files could be relied upon to be reasonably accurate at least regarding chronology and statistics. Indeed, the Resident's Fortnightly

Reports alone, from approximately 1911 to 1947, provided many hours of very exciting and rewarding reading.

Compared to the India Office Library, the Andhra Pradesh State Archives proved to be disappointing. The Tarnaka Repository contained a wealth of printed Government reports (on revenue, education, agriculture, trade, communications and so on) which were naturally of interest but, like most such reports, were somewhat lifeless and gave little information regarding actual political developments. I was told that the Interim Repository at the Hyderabad Secretariat contained more directly relevant material—the files of the Home Department of the former Hyderabad Government in particular—but there were no proper indexes or catalogues to these files. The most promising ones seemed to be missing and I could achieve little in the time I could spend in Hyderabad. In both Repositories, however, the staff did their best to help me and for this I am grateful. During my stay in Hyderabad, I was fortunate enough to meet various people in all walks of life who had much to say about what they remembered of that period, some eminent scholars of Osmania University from whose knowledge I greatly benefitted, and many others who made me feel welcome with inimitable Hyderabadi hospitality. My special thanks are due to: Mr M. Asadullah Khan and Mr H. Ansari (and through them to Mr Jah), Mr M. Latif, Professor L. R. Penna, Dr G. Pandey, Professor Sarojini Regani, Dr M.A. Khan, Mr (former Justice) Ekbote, Dr V.K. Bawa, Mr Zahir Ahmed, Pandit Krishna Dutt and Mr Tyabji. I also thank Ami Chand & Sons of Secunderabad and Mr Mohammad Safiullah for their kind permission to reproduce their excellent photographs in this book.

At the National Archives of India in Delhi, I was able to consult some unpublished documents of various departments of the Government of India—Foreign and Political Departments, Internal Branches A and B in particular, which dealt with relations between the British, the Government of India and the princely States—as well as some copies of documents from the Hyderabad Residency.

In Delhi, the resources of the Nehru Memorial Museum and Library were most useful. They included papers of political and religious organisations—All India Congress Committee, All India States' People's Conference, All India Hindu Mahasabha—and private collections. For all their help, I thank in particular: Dr D.E.U. Baker (St Stephen's College, Delhi University); Professor R. Kumar,

Mr S. Mahajan and the staff of the Nehru Memorial Museum and Library; Professor Rasheeduddin Khan (Jawaharlal Nehru University); Ms Kapadia and the staff of the National Archives of India.

After I reached London, it seemed as if the further away I was from Hyderabad, the richer the resources. I spent my time in London mostly at the India Office Library with the exhilarated feeling of a fossicker who has finally struck gold. There I discovered all the Fortnightly Reports of the Hyderabad Residency impeccably classified, as well as the parallel files of the British and Government of India departments. The European Manuscripts Section contained three important collections of papers of former British officials connected with Hyderabad. My stay in London was by far the most fruitful, and I am most grateful to Dr Richard Bingle and the staff of the India Office Library, and to Mike and Vanessa Hawkins for their kind help and hospitality.

In Australia, my greatest debt is to Dr H.F. Owen who first roused my interest in South Asian history and, over the years, encouraged me towards this book. I am most grateful to him for his constant interest, friendship and patience. Professor Peter Reeves, Dr Ken McPherson, Dr Gill MacDonald, Dr Brian Stoddart, Ms Sue Simon and many others were most generous with their time and advice and deserve my heartfelt thanks.

My thanks are also due to the Australian Commonwealth Education Department which provided me with a Postgraduate Research Award and to the History Department of the University of Western Australia for its subsidy towards travel costs and research. I would also like to thank Ms Phyllis Langley and Ms Pamela Low who, as secretaries to the History Department, were most helpful and sympathetic.

Ms Mary Alexander of the Reid Library, as well as Ms Ko and all the staff, rendered invaluable help in tracing material and helping me to obtain it through inter-library loans.

My most grateful thanks to Ms Nancy McKenzie who kept a warm and cheerful composure even when faced with the awesome task of deciphering and typing my manuscript, and to Mr Viv Forbes who drew the maps and assisted me in the reproduction of photographs.

The publication of this book would not have been possible without the help of Mr Mahmood bin Muhammad and Dr V. K. Bawa of Hyderabad whose wonderful warmth and encouragement, many years after this thesis was completed, finally led to fruition. I also want to thank Orient Longman Ltd and Ms Nandini Rao in particular for accepting my manuscript and showing great forbearance with me throughout the prepatory stages of the publication.

Finally, my greatest debt is to my wife, Jaye, who suffered stoically through my years of absent-mindedness.

HYDERABAD STATE AND INDIA
N
Delhi
INDIA
Calcutta
Bombay
Hyderabad
ARABIAN
SEA
BAY
OF
BENGAL
Madras
INDIAN
OCEAN
1938–1948 boundary
Hyderabad State

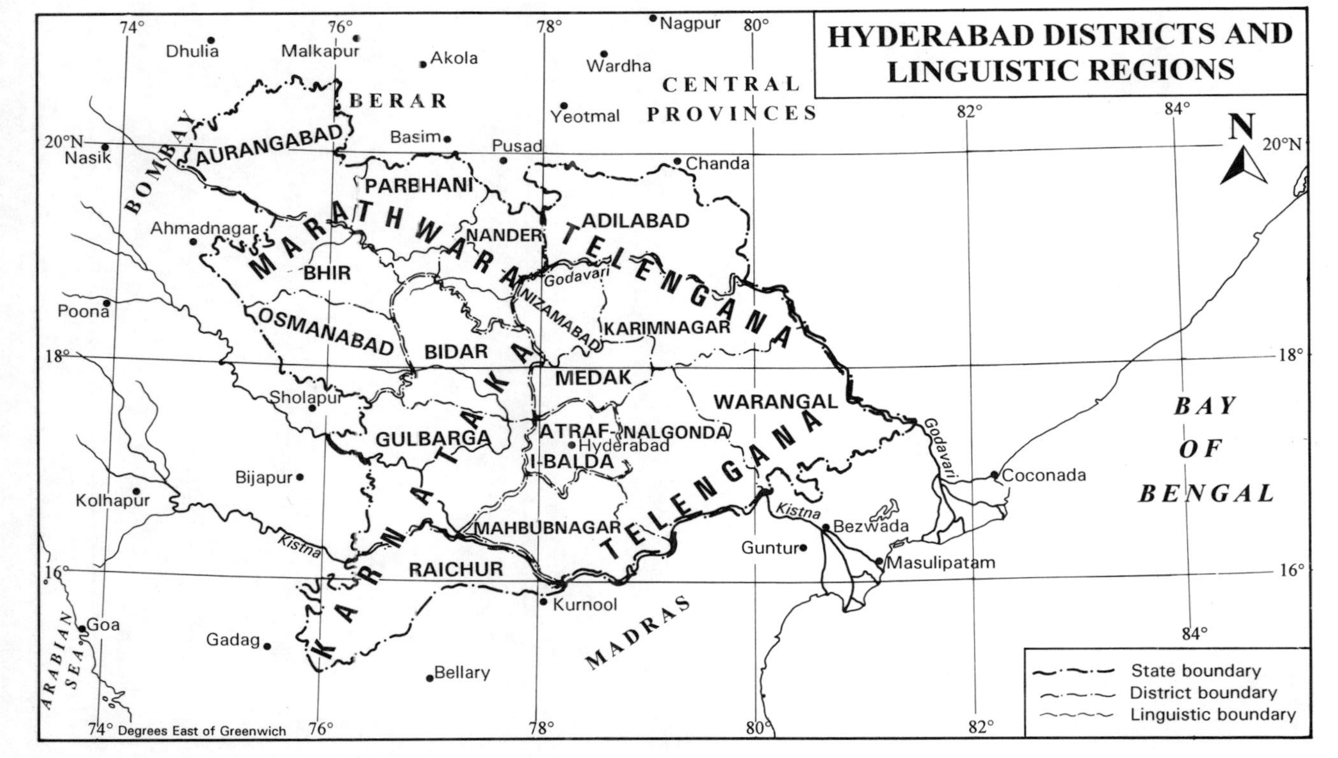
HYDERABAD DISTRICTS AND
LINGUISTIC REGIONS
N
CENTRAL
PROVINCES
BERAR
BOMBAY
MADRAS
BAY
OF
BENGAL
ARABIAN
SEA
MARATHWARA
TELENGANA
TELENGANA
KARNATAKA
KARNATAKA
AURANGABAD
PARBHANI
NANDER
BHIR
OSMANABAD
BIDAR
ADILABAD
NIZAMABAD
KARIMNAGAR
MEDAK
WARANGAL
ATRAF-
I-BALDA
NALGONDA
GULBARGA
MAHBUBNAGAR
RAICHUR
Nagpur
Wardha
Yeotmal
Dhulia
Malkapur
Akola
Basim
Pusad
Chanda
Nasik
Ahmadnagar
Poona
Sholapur
Bijapur
Kolhapur
Goa
Gadag
Bellary
Kurnool
Hyderabad
Guntur
Bezwada
Masulipatam
Coconada
Godavari
Godavari
Kistna
Kistna
74°
76°
78°
80°
82°
84°
20°N
18°
16°
74° Degrees East of Greenwich
State boundary
District boundary
Linguistic boundary

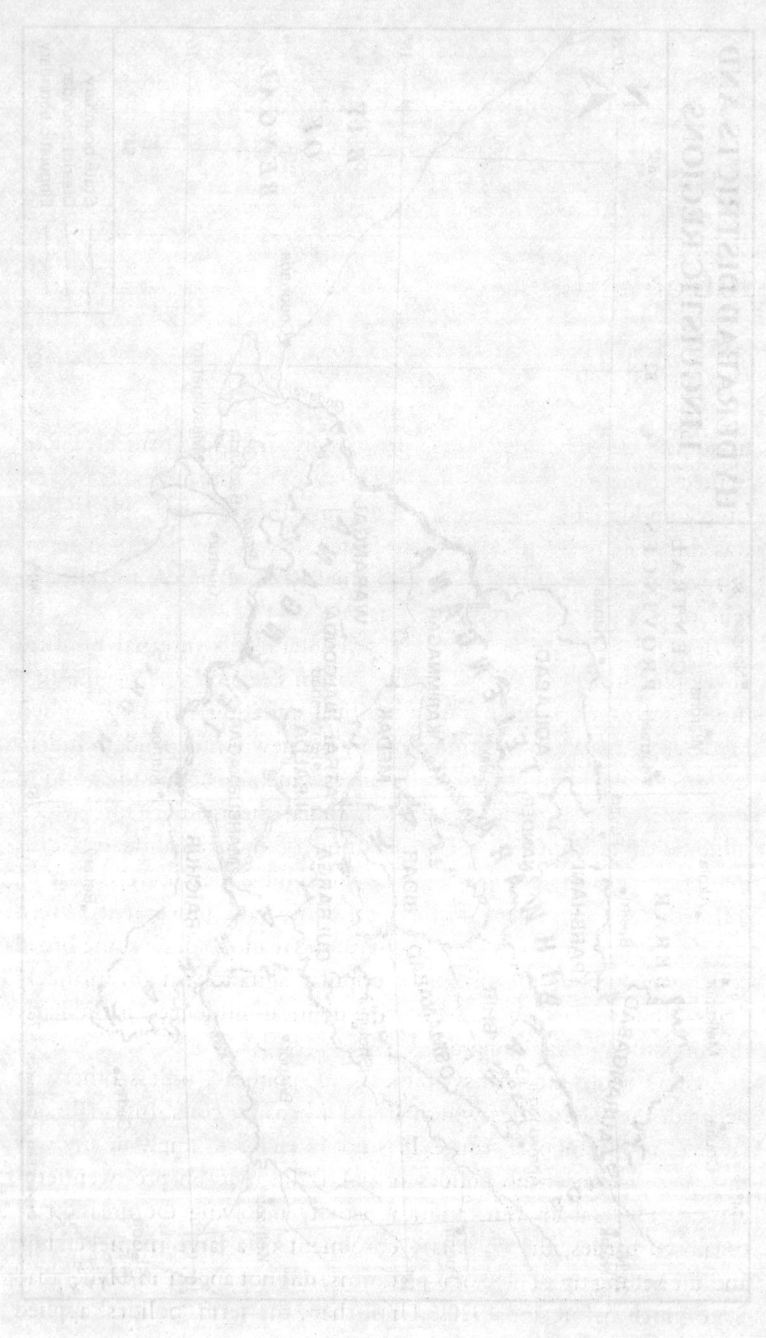

Introduction

In some ways, Hyderabad was the archetypal Indian princely State. In the twentieth century its ruler, the Nizam, still had autocratic powers largely undiluted by constitutional reforms. In other ways, Hyderabad was different from other princely States. It was the largest in terms of revenue and population,[1] 'the premier State of India', and the last relic of Muslim rule in the Deccan.

Because of these characteristics, Hyderabad's internal political development from 1938 (when the Nizam's regime was for the first time confronted with popular political agitation) to 1948 (when Hyderabad was taken over militarily by the newly-independent Indian Union) vividly highlights the differences which existed in the political atmospheres of princely and British India; the main factors which inhibited or encouraged the penetration of Indian nationalist ideas into princely India; and the extent to which these ideas were similar to, differed from, or influenced the local democratic movements. From a study of these features, an attempt can be made to draw some broad conclusions about the origin of popular agitation in the princely States, and the part played by outside political influences, particularly the Indian National Congress.

In this book, the terms 'politics' and 'political', unless otherwise defined, mean activities which are of a broadly constitutional, agitational, or institutional nature. It is not intended to imply in any way that there had been no politics or political activity in pre-twentieth-century Hyderabad. But, political activity involving the creation of organised parties, the voluntary enrolment of a large memebership, and the setting up of electoral platforms, did not appear in Hyderabad State much before the 1920s. Until then, the term 'politics' applied mainly to the interactions between the various centres of internal power—the Nizam, the members of his Council and the British, as well as the power relations between social classes—rather than to the activities of political organisations as such.

Politics, thus, followed a particularly intricate pattern in Hyderabad. The State was dominated by a Muslim minority ruling over a predominantly Hindu population and, from 1938 at least, communalism, with the resultant antagonism between the Hindu and Muslim communities, clouded all political issues. The reaction of the Muslims to Congress and Hindu militancy in the State is of particular historical interest, as it gave rise to the formation of a local Muslim political party devoted to the maintenance of princely rule. At the time the only party of its kind and size in India, it reflected the feelings of Muslims towards the prospect of 'Congress Raj' and indicated the place which communalism came to occupy in the politics of some of the princely States.

In the circumstances, it is difficult to establish whether the local 'popular' movement for constitutional reforms and responsible government in Hyderabad can be understood merely in terms of its avowed political aims or whether it should be seen as a parallel to the communal conflict in British India between the Indian National Congress and the Muslim League. Can this movement be considered a part of the Congress struggle for freedom? This is how it has overwhelmingly been presented by Indian historians and chroniclers, those of the 'Freedom Struggle Series' in particular. Or, was it a local movement expressing the ambitions of some Hindus of the State to overthrow the Muslim ruling elite, for their own purpose and not necessarily in the context of the all-India freedom struggle?

The issue was further complicated by a number of other factors: the emergence and success of the Communists in Telengana (the eastern half of the State) who opposed but later allied with the 'reactionary' forces supporting the Nizam's rule; a short idyll between the Socialists and the Hyderabad State Congress; the pervading and unpredictable influence of the Nizam; the consummate art of the paramount power at pulling strings from behind the scenes; and the shrewdness of Mahatma Gandhi at some crucial moments. It was to take a decade of internal conflicts often manoeuvred from outside, of an utterly unrealistic stance adopted by the local Muslims in a steadily deteriorating communal atmosphere, for the 'Hyderabad case' to mature.

By 1947–48, Hyderabad was one of the three princely States which continued to refuse accession to India as demanded by Sardar Vallabhbhai Patel and the Government of India's States Department. The other two were Junagadh and Kashmir. While Junagadh's case was easily settled in 1947 after its ruler fled to Pakistan, Kashmir's was a long drawn out problem. But the refusal of Hyderabad to join the Indian Union was, because of the State's size and location, perhaps the greatest impasse which the Government of India had to try and solve through negotiation. When this finally failed, military takeover appeared to be the only solution. However, the integration of Hyderabad was a turbulent chapter in the history of post-Independence India and it provides, therefore, a dramatic case study of some of the problems which accompanied the transfer of power from British to Indian hands.

Finally, a survey of the aftermath in Hyderabad State provides a glimpse into the consequences of India's policy of integration of princely States—in terms of immediate shifts in the balance of power at the local level and of later demands for a linguistic reorganisation at the national level. How the people in the princely States adapted to the new political and linguistic set-up is a question of central relevance to the viability of a united contemporary India.

It is worth pointing out at the outset that princely States are an area of study where conflicting notions abound. This needs to be stressed, because some of these ideas, arising from the bias of supporters and detractors of princely rule, have remained largely unchallenged and often continue to have currency in the field.

There is, for instance (although mainly in popular works), the 'romantic' bias which depicts even the worst characteristics of princely rule sentimentally and nostalgically. In these works, autocracy appears as a form of benign paternalism, and the princely States are pictured as worlds of turbanned and bejewelled nawabs and maharajas periodically throwing handfuls of gold coins from atop decorated elephants to the delighted multitudes below (Karaka 1955; Lynton and Rajan 1974). But this romanticism is wide off the mark in regard to the Hyderabad of later years, as fast living and extravagance, to say nothing of benign paternalism, were hardly the manner by which the reign of its last ruler could be remembered.

To others, conservative British writers in particular, the princely States were mere pawns and victims of British political expediency, which went into historical oblivion for no fault of their own. But, though there is no doubt that Britain in the end made only feeble attempts to protect the future of the Indian rulers, it is also true that for the princes themselves, the writing was clearly on the wall long before the hurried British departure from the subcontinent (Manor 1978, pp. 306–38).

Most significant, however, is the totally different view expounded at length in pre- and post-independence Indian literature. This is clearly stated in the Government of India's *White Paper on Indian States* (1950, p. 145) that

> the policy of integration and democratisation which the Government of India have applied to the States constituted ... the only solution of the problem of the States and the only method of fitting in the State in the new set-up of India.

This categorical statement has been the pivot of the Government of India's policy towards the princely States and has often been considered axiomatic in the historical approach to the States' question. It must be noted, however, that this argument rests basically on two broad assertions. The first is that integration was 'the only solution' to the problem of the States because it was something of a natural corollary to the Indian struggle against British rule. That is, the democratic movement in the States was a substantial and long-standing, self-generated movement against princely rule waged in tandem with the nationalist agitation in British India. And that by 1947, the people of the princely States could accept nothing but the 'full democracy' which had come into being beyond their borders.[2]

The second assertion is that integration was 'the only method' of fitting the States into the new India because toleration of the survival of any of these territories as independent entities would have led to an 'insuperable Balkanisation of India'. The creation of Pakistan had been accepted as the very last resort to end communal strife in the subcontinent, but any further tampering with the territorial integrity of the new India would have struck at the roots of the long-nurtured ideal of national unity and put the future of the whole Indian Union in jeopardy.

Thus, for the Government of India at the time and many of its supporters subsequently, the issue regarding princely States was an open-and-shut case in favour of integration.

Yet, as I will attempt to show, even at the risk of arousing controversy, both these assertions are disputable, in regard to Hyderabad at least.

On the one hand, integration was unilaterally imposed from the top and, despite earlier promises, no plebiscite was ever held in Hyderabad (Menon 1961) to confirm that the State's population saw integration as the only solution fulfilling the aims of the preceding agitation against the Nizam's regime. Indeed, even the nature and extent of this agitation are not yet known reliably. The largest body of literature devoted to pre-integration political developments in Hyderabad State has been written by nationalist leaders and participants, and following them by Indian nationalist historians who, perhaps guided by a natural patriotic feeling, have often oversimplified issues *a posteriori* so as not to mar their accounts with past discordances and differing political points of view.[3]

On the other hand, as India's political conditions show today, it is not certain any longer that the integration of the princely States, which opened the door to a linguistic reorganisation of the whole of India and thus helped the development of linguistic and regional loyalties (resulting in the contemporary trend towards increased regionalism), was in the best long-term interests of Indian unity.

It is neither easy nor worthwhile to suggest that the problem of the princely States could have been solved differently. However, to understand the issue, it is necessary to place it in its proper context, without being influenced by past preconceptions and readymade conclusions.

In the twentieth century, Hyderabad was still ruled by a Muslim elite, as it had been since the eighteenth century. Most other large princely States of pre-1947 India (for instance, Mysore, Travancore, Baroda, the Rajput States, Gwalior and even Kashmır) had developed an indigenous counter-elite to the old princely aristocracy, from bases of modern education and middle class ownership of land. However, the formation of such a counter-elite was much delayed in Hyderabad, as Chapter 1 will show.

As a result, internal political developments in Hyderabad throughout the 1920s and 30s remained weak and, as will be seen in Chapter 2, dominated by the towering personality of the Nizam. However, from the late 1930s onwards, the political atmosphere in British India had an increasing impact on all princely States including Hyderabad.

In 1938, an attempt was made to launch a full-scale political agitation in Hyderabad but, lacking in popular support, this *satyagraha* movement did not spread and was sustained largely through the active help of organisations in British India. Chapter 3 will show that the events of 1938–39 owed much to outright 'importation' rather than to any spontaneous movement within the State.

This forceful intrusion in Hyderabad's political scene, even if it provoked only a poor local response, seriously disturbed the communal harmony which is often referred to as a 'proud tradition' of the State. Chapter 4 analyses one of the consequences of the 1938–39 satyagraha—its effects on the local Muslim population. Vindictiveness resulting from what was seen as a concerted pan-Indian Hindu attack on Hyderabad, uncertainty about the future, and the impetus given by an energetic leader, all contributed between 1939 and 1944 to an increasing political mobilisation of the Muslim community and opened the way for the unrealistic Muslim extremism of later years.

Meanwhile, insofar as the nationalist movement took root in Hyderabad, it will be shown in Chapter 5, that between 1939 and 1946, no consensus as to its meaning was achieved between the various militant Hindu groups of the State. In Telengana, the Communist party was able to challenge the influence of the Hyderabad State Congress successfully, and events in the region followed a course altogether different from that in the rest of the State. As the political situation evolved in British India, communalism increasingly tainted political decisions in Hyderabad and the movement of opposition to the Nizam's rule led to an intensifying of Hindu–Muslim antagonism which involved growing numbers of participants in violent confrontations.

After 1946, however, the importance of internal political developments paled in significance in the momentous context of the impending liberation of British India from foreign rule. Chapter 6 deals with the delicate period of the first phase of negotiations between the Hyderabad and Indian Governments, ending in November 1947 with the signing of a reciprocal Standstill Agreement. By then, as Chapter 7 will illustrate, the die was already cast for Hyderabad, although negotiations with the Indian Government continued desultorily. Within the State, extremist Muslims were as determined to safeguard the privileges of their community as extremist Hindus were to wrench these from them, and the situation degenerated into further violence on both sides. Meanwhile, the Standstill Agreement was followed by an economic blockade of the State, and, when further negotiations proved to be sterile, it was finally left to the Indian army to settle, in one stroke, both the recalcitrance of the Hyderabad State in regard to accession and the internal dispute for power between the Hindu and Muslim groups.

How this was done and with what short-term consequences at the local level and longer-term consequences at the national level is outlined in Chapter 8.

NOTES

1. Hyderabad (approximately 82,700 square miles) was the second largest Indian State after Kashmir (85,885 square miles); it was, however, first in terms of population and revenue (14,436,148 persons and Rs 84,213,000 in 1931) followed by Mysore (6,557,032 persons and Rs 35,441,000 the same year). See *What Are the Indian States* (1949), pp. 52, 74 and 94.
2. Sir Percival Griffiths (1965, p.118) notes the statement made in the *White Paper on Indian States* that,

   > with the advent of independence, the popular urge in the States for attaining the same measure of freedom that was enjoyed by the people of the Provinces gained momentum and unleashed strong movements for the transfer of power from the rulers to the people ...

   and comments:

   > the present writer believes that this account of the popular movement in the States was exaggerated and that the urge for change operated in Delhi rather than amongst the peoples of the States.

3. Gopal Rao Ekbote, Vice-President of the Hyderabad State Committee of the History of the Freedom Struggle in India, himself warns in the preface to *The Freedom Struggle in Hyderabad, Vol. I: 1800–1857* (Hyderabad, Andhra Pradesh State Committee, 1966):

   > No doubt it is a fact that an endeavour to compile the history of such a colossal phenomenon so early will not give a dispassionate and correct picture of the whole struggle.

   S.P. Sen (1977, p. vii, viii) says in his introduction,

   > After independence the Nehru Government had taken up an official plan for a comprehensive history of the freedom movement .... Historians were asked to write only what the party or group in power wanted them to write .... When ... Dr R.C. Majumdar who was in charge of the project resisted the attempt ... the Nehru Government ... abandoned the project .... Curiously ... after getting rid of ... Dr R.C. Majumdar, the Nehru Government entrusted the task ... to Dr Tara Chand whose principal virtue as a historian was his willingness to toe the line ... Dr Tara Chand produced his three volume history of the freedom movement in India which is to be considered the official version of the freedom movement. Volume I of Dr Tara Chand's work is sheer nonsense and has nothing to do with the freedom movement. The other two volumes have some bearing on the freedom struggle but the accounts given are wholly biased in favour of the official line and are thus treated with contempt in academic circles.

1

Hyderabad State: The Context

Part 1
The Physical, Historical and Economic Background

'God began creating the world in Andhra Pradesh.' On a journey eastward from Hyderabad, the guide points at the colossal boulders dotting the parched countryside and quips that this was the site of the primeval quarry from which all mountains in the world were made and that only the rocks, which divine intervention itself could not move, now remain. And indeed, these enormous rocks, often fantastically and precariously piled on one another, are awesome.

The region is Telengana, once part of the princely State of Hyderabad. Until its dissolution in 1956, the State occupied most of the vast *doab* area of two great Indian rivers, the Godavari and the Krishna, on the Deccan tableland. Hyderabad also encompassed two other regions—Marathwara (Marathwada) and Karnataka (now in Maharashtra and Karnataka respectively)—different from Telengana not only in geology and agriculture but also in ethnology and language. Indeed, three languages, Telugu, Marathi and Kannada, were spoken in the erstwhile State of Hyderabad.[1]

In Telengana, because the red soil does not retain much moisture, irrigated agriculture is the rule and the spectacular rocky tracts alternate in the landscape with green areas of rice, millet and oilseeds grown around artificial tanks and lakes.

There are no natural lakes in the region but the dams built across hills and low grounds over the centuries have resulted in a myriad reservoirs, some of impressive dimensions. The ancient Pakhal lake in Warangal district, for instance, stretching from a dam 2000 yards long, covers an area of 13 square miles and the more recent Nizamsagar lake in Nizamabad district stretches over 50 square miles. In addition there are literally thousands upon thousands of constructed tanks, particularly in Telengana (Iyengar 1951, p. 17). But despite all this, irrigated land constituted only 5 per cent of the total cultivated area in the State, and 80 per cent was devoted to rain-fed crops.[2]

Hyderabad was rich in minerals, which were under-exploited 'owing to lack of industrial enterprise and insufficiency of technical skill and capital' (Qureshi 1947, p.15). There was coal, gold, marble, mica, garnet and limestone but only coal was worked on a reasonably large scale. The collective output of the State's three main coalfields (Kothagudum, Tandur and Singareni) exceeded 1,000,000 tons in 1948.

Most industries in the State were based on local raw materials. There were six textile mills producing cotton yarn and machine-woven goods, a government-sponsored handloom and dyeing industry (traditionally the part-time occupation of cultivators) providing clothes for 'nearly half the population of the State', and cottage and handicraft industries like carpets, blankets, silk goods and metal-inlay articles.

The State also produced edible oil from groundnut, castor and other oilseeds, leather for the local market and for export through 84 tanneries, 'more matches than [could] be consumed locally,' soap, alcohol, cement, cigarettes (3.5 million of which were produced annually by 1948), glass, stoneware pipes and other sundry products (see Appendix 2). The railways, electric, telegraph and postal systems were all introduced in the State in the late nineteenth century (Bawa 1965, pp. 307–40).

However, the State was predominantly agricultural and in terms of acreage was (in 1937) the first in India for its cultivated area of castor (48 per cent of total area under this crop in India) and jowar (27 per cent), third for cotton (15 per cent), sesamum (9.6 per cent), and groundnut (14.7 per cent), and fourth for linseed (9 per cent) (*F & F*, p. 9; Qureshi 1947, pp. 39–60). But the yields in general compared unfavourably with the rest of India.

Nevertheless, the State was generally in a favourable position in terms of balance of trade, as exports exceeded imports in most years. Internally, Hyderabad had enough income from taxation—mainly land revenue, excise, opium, customs, forests, stamp registration, railways and mines—to have surplus budgets even during the Depression and the Second World War (Munshi 1957, p. 278–79).

Hyderabad suffered, however, from a 'fundamental weakness'[3] in its system of taxation since income tax, which was introduced in British

India as early as 1860 (Kumar, 1983), did not exist in the State until 1947–48.[4] The bulk of the taxation fell mostly on low-income earners while the wealthier classes escaped it almost entirely. In the words of an analyst:

> The tax burden on the poor classes, including agricultural and industrial labourers, small-scale farmers, petty artisans and low grade staff is fairly high relative to their income as these classes have to bear the burden of excise duties, customs duties and land revenue in the case of farmers. In the middle classes certain sections are lightly taxed, e.g., the traders and landlords. In the upper section, the substantial land-holding classes escape lightly including the professional classes, merchants, and industrialists.[5]

A plan to introduce moderate income tax was proposed to the Nizam by his Government in 1943 but it aroused strong opposition from large landowners, lawyers and business persons, and the Nizam was persuaded to reject it on the plea that it would mark 'too great a departure from the fiscal and administrative tradition of Hyderabad'.[6]

In this instance, as often, custom prevailed over reform, a tendency which was not specific to Hyderabad but was generally representative of princely India where the upper socioeconomic groups jealously guarded the traditions (and privileges) inherited from the past. From that point of view, twentieth-century Hyderabad was still very much a princely State.

The socioeconomic pattern of Hyderabad State reflected strongly its princely (quasi-monarchical) set-up with clear distinctions between the governing and the governed, the high (few) and the low (many)—in brief, between the minority ruling elite and the rest of the population.

It was also a characteristic of princely India, and *a fortiori* of Hyderabad State, that access to high governmental positions was generally the privilege of the local ruling elite and was more or less closed to those who did not possess the requisite qualifications of 'birth' and wealth. Being of the same religion as the ruler did not automatically warrant elevated employment nor was the converse true, for high officials and even prime ministers in Hyderabad had sometimes been Hindus. But, historically it had become a tacit tradition that high governmental employment was the prerogative of the Muslim elite. Further, as those in high positions tended to employ men of their own religion in subaltern posts (deputies, clerks and peons), State Government service as a whole came to be considered as the preserve of Muslims.

This preferential recruitment of Muslims in State services was not a new phenomenon in this area of the Deccan. It was intrinsically linked with the continuous sway of the Muslims over the region since the fourteenth century (see Sherwani 1973; Gribble 1896). Muslims, led by Alauddin Khilji, later Sultan of Delhi, had plundered the Deccan even earlier, but it was during the reign of Muhammad bin Tughluq that Muslim authority, after a prolonged and bloody struggle, finally prevailed over the local Hindu (then Kakatiya) rule. The Tughluqs were succeeded by the more benign Bahmanis and Qutub Shahis, and then by the Mughals in the mid-seventeenth century. But it was only in the troubled period of succession which followed Emperor Aurangzeb's death in 1707 that the future founder of Hyderabad State, Mir Qamruddin (a Mughal general of note, afterwards known as Nizam-ul-Mulk) was first appointed Governor of the Deccan and the Carnatic. He occupied his post only long enough to 'pacify' the region, by which time he realised that there was an opportunity in the Deccan afforded to him by the decline of the Mughal Empire. Recalled to the capital by the Sayyid brothers who dominated the court at Delhi, Mir Qamruddin remained inactive till the early 1720s, when, after the Sayyids' violent death, he was appointed *wazir* of the Mughal Empire. However, he returned to the Deccan in 1723 to carve a domain for himself (see Ikram 1964, p. 257–58).

Nizam-ul-Mulk quickly consolidated his position and a decisive victory in 1724 over a Mughal rival to his governorship finally removed all threats to his rule (Husain, 1963).

At the time of his death in 1748, Nizam-ul-Mulk, now Asaf Jah I, was according to the *Imperial Gazetteer of India* (1909, p. 15), 'fairly established as an independent sovereign of a kingdom' which extended 'from the Narbada to Trichinapali and from Masulipatam to Bijapur'.[7] Asaf Jah I's succession was fiercely disputed by two claimants (his second son and one of his grandsons) who had secured the respective support of the French and the British then vying for power in south India. In the intrigues which followed (Gribble 1896, vol II), the French initially emerged victorious, but by 1761 British successes in the Carnatic turned the tide of events.[8] By 1798, England was the decisive master of the field and henceforth the 'protector' of the Nizam's rule over Hyderabad State.[9]

From the late eighteenth century the Nizam's authority was, therefore, under British tutelage but as this control was mainly confined to the political field, it was not followed by major social changes. It could be said that the socioeconomic structure which emerged in the days of Asaf Jah I survived in its main outlines until the end of the princely era in 1948 (see Leonard 1971, pp. 569–82).

Under the same strategic compulsions as the Bahmanis and Qutub Shahi kings before him, Asaf Jah I entrusted military positions mainly to Muslims, leaving administrative work and cultivation of the land to the Hindus (Gribble 1896, II, p. 22). Once he became independent of Delhi, he also created his own court and nobles by rewarding all those who served him well, regardless of community. Gribble gives a glimpse of this process in the following oft-quoted passage:

> Asaf Jah had brought with him from Malwa a number of followers, Mahomedans and Hindus, who were attached to his person and fortunes. To the Mahomedan nobles he granted *jaghirs* or estates on military tenure and employed them as his generals .... The Hindus ... he employed principally in administrative work in the departments of revenue and finance. To them he also granted *jaghirs* as a remunerations [*sic*] for their services, and all these *jaghirs*, whether granted for civil or military purposes, came to be considered as hereditary in the different families.[10]

Karen Leonard points out that the inheritable character of *jagirs* in Hyderabad differed from the Mughal practice of transferring jagirs regularly, and that 'the contrast assumes some importance in the context of the establishment of Hyderabad's independence' because 'the Nizam's policy ... would have given men an incentive to transfer their allegiance to the Nizam, and ... destroyed an important link to the Central Mughal administration' (Leonard 1971, p. 577). Indeed, the institution of hereditary jagirs served to form a nucleus of loyalty around the Nizam for centuries to come and kindled the notion of Hyderabad as a separate Deccani entity, the basis of its later claims to independence from the rest of India.

Asaf Jah I also recognised a large number of native Hindu rajas and chiefs 'who held sunnads or grants from former Kings, many of which had been confirmed subsequently by the Delhi Emperors' (Gribble 1896, p. 6) and included them in the local nobility. By the late eighteenth century, a 'distinctively Hyderabadi nobility'[11] had emerged and with it a certain style of life which combined the old Mughal culture with the new customs of the Nizam's eclectic court. In this new order, Muslims continued to monopolise the highest positions, but Hindus played an important role not only in administrative functions but also in banking and money-lending. Local Telugu-speaking Komatis and other non-Muslims from northern and western India— Marwaris, Jains, Agarwals, Goswamis—provided essential assistance to the household of the Nizam and the nobles and thus often controlled the pulse of local politics (Leonard 1971, p. 574; Gribble 1896, II p. 254).

Britain's supremacy in India and its treaties with Hyderabad guaranteed the survival of the Nizam's rule and preserved the political and social traditions of the State. As a result, twentieth-century Hyderabad had remained, in Smith's words, 'a major area in India where a political and social structure from medieval Muslim rule had been preserved more or less intact' (1950, p. 28).

Strictly speaking, the term 'medieval' is inappropriate here as it relates only to the Mughal model which constituted the original blueprint for the social and political system of Hyderabad. It does not take into account the significant social changes which occurred in the late nineteenth century—a general rise of the administrative classes and a decline of the military and Mughal bureaucracy (Leonard 1978a, 1978b). But in general terms it is true that the original characteristics of the social and political system put in place by Asaf Jah I (particularly the position of Muslims in the system) were still the fundamental features of twentieth-century Hyderabad.

The Muslims, a minority averaging little over 10 per cent of the total population, had retained their privileged position in the State and continued to dominate the approximately 85 per cent Hindu majority.

This is not to say, however, that all Muslims in Hyderabad were wealthy and/or influential. Most were, in fact, found at the lower levels of the State's socioeconomic order. In 1911, for instance, although Muslims accounted for 10.3 per cent of the total population, they constituted approximately 70 per cent of the urban police force, 55 per cent of the army and 26 per cent of the public administration.

Three decades later, a report on the Civil Service in Hyderabad indicated:

> Of officers drawing Rs 600/- a month or less, 930 are Muslims, 340 are Hindus, and 74 others. Of officials, drawing between Rs 600/- and Rs 1200/-, 59 are Muslims, only 5 Hindus, and 38 others. This means that of the 1,765 gazetted officers in the State, 1,268 are Muslims, 421 Hindus, and 141 others. The largest number of Hindus in the lower ranks shows some headway being made with reducing Muslim preponderance. But the number of Hindus in the higher posts remains very low. Figures are not available for the clerical and menial services but even there Muslims have monopolised at least 75 per cent of the posts.[12]

In the civil administration, thus, Muslims were most concentrated both at the highest and lowest echelons, the middle ranks being shared somewhat with Hindus. The Nizam and the local nobility—a landed gentry which included some Hindus—together owned approximately forty per cent of the total area of the State,[13] and occupied the very apex.

Among the next wealthy classes (large landowners, high-ranking officials and administrators, bankers and financiers, cadres of the army and the police), Muslims were prominent only in the second and fourth categories (bureaucrats and army officers), while among the well-to-do, educated middle classes their numbers were fewer, depending on the field. For example, in 1911 Muslims employed in the professions and liberal arts (law, medicine, instruction, arts, letters and science) accounted for only 1.7 per cent (aggregate) of their community (24,268 persons) and for an average of 27.7 per cent of all those in that category. Hindus in the same professions (81,222 persons) accounted for 0.7 per cent of their community but for 77 per cent of the workforce. On the other hand, 6.7 per cent of all the Muslims in the State were employed in public administration. In terms of literacy, Muslims (5.9 per cent literate) accounted for 22 per cent of all literates in the State (see *C of I* 1911; Appendix 6).

However, the majority of Muslims were found at the lower socio-economic levels as petty traders, subaltern clerks, office staff and peons, artisans (tailors, carpenters, cooks, blacksmiths), workers, cultivators, soldiers, bearers and domestics. It is striking to note (again in 1911) that Muslims accounted for 45.2 per cent of the total number of domestics in the State (13.8 per cent of the community). Approximately 28.6 per cent of them were classified under 'Domestic Service' and 'Farm Servants/Field Labourers'. Although 24.3 per cent of the community were classified as 'ordinary Cultivators', it should be borne in mind that 'the lower class Muhamedan as a rule did not own land'.[14]

Overall, because Muslims derived income mainly from employment in government and administration, the police, the army, trade and service, they tended to be found mainly in urban centres. In 1941, for instance, Muslims accounted for 37.8 per cent of the total urban population of the State and for approximately 46 per cent of the population of Hyderabad city (*C of I* 1941, Part I, p. 60). Muslims were also found in large numbers in the cities of Aurangabad, Gulbarga and Bidar which were 'intimately associated with the early history of Muslim conquest and supremacy in the Deccan'.[15]

Thus, Muslims tended to be urban dwellers which, according to the Census commentary, 'was not any peculiar feature of Hyderabad State but a phenomenon recorded in almost all parts of India'.[16] Peculiar to Hyderabad, however, was the fact that 'by far the greatest proportion of this community depended on government service'.

Hindus, on the other hand, derived their income predominantly from agriculture, although in the urban areas they accounted for the largest number among the well-to-do classes in trade and commerce, banking and finance, the professions and liberal arts, and in the middle levels of the civil service and administration. In district headquarters they were government officials of middle and low rank, traders, moneylenders and pleaders in local courts. Overwhelmingly, however, they were found at the village level where they were landowners, large and small (the former often combining cultivation with local money-lending), headmen, *patel*s, *patwari*s, watchmen, as well as agricultural tenants, farm servants and field labourers.

In 1931, approximately 57 per cent of the earners and working dependents were engaged in the 'exploitation of animals and vegetation', pointing to the predominant place of agriculture and agrarian classes in the economy. To give exact figures of the distribution of Hindus among these agrarian classes is not easy, but it appears that those deriving income from 'rent of land' and 'field labour' respectively were approximately 89 and 94 per cent non-Muslim. As people of religions other than Muslim or Hindu—Jains, Parsis, Christians—accounted for only a very small proportion of the total population in the State (approximately five per cent in 1931), and as the occupation of these communities was generally not agriculture but money-lending and the professions, the figures obtained above can be taken as reasonably applicable to Hindus.

In brief, Hindus accounted for the greatest percentage in all agrarian classes of the State and their economic predominance at the rural level was complete. In urban areas, they were strongly represented in the well-to-do and middle classes and they also vastly outnumbered all other communities at the less affluent socioeconomic levels.

In effect, Hindus as a whole (85 per cent of the population) dominated the State economy. While the Muslims had long monopolised State services, they had shunned many other activities like agriculture, banking and, with few exceptions,[17] the loftier levels of trade, which could have often been far more lucrative for those with the necessary wealth and/or abilities.

The sentiments of the Muslims regarding the socioeconomic order of Hyderabad are rarely found in print, as opposed to the Hindu 'grievances' which have received ample coverage, and it is worth quoting at some length what Salam, an apologist for the Nizam's rule, wrote in 1941:

> As things stand today, the top-class Hindus have got almost everything they want. Almost all the commercial and business concerns are in the hands of the Hindus. The learned professions are in the hands of the Hindus. All the State and private contractors are Hindu .... For centuries, very much to the detriment of the community, Muslims have been content with Government service, be it of the lowest kind, leaving the various other fields of economic enterprise to the exclusive exploitation of the Hindus. Those, therefore, who complain of Muslims as having monopolised the public administration are either deliberately blind to the facts of the situation or have never been genuinely anxious to know them.
>
> As can be seen from the Census figures, a preponderating majority of the Hindus is spread over 21,708 villages of the Dominions and prefers agriculture and other rural pursuits to the economically less tempting service in the towns and cities. Those Hindus who live in urban areas are more attached to trade, banking and other paying professions such as law and medicine than to Government service where the prospects, though secure, are extremely limited in scope. The Muslims, on the other hand, may be classified under a landed aristocracy singularly devoid of business enterprise, poor villagers who live as land serfs, and Government servants from the lower ranks of chaprasi upwards (Salam 1941, pp. 36–38; 137–38).

As will be seen, by 1941 relations between Hindus and Muslims in the State had become vitiated by communalism, although to a lesser extent in Hyderabad than in the rest of India. But what is striking in the above quotation is the clear occupational delineation between the two communities in the State's socioeconomic system.

However, it does seem that this system worked smoothly in twentieth-century Hyderabad, perhaps because it had evolved over the centuries and entailed a division of labour, a 'sharing' of resources, which eliminated economic competition and friction between the communities.

For the Hindu majority, perhaps this system worked smoothly because it had principles akin to those of the caste system, each caste being bound by its traditional occupation to a specific sector of the economy. More importantly, it was not a rigid differentiation on the basis of religions but a local tradition amenable to personal enterprise. For instance, Hindus with sufficient education could, and did apply, for the Civil Service and would, if qualified, be preferred to less suitable Muslims (Salam 1941, p. 141). But, employment in the Civil Service was of interest only to those for whom it represented an improvement in their existing conditions. For wealthy young Hindus, it was generally far more profitable to follow their father's occupation in agriculture, trade, or money-lending than to take up comparatively poorly-paid government employment. As for those aiming at higher education, sons perhaps of doctors or lawyers, they would also proceed by preference towards the professions and liberal arts. When competition existed, it was mainly among those with a modest education who accounted, as will be seen, for a tiny minority of the total population of the State.

Thus, the socioeconomic order of Hyderabad might have appeared static and inequitable, but for the Hyderabadis it was familiar and secure. It was a system which was accepted both by Hindus and Muslims, by the wealthier elements because they were well satisfied with their respective shares, and by the poorer sections because their condition was devoid of any choice and because competition from other communities was hardly an important part of their plight.

Relations between the communities in Hyderabad were also kept harmonious by the spirit of religious tolerance which was proverbial in India,[18] at least until the late 1930s.

This, it must be noted, was not the result of a policy of religious *laissez-faire* but, on the contrary, that of a careful management of communal matters by the Nizam's Government. The principle in the State, first enunciated by Nizam Mir Mahbub Ali Khan (1884–1911), was that the Government should have 'nothing whatever to do with [the] religious or quasi-religious practices of its subjects'; but 'when any such practice of any community gives offence naturally to the real susceptibilities of any other community, the Government must prevent it in the interests of peace and public tranquility'.[19]

Since the time of Sir Salar Jung I (1853–1883), Regent from 1869 to 1883 and the most celebrated Diwan of Hyderabad, a special government department, the Department of Religious Affairs, had been created specifically to supervise all religious activities in the State.

The jurisdiction of this Department extended to all places of worship and all practices, but it was stipulated that the Department should intervene only if 'something new' was proposed, which as defined in the original text included,

(a) non-customary practices against which any other community complain[ed];
(b) extension of the old buildings of temples and mosques, by new buildings;
(c) taking out processions on non-customary roads;
(d) playing music near, at, or before non-customary roads.

As to what was 'customary', it was a question which the Department was to decide after 'due inquiry into the circumstances of each particular case'.[20]

The Department of Religious Affairs was responsible to the Home Secretary and functioned through the network of the Police and Revenue Departments. Revenue officers kept special registers of all information relating to each place of public worship but it was never a simple affair (particularly from the 1930s onwards when serious deterioration in the communal atmosphere in the rest of India began to affect the State). There were, in 1931 for example, 31,372 temples, 5,191 mosques and 110 churches in Hyderabad (*C of I*, 1941, Part I, p. 242).

Nizam Mir Osman Ali, who succeeded his father in 1911, continued to uphold the principle of communal impartiality of his Government. In addition, he made personal efforts to assuage religious feelings in his State. In 1923, in a measure which was acclaimed throughout India, he decreed that the slaughter of cows in public places was henceforth forbidden in Hyderabad State. A crowded meeting in Hyderabad enthusiastically 'thanked the Nizam ... and assured him of the staunch loyalty of Hindus', while an Indian newspaper asserted that this decision had 'placed the entire Hindu community under a deep debt of gratitude'.[21] The *Express* (8/2/1923) of Bihar stated:

> Every Moslem in this country should follow the example of ... the Nizam who has done more to promote Hindu–Muslim unity than any other prince in India. The Hindus will ever remain grateful to His Exalted Highness and pray for his long life and prosperity for the generous and sympathetic consideration which His Exalted Highness had displayed for their religious sentiments.

The Nizam also made gestures of lesser import but of unprecedented originality such as that of 29 May 1926 when:

> in connection with [a] religious festival at [a Hindu] shrine of Gulbarga, the Nizam ... carried on his head, to the astonishment of all beholding, the tray containing offerings of sandal and flowers to the shrine. He walked thus a long distance barefooted followed by a large crowd. His sons and brothers also carried the tray ... the usual custom [was] for the *subadar* of the division to perform this duty and it [was] the first time that the custom had been departed from.[22]

This harmony between the communities in the State endured through the 1930s despite sporadic reports of communal clashes in districts where the Arya Samaj and the Anjuman-i-Tabligh-i-Islam conducted competitive conversion movements, and even though the communal atmosphere in the rest of the country had by then seriously deteriorated.

By 1938, Hyderabad too fell prey to communalism, when Hindus in the State, helped by political and communal organisations from outside, launched their first agitation against the Nizam's regime. This agitation made a serious impact on the minds of some of the local Hindus while it led to a general feeling of defensiveness among the Muslims—a prelude to their extreme political stance of the 1940s, and hence to their total downfall in 1948.

Part 2
Socio-political Conditions of Hindus in Hyderabad State

Hindus in Hyderabad outnumbered Muslims by an average of 8 to 1 and dominated many sectors of the State's economy. But, despite their numbers and resources, no important political movement emerged from among their ranks and, throughout the period under study, Hyderabadi Hindus as a whole did not unite politically. No doubt, political development in British India at the time gave little scope for the emergence of strong popular movements within the princely States. But in Hyderabad, perhaps more than in the other princely States, local conditions were also such that divisions arose within the Hindu majority. In addition, there were schisms commonly found elsewhere among the Hindus.

Caste naturally comes to mind here since the traditional occupations of the different castes made for diversity in social standing, economic interests, and, often, political sympathies. However, in Hyderabad caste itself did not lead to political divisions as it did in Mysore, Travancore, Bombay, or Madras where brahman monopoly over education and administrative power was a source of anti-brahman feelings and caste conflicts (Jeffrey 1978; Kothari 1970; Manor 1977; Patterson 1954). Indeed, caste antagonism was much less in evidence in Hyderabad because both brahmans and non-brahmans were generally absent at the higher levels of administrative or political power under the Nizam's regime (Regani 1978).

Caste might have played its part to a certain extent later when brahmans (mostly) took the lead in a local movement for political reforms but were eventually displaced by non-brahmans (mostly Reddys). However, as will be seen, the reason for this change lay more in disagreements over how to conduct the agitation than in actual caste conflicts.

More than caste, Hindus were divided by language. Three different vernaculars—Telugu, Marathi, Kannada—prevailed in Telengana, Marathwara (now Marathwada) and Karnataka respectively and, in 1921 for instance, the State's population was linguistically distributed as follows:

Table 1

Linguistic group	*Numbers*	*Percentage of total population*
Total population	12,477,770	100
Telugu speakers	6,015,174	48.2
Marathi speakers	3,296,858	26.4
Kannada speakers	1,536,928	12.3
Urdu speakers	1,290,866	10.3
Others	337,944	2.7

Source: Census of India, 1921

Since Muslims overwhelmingly described Urdu as their mother tongue,[23] the figures for the other linguistic groups can reasonably be assumed to refer mainly to Hindus, the minorities in non-Hindu groups which claimed these vernaculars as their mother tongue being negligible.

Hindu Telugu speakers, thus, accounted for nearly half the total population and their concentration in Telengana was markedly higher than that of Marathi or Kannada speakers in their respective regions. District-wise, over 95 per cent of the population in Nalgonda, almost 95 per cent in Karimnagar, 87 to 89 per cent in Warangal, Medak and Nizamabad, 85 and 80 per cent respectively in Mahbubnagar and

Atraf-i-Balda, described Telugu as their mother tongue (*C of I*, 1921, Part I, p. 86).

In contrast, Marathi speakers, even in the distinctively Marathi districts of Aurangabad, Bhir, Parbhani and Osmanabad averaged only about 80 per cent of the total population, the rest speaking mainly Telugu and Urdu.

As for the Kannada speakers, they constituted only a small percentage of the population and were found mainly in the three districts of Raichur, Gulbarga and Bidar where they accounted for 64.6, 54.6, and 29.8 per cent respectively of the total population. Marathi and Telugu were also spoken in varying proportions in these Kannada-speaking districts, and in Bidar, for instance, Marathi speakers were more numerous than Telugu speakers, the position being reversed in Gulbarga and Raichur.

The density ratio of the three vernaculars in their respective regions will be evoked later as a factor which almost certainly affected the entry and dissemination of political trends in Hyderabad from British India and contributed to a 'blotting-paper effect', encouraging the linguistic regions of the State to align politically with co-linguistic provinces of British India.

It will suffice to say here that, by the late 1930s, linguistic divisions among the Hindus had crystallised into quasi-political divisions along linguistic lines. The educated sections of each linguistic group, often high-caste lawyers as in British India, constituted a separate regional elite and there were, therefore, not one but three sets of Hindu elite in the State. Among these, the Marathi-speaking elite, perhaps because it had the example of the active Marathi brahmans of the Bombay Province, was the most energetic and influential, at least in the early 1920s. Marathi was the most important second language in Karnataka and probably because of the influence of Marathi speakers in the region, the numerically insignificant Kannada-speaking elite joined forces with them from the outset.

The Telugu-speaking elite, on the other hand, seems to have been more conscious of its separate identity or, perhaps, was not willing to be dominated by Marathi speakers. This became evident as early as 1921, when a Social Reforms Conference broke down precisely on the issue of language. According to Regani (1972, p. 177):

> The Nizam State's Social Reforms Conference was held in Hyderabad on 11 and 12th November, 1921 .... The proceedings of the Conference

> for the most part were conducted in English, Urdu,[24] and Marathi as the greater part of the social and political leaders up to this period happened to be mostly Maharashtrians ... One of the delegates at the Conference ... wanted to move a resolution in Telugu [but] his attempts ...were hooted down by the audience .... [This] was taken as a great affront by those Telugu members who happened to be present at the Conference. So, that very night they formed an association called the *Andhra Jana Sangh* .... This was the beginning of the Andhra movement in Hyderabad State.

The lead given by Telugu speakers was later followed by the other two linguistic groups, and by 1938 three separate regional organisations had sprung up, each standing in defence of its own vernacular and the social and economic welfare of the linguistic group it represented. These 'cultural' organisations were intended, in reality, as a substitute at the regional level for a Statewide Congress party repressed by the Government. But their basic parochialism was an important factor in preventing the political unification of the Hindu community in the State, and seriously affected the development of a local Congress movement.

However, linguistic differences were not the only factor which hampered the emergence of Hindus as a strong political force in Hyderabad. The isolation of the State, the nature of its political regime, widespread illiteracy, and the prevalence of a static socioeconomic order, all these did little to encourage political movements of any kind, let alone the political mobilisation of Hyderabadi Hindus.

The geographical position of Hyderabad, in the heart of the Deccan plateau, had long presented a major natural barrier to the penetration of ideas from the rest of the subcontinent. Sheltered from direct impact of changes beyond its borders, Hyderabad in the early twentieth century continued to live at the pace of its own tradition and values and, until the late 1930s at least, remained largely unaffected by the political upheavals occurring in British India.

This, however, can be attributed also to the repressive nature of the Nizam's rule which, in contrast to the regimes of Mysore, Travancore or Cochin for example, allowed little room for the development of popular political activity. Stringent rules regarding freedom of speech, of the Press, and of association had been passed in the early 1920s, when some tremors of the Khilafat and Non-Cooperation movements were felt in Hyderabad. From 1921, for instance, the holding of political meetings and the entry of leaders from British India had to be formally authorised by the State authorities. From 1923, the 'printing or publishing [of] any words, signs or visible representations ... likely to excite dissatisfaction against HEH the Nizam's or the British Governments' was prohibited.[25]

It is clear that the Nizam's Government, aware of the watchful eye of the British Resident, was anxious to prevent public displays of anti-British sentiment in the State. It was also naturally concerned over a possible spread of 'rebellious' ideas—such as those of the Indian National Congress and Gandhi—among the hitherto politically quiescent population. This combination of self-preservation and deference for the British alliance remained, throughout the 1930s and 40s, the policy guideline of the Nizam's Government with regard to political activities within the State.

In the circumstances, information about outside political developments trickling into the State—through British Indian newspapers (when they escaped government censorship or were smuggled in), the radio, or individual reports from travelling businessmen and professionals—made little headway beyond Hyderabad city as it was denied publicity in the local press. More importantly, such news could not be disseminated to the largely illiterate masses in district areas through political meetings or public gatherings which would have been the most effective means of communication. This posed a much greater hurdle to political mobilisation in Hyderabad than in British India where there was greater freedom to organise peaceful political activities, and where the popularity of leaders such as Gandhi, Nehru and Patel also helped to rouse the people. In Hyderabad, on the other hand, there were no such figures of all-India standing.

The leaders had to contend, in addition, with a level of literacy which was among the lowest in the important princely States and provinces of British India. In fact, Hyderabad remained till the end one of the least literate regions of India. To explain this phenomenon, which throughout the period under study stigmatised Hyderabad as a 'backward' region, it is not enough to say that the State's population was and remained mainly agrarian, with nearly ninety per cent living in small villages, lacking exposure to the stimulating influence of large cities. Nor is it enough to assert that the State's economy was primarily agricultural and deficient in 'nation-building activities'.

Certainly, these factors must have inhibited the growth of literacy in Hyderabad and, with it, interest in wider political issues. But figures for other princely States and provinces of British India show that the differences between Hyderabad and these other regions, in terms of distribution of population, urbanisation or economy, were not so great as to justify this explanation.[26] Comparative figures of expenditure on education do not help as, it appears, the Nizam's Government addressed the problem of illiteracy in the State repeatedly and at great expense. The Economy Committee, nominated by the Government of India in 1950 to overhaul and streamline the finances of Hyderabad State, remarked that the Nizam's Government had been 'most generous in the matter of grants-in-aid, the permitted ceilings being higher than in any other State of India'. It also noted that school fees were 'considerably lower [in Hyderabad] than in neighbouring States', that twenty per cent of the students in all high schools in the city and thirty per cent in district high schools paid no fees at all (and that forty per cent in the former and sixty per cent in the latter paid only half fees), and recommended drastic reductions of these percentages.[27] Why then did literacy not progress faster in Hyderabad? The basic answer to this seems to lie in the local socioeconomic order which did not encourage literacy to permeate downwards to the lower socioeconomic groups, even to the limited extent that it had done in some other regions of India.

In twentieth-century Hyderabad, perhaps more than elsewhere, traditional occupations were still followed from generation to generation, within a socioeconomic order which offered little upward social mobility. Education, which in British India and some princely States provided the key to higher employment (and social elevation), presented no such incentive in the State because all professions requiring a modicum of education had long been monopolised by Muslims and by Hindus of the higher castes. For those outside these groups, and more particularly for Hindus of the traditionally agrarian castes constituting the vast majority of the population, education seemed utterly disconnected from the realities of life on the soil and, thus, of little practical value. From 1915, most villages with a population of over a thousand inhabitants were provided with a school (using the local vernacular) and in 1921, primary education was declared free. However, despite official figures to the contrary, the impact of these measures on rural illiteracy was negligible. Explaining the reason, Census surveyors in 1931 remarked that:

> Once a boy leaves the institution and goes to share with his father the toil of earning daily bread for the family [*sic*], he has no opportunity for keeping up even the elementary knowledge which he acquired at

> school. Thereafter, there is, in fact, no demand for putting into use his skill in reading and writing, much less in accounting. Printed books and newspapers are hard to get and, even if they are available, their contents are not of interest to the ordinary villager nor is the language intelligible to the average reader. Therefore, excepting the few priestly and trading classes, others, not having tried their hand for a long time, unconsciously slip into illiteracy (*C of I*, 1931, Part I, p. 200).

This phenomenon, recorded as 'temporary literacy', affected all those who did not have the means to avoid family labour, that is to say, the majority of the agrarian classes. As for those among them who could afford (through their own means, government grants, or exemption from fees) to send their children to school, yet another hurdle existed in the long term. It was that, since 1921, higher education, obtainable at the newly created Osmania University (in Hyderabad), was imparted through the medium of Urdu. This deliberate government measure to reduce the need to import qualified personnel from outside created additional problems for all those whose mother tongue was not Urdu, and further eroded the already poor incentive attached to education. To be sure, the University was open to all and attracted a good number of students, but because higher education in Urdu was only relevant to Hyderabad, it could not guarantee a job outside the highly competitive field of local employment where Muslims and Hindus with the proper (urban) connections had the upper hand. Higher education in Urdu was thus entered into, for want of a better alternative, only by those who could not afford an education in English—children of petty traders and landowners, of school teachers and subaltern officials. It will be seen later that Osmania University, for this reason, bred many a politically discontented Hindu.

Tertiary education in English, more highly prized for prestige value and practical reasons, could be obtained at the Nizam's College, an institution affiliated to the Madras University, but it was so small and its hostel so expensive that the poorer students who came from outside Hyderabad city were not able to take advantage of it (*Imperial Gazetteer of India. Provincial State* (hereafter, *Imperial Gazetteer*) 1909, p. 75).

The alternative for all others desiring an education in English was to seek it in British India, but as this also entailed considerable expense, it was again available mainly to the well-to-do.

Thus, from basic literacy to higher education, the road was paved with difficulties for the majority. As a result, public interest in education remained generally low in Hyderabad and 'permanent literacy' was found mainly among those who possessed wealth and/or a background of literacy.

The physical isolation of Hyderabad State, the repressive nature of its regime, the linguistic differences within its population and the low level of general literacy were all factors which impeded the development of strong internal popular movements, especially among the Hindus.

Lack of access to education was a hindrance with multifaceted consequences, first, because the goals of political parties in British India could not be readily assimilated by the illiterate majority of the State's population. This was especially so when these objectives required familiarity with Western political concepts and seemed to have relevance only in British India. The Congress party's goals of 'democracy', 'responsible government' or 'electoral franchise' could be summed up under the general heading of 'struggle against foreign rule'. But in Hyderabad, these notions had to be re-examined in the context of a princely State and often ran contrary to centuries of traditional respect, or apathy, towards princely rule.

Second, because higher education attracted only a few segments of the general population, the contacts between the masses and the highly educated minority were extremely limited. On the one hand, political meetings were prohibited by the Government; on the other, the State's educated elite were concentrated in Hyderabad city and the important district centres. As a result, 'educated people' were known in the countryside only when they had business, property, or family ties in rural areas. Some belonged to communities non-indigenous to the State—Marwaris, Gujaratis, Sikhs, Parsis—and were involved mainly in trade or money-lending; others generally owned land, either recently acquired or hereditary. Thus, the impression among the rural people was that all educated native Hindus were primarily landlords. Indeed, most of the early (conservative) Congress leaders in the State were influential Marathi-speaking lawyers who also owned land.[28] To the masses their advocacy of 'constitutional reforms' and 'responsible government' appeared merely as the political leanings of the landlord class, and attracted little popular support even in Marathi-speaking areas. In Telengana, where feelings against landlordism ran highest on account of the dominance of the *deshmukhs* (large landowners) and the abuses they practised (see Pavier 1981; Sundarayya 1972), the Congress failed altogether. By contrast, the Communists (whose leadership was mainly local and who were modestly educated and committed to defending the landless) were highly successful in Telengana. The later unsuccessful appeals to Hindu communal loyalty made repeatedly by the Arya Samaj and the Hindu Mahasabha (and supported unofficially by the conservative leadership of Congress in the State) might have been attempts to defuse the antagonism of the poorer section towards the local Congress leadership.[29] In Hyderabad, the Hindus remained divided by class conflicts as well as the other factors already mentioned.

NOTES

1. Most of the factual information in this section is drawn from Part 3 of *Census of India* (hereafter *C of I*) for 1941 unless otherwise indicated, and *Some Economic Facts and Figures of HEH the Nizam's Dominions* (Hyderabad-Dn, Government Central Press, 1937) (hereafter *F & F*).
2. See Qureshi 1947, p. 88. In 1941, the land was classified as follows:
   Net area sown: 53.2%
   Forests: 8.8%
   Culturable waste: 5.9%
   Current fallow: 11.7%
   Not available for cultivation: 20.4%
   Source: *C of I* (1941), I, p. 10.
3. India Office Library (hereafter IOL), L/P & S/13/1209 (1944), p. 58.
4. Income tax was introduced by the Nizam's Government early in 1948. Even then the rates of income tax were lower than those prevailing in British India. After police action, income tax became a Central subject and rates were levelled up. (See Narayan 1973, p. 31).
5. Finance Department, Hyderabad Government, *A Review of Hyderabad Finance* 1951, p. 292.
6. IOL, L/P & S/13/1209 (1944), p. 58.
7. Malleson, (1875, pp. 277–96). Nizam-ul-Mulk, however, 'never openly claimed severance of the Deccan from the Central Mughal Government although from 1724 his allegiance to the Emperor was purely nominal', Husain, (1963, p. 132 fn).
8. On 17 January 1761, Pondicherry, the last French outpost in south India, fell to the British. With this, French ambitions in India were thwarted forever although Pondicherry was restored to France in 1768. Gribble, (1896, p. 61); also Malleson (1875, p. 72–3).
9. In the 1780s, the Nizam partly manipulated the British into an alliance against Mysore. In the 1790s, he employed the French officer Raymond to train his army. In 1795, he was heavily defeated by the Marathas and in 1798, he was brought into subordinate alliance by Wellesley. See V.A. Smith (1958, pp. 542–43).
10. See Gribble, (1896, p. 5); Khusro (1958, p. 2)) uses this passage to account for the origins of jagirs in the State. (Gribble's spelling of *jaghir* is obsolete).
11. 'Only one of the ten families most often counted among the highest nobles was Sunni; 5 were Shia; and 4 were Hindu ... these ten families will represent the nobility eventually constituted in Hyderabad', Leonard, (1971, pp. 579–82).

12. IOL, L/P & S/13/1209 (1944) p. 53; "Others" were presumably Christians, Parsis, Jains, and Sikhs, as other groups (Adi-Hindus, tribals) were overwhelmingly illiterate.
13. There ware approximately 1400 jagirs attached to this nobility, Khusro (1958 p. 4). 'Jagirs including the Nizam's *sarf-e-khas* [private estate] constituted about 33,700 sq. miles out of the total State area of 82,700 sq. miles', (*ibid*., p. 1).
14. IOL, L/P & S/13/1209 (1944), p. 406.
15. *C of I* (1931), Part I, p. 240. In 1931, the percentage of Muslims in these district headquarters was: Aurangabad, 43.6; Gulbarga, 48.1; Bidar, 55.2. (Calculated from *C of I* [1931], Part II, Table V, pp. 15–25.)
16. *C of I* (1941), Part I, p. 62; the reason was that 'in the major industry of the country which alone can bind the individual to the soil, viz. agriculture, Muslims have comparatively little share. For their means of livelihood, they depend mostly on trade and to limited extent on industry and services'.
17. The most notable of these was Mir Laik Ali, a business magnate of the State, who was later to be the last President of Hyderabad's Executive Council. Others were Ahmed Alladin, Comar Tyabjee, A.K. Babu Khan and Salar Jang. See *The Hyderabad Problem: The Next Step* (Hyderabad, Socialist Party Publication, 1948), Appendix II.
18. Padmaja Naidu (Congress) for instance refers to the 'long tradition of real communal harmony' in Hyderabad in her despatch to Gandhi of November 1938. (See Chapter 3), NMML, Private Papers, Padmaja Naidu Collection. The British Resident also confirms this repeatedly.
19. IOL, R/1/29/1921 (1939), p. 123.
20. IOL, R/1/29/1921 (1939), p. 124.
21. IOL, R/1/29/42 (1923) Indian New Agency Telegram 6D, 4 January 1923 and *Kisan Mitra* (Patna), No. 7, 1923.
22. IOL, R/1/29/200, FR 1/6/26. A few years later, the Nizam wrote and published a poem in Persian celebrating the glory of Christ and declared 25 December a public holiday in Hyderabad (IOL, R/1/29/1134, FR 1/8/34).
23. In 1921 the number of Muslims was 1,298,277 and that of Urdu speakers 1,290,866. They spoke Deccani Urdu which sounded 'antiquated' to north Indian Urdu speakers, (Leonard 1978a, p. 71).
24. Urdu was often used as lingua franca at meetings of leaders who otherwise spoke only their vernaculars (Justice Gopal Rao Ekbote, pers. comm. 1980).
25. *A Peep into Hyderabad* (Bombay, Indian States' People's Conference, 1938), p. 26.
26. For Mysore, Travancore and Baroda in 1931, see *C of I*, Vols. XXV, XXVIII and XIX.
27. *Report of the Economy Committee*, p. 42.
28. Interview with Pandit Kishen Dutt (former Arya Samaj leader), Hyderabad, September 1980.
29. An insight into this is given by Salam's comment:

> As far as class affiliations were concerned, the Arya Samaj and the Hindu Mahasabha were purely capitalist organisations which were not so much keen on establishing a rule of the masses as of the top class Hindus of Hyderabad (1941, p. 36).

2

Hyderabad State: The Political Developments

Part 1
Internal Political Developments till 1938

Upto 1920, no popular political party or organisation of any sort existed in Hyderabad. In fact, had it existed, it is difficult to see what useful role it could have played in the local political scenario as the Nizam's executive machinery was not given to calling for or welcoming consultations with non-official bodies in its decision-making process.

Outwardly, the State had long been 'modernised' with the establishment of a Legislative Council in 1893 and of a Cabinet Council the same year with a 'Prime Minister' as its president. But the regulations framed for the guidance of these Councils were good examples of the hegemony of the Nizam. It was laid down, for instance, that the Councils would not question the royal prerogatives, which the Nizam could still use 'at any time and in any manner as he pleased'; these prerogatives also left him free 'to modify or reject any decisions of the Councils', again 'as he pleased'. The Councils, moreover, contained no elected non-official element.[1]

Nizam Nawab Osman Ali Khan Bahadur inherited these wide powers when he succeeded his father in 1911; from 1914, he acted as the State's Prime Minister for nearly five Years. In 1919, however, largely under British pressure (see D. R. Rao 1926, p. 65), the Nizam reverted to government in consultation with council—now to be called the Executive Council.[2] And in 1920, perhaps to be seen at one with the spirit of the Government of India at the time, he issued a *firman* appointing a special officer to investigate possible constitutional reforms and the feasibility of a future expansion of Hyderabad's Legislative

Council. This momentous firman directed that particular attention should be paid to:

(a) substantial introduction of the elective element
(b) direct voting
(c) representation of all important classes and interests
(d) effective protection of minorities
(e) conditions of franchise
(f) the official element
(g) powers and functions [of the future Legislative Council][3]

For the first time in Hyderabad, the possibility of some popular participation in the government had been mooted by the Nizam, although the implementation of the scheme was not envisaged immediately. In fact, procrastination in constitutional reforms remained a source of political contention in Hyderabad for the next twenty-nine years.

The prospect of the introduction of an elective element in the Legislative Assembly, direct voting, wider franchise and so on, provoked enthusiastic public reaction in Hyderabad, particularly among the 'important classes' of the well-to-do and the educated who were most likely to benefit by them.[4]

Affluent Hindus and Muslims (mainly from the legal profession) organised a meeting on 18 February 1920, at a well-known local venue, the Viveka Vardhani Theatre, and passed a resolution expressing the 'loyal greetings and thanks of the people of Hyderabad to His Exalted Highness for his *firman* adumbrating constitutional reforms'. As they expected that Rai Balmukund (a retired High Court judge) who had been appointed the Reforms Officer by Sir Ali Imam, the first President of the Executive Council, would consult the public in the course of his work, they also decided to create an organisation—the Hyderabad State Reforms Association (hereafter HSRA) with these objectives:

1. to educate the people of Hyderabad regarding the nature and importance of constitutional reforms and the rights and duties attendant on the inauguration of reforms in the State
2. to canvass public opinion in favour of the Government and secure their cooperation in the successful inauguration of constitutional reforms in the State
3. to create public opinion on matters of public welfare and endeavour to develop the spirit of loyalty to the King
4. to prepare and publish the material necessary for constitutional reforms

5. to establish proper institutions at different places in the State with a view to attain the above objects.[5]

As the government did not find these aims objectionable, the Association was allowed to function without hindrance for a while. Meetings were thus organised in Gulbarga, Aurangabad, Warangal, Nander and Osmanabad where branches of the HSRA were also established.[6] In October 1920, the HSRA passed a resolution requesting the Government to publish matters regarding constitutional reforms for public comment. However, as the Rai Balmukund Committee had not yet produced its report, the Nizam's Government took no action.

The following year, the HSRA announced its intention to convene a Hyderabad State Reforms Conference on 11 and 12 June 1921, to take stock of the situation. But, by then, the Government, weary of the Khilafat and Non-Cooperation developments in British India, was considering a ban on political meetings in Hyderabad, and refused permission. (It was passed later, on 8 September 1921.)

When Rai Balmukund submitted his report on 6 September 1921, the HSRA presented a second petition for the holding of a 'Political Conference' in Hyderabad State, with the warning that should this be refused, the Conference, reluctantly, would have to be held outside the State. The Nizam's Government, this time, simply ignored their request, as it did their presentation two years later of a scheme for the expansion of the Legislative Council. By 1923, the HSRA still existed in name but had ceased to function as an active organisation.

In fact, it was the HSRA's unfulfilled demands for constitutional reforms that provided the basis for successive 'popular' political endeavours in the State, eventually leading to the creation of a local Congress organisation. Interestingly before 1920 and the HSRA, Hyderabadis of education and standing had never ventured to articulate political opinions or demands regarding decisions announced by the Nizam's Government. Hyderabad was an autocratic State where, it was known, public participation in governmental decision-making was not welcomed and where, in ordinary circumstances, attempts to pressurise government would have been futile and possibly dangerous. What, thus, had changed in Hyderabad's political scene by 1920?

Part of the answer is, undoubtedly, that the Nizam's firman that year was a remarkable departure from tradition as it showed an unprecedented willingness to mitigate the State's autocratic regime. Although the firman did not specifically call for public opinion, it did not forbid its expression either. It was, therefore, a rare—and safe—opportunity for the politically-minded in the State to make their opinions known.

This surge of 'popular' political activity in 1920 can also be seen as an early manifestation of the slow permeation into the State of trends and ideas from British India, a phenomenon which will be observable throughout the period under study.

This outside influence penetrated the State at all levels. The Nizam himself, for instance, was constantly aware of political developments in British India and of his 'alliance' with the paramount power. Hyderabad's internal policies were, thus, often framed with an eye to the British and, no doubt, the Nizam's firman of 1920 owed a great deal to the lead given by the Government of India with the Montagu–Chelmsford Reforms of 1919. It will be seen later that this applied also to the repression of anti-British and/or 'democratic' agitation in the State.

The effects of such outside influence on Hyderabad's population were not immediately tangible. The ideological trends of the political scene in British India penetrated slowly, affecting the educated elite first and filtering downwards to the masses with varying speed and success. Its communal messages, on the other hand, although tempered by the State's traditional communal harmony, spread faster and generally affected the masses first. In both cases, however, Hyderabad consistently lagged well behind the rest of India.

Thus, by 1920, a 'democratic movement' headed by a moderate elite was making a very timid debut in Hyderabad, when in British India agitation for constitutional reforms had gone way ahead and was, in fact, about to turn into a mass movement of non-cooperation and civil disobedience. In other words, it was only after the idea of turning to the masses had thoroughly taken root in British India—through the precedents of the *swadeshi* agitation following the partition of Bengal in 1905 (see H. and V. Mukherjee 1958; Pal 1954) and the Besant–Tilak Home Rule Movement (see Owen 1968) begun in 1915—that the educated elite of Hyderabad began to slowly participate.

The swadeshi and Home Rule Movement had, however, only given rise to some sympathetic but politically insignificant activity in the State.[7] But, the developments of 1919–20 in British India were to result, for the first time in the history of the State, in the formation of an organisation aimed at obtaining constitutional reforms. In effective terms, the HSRA was not an internal political development of major importance. Nevertheless, it was the first step in the direction of a Congress party in Hyderabad State.

The Hindu and Muslim elite in the State were joining hands too, as were their counterparts in British India, over the Khilafat issue. The quid pro quo effected by Gandhi in British India—Hindu support on the Khilafat question in return for Muslim participation in the agitation against the British—encouraged hopes that a similar spirit could be generated at the local level and, altogether, the atmosphere seemed ripe to try and sway educated Muslims towards a democratic movement in the State on Congress lines.

> The anxiety of Muslims on behalf of Turkey had waxed and waned during the interval which elapsed between the declaration of the Armistice and the end of the year 1919 .... during the latter half of 1919, feelings had risen steadily among the more advanced sections of the Muhammadan community and ... Mr Gandhi had taken what was, for a Hindu, the unprecedented step of identifying himself with a Muslim religious movement (Rushbrook Williams 1921, p. 31).

It was at this juncture that the HSRA came into being. Within it, Hindus and Muslims—Hyderabad's elite of lawyers and landlords—freely mingled. Addressing the public on behalf of the HSRA were, for example, Mohammed Asghar (barrister-at-law), Pandit Keshav Rao Koratkar (lawyer, later judge of the Hyderabad High Court), Khaleeluzaman Siddiqui (barrister-at-law), Waman Naik (jagirdar) and Raghavendra Rao Sharma (pleader). The same M. Asghar who presided at the meeting of 18 February 1920, when the HSRA was formed (and who, in fact, became the first president of the Association), also presided the next month at the first Khilafat mass meeting in Hyderabad. In the audience were again K.R. Koratkar, W. Naik and R. Sharma.

The Khilafat spirit also spread to the districts, at the initiative generally of Muslim *vakils* who organised meetings attended by both communities, notably at Mahbubnagar and Raichur. Shaukat Ali, one of the leading lights of the Khilafat movement in British India, was greeted at Gulbarga, when he passed through the State in April 1920, by 'a crowd of three thousand people consisting of Musalmans, Hindus, *vakils* and government officials'. *Youm-e-Khilafat* (Khilafat Day) was observed in March and April 1920 under the direction of M. Asghar, and when, at one of the Khilafat meetings, 'the chairman [Asghar] had suddenly to leave the chair for some important business, Pandit Keshav Rao, *vakil*, was requested to occupy the chair.' (Ramesan 1966, p. 38–42). As in British India, a spirit of rapprochement thus reigned between the Hindu and Muslim elite in Hyderabad State.

The Nizam and his Government, meanwhile, kept a close watch on all activities inside and outside the State. In May 1920, the terms of the Treaty of Sevres became public and confirmed the worst fears of the Khilafatist Muslims. The Turkish Empire was to be partitioned and the spiritual leadership of its Sultan as Caliph of Islam was permanently undermined. In India, the Central Khilafat Committee met in Bombay on 12 May 1920 and decided in favour of Non-Cooperation (Minault 1982, p. 100). A fortnight later, the Nizam issued a firman banning Khilafat meetings in his Dominions.[8]

Writing to Lord Chelmsford in June 1920, the Nizam claimed in his usual style,

> So long as [the Khilafat agitation] had not passed out of sober reasoning and judicious restraint, it was entitled to my sympathy. As a Musalman ruler it is but natural that I should feel the break up of a Muhammadan power but it is impossible for me to countenance proceedings that have avowed intentions of resistance ... to British authority, indeed against all authority .... I am responsible for the peace of my Dominions and ... I had no option but to nip the exotic in the bud. I am glad to say that ... as far as my Dominions are concerned, the horizon is clear. Barring a few outsiders who are of little consequence, there is not even a murmur anywhere.[9]

Despite this sweeping statement, however, Khilafat activity continued for a while. Subdued forms of Non-Cooperation, advocated by the Indian National Congress after its decisive sessions at Calcutta and Nagpur in September and December 1920 (Aggarwala 1965, pp. 33–34), also made an appearance in the State. By mid-1921, the Police Department 'urgently called the attention of government' to the 'rapid growth and progress of the political agitation in its many and varied aspects' in Hyderabad. These included the distribution of Khilafat pamphlets, the making of political speeches, the sale of *charkha*s and of photographs and brooches of Mahatma Gandhi and the Ali brothers, the wearing of Gandhi caps, the boycott of liquor and foreign cloth shops, the creation of 'national schools', and so on (Ramesan 1966, p. 16).

However, the more extreme forms of Non-Cooperation never reached Hyderabad (Aggarwala 1965, pp. 134–35). There was no reaction among government officials, no resignations from office, little if any withdrawal of children from government schools, and, even as admitted by the chroniclers of *The Freedom Struggle in Hyderabed State*, 'no glaring examples of persons who had given up their legal practice' (Ramesan 1966, p. 24).

Nevertheless, the policy of 'wait and see' then adopted by the Government of India was considered inadvisable in Hyderabad, and Sir Ali Imam,[10] President of the Executive Council, moved quickly to devise adequate preventive measures. The result was the famous Government Order (*Gashti*) No. 52 of September 1921 slapping a ban on any political or social meeting 'creating political issues' and on 'the entry of political outsiders into the State without prior permission from Government' (Ramesan 1966, pp. 26–8; Regani 1972, p. 177).

Gandhi's birthday was, however, celebrated with enthusiasm in October 1921. Over 3000 Hindus and Muslims gathered, listened to numerous speeches in favour of Hindu–Muslim unity, and parted in an extravagant display of mutual good-will.

> After the close of the meeting the audience and the speakers proceeded to ... Tulja Devi Temple in Murlidhar Garden [Hyderabad] .... all Hindus and Muslims entered it without any racial distinction ... on entering the temple Mr Asghar changed his 'fez' for a Gandhi cap and a Poojari approached him and applied 'sendhur' on [his] forehead. The Hindus then shouted 'Musalmanoki Jai' and great enthusiasm was exhibited by embracing one another.[11]

By 1922, however, Non-Cooperation in British India came to a head with the incident at Chauri Chaura (UP) in February, following which Gandhi ordered the immediate suspension of the movement. His arrest shortly afterwards, amid public indifference in British India, was of no consequence in Hyderabad. With the abolition of the sultanate in Turkey the same year (Minault 1982), much of the impetus of the Indian Khilafat movement also disappeared. In such a situation, 'what was left of the tenuous alliance between Hindus and Muslims ... collapsed' in British India (Minault 1982, p. 187).

In Hyderabad too, unity among the Hindu and Muslim elite was no longer in evidence after 1922. For instance, when at the initiative of Waman Naik and others, it was proposed that a Hyderabad Political Conference should be held in 1923 concurrently with the Indian National Congress session at Kakinada, only one Muslim, Abdul Kareem, a pleader of Gulbarga, responded to the call.[12] Even so, Kareem's attitude throughout the Conference was one of dissociation from the proceedings. In subsequent Hyderabad Political Conferences (at

Bombay in 1926, Poona in 1928, and Akola (Berar) in 1931) there was practically no Muslim attendance at all.[13]

After the Government Order No. 52 of September 1921, most aspiring political leaders prudently avoided attracting the attention of the authorities. Some redirected their energies into social and educational work among the masses. Curiously, although Marathi speakers (mainly Hindu lawyers) had been the first to take active interest in Hyderabad's public affairs and had so far been prominent in the organisation of political activities, it was Telugu speakers who now came to the fore (Narayana Rao 1973, p. 273).

The Andhra Jana Sangh had been created in November 1921 after the stormy meeting of the Nizam State Social Reforms Conference already related. The leaders of the new organisation perhaps felt that political awareness among Telugu speakers lagged behind that of other linguistic groups in the State and turned their efforts to working among the masses. Whatever the case may be, they began 'forming new associations, helping the existing ones and ... convening public meetings and other allied activities' to bring about 'progress of the Andhras' (Ramesan 1966, p. 43).

From an initial membership of twelve in 1921—prominent among whom were M. Hanumanth Rao, B. Ramakrishna Rao (later Chief Minister of Andhra Pradesh) and M. Narsing Rao (journalist)—the Andhra Jana Sangh developed into an organisation of a hundred members by 1922 (Regani 1972). Its general programme was professed to be the 'social, economic and cultural revival of the people of Telengana'. And, to fulfil this goal, the organisation proposed to encourage students to collect historical manuscripts and conduct research; print handbills and booklets and organise public speeches; propagate Telugu, to encourage fine arts and physical culture; and somewhat less precisely 'to accord respect to scholars' and 'help the helpless' (Ramesan 1966, p. 44).

Itinerant workers, presumably schoolteachers and students, began to open libraries and reading rooms in rural areas and, in 1925, convened a special Library Conference to coordinate all educational activities.

The Andhra Jana Sangh's work included interventions, as when in 1922 it urged the merchants of Telengana, who were bound by convention to charge supplies to travelling government officers at reduced rates or nothing at all, to resist the practice and stand up for their legal rights. A booklet entitled *Freedom of the Merchants* was published and distributed.

The Sangh also opposed the prevalence of *begar* in Telengana, through which government officials, patels, deshmukhs, and other persons of local influence could, on the strength of social traditions, exact free labour from skilled and unskilled labourers of the lower castes (Sundarayya 1972, pp. 11–16). This practice had been prohibited by numerous firmans but continued to flourish. Again, a booklet in Telugu listing relevant firmans and their provisions was published and circulated among the affected classes.

Alarmed by the extent of such activities over the years, the Nizam's Government reacted in 1928 by trying to prevent the convening of an Andhra Jana Sangh Conference along with a proposed second Library Conference at Suryapet (Nalgonda district) on the grounds that permission to hold these meetings had not been sought (Regani 1972, p. 180). The Government injunction was successfully defeated by an appeal to the courts, and both Conferences took place.

The following year, however, the Government passed Order No. 53, superseding Order No. 52, regulating the holding of political meetings. Now, the convening of any public meeting without prior sanction was prohibited; the agendas of proposed assemblies, together with due applications for sanction, were to be forwarded to the authorities at least ten days in advance and Government alone would determine their nature—political or not.

Under the moderate leadership of Hanumanth Rao, B. Ramakrishna Rao and W. Naik, the Andhra Jana Sangh, however, 'always took great care to see that their meetings did not come under the gagging order (Regani 1972)'. It focussed more on social work. The organisation, now renamed Andhra Mahasabha, passed resolutions on issues such as protection of *ryots* in times of drought or penury, women's education, abolition of the *devadasi* system, uplifting of the Harijans, abolition of *purdah*, introduction of elected elements in municipalities, promotion of primary education, revival of the indigenous Ayurvedic and Unani systems of medicine, introduction of cooperatives, and so on, but drew little response from Government (Ramesan 1966, pp. 46–49).

Andhra Conferences continued to be held yearly through the 1930s and 40s, but from 1937 onward, the Andhra Mahasabha turned to politics. At the Nizamabad Conference, presided over by M. Narsing Rao that year, the first political resolution of the organisation was passed, calling for the introduction of responsible government in the State. The Andhra Mahasabha increasingly developed along the lines of a political party rather than a social and cultural organisation.

But, differences appeared between moderates (led by M. Ramchandra Rao) and extremists (under the younger leadership of Ravi Narayan Reddy, the son of a Telangana landlord) which were to have momentous consequences on the political direction taken not only by the Andhra Mahasabha but by the whole of the Telengana region.

The Andhra Mahasabha's move towards politics also prompted the creation of 'sister' organisations in Marathwara and Karnataka—the Maharashtra and Karnataka Parishads—in 1937. As will be seen, however, with the rise of Congress activity in 1938 both organisations became largely redundant, their aims and leadership being indistinguishable from those of the Hyderabad State Congress (HSC).

The Muslims, in the meantime, made no effort to organise themselves politically. As the minority community, they were against any idea of reform. Their educated elite also did not feel the need to create a specific political organisation to defend Muslim interests in the State, as the Nizam's Government seemed to have Hyderabad affairs well in hand.

Besides, in the absence of a direct threat, the idea of a political party of all Muslims regardless of status ran against the strong sense of social hierarchy and tradition which still prevailed among the Muslim community. As Rasheeduddin Khan (1971, pp. 786–87) put it:

> A political party was considered not only anti-social and 'uncultured' but also below the dignity of the elite who visualised it as being contrary to their basic values of life, in which 'association' for political or economic demands was recognised as a big comedown from the high pedestal of noble 'individualised' living .... Then the inevitable democratisation involved in a party organisation, which would have dismantled the hierarchical order and disrupted the ... sense of rank and respect ... was anathema to the Hyderabad Muslim society. How can the high-born and well-bred, the successors of the 'renowned and decent families' rub shoulders with the lowly, the wretched 'have nots', sons of the soil?

While the Hyderabad Muslim elite, thus, took no step towards political activity, the entire community was concerned about religious issues. The Arya Samaj, a Hindu reformist movement, had engaged in a forceful programme of conversion—or reconversion—from Islam to Hinduism (*shuddi*) since the turn of the century. Its success among the Malkana Rajputs (a sub-caste of Rajputs converted to Islam during the reign of Aurangzeb) in the Agra region attracted the attention of Muslims all over India. Eighteen thousand of these had been reconverted to Hinduism in 1923, and it was the application of shuddi to mass rather than individual conversion which particularly provoked Muslim alarm in British India.

The Arya Samaj had established itself in Hyderabad State in the 1890s (in the Bhir and Bidar districts), and in 1923 opened a branch of the Arya Pratinidhi Sabha (or Shuddhi Sabha) in Hyderabad city. By 1924, work on mass reconversion from Islam had begun (M.A. Khan 1980, p. 48), and in the same year the first major clash between Hindus and Muslims occurred in Hyderabad State.[14] This incident was perhaps not a direct reaction of Muslims to Arya Samaj activity; it was nevertheless an indication that, despite the State's traditional communal harmony, communal issues could lead to serious trouble in Hyderabad as in any other region of India.

In fact, communal incidents remained rare during the rest of the 1920s, but in 1926, the idea of a Muslim religious organisation uniting all sections of the Muslim community was put forward by a few religious leaders.[15] And, in 1927, the Majlis-e-Ittihad-ul-Muslimeen (Council for the Unity of Muslims) was created. Its stated objectives were:

1) to unite and help the various Islamic sects for the solution of their common problems within the principle of Islam
2) to protect the economic, social and educational interest of the Muslims
3) to express loyalty to the land and to the Ruler and to respect the prevalent laws of the realm (R. Khan 1971, pp. 786-7)

However, the Majlis-e-Ittihad-ul-Muslimeen (hereafter the Ittihad) did little apart from making an occasional representation to the Government and convening the *Milad-un-Nabi* (commemoration of the Prophet's birthday) in the first decade of its existence. It made no attempt at building a mass following and, until much later, abstained from intervening in current political issues. The Ittihad was nevertheless the 'watchdog' of Muslim interest. In 1933, for instance, it emphasised the Islamic character of the State to the Hindu Mahasabha (an all-India orthodox Hindu organisation with branches in Hyderabad), and vigorously defended the privileged position of Muslims in government and administration (M.A. Khan 1980, p. 50).

This issue was an area of growing contention among Hyderabadis, not merely because it was Muslims who occupied these positions but because many of these Muslims were not *mulkis* (Hyderabad-born). It was felt that the mulkis—both Hindus and Muslims—were being deprived of employment in their own State. In 1933, there were

46,800 non-mulkis in Hyderabad. Both the President and members of the Executive Council were non-mulkis. Mulki organisations such as the Osmania Graduates' Association or the Society of Union and Progress had been created in the 1920s (Leonard 1978a, p. 88). But, they had been largely ineffective in their aims of 'replacing non-mulkis with mulkis in a responsible government, avoiding British advice and pressure, and retaining the Nizam and the old aristocracies as allies' (Leonard 1978a, pp. 88, 89). That year, at the initiative of Nawab Ali Nawaz Jung (Chief Engineer of the State), Sir Nizamat Jung (Minister of Political Affairs) and Abul Hasan Syed Ali (a leading advocate), a new mulki association, the Nizam's Subjects' League, was formed. It was the first organisation in which Hindus and Muslims representing the well-to-do educated and landowning classes united on the mulki issue. Important leaders such as Waman Naik, M. Hanumanth Rao, Mir Akbar Ali Khan (barrister, *jagirdar* and newspaper editor), B. Ramakrishna Rao, Nawab Bahadur Yar Jung (jagirdar), M. Narsing Rao and Kasinath Rao Vaidya among others, participated.[16] The so-called Mulki League, the Ittihad-ul-Muslimeen and the State administration were in agreement on the fundamental point that,

> since Hindus dominated in all other lucrative occupations in the state such as trade and money-lending, the liberal professions, the landed *zamindars* and agriculturalists, they could agree upon a continuation of the 'historic' share of official government positions for Muslims (Leonard 1978a, p. 90).

Very soon, however, the Mulki League, under the influence of its Hindu element, brought up the subject of introducing responsible government in Hyderabad. Despite its otherwise professed 'loyalty to the Nizam' and to 'Deccani nationalism', it thus incurred Government displeasure. Its Muslim members, who were not for this new stand, resigned (M.A. Khan 1980, p. 52). By 1937, the Mulki League had lost credibility as an organisation representing both communities. Its membership was divided on the topic of the mention of responsible government in its Statement of Creed demanded by the authorities; one group demanded that the Creed be scrapped and a short, vague statement of objects be adopted instead, while another group wished to adopt the rest of the Creed with no amendment. A futile discussion with no agreement followed.

The same year, the Hyderabad People's Convention, a prelude to the State Congress, was formed.

Part 2
The Nizam in the 1920s and 1930s

Overall, the 1920s and 1930s gave the Hyderabad Government little cause for concern about internal political developments. The period, nevertheless, was far from uneventful from the Nizam's point of view. His activities at the time give a good insight into his personality.

Nizam Osman Ali Khan began his reign much in the usual style of Indian princes, but he also showed quickly that he did not take the prerogatives and authority of his new position lightly. In 1912, the British Resident reported,

> the young Nizam [works] steadily and [passes] all the necessary orders under the advice of the [Prime] Minister and myself.[17]

However, this statement was a bit of an exaggeration. In fact, Lt-Col Pinhey, the British Resident at the time, Sir Faridoon-ul-Mulk, a courtier who had served the previous Nizam and Sir Kishen Pershad, also an old courtier and the first Prime Minister of Hyderabad, already had difficulties in controlling the young Nizam's tendency to act independently of the Cabinet Council.

In another report the same year the Resident remarked,

> [the Nizam] often consults me before passing his orders. This is apparently very galling to the [Prime] Minister because he imagines that there is some 'power behind the throne' which is undermining his authority.

The British were, beyond doubt, the power behind the throne in Hyderabad, as in other princely States (see Copland 1966 and 1982; Low 1978), but the Nizam skilfully used the technique which was to become his political trademark later. He took sides strategically, neutralising to the extent possible the power most cumbersome to his authority. 'The less effective the Resident was, the more assertive became the Nizam' and vice-versa (K. P. S. Menon 1965, p. 82). The balance between the three poles of power in Hyderabad—the Nizam, the Resident and the Prime Minister (later President of the Executive Council)—was maintained until the end.[18] Naturally, the Nizam preferred a weak Prime Minister whom he could influence, since appointments at the Residency were beyond his control.

Thus, in 1914, when Sir Kishen Pershad was discredited over a past alleged conspiracy against the throne,[19] he was succeeded at the

Nizam's suggestion by the twenty-three-year-old Salar Jung III, a scion of the illustrious family of Hyderabad State servants. The new minister 'though boyish in certain ways ... [had] earned good opinion all around and everyone was confident that he [would] make a good minister', particularly as Sir Faridoon-ul-Mulk who had 'practically been Minister of Hyderabad for many years' was there to help him. Shortly, however, the Resident reported:

> the Nizam has grown jealous of [Salar Jung III's] popularity and goes out of his way to treat him as a boy. He never sees him about business and angrily rejected a recent suggestion from [a courtier] that he should do so.[20]

Salar Jang III 'retired' within the year, and the Nizam then suggested that he should become his own Prime Minister. The British agreed with the idea as Sir Faridoon-ul-Mulk and the British officers in charge of Finance, Revenue and Police would be retained. They therefore thought work would carry on precisely as it did at the time. However, the Nizam's interference in the working of the Cabinet Council increased and so did his defiance of all control over his authority. But, between 1914 and 1918, the successive British Residents, while they kept close scrutiny over the Nizam's actions, did not intervene, perhaps because he had generously contributed to the war effort. In fact, as a reward for his support, the Nizam received the hereditary title of 'His Exalted Highness' on 1 January 1918, to which was later added 'Faithful Ally of the British Government' by an autographed letter from the King.[21] In the same year, however, Nizam–British relations entered a new phase as the British felt that the 'Faithful Ally' was now definitely beginning to overstep his boundary. A first report of the Resident disclosed that,

> His Exalted Highness the Nizam returned from Bombay on the 18th March [1918], his mind unfortunately ... warped and upset by ... flatterers, politicians and others who influenced him to believe that he must make a show of independence or he would be dubbed the puppet of the British Government .... The result was the immediate dissemination of the idea that all Europeans in the service of Hyderabad State were to be got rid of and orders were passed about two of the most prominent which gave colour to the popular belief.[22]

Proper procedure demanded that the Nizam should consult the Resident before taking action on important internal matters. The Resident, in turn, would consult the Political Department of the Government of India which would, if need be, refer to the Viceroy before instructing the Resident. The Resident would then 'advise' the Nizam accordingly.

One month later, the Nizam, again 'influenced by journalists, lawyers, merchants and others ... [who] played upon his almost incredible vanity,' let himself be convinced that the title of HEH he had received '[was] nothing and that he ought to be created "His Majesty, King of Hyderabad" and have the Berars[23] restored to his Dominions in virtue of his commanding position among the Princes of India and his services during the war.'[24] This time, a stormy meeting with the British Resident followed, in the course of which the Nizam not only retracted from his position but, at the Resident's suggestion that a message of loyalty from HEH to the Viceroy would be appropriate, immediately 'borrowed a pencil and a scrap of paper from his small son, himself added in the draft an offer of £100,000 and had the message dispatched without delay.'

> It is a pleasure to me [commented the Resident] to be able to record so characteristic an instance of that impulsiveness which ... has its wise and generous moments as well as those others which it has been my duty to criticise during the past strenuous few weeks.[25]

The Nizam's 'impulsiveness' remained, however—unpredictable in money matters and abusive in many others. In 1919, it was reported to the Government of India that the Nizam was again interfering in the working of the Cabinet Council; that official and non-official appointments were 'for sale to the highest bidder'; that private estates of nobles and jagidars were being appropriated at the slightest pretext; that the ancient custom of presenting *nazar* to the Ruler had been streamlined into a regular money-making enterprise.[26] In March 1919, the Nizam was summoned to Simla by the Viceroy Lord Chelmsford, who did not mince his words: the Nizam had attempted to govern Hyderabad without a minister and Lord Chelmsford said the experiment had been 'a costly mistake'; the administration had rapidly deteriorated and

> no one possessing property felt safe from the inquisition of special commissions appointed by the Nizam under no process of law to report on estates alleged to be without near heirs and so liable to escheat .... You have estranged your nobles; you have alienated your officials ... you have undermined the respect and love of your people. Needless to say you have thereby shaken the confidence of the Government of India

> in your rule .... It has always been clearly laid down that we cannot tolerate misrule; and results such as I have indicated are to my mind clear evidence of personal misrule.[27]

Following this, intimation was given that a new Constitution and the setting up of an Executive Council under a President were imperative priorities, and Lord Chelmsford insisted that it was necessary for the Nizam to support the Council and his officers.

An Executive Council and a new Constitution were thus duly set up, but the Nizam himself, although he followed the Viceroy's recommendations for a while, gradually reverted to his old habits.

The British Residency was then headed by Sir Lennox Russell, a man punctilious about Treaty Rights and the British policy of non-interference in the affairs of the princely States. He 'adopted an attitude of comparative detachment to the existing abuses'.[28] As a result, most of Lord Chelmsford's admonitions went unheeded until 1925, when Sir William Barton, transferred from the North-West Frontier Province, replaced Sir Lennox. Barton was 'a compact well-knit man ... as hard as nails ... every inch a Frontier officer' (K.P.S. Menon 1965, p. 83)) who took a much sterner view of the Nizam's idiosyncracies and lost no time in exposing them to the Government of India. Writing in December 1925, he said in a voluminous despatch,

> The situation is, I regret to say, infinitely worse than in 1919. Distrust and apprehension have deepened; the estrangement between the Nizam and his nobles and subjects has increased; oppression and corruption are rampant everywhere .... [T]he Council is now in a state of paralysis and has practically ceased to function. Money will buy everything .... [T]he judiciary ... is now corrupt from top to bottom. The Revenue Department is honeycombed with corruption; Customs officials are a byword for rapacity; the Police are more concerned to line their pockets than to suppress crime. The Ruler interferes constantly in the course of justice by the issue of extra-judicial commissions ... the estates of deceased persons are frequently seized even when there are heirs ... the extortion of *nazars* has been reduced to an organised system and has perhaps caused more disaffection than any other of the Nizam's malpractices .... The Ruler is prepared to intervene in almost any matter on receipt of a *nazar* .... Most of the important appointments are filled by men who have paid the highest *nazars*.[29]

But, while Barton was busy reporting, Sir Ali Imam and the Nizam had, in September 1925, sent a carefully worded despatch to the Viceroy (then Lord Reading) not only asking that the case for the retrocession of Berar be reopened but asserting that the matter should be discussed between the State and the British Government as equals.

The Nizam wrote,

> Save and except matters relating to foreign powers and policies, the Nizams of Hyderabad have been independent in the internal affairs of their State just as much as the British Government in British India .... The Berar question is not and cannot be covered by that reservation ... and thus the subject comes to be a controversy between the two Governments that stand on the same plane without any limitations of subordination of one to the other.[30]

The reply of the Government of India to this was concise and decisive, shattering the Nizam's greatest ambition. As far as Berar was concerned, the Nizam had requested the appointment of a Commission of Enquiry. Lord Reading replied that a recent provision had been made in British India for the appointment of a Court of Arbitration in cases where a State was dissatisfied with a ruling given by the Government of India; there was, however, no provision for the appointment of such a court in cases which had been decided by His Majesty's Government, and the Berar case could therefore not be reopened. As regards the parity between Hyderabad and the British Government, Lord Reading made a statement which was to be a milestone in the relations between Britain and the princely States,

> The Sovereignty of the British Crown is supreme in India, and therefore no Ruler of an Indian State can justifiably claim to negotiate with the British Government on an equal footing (see Copland 1982, pp. 262–63).

This paragraph was later to weigh heavily against Hyderabad's bid for independence from the Indian Union; for the present, it merely re-affirmed the subordinate position of princes *vis-a-vis* the paramount power and closed unilaterally any possibility of discussing the retrocession of Berar to Hyderabad.

The Nizam was, however, yet to get retribution from the paramount power for the 'misdeeds' reported by the Resident. Throughout this period, the Nizam's behaviour in Hyderabad affairs had received wide and often exaggerated press coverage in British India. By 1926, newspaper articles written (since 1920) about Hyderabad and the Nizam were numerous enough to be published as a book under the title, *Misrule of the Present Nizam*. The book 'threw light' on issues such as the system of governance in Hyderabad, the composition of its public services, constitutional reforms, freedom of the press, of person and of speech, the ruler's eccentricities, and included an article from the *Milap* in Lahore that 'the Nizam should be dethroned' (D. R. Rao 1926, p. 43).

While not going that far, the British reaction was severe. In July 1926, Barton was authorised to convey to the Nizam that the Government of India had decided to restrict his power and prerogatives.

As regards his prerogative to nazars, the Nizam was advised:

(a) to accept nazars only from nobles and high officials and even from them only at the traditional rates which are little more than nominal, and
(b) to abolish the practice of accepting nazars from officials on appointment which has been carried to such excess ... that practically all appointments are the prize of the highest bidder.

As to general administration, the Nizam was asked to agree to:

(a) the appointment of an efficient President and Council, and
(b) the necessity of placing the Revenue and Police Departments under British officers (for five years in the first instance).[31]

British officers had manned the Revenue and Police Departments for a number of years and there had long been an Advisory Council in Hyderabad. But the difference now was that the appointment and dismissal of President and Members of the Executive Council were to be made with the approval of the Government of India.[32] This, the Nizam particularly resented and he made many attempts in the following years to have the restriction removed. In 1926, however, he had little choice but to abide by British orders. A firman on nazars was immediately passed, and in 1927 a new Council and President were appointed. The latter position, however, was again occupied by Sir Kishen Pershad, the old courtier, as he was considered to be the most suitable person in the Dominions. The appointment of an outsider was not considered. British officers were also duly placed at the head of the Finance and Revenue Departments, in addition to those already in charge of the District Police and the Commerce and Industries Department.[33]

In hindsight, it is difficult to know whether the Government of India's increasingly hardening attitude towards the Nizam from 1925 onwards was justified by the abnormally high level of inefficiency and corruption in Hyderabad, or whether it merely followed the alarmist reports streaming in from the Residency since the appointment of W.P. Barton. Relations between Barton and the Nizam had been strained from the start perhaps because both men had high notions of the authority stemming from their respective positions. It might also have been that Barton's 'Frontier attitude' was ill-adapted to the atmosphere of courtly Hyderabad and to what Barton saw as the Nizam's 'characteristic oriental mentality'.[34] Colonel Terence Keyes, who succeeded Barton in 1930, was to prove that the impression of Hyderabad affairs and of the Nizam could be somewhat milder. But, until then, tension between the Residency and King Kothi steadily escalated. By September 1929, Barton's reports bordered on vituperation:

> Everyone who knows the Nizam realises that his attitude towards the efforts of the Government of India to introduce good government into the State is one of undying repugnance and hostility .... He is incapable of keeping a promise; he regards deceit, lying, obstructiveness and intrigue as legitimate weapons with which to meet the well-meant efforts of the Government of India for the benefit of himself and his people. He is determined to get back to the old tyranny and in this, his dominant motive is loot, pure and simple.

Two months later, and although his term in Hyderabad was nearly over, Barton stated unhesitatingly that,

> the time has come when it may be necessary for the Viceroy to tell [the Nizam] in unmistakable terms ... that unless he accepts the Government of India's advice and unless he can give them satisfactory assurances that he will work the reforms in the right spirit, they will be compelled to offer him one of two alternatives, abdication or an enquiry into his rule during the last ten years.[35]

C. C. Watson of the Government of India's Political Department advised:

> I do not altogether like the line suggested in the Resident's letter .... We might be rushed into delivering an 'ultimatum' to the Nizam just when we are changing Residents—a most undesirable position and one which *I find little in the conditions to justify* [emphasis added]. So far as I can discover, it would have to be founded on:
>
> (1) No change of heart by the Nizam. (But no reasonable person can ever expect this.)

(2) Instances of failure to observe the spirit of the *nazar* firman. (Too petty as compared to what went on before 1927.)
(3) Nizam works against the reforms secretly and tries to obstruct. (This is only to be expected. It is up to us to counter his obstruction and only when we fail to do so would an ultimatum be considered.)
(4) He has tried to appoint unfit and unsuitable nominees to high posts in the hope of preventing reform and reintroducing corruption. (But we have objected and so far always succeeded in enforcing our objections. Until we fail and find that we cannot expect any reasonable progress with the Nizam, we cannot seriously consider the drastic step of removing him altogether.)

And he concluded:

> I rather feel that Sir William Barton, possibly inevitably owing to his impending departure, ... is inclined to rush us into an extreme policy so that he may depart with banners flying ... even if our complaint against HEH were stronger than I believe it to be, I should advise against committing ourselves to a crisis until Colonel Keyes has tested his seat in the saddle.[36]

Sir Terence Keyes occupied the Hyderabad Residency for three years (to June 1933) and seems to have had an easier relationship with the Nizam, although he too drew him in rather unflattering light. Towards the end of his term, he wrote, for instance:

> There is much in Barton's description of the Nizam with which I am not in agreement .... His [the Nizam's] miserliness is only one symptom of a fairly common type of mental disease—the hatred of the interference of any other person in the absolute control of everyone and everything he considers his own. His miserliness in money matters is extreme, though nearly all the grotesque stories about it are untrue .... Strangely enough he is very jealous of his reputation as a keeper of promises; and I believe, can always be made to honour his bond; but he is an unblushing liar in negotiations or in narrating a case and totally unashamed when bowled out .... For all his unpleasant characteristics, and he is in many ways mean and sordid, I have real affection for the queer little creature. He has distinct powers for good, ... a quick sense of humour, an unexpected capacity for friendship ... and a pathetic craving to be liked and understood.[37]

Rightly or wrongly, Keyes could thus see some redeeming features in the Nizam's character, and the contrast between his and Barton's opinion merely illustrates the part subjectivity could play in the Nizam–Resident relationship.

It is true that for most of Keyes' term the attention of the Nizam had shifted from internal concerns to the broader preoccupations of the All-India Federation scheme. A delegation from Hyderabad attended the Round Table Conferences conducted in London in 1930 and 1931. Perhaps during this period the Nizam calculated that better relations with the British, and support of the Federation scheme, could further the cause of the State and help obtain special consideration on the question of Berar.[38] Hence perhaps the slightly better impression of the Nizam reported by Keyes. But it is also possible that the Nizam had genuinely amended his ways—or at least their most blatant manifestations. Indeed, Sir Duncan MacKenzie, who succeeded Sir Terence Keyes from 1934 to 1937, reported in 1934:

> There is no doubt that HEH has been regaining his position in general esteem. After the recalcitrance of 1927–28, His Exalted Highness has retired into his tent and the negative period which followed was of great value in that it induced partial forgetfulness in the public mind and allowed administrative reforms to proceed. By 1930 the Nizam's main attention became taken up with Federation and with the Berar and allied questions. He became in popular view the exponent of the simple life in contrast with other Princes and his own sons.[39]

However, the Resident noted that the Nizam made no attempt to bridge the gulf between himself and the members of the Council and the concern remained that autocratic intervention or direct action by firman could resume at any time.

The Nizam's basic attitude towards other poles of authority in the State, indeed, changed little through the 1930s.[40]

Clearly, he had remained unmoved by the extent of popular politics within his Dominions as also by the two Civil Disobedience campaigns in British India at the time of the first and third Round Table Conferences in 1930 and 1932. At that time, although he professed complete support of the idea of an All-India Federation, his position towards the scheme was guarded, like that of many other important rulers (Handa 1968). Under his instructions, Sir Akbar Hydari,[41] who headed the State's delegation in London, stated that Hyderabad would join the proposed Federation 'provided that the sovereignty of the Nizam be maintained ... federal subjects [be] very closely defined and provided the Crown affirm[ed] the obligation and retain[ed] the power to fulfil its treaties.'[42]

The Government of India Act of 1935—the careful synthesis of all discussions and proposals since 1927—comprised fourteen parts and ten schedules and came into force in April 1937 (Coupland 1942). Its main feature was provincial autonomy or the liberation of the provinces in British India from the control of the Central Government. In all the provinces, which, with the new provinces of Orissa and Sind, now numbered eleven, full responsible government was established subject only to certain 'safeguards' retained by local Governors. Part II of the Act, which dealt with the creation of the All-India Federation, was, however, held in abeyance as its implementation required the voluntary accession of a specific number of States (Coupland 1942). Despite further efforts by Lord Linlithgow in 1937 and 1938, the rulers continued to stall the issue and with the advent of war in 1939, the whole proposal of an Indian Federation was shelved indefinitely. It was, in fact, never to emerge again in the same terms.

Meanwhile, elections to the new legislatures held in British India (in the winter of 1936–37) resulted in a sweeping Congress victory, following which Congress ministries were installed in seven of the eleven provinces.[43] For the first time, popular Indian governments and Indian autocracies existed alongside each other.

This changed the attitude of the Indian National Congress (INC) towards the princely States. So far, the INC had abstained from interference in the internal affairs of the States, although from 1928 it had sided with the All-India States' People's Conference (an organisation created the year before to look after the interests of the people of the States). Its goal of 'responsible government for the people of the Indian States through representation institutions under the aegis of their Rulers' had been officially adopted (Coupland 1942, p. 91). This statement had been reiterated every year at INC sessions, purely as moral support, and it was understood that it was for the people of the States themselves to launch and sustain struggles for responsible government. After 1937, however, the success of Congress at the provincial elections seemed to authorise a bolder attitude. Gandhi and the right wing of the INC were, however, opposed to an escalation of Congress involvement in the princely States, whereas the Left and Nehru favoured it (Coupland 1943, pp. 171–72; Manor 1977, p. 107). But Gandhi's influence prevailed at the next Congress session, in February 1938 at Haripura (Gujarat), and the new policy of Congress towards the princely States was in the end couched in altogether moderate terms:

> The Congress stands for the same political, social and economic freedom in the States as in the rest of India and considers the States as integral parts of India which cannot be separated .... Purna Swaraj or complete independence, which is the objective of the Congress, is for the whole of India inclusive of the States ...

But, it added,

> under existing circumstances, the Congress is not in a position to work effectively ... within the States .... [T]he burden of carrying on the struggle for freedom must fall on the people of the States .... Individual Congressmen ... will be free to render ... assistance in their personal capacity [but] internal struggles of the people of the States must not be undertaken in the name of Congress (Banerjee 1965, pp. 324–25).

In appearance, thus, this resolution seemed little different from the previous Congress policy of non-interference. But, as Coupland pointed out, it was, in fact, 'markedly more 'activist'':

> In the first place, the support given to popular agitation in the States was more outspoken and there was no suggestion ... that the Rulers would give up any of their power except under compulsion. Secondly, while the Congress as a body would restrict itself to moral support ... the direct intervention of individual Congressmen was to be permitted and thus in fact encouraged (Coupland 1943, p. 172).

The Haripura resolution had immediate effect in Mysore State, south of Hyderabad. In defiance of the terms of the resolution, a Mysore State Congress was formed in March 1938 without any demur from the Congress high command. In April, as a result of a serious clash between a crowd led by Congressmen and the Mysore authorities, at least 30 persons died and many more were injured (Manor 1977, pp. 108–09). Following this, the Mysore Government hastily recognised the Mysore State Congress, agreed to associate it in the work of a Reforms Committee, and allowed the Congress flag to be flown side by side with the flag of Mysore on ceremonial occasions (Coupland 1943, pp. 172–73).

Spurred on perhaps by this success, agitation for political reform spread widely through the States in the summer and autumn of 1938. In Hyderabad, it began in earnest on 24 October 1938.

NOTES

1. *Report of the Reforms Committee 1938 (1347F)* or the so-called Iyengar Committee. (Hyderabad-Dn, Government Central Press, 1938), p. 5.
2. See IOL, L/P & S/10/743 (1919), Doc. No. 8531, Fraser to Holland, 25 Nov 1919 where the Resident reports that 'the Nizam's Executive Council ... is at last a *fait accompli*'. The Executive Council was to be composed of eight members and a 'President ... subject to [the Nizam's] ultimate control and authority'. IOL, L/P & S/10/743; see also *The Freedom Struggle in Hyderabad State*, Vol. III, pp. 236–39.
3. *Report of the Reforms Committee 1938*, p. 33.
4. There is no evidence of a similar reaction from the 'minorities' which were to be 'effectively protected'.
5. NMML, P. Naidu's report to Gandhi, 1938, Appendix IA, p. 1. A previous organisation also known as the Hyderabad State Reforms Association had been created in 1918 but was inactive. See *The Freedom Struggle in Hyderabad State*, Vol. III, p. 236.
6. Little is known of the personnel in district branches but the HSRA presumably relied on the scant educated element in district headquarters.
7. See *The Freedom Struggle in Hyderabad State*, Vol. III, Chapter IX; this chapter indicates that the swadeshi movement was promoted in Hyderabad mainly by Marathi-speaking brahmans; this information is confirmed in police reports of the period. A confidential report, Hankin to Faridoon Jung of 18 October 1909, states, for instance, 'In spite of a government school already existing here, the local brahman *vakils* [pleaders] ... collected funds and opened a school in Brahmanipura .... To all outward appearances this is only an ordinary school but in reality it is ... a *swadeshi* school'. (IRH, Home Department Special Branch Documents, File No. 12 of 1317F).

   As regards Home Rule agitation in Hyderabad, the British Resident states, 'Home Rule is not, of course, a burning question in a State governed by an absolute autocrat like the Nizam. The Hindus are alarmed at indications that the present Ruler is departing from the even-handed policy of his father and means to give Hindus even fewer appointments than before. The younger Muhammadans, on the other hand, are elated and think at the bottom of their hearts: since Home Rule in British India under the British Government would mean the rule of the Hindus over the Muhammadans, better that Home Rule should be Muhammadan rule under a Moslem Power'. (IOL, L/P & S/10/743, Letter No. 58F, Fraser to Holland, 15 April 1918).
8. For the full text of the firman see Aziz (1972). This contrasts with Mysore where Gandhi was allowed to speak on Khilafat and Non-Cooperation (in August 1920). See *The Collected Works of Mahatma Gandhi*, Vol. XVIII (Delhi, Government of India, Publications Division, 1965), pp. 185–86.
9. Letter, Nizam to Lord Chelmsford, quoted in Ramesan 1966, Vol. IV, p. 3203.
10. Sir Ali Imam (1869–1932) was appointed President of Hyderabad's Executive Council in August 1919. Born at Neora (Patna district), he was called to the Bar (Middle Temple) in 1890. Appointed Standing Counsel to the Government of India in Calcutta High Court and then Law Member of the Governor-General's Executive Council in 1910, he became a judge at Patna High Court in 1917 and

a member of the Executive Council of Bihar and Orissa in 1918–19. As President of Hyderabad's Executive Council, 'he worked hard but unsuccessfully for the retrocession of Berar to the Nizam' but his tenure has been characterised 'not as fruitful as it deserved to be'. In 1920, Sir Ali Imam was the first Indian representative to sit at a meeting of the League of Nations. He resumed practice in Patna in 1923 and died in Ranchi on 27 October 1932 (see Kabadi 1935 and Sen 1972, Vol. I).

11. IRH, Home Department, Special Branch Documents, File No. 3 of 1331F, Part V.
12. Others who attended were: Raghavendra Rao Sharma, Madapati Hanumanth Rao (lawyer); Kasinath Rao Vaidya (pleader) and Digambar Das (pleader), (Ramesan 1966, p. 53).
13. The only Muslim present at Akola was Sirajul Hasan Tirmizi.
14. It was at Gulbarga (Karnataka) where riots occurred between 11 and 14 August 1924 resulting in 'widespread desecration of mosques and temples and to 5 deaths and 8 serious injuries'. IOL, L/P&S/11/240, Viceroy to Home Office, 28 Aug 1924.
15. Ittihad leadership 'was mainly in the hands of ulema and *mashaiqeen* (religious leaders of non-Sunni sects)' M.A. Khan 1980, p. 48.
16. NMML, P. Naidu, *op.cit.*, Appendix Id, pp. 1–2.
17. IOL, R/1/11/1111 (1912), Pinhey to Viceroy, 22 Feb 1912.
18. Reminiscing, Tasker, one of the British officers 'lent' to the Hyderabad Government, wrote in 1972: 'It must be realised that there was a gulf between the Palace and the Council. Under the constitution, the Council had to get certain final orders by *firman* which had the force of law. Departmental proposals with Council's recommendations were ... sent up to the Nizam's 'Peshi Office', over which Council had no control. The Nizam did not send for the Resident in case of doubt. It was at this unpredictable stage that intrigue had its opportunity. One member of Council described the Nizam as 'the permanent opposition' .... Much depended on the relations between the Nizam and the Resident and on the extent to which the Nizam ... felt he could ignore Council without risk of advice from the Resident. This, of course, only rarely came into play when the principles of Intervention were at stake.' IOL, Mss. Eur D798/1–36, Tasker Collection, Box I.
19. IOL, R/1/1/1100 (1912), (Strictly Confidential) Memorandum Nizam to Viceroy, 17 Aug 1912.
20. IOL, R/1/1/1118 (1914), Fraser to Wood, 23 March 1914.
21. IOL, *Hyderabad Political Notebook*, Vol. II, p. 3 from Mss. Eur F144/63.
22. IOL, l/P & S/10743 (1918), Fraser to Holland, 1 April 1918; the two officers were Mr Wakefield, Director-General of Revenue, and Mr Hankin, Director-General of the Nizam's Police.
23. The Berars or Berar was a region of Hyderabad State which had been incorporated into British India since the days of Lord Curzon. See, A.P. Nicholson 1930.
24. IOL, L/P & S/10/743 (1918), Fraser to Holland, 4 April 1918.
25. *ibid.*, Fraser to Holland, 16 April 1918.
26. IOL, R/1/29/144 (1926), Barton to India Office, 11 Dec 1925. A nazar was a gift showing goodwill towards the ruler on festive occasions. It was a dated tradition, and nazars had become mere token presentations under the previous Nizam. But, Osman Ali revived the practice.
27. IOL, R/1/29/144/(1926), Barton to India Office, 11 Dec 1925.
28. IOL, R/1/29/144 (1926). See also K.P.S. Menon 19 , pp. 81–82.
29. IOL, R/1/29/144 (1926).

30. Quoted by the Viceroy in his reply to the Nizam on 27 March 1926. For the full text of Lord Reading's letter see *Report of the Indian States Committee 1928–29* (London, HMSO, 1929) pp. 56–58.
31. IOL, R/1/29/144 (1926).
32. IOL, L/P & S/13/1209 (1933), Mackenzie to India Office, 2 Nov 1933.
33. *ibid.*, Sir R. Trench was appointed Revenue Member (Minister) with Sir T. Tasker as Director-General and Secretary. Mr Armstrong was in charge of the District Police and Mr Collins headed the Commerce and Industries Department.
34. IOL, R/1/29/306 (1927), Barton to Political Department, 31 March 1927.
35. IOL, R/1/29/416 (1929), Barton to Political Department, 17 Sept and 8 Nov 1929. Keyes replaced Barton on 8 Feb 1930. The Nizam did not give Barton the traditional farewell dinner. See IOL, R/1/29/515. Fortnightly Report (hereafter FR) for the first half of February 1930 (hereafter abbreviated thus: 1/2/30).
36. IOL, R/1/29/416 (1929), *op. cit.*, 'Extract from file No. 12-P' following Barton's letter.
37. IOL, Mss Eur F131/31(b), pp. 1–5, Keyes to Watson, 1 March 1933.
38. The Nizam never relinquished his rights over Berar and, within the scheme of Federation, amalgamation of the region with the Central Provinces on the condition, among others, that 'HEH's sovereignty over the Berars should be recognized by some significant style and title for the Nizam and his successors; ... the heir apparent ... should in future be known as 'His Highness the Prince of Berar'.' In 1936, under the Berar Agreement, the Nizam was given the dynastic title of 'HEH the Nizam of Hyderabad and Berar' but never regained real sovereignty over the latter territory. In 1947, Berar passed to the Indian Union without appeal. IOL, Mss. Eur F131/31(b), Hydari to Keyes, 2 Jan 1933.
39. IOL; R/1/29/1189 (1934), Mackenzie to Political Department, Secret Report 17 Dec 1934, Appendix F, pp. 130–31.
40. His attitude in money matters also seems to have changed little. In July 1936, Mackenzie reported an 'increasing tendency of the Nizam to hoard his private wealth and debit the State with all manner of expenses on account of himself and his family which ought to be defrayed from his own pocket.' He continued: 'It is doubtful whether any Ruler in the world ... has ever possessed so large a private fortune .... The Nizam could without difficulty live on the interest of his income .... He still manages to take some two lakhs [200,000 rupees] a year in *nazars* and a good deal more in bribes .... In 1935, his receipts in bribes and *nazars* reached a grand total of 13½ lakhs.' IOL, R/1/29/1438 (1936), Mackenzie to Glancy, 23 July 1936.
41. Sir Akbar Hydari, B.A., LL.D (born 1869 in Bombay) came to Hyderabad in 1905 as Accountant-General. In 1906, he was appointed Finance Secretary and in 1907 acted as Finance Minister. Home Secretary in the Judicial, Police and General Departments in 1911, he took over the Finance portfolio from Sir R. Glancy in 1920. He represented Hyderabad at the first and second Round Table Conferences (voting in favour of the All-India Federation) and became President of the Executive Council in March 1937. *Hyderabad Directory and Diary, 1936* (Secunderabad, West End Craft, undated) and IOL, R/1/29/1527 (1937).
42. IOL, Mss. Eur F131/31(a), Keyes to Glancy, 16 Sept 1932.
43. Congress won a majority in Madras, the United Provinces, the Central Provinces, Bihar, Orissa, the NWFP and (in conjunction with a pro-Congress group) in Bombay (Coupland 1943, p. 308).

3

The Beginnings of Popular Political Agitation: The 1938–39 Satyagraha

Agitation in Hyderabad State was launched on two fronts. On the one hand, a newly-created Hyderabad State Congress pressed the Government on the issue of constitutional reforms; on the other, two communal pan-Indian organisations—the Arya Samaj and the Hindu Mahasabha—jointly put forward a demand for greater civil and religious liberties. Both movements escalated and finally coincided in a declaration of satyagraha on the same day, 24 October 1938.

The Congress rationale for agitation was that an announcement of constitutional reforms had been made in the State as long ago as 1920 but that, some seventeen years later, it had still not produced any result. Now, the Nizam's Government—no doubt again influenced by political developments in British India (the Act of 1935 and the introduction of responsible government in the provinces)—was repeating the same motions as in 1920, but with even less credibility. A Constitutional Reforms Committee had been appointed in September 1937 and, this time, relevant representations from the public had been invited. Yet, the orders dating from the late 1920s,[1] curtailing the liberty of the press and restricting speeches and public meetings had not been relaxed. Newspapers both within and outside the State had clamoured against these restrictions, but to no avail. Further, the members of the new Reforms Committee—two Hindu lawyers and four Muslims, all men of moderate views—and its vague terms of reference gave little hope that the granting of 'Responsible Government under the Asaf Jahi Dynasty', which had figured in the agendas of pre-Congress organisations in Hyderabad, would now be seriously considered.

The latest of these, the Hyderabad People's Convention, had been created (principally by educated Hindus) specifically to prepare an alternative scheme of constitutional reforms to that of the Aiyangar Reforms Committee.[2] A Working Committee consisting of 23 leading Hindus (mostly lawyers) and five Muslims had been elected in November 1937[3] and a report, duly ratified by a General Assembly of the Hyderabad People's Convention, was submitted to the Aiyangar Reforms Committee in January 1938. However, as four of the five Muslim members of the Working Committee had refused to sign it, this report lost much of its credibility with Government.

Subsequently, the Hyderabad People's Convention dissolved itself, after having appointed a Standing Committee of ten (nine Hindu Lawyers and one Muslim, under the presidentship of M. Hanumanth Rao, the well-known political figure) to pursue its work.

Less than a month later, the Indian National Congress stated, in its famous Haripura resolution, that it stood for 'the same political, social, and economic freedom in the States as in the rest of India' and considered the States 'an integral part of India'. In Hyderabad, the resolution was considered distinctly encouraging by the members of the Standing Committee[4] who decided forthwith on the conversion of their organisation into a new one, to be called the Hyderabad State Congress. This decision, however, provoked a furore in the local Muslim press. As a result, it was hastily replaced, Padmaja Naidu reported to Gandhi, at an emergency meeting of the Standing Committee, by an appeal merely 'urging the necessity for the formation of ... a political organisation for the attainment of Responsible Government'.

Members of pre-Congress organisations rallied to the call, and informal meetings began. By June, the intention to start an organisation to be known as the Hyderabad State Congress (HSC) was declared again by the Standing Committee. Later that month, a Congress Provisional Committee of six Hindus (R. Dhoot (Convener), B. Ramakrishna Rao, M. Hanumanth Rao, P.V. Joshi, Ramachari, and Janardhan Rao Desai) and one Muslim (Sirajul Hasan Tirmizi) was formed to supervise the enrolment of members and to start preparations for the general meeting, planned for August 1938 or after at least 500 ordinary members had been enrolled.

By the end of July 1938, the Committee claimed to have enrolled 1200 primary members in the city and districts, and an announcement was made in the press that an election of office-bearers would soon be held. Statewide appeals were also made, urging the public to join the HSC in great numbers and exhorting Hindus and Muslims 'to shed ... mutual distrust and join the cause of Responsible Government under the aegis of the Asaf Jahi dynasty'.

Having thus publicly adopted a non-communal stance and affirmed non-allegiance to outside political bodies—pre-conditions of recognition by Government—the HSC awaited official response.

To the State authorities, however, the HSC, with its almost exclusively Hindu membership and constant, if discreet, consultations with Congress headquarters in British India, was not the 'purely non-communal and national body, having no connection with the Indian National Congress' (Regani 1972, p. 190) it purported to be. Accordingly, the Nizam's Government planned to introduce a new Public Safety Act before 9 September 1938, the date fixed for the election of the HSC's office bearers.

This Act, modelled on the Act passed in British India during the previous Civil Disobedience Movement, was promulgated on 6 September 1938.[5] Two days later, it was followed by orders that, should it be formed, the HSC would be declared unlawful.

At the same time, the State Government made a show of even-handedness. Against the accusation that it was unjustly favourable to Muslim organisations (since State officials were allowed to join them), the Government published a list of nine organisations and institutions—both Hindu and Muslim—which were henceforth to be considered communal, and prohibited all public servants from participating in their activities.[6]

The list, however, did not include the Hyderabad State Congress, and its members continued lobbying ministers and officials of the Hyderabad Government to lift the ban on their party. On his way back from an official visit to Simla, Sir Akbar Hydari, the President of the Hyderabad Executive Council, met M. Nurie and K. M. Munshi, Congress ministers of the Bombay Government, and Shankar Rao Desai, of the Working Committee of the Indian National Congress, to consult with them on Hyderabad affairs. But these consultations did not allay Sir Akbar's suspicions that the HSC was a communal organisation.

Meanwhile, attempts were being made by local political leaders to defuse the tension which had followed a communal riot in Hyderabad city in April 1938. Narsing Rao, a respected moderate journalist and editor of the newspaper *Raiyat*,[7] and Bahadur Yar Jung, jagirdar and prominent Muslim leader, had for some time informally discussed religious and political matters, particularly mass conversion and demands for responsible government. Now, both Narsing Rao and Bahadur Yar Jung felt that, before entering actual negotiations, they should receive a mandate from the important leaders of their respective communities. Bahadur Yar Jung also proposed that, for their talks to be pursued in a propitious atmosphere, there should be no communal propaganda on either side during the period of negotiations. Hindu leaders replied, however, that so long as the ban on the HSC continued, the necessary calm atmosphere would be difficult to ensure.

Narsing Rao then personally approached Ali Yavar Jung, Secretary of the Constitutional Secretariat of the Hyderabad State, and suggested that, for the purpose of his talks with Bahadur Yar Jung, the ban on the HSC should be lifted. Ali Yavar Jung consulted Sir Akbar Hydari, who, before giving further consideration to the question, requested that the meeting of the General Body of the HSC be postponed indefinitely; that the name of the Hyderabad State Congress be altered so as to delete the word 'Congress' which was not approved by the Executive Council because of its political implications; that a detailed report of the points under discussion between Narsing Rao and Bahadur Yar Jung be given, with the assurance that there was at least a 50 per cent chance of the talks succeeding. Points on which agreements and disagreements were likely to occur had to be clearly stated.

The Provisional Committee of the Hyderabad State Congress met on 22 September 1938 to deliberate Sir Akbar's request. It resolved that the word 'Congress' could not be deleted; it also refused to commit itself as to the result of the talks between Narsing Rao and Bahadur Yar Jung; and, as a reply to Sir Akbar, it submitted an unsigned application to the Government requesting the lifting of the ban. Only a general assurance was given that the 'unity talks' had made a 'favourable start', and that there was 'every hope of a settlement' (Naidu 1938).

Nawab Ali Yavar Jung flatly rejected the terms of the application and reminded Hanumanth Rao and K.S. Vaidya that a detailed assurance was required, as well as the signatures of at least three leaders, namely B. Ramakrishna Rao, M. Ramachari and Janardhan Rao Desai, all members of the Provisional Committee. However, as no member of the Provisional Committee was prepared to sign, the negotiations with Government came to an end.

On 26 September 1938, the Executive Council decided that the ban on the HSC could not be lifted, and the next day Narsing Rao and Nawab Ali Yavar Jung agreed that their negotiations should be closed. The confrontation between the Hyderabad State Congress and the Nizam's Government had entered a new phase.

Subsequent meetings of the Provisional Committee now considered plans for a future political 'programme of action', while the Hyderabad issue was widely discussed in newspapers in British India. As a last concession to the personal request of Narsing Rao, the HSC General Body meeting had been postponed for a fortnight. But, in the meantime, P.M. Bapat, a Congress leader from Poona (Pune), had entered the State and had been promptly externed. Following this, Bapat stated to the press that he would personally launch satyagraha in Hyderabad and start sending in batches of volunteers, or *jathas* from 1 November. In parallel confrontations with the Government, the Arya Samaj was preparing to start satyagraha in December on the issue of Hindu civil rights, and Sanatanists (Hindu Mahasabha) were planning a procession through the streets of the city earlier, on the second anniversary of Waman Naik's death in October. As it was against Government orders, the issue would be used to precipitate a campaign of satyagraha against the State authorities. Satyagraha was thus 'in the air', and this is perhaps what prompted some members of the Congress Provisional Committee to include it in their programme of action. On 17 October 1938, a last meeting of the Provisional Committee was held, following which a 'manifesto' and a scheme for a campaign of satyagraha were issued. Several members of the Provisional Committee had declared their unwillingness to take any active part in the proposed satyagraha. The Provisional Committee was formally dissolved, and a Committee of Action, whose members would be the first to be dispatched, was formed.[8]

On 24 October 1938, the Committee of Action courted arrest at Sultan Bazar in the city, by announcing to the crowd that they represented the HSC. Two days later they were arrested. The Nizam's Government issued a communiqué that the HSC was henceforth an unlawful association within the meaning of the Public Safety Act.

The events leading to the Arya Samaj satyagraha followed a rather more incisive pattern as, unlike the HSC the Arya Samaj was not a new organisation in Hyderabad. By 1938 it had, in fact, some 250 branches in the State (twenty of which were in Hyderabad city). It was in opposition to the Anjuman-i-Tabligh-i-Islam, a proselytising Muslim society for the conversion of Hindus to Islam, created in 1932 by Bahadur Yar Jung. Conversions to Islam (of Untouchables and tribals mainly) were often followed by reconversion to Hinduism, thanks to

Arya Samaj efforts, and on the whole the Arya Samaj's movement (shuddi) seemed to retain the upper hand. Naturally, shuddi was served by the fact that the State's population was overwhelmingly Hindu and that new Arya Samaj converts could be 'supervised'. On the other hand, converts to Islam could be subjected to general harassment and economic boycotts, once the Islamic preachers had gone away. It was also strongly supported in the Indian press and, when incidents between the two communities occurred, they were exploited to the full. For example, the death, early in 1938, of a certain Ved Prakash—weaver and Arya Samaj member of Ganjaoti (Osmanabad district), allegedly murdered for having refused to embrace Islam—gave rise to a long campaign of protest both within and outside the State.[9]

The political alliance between the Arya Samaj and the Hindu Mahasabha was also evident in this context, although the two organisations were opposed—the first being reformist and the second orthodox—at the religious level.[10] V.D. Savarkar, President of the Hindu Mahasabha (then in session at Ahmedabad), was immediately notified by the Hyderabad Arya Samaj of the death of Ved Prakash. The topic was hotly discussed by the Hindu Mahasabha and it was decided that three leading Mahasabhaites, Sir Gokul Chand Narang, Dr Moonje and Bhai Parmanand, would apply for permission to conduct a general inquiry into the 'grievances of Hindus' in Hyderabad State.

Telegrams in great numbers protesting the 'murder' of Ved Prakash were also sent from different parts of India to the Viceroy in Delhi and to the British Resident in Hyderabad. Bhai Parmanand himself arrived in Hyderabad in March and was greeted at the railway station by a crowd of about 4,000 Arya Samajists. He was received by the President of the Executive Council, Sir Akbar Hydari, and addressed several meetings at which he advocated the creation of Hindu Mahasabha branches all over the State.

'The April Riots' occurred shortly after in Hyderabad city. They began on 5 April 1938, and lasted four full days. Regarding the origin of these riots, G. A. Anderson (Deputy Director-General, HEH the Nizam's CID) stated in his report:

> On [5 April], celebrations of the *urs* of a Muslim saint were in progress and included processions through the Jinsi Chouraha locality of the city inhabited predominantly by Hindu Lodhas, some of whom were staunch Arya Samajists. As there had been a rumour that the Lodhas were looking forward to picking a quarrel with the procession, the

> Muslims made their own arrangements: 10,000 armed with *lathis* and swords attended the procession. As they were passing through Jinsi Chouraha, throwing of stones began which prompted a Muslim counter-attack, and soon a chain of riots began which affected six or seven densely populated localities of the city (until 9 April 1938). For a while, panic and wild rumours regarding the numbers of persons killed and wounded prevailed over the whole city. In fact, the exact number of casualties was remarkable low, considering the extent of the riots: four killed (two Hindus and two Muslims) and 200 injured.[11]

The Resident added:

> There would appear to be little doubt that the spark which started this particular flame was the apparently unprovoked hostility of the Hindus to the procession of 5 April, a procession which had taken place for a considerable number of years without any objection being taken.
>
> Notwithstanding who had been responsible, these riots led to a storm of protest in the press in British India and to an increase in the allegations of 'oppression of Hindus' in Hyderabad State.[12]

The Nizam's Government, for its part, was of the opinion that 'much of the tension is due to the machinations of outsiders who have attempted by propaganda and teaching to poison the mind of the communities here'.[13] Bans were imposed on communal speeches and on preachers of any persuasion, from outside, lecturing in the State without prior authorisation.[14] The conflict with Hindu organisations was now an open one, and the pace of events accelerated rapidly.

At the end of April 1938, the International Aryan League (Arya Samaj) of Delhi discussed, in a Working Committee meeting, the 'grievances' of the Arya Samaj in Hyderabad and passed a resolution 'demanding an early settlement' on 14 points, the most salient of which were:

- Gashti (Order) No. 53, prohibiting public meetings, should be cancelled
- Restrictions regarding religious ceremonies should be removed
- Laws prohibiting the opening of *akharas* [gymnasiums] should be repealed
- Circulars prohibiting the opening of private schools should be cancelled
- Cases relating to communal disturbances should be investigated by an impartial tribunal
- Bans on religious workers should be lifted

- Books should not be proscribed without any scrutiny
- Restrictions on the publication of Arya Samaj newspapers should be removed
- Complete freedom for the observance of Hindu and Arya Samaj festivals when these coincide with Muslim festivals
- Hindu prisoners in the State prisons should not be converted to Islam, and Arya Samajists should be allowed to impart religious teaching to such prisoners
- No victimisation of Arya Samajists in the State service should be allowed
- Arya Samajists should have complete freedom for hoisting and flying 'Om' flags on their houses and Arya Samaj temples.

The resolution then concluded:

> This League declares that if State officials are not going to alter their policy in regard to the Arya Samaj, then the entire community shall be called upon to undertake all peaceful and legitimate means including satyagraha to defend their religious rights.[15]

The Nizam's Government, in response, withdrew Gashti No. 53 and granted that meetings of a non-political character could be held without permission; it also allowed G.S. Gupta, Speaker of the Central Provinces Assembly and President of the International Aryan League in Delhi, to visit Hyderabad between 29 June and 3 July 1938. G.S. Gupta had interviews with leading Hyderabad officials and local Hindu leaders, and was invited to inquire into the allegations of anti-Hindu discrimination in the State. The authorities (and the Resident) were hoping that such a visit would serve to dispel some of what the Resident termed the 'wildest exaggerations and distortions of the truth'[16] which had appeared in newspapers in British India, but G.S. Gupta declined to make a statement.

The Arya Samaj had, however, met again and it was soon learnt that a large scale anti-Hyderabad State campaign was being organised for September 1938 under the presidentship of G.S. Gupta himself!

This project was, in fact, abandoned in favour of a joint Arya Samaj–Hindu Mahasabha plan of action which would begin late in December 1938 with an Arya Samaj Conference in the vicinity of Hyderabad State, most probably in Sholapur. The All-India Hindu Mahasabha, at its Nagpur session in January 1939, would then adopt the resolution of the Arya Samaj Conference and both organisations would observe a 'Hyderabad Day' throughout India. Following this, satyagraha would be launched in Hyderabad, with outside assistance in the shape of funds and volunteers. It was reported that V.D. Savarkar, President of the All-India Hindu Mahasabha and G.S. Gupta, President of the International Aryan League, had personally devised this plan.[17]

The Nizam's Government took the threat seriously and prepared to meet it with a firm hand. Newspapers published in adjoining provinces in British India were closely scrutinised, and about half a dozen published in Bombay and Poona were prohibited entry into the State. The counter-move of the newspapers was to close down and resume under a different name and sometimes at different places.

By September, the Hyderabad State Congress was banned and a list of organisations considered to be communal (the Arya Samaj and the Hindu Subjects' Committee—the Hindu Mahasabha organisation in Hyderabad—were included) was published with the appending order to civil servants of the State Government not to participate in their activities.

Arya Samajists, in the meantime, had formed a 'War Council' which was to lead the satyagraha campaign planned to begin shortly after the Arya Samaj Conference of December 1938, and had begun collecting funds both in British India and in Hyderabad. By the second half of September, it was reported that Rs 24,000 had already been collected and deposited at Sholapur, the satyagraha headquarters-to-be. Lists of volunteers and a payment scheme for them and their families were being prepared. Meanwhile, there were rumours that the Arya Samaj Conference would be held in Nagpur along with the Hindu Mahasabha session, and not separately at Sholapur.[18]

The Nizam's Government decided to strike immediately and took two steps which, the President of the Executive Council said, 'appear likely to either "call the bluff" of the Arya Samajists or precipitate the threatened satyagraha': Narender Pershad Saxena, a Hyderabadi Kayasth and one of the most prominent Arya Samaj leaders in the State, was arrested for breaking the ban on communal speeches and for possession of prohibited newspapers. And, an announcement was made that a White Paper 'trouncing the Arya Samaj for its political activities under the guise of religion and giving chapter and verse for the charges against it' would be prepared.[19] The Arya Samaj and the Hindu Mahasabha went ahead with their plans, however, and satyagraha was declared on 24 October 1938.

Regarding the coincidence of the declarations of satyagraha by the Hyderabad State Congress and the Arya Samaj–Hindu Mahasabha, it is difficult to affirm collusion between the two blocks. The HSC denied links with communal organisations (although many of its leading personalities had been or were still involved with either Arya Samaj or the Hindu Mahasabha).[20] Nevertheless, the reason given by the Arya Defence League of Hyderabad for the coincidence in the day of declaration sounds rather unconvincing:

> When it became known that the Hyderabad State Congress proposed to start a campaign of *satyagraha* on the 24th October 1938, the younger workers of the Arya Samaj threatened that they would join in the other two campaigns unless the Aryan League *satyagraha* was started immediately. Therefore it was launched on the 24th of October 1938, on the same day as the Hyderabad State Congress started its *satyagraha* (Naidu 1938, p. 5).

As for the Hindu Mahasabha, it seized on the refusal of Government to allow a procession commemorating the second anniversary of W. Naik's death—to be led on 21 September 1938 by Y.D. Joshi of the extreme wing of the Mahasabha—to declare that satyagraha would be launched in one month (21 October 1938) and this date was later adjusted also to 24 October.[21]

Congress began its offensive at the end of November 1938, launching the agitation in most of the districts at once:

> The procedure adopted was everywhere the same. Congress literature was distributed secretly on the evening of 22nd November in district headquarters and important towns, calling on the public to observe *hartal* and announcing that the 23rd November would be marked by processions, public meetings, and the courting of arrest by volunteers.

The comment was made, however, that,

> the performance of this programme was nowhere completely achieved and varied from being a total failure in several districts to partial success in a few .... Nowhere did the police find it necessary to use force in effecting arrests or dispersing crowds.[22]

The State authorities remained vigilant, nevertheless, as there was, behind the ease with which the agitation was being kept under control (and so far there had been only threats of jathas), 'a general feeling that these somewhat farcical proceedings were in the nature of an overture' and that 'the symphony would begin with the Arya Samaj Conference at Sholapur on Christmas week'.[23]

At this juncture, some of the Osmania University Hindu students became involved in a confrontation with the University authorities and later with Government, over the singing of *Vande Mataram*, a song judged to have objectionable political connotations by the Nizam's Government. Some 300 of them were expelled, drawing further all-India attention to Hyderabad (Ramesan 1966, pp. 103–05). The expelled students, who were sympathetically received by Nagpur University, called on the Indian National Congress (INC) to take a definite stand on the Hyderabad issue.

The INC, however, already divided at Haripura as the election of Subhas Chandra Bose showed (see Majumdar 1969, p. 562), was in a difficult position. Gandhi and the conservative section had retained sufficient control to ensure that the INC would stay away from too direct an involvement in the princely States. Calls for support to the lukewarm satyagraha campaign of the Hyderabad State Congress, which coincided with that of two communal organisations, were therefore an embarrassment. The Congress high command did not want to be construed as actively supporting a communal struggle. Besides, 'unity talks' between Narsing Rao and Nawab Bahadur Yar Jung were again in progress and still had credibility. It was felt at Wardha that an agreement reached by the two leaders would be preferable to a continued fight and further embittering of relations between Hindus and Muslims in the State, particularly as, in British India, Muslims were following attentively what was beginning to look like a concerted Hindu attack on Hyderabad.[24]

Satyagraha was also dampened by the efforts of Bahadur Yar Jung. Abul Kalam Azad (member of the Working Committee of the INC) had, on two occasions, provided him the opportunity of talking about conditions in Hyderabad directly with Jawaharlal Nehru.[25] The Viceroy himself had spoken to Birla (the Indian magnate who had influence with Gandhi) to convey to Gandhi the seriousness of the view the Government of India took towards political developments in Hyderabad. Birla also talked to Gandhi and Patel about 'the advisability of preventing so far as possible any jathas or individuals marching on Indian States for offering [*sic*] satyagraha'. Judging the Indian National Congress' sentiments at the time, he reported back to the Viceroy that, 'as Gandhi and Patel already held views similar to those of His Excellency, I found my task very easy.[26]

Shortly before Birla's visit, Gandhi had also received the report on the internal situation in Hyderabad prepared, at his request, by Padmaja

Naidu (the daughter of Sarojini Naidu, Hyderabadi poet and a well-known INC figure) in November 1938.

Naidu's report (a 12-page letter with 13 appendices) contains a wealth of information on the local political scene and organisations. Her most damning comments concern the early State Congress leadership, which she bluntly accuses of communalism and callousness, and the State Congress itself, which she says, was unrepresentative. Her letter to Gandhi begins, however, with her views on the appearance of communalism in Hyderabad since the April riots. She says:

> I still find it almost incredible, that in this short space of time, there could have been established in Hyderabad with its long tradition of real communal harmony, the bitterness and hostility, the demoralising distrust and suspicion, that are abroad. I am not referring to the masses or to those large sections of the people throughout the dominions who have been relentlessly corrupted during the last few years by the avowed communalist organisations like the Arya Samaj and the Tanzim Societies who have been carrying on their rival programmes of mass conversion (1938, p. 1).

Naidu here ascribes responsibility for the deterioration of the inter-communal atmosphere in Hyderabad to Hindu and Muslim competitive conversion movements rather than to the 'oppression of Hindus in Hyderabad State' as claimed by the Arya Samaj, the Hindu Mahasabha and a section of the press in British India. She continues:

> I am now referring specifically to the Hindu and Muslim intelligenosia [*sic*], and especially to [its] recognized leaders ... who have been making sincere if not very strenuous efforts to build up such public life as exists in Hyderabad on a non-communal basis, and all of whom ... have been intimately associated ... in every organised effort at political work there has been in Hyderabad during the last twenty years. I am shocked ... beyond measure to find these men, both Hindus and Muslims, openly expressing suspicion and distrust of each other [*sic*] *bona fides* on the question of communalism.

Thus, by 1938, it appears that feelings of communalism, which had permeated the masses for some years, had gradually affected even the top layers of Hyderabad's society. Naidu, however, blames not only the communal organisations for this but also the State Government which, she charges, was 'in no less measure responsible for creating this mutual distrust' and was 'using every subtle, underhand method possible to exploit it for its own political purposes' (p. 2). She was referring here presumably to the covert but well-known support given by the Nizam himself to the Ittihad.

Turning to the Hyderabad State Congress, she says:

> Sitting in Delhi and moved by righteous indignation at what I believe to be an unjust ban on it [Hyderabad State Congress] I could have made out a much stronger case for it than I am able to do today seeing it clearly in relation to its surrounding ... I must confess ... that apart from the justice of the fight against the ban placed on it, I find it difficult to pretend that I am, personally, in sympathy with its methods of work ... or with its vague unpractical attitude about plans for the future .... [The State Congress] comprises three different groups: (1) the original founders who formed the Provisional Committee (2) the Shadow Cabinet that is conducting the present fight (3) the members who have volunteered for *satyagraha* .... There has been throughout, from the beginning, a deplorable lack of honesty and trust and understanding among the members themselves which ... is still handicapping them in their struggle today because, obviously, it entails a lack of coordination between the three different groups involved. Above all, I cannot reconcile myself to the fact that nearly all the prominent leaders who were involved in starting the Hyderabad State Congress, who were intimately concerned in all its dealings with the Government, and who made all the decisions with regard to the policies of the State Congress, and are thus morally responsible for precipitating the struggle against Government, have openly disassociated themselves from the *satyagraha* movement and are sitting idle at home while batches of young volunteers that they are personally responsible for involving in the fight are being sentenced to jail for long periods .... Another thing that I personally find difficult to accept is the amazing lack of political perspective that has been shown throughout, as is proved by the utter apathy of the members of the State Congress with regard to the question of the minorities .... They realize that they have earned, owing largely to their own carelessness, the active resentments of the Muslims and the Depressed Classes. But they do not ... make any step ... to inspire confidence .... The original founders of the State Congress consisted almost exclusively of men who had all been openly connected in some capacity or the other, either with definitely communal or else preponderately [sic] Hindu organisations .... These members admit ... that they deliberately made no effort ... to approach the Muslims and seek their cooperation ... they express frankly to me their distrust and dislike of the Muslims .... I must say ... that even if such an organisation [State Congress] cannot be proved to be communal in the Government's

sense of the word ... it ... still remains communal in my sense of the word (pp. 4–6).

And she concludes:

> Any real enduring fight for Civil Liberties or Responsible Government must be based on some legitimate claim to make a demand on behalf of the people. I do not feel that there is any real sanction behind the claim of the State Congress to represent the people of Hyderabad (p. 8).

It is difficult to affirm that it was only due to personal meetings (such as Bahadur Yar Jung's or Birla's) or reports (such as Naidu's) that the Indian National Congress declared an 'unconditional suspension of anti-Hyderabad activities' by mid-December 1938. Naidu's report is specifically cited by the British Resident in Hyderabad as a factor 'believed to have influenced Gandhi and the Congress High Command in coming to this decision'.[27] But, it is probable that this report merely confirmed the fears of the INC that agitation in Hyderabad could rapidly become communally-rather than politically-based. The Haripura resolution of February 1938 had been a compromise between the two groups within Congress which disagreed on the extent to which the party as a whole should support agitation in the princely States (see Jeffrey 1978, p. 18). Some favoured active support in order to hasten the process leading to responsible government in the States (and thus increase Congress chances to dominate at the federal level).[28] Others—like Gandhi— remained wary of too direct an involvement as they doubted whether, once begun, 'non-violent' agitations in the States could be prevented from degenerating into violence. Since then, agitations of varying degrees had been launched in Mysore, Travancore, Kashmir, the Orissa States, Rajkot, Mewar and Baroda as well as in Hyderabad (Jeffrey 1978) and, on the whole, the form of the Haripura resolution had been observed. However, in States such as Travancore, Kashmir and Hyderabad, indications were that the agitation was quickly assuming a communal colour and, by December 1938, the INC was probably already anxious to dissociate itself urgently from further developments (Coupland 1943, p. 175).

Whatever the case may be, Dr Abdul Hamid, a member of the INC Working Committee, was deputed by Abul Kalam Azad to Hyderabad 'to study the situation and restore cordial relations between the Hindus and the Mussalmans'.[29] After an interview with Sir Akbar Hydari, Dr Hamid announced that the State Government would accept, with regard to constitutional reforms and franchise, an agreed settlement between the two communities.[30] Negotiations between Bahadur Yar Jung and Narsing Rao would be continued and, Dr Hamid said, 'a successful outcome to them was expected'.[31] What was still hoped was a sort of 'Lucknow Pact' in Hyderabad State, and the Nizam's Government (relying on Bahadur Yar Jung to clinch the deal on behalf of the Muslims) would welcome 'a solution reached in direct negotiations by known officials of both communities'.

As expected, the HSC bowed to the recommendations put forward at Wardha and, on 24 December 1938, Kasinath Rao Vaidya, the sixteenth and last 'dictator', announced rather lamely that the satyagraha movement of the HSC was suspended 'temporarily'.[32] He was promptly arrested.

The satyagraha in Hyderabad State had lasted two months to the day, and according to HSC sources, 300 satyagrahis were in jail. The Nizam's Government, as a goodwill gesture in response to the unconditional suspension of anti-Hyderabad activities by the INC, had accepted in principle the liberation of imprisoned Congress satyagrahis. A distinction between the State and the Indian National Congress was drawn, however, and only INC satyagrahis numbering fifty or sixty would be freed. There would be no general amnesty.[33]

Thereafter, the anti-Hyderabad movement was entirely controlled by the Arya Samaj and the Hindu Mahasabha. Predictably, it developed on clearly communal lines.

Throughout its satyagraha, and despite all pretence of dissociation from organisations in British India, the Hyderabad State Congress had received guidance and advice from Congress headquarters in British India; Congressmen had organised meetings in their respective provinces calling for money and for volunteers to further the movement, and a number of these volunteers from British India had entered the State to take part in the agitation. But at no time was responsibility for the Hyderabad satyagraha acknowledged by the INC. The abandonment of satyagraha by the HSC, therefore, did not mark the end of agitation in Hyderabad State. The field was now left to the Arya Samaj and the Hindu Mahasabha which, by contrast, had been openly backed by their all-India bodies, with their respective presidents involving themselves personally in organising joint agitation.

V.D. Savarkar, President of the All-India Hindu Mahasabha (Poona), was making arrangements with G.S. Gupta, President of the International Aryan League (Delhi), as early as July 1938, to combine their next sessions and prepare a common programme of agitation. Savarkar said,

> The dates should be somewhere at the beginning of the Xmas [*sic*] vacation so as to suit the session of the Hindu Mahasabha at Nagpur .... That will enable the representatives of the Arya Samaj from the North to proceed from Sholapur directly to Nagpur to attend the Hindu Mahasabha session ... as soon as the Sholapur Arya Samelan is over .... A protest should be organised all over India and the common programme of hartal, black flag processions, meetings and resolutions backing up the Arya Samaj and the Hindu Mahasabha resolution on the subject and the ultimatum sent to the Nizam by them. If the Nizam fails to satisfy the demands, then a campaign of civil disobedience should be taken up forthwith by both the organisations so as to render it a Pan-Hindu Aspect [*sic*].[34]

Agitation had thus not been planned to begin before these December sessions, but the intrusion of the HSC on the scene and its declaration of satyagraha to begin on 24 October 1938 set the wheels in motion, and both the Arya Samaj and the Hindu Mahasabha then followed suit although they had not yet fully prepared their own movements by that date.[35]

This probably explains why the Arya Samaj–Hindu Mahasabha agitation really got under way only by March 1939. At the Sholapur and Nagpur sessions of December 1938, both organisations had displayed 'wild enthusiasm' and their members delivered 'fiery speeches', but jathas, which began courting arrest in January and February, rarely exceeded five persons.[36]

Savarkar was appealing to all Hindu Sabhas in India to recruit volunteers, while the Arya Samaj decreed the twenty-second of each month to be a day of particular anti-Hyderabad demonstration ('Hyderabad Day') throughout India. But jathas from British India, which arrived principally at Hyderabad and Aurangabad, remained unimpressive. For example, a jatha arrived by train at Aurangabad (from Poona) on 4 February 1939 consisting of five students aged 21, 15, 14, 13 and 12. They said that the editor of the *Mahratta* of Poona had given them Rs 40 to go to Aurangabad and demonstrate on behalf of the Hindu Mahasabha. Another jatha of eleven youths also arrived at Aurangabad (from Bombay), and said that they had received Rs 50 each from one M.C. Gokhale for the same purpose. Both batches apologised, promised never to return, and were sent back on the first available train.

In Hyderabad, too, the response of the Hindus to agitation was poor, the arrival of jathas being generally greeted 'by a few idle onlookers with bored interest'.[37] The figures for February show that out of a total of 284 arrests, 212 came from British India and only 72 were residents of the State. The State authorities asserted that:

> The actual number of demonstrators who have come forward on their own initiative from within the State had been extremely small and of these the men of any status have been nil. It can be said with certainty that, if the influx from outside could be stopped, there would be practically no Arya Samaj or Mahasabha satyagraha in Hyderabad.[38]

This absence of local 'men of status' in the jathas was probably due to the fact that they had too much at stake to risk imprisonment. That they were perhaps prepared to extend some help to their co-religionists did not mean that they would actually court arrest themselves, any more than they had been willing to do so at the time of the Congress satyagraha.

There were also the Hindus attached to the Nizam who saw the dangers of change in the power structure, and those, whatever their social rank, who were plainly unmoved by communal propaganda. In April 1939, for example, Sir Kishen Pershad, former President of the Executive Council, 'denounced in a lengthy statement the agitation of the Arya Samajists and Hindu Mahasabhites and refuted their arguments.' Later,

> a mass meeting of citizens of Hyderabad and Secunderabad was held and the recent message of communal harmony and political progress by constitutional means given by Sir Kishen Pershad was moved by Raja Jaswantrao Bahadur and seconded and supported by representatives of Hindus and Muslims, including Baji Krishan Rao, an Arya Samajist (*Review of the Hyderabad Agitation* (hereafter, *RHA*) 1939, p. 35).

Those most likely to fall prey to propaganda were the uneducated and the poor, often Untouchables, as they could be more easily manipulated by prospects of remuneration, or of various immediate advantages. At the same time they were less able to use critical reasoning in regard to the deeper political or communal motives of propaganda, whether Hindu or Muslim.

The Muslim population, for its part, was reacting variously to the onslaught of Arya Samaj and Hindu Mahasabha activities. In general there was forbearance, but here and there a flare-up would occur such as that on 5 March 1939, when satyagrahis arrived by bus in Hyderabad city, and began shouting slogans on alighting. They were

> set upon by irate bystanders, three being severely injured. But for the prompt interference of the policemen on point duty, and others who rushed to the scene from the vicinity, a serious situation would have quickly developed. In fact, if outside satyagrahis were not promptly arrested, they would have been given short shrift by the Muslim public (*RHA* 1939, p. 37).

The extremist Muslim parties, such as the Anjuman-i-Ittihad-ul-Muslimeen and the Khaksars, had advocated the organising of the Muslim community, and from the end of 1938 had staged counter-propaganda demonstrations. Two thousand Khaksars, for instance, had taken out a procession at Nander (Nanded) in November 1938, brandishing swords, guns and other weapons, and shouting slogans such as 'Nizam Zindabad' and 'Hindu Sabha and State Congress Murdabad'. According to the *Review of the Hyderabad Agitation*, they then submitted a memorandum warning that 'if the [Arya Samaj–Hindu Mahasabha] Movement was not suppressed within a fortnight, they would come forward to combat the agitation ... irrespective of the consequences that might follow' (*RHA* 1939, p. 38).

However, other than stray assaults on parties of satyagrahis entering Hyderabad and isolated clashes with local Hindus, the Muslims did not follow up their threats of violence with organised opposition; but the situation remained tense and dangerous.

In British India too, Muslims were reacting to the Hindu attack on Hyderabad. Religious and political organisations—the Jamiat-ul-Ulema-i-Hind, the Ittihad-i-Millat, and the Muslim League—assured the Nizam's Government of Muslim help from British India, and staged demonstrations in favour of Hyderabad. The *RHA* also reported (p. 4) that,

> ... the Majlis-i-Nawajawan-Islam of Amritsar offered the services of 500 Muslims who pledged themselves to sacrifice their lives for the cause of the State .... At a Muslim League meeting on March 19th, a suggestion was made to lead a *jatha* to the Lahore Railway Station to prevent Hindu *satyagrahis* from proceeding to Sholapur .... A busload of *satyagrahis* proceeding to the State was attacked by Muslims at Karachi on March 30th 1939 and many were injured ... (*ibid.*, p. 40).

Similar incidents occurred at Delhi, Bombay, Nagpur, Pusad (Central Provinces) and Ahmedabad, but it was at Sholapur, the headquarters of the anti-Hyderabad agitation, that feelings were running the highest. Muslims often attacked Arya Samaj and Hindu Mahasabha meetings with stones. Trouble was frequently feared as, for instance, before a Muslim League procession through Hindu localities which had been planned for 3 May 1939, at a time when 'Muslims [were] definitely on the warpath and [were] reported to have stored up weapons of offence for such an occasion' (*ibid.*, p. 41). A cause for further alarm during that period was the Bombay Provincial Muslim League meeting at Sholapur planned for 5 and 6 May 1939 'as a counter-blast to the Arya Samaj activities'. Fearing trouble, Arya Samajists were warned by their leaders not to send any jathas to Hyderabad during the period of the Sholapur Conference of the Muslim League. But this did not prevent rioting of some consequence later in the month, on 21 May. Total casualties amounted to six deaths and over sixty injured; British troops were called in from Poona, and the Sholapur district magistrate ordered the removal of Arya Samaj volunteers from Sholapur city and district, to which K.M. Munshi (Home Minister, Government of Bombay) agreed after some hesitation.[39]

Yet, Professor Sudhakar, General Secretary of the International Aryan League, made statements in the all-India press that 'no slackening of activity was to be allowed and still greater exertions were to be made ...' (*Madras Mail*, 13 May 1939) and that, 'the *Satyagraha* Committee had directed all Arya Samaj centres to direct *jathas* to Pusad [Berar] instead of Sholapur'.[40]

This displacement of the centre of agitation from the Bombay Province to the Central Provinces particularly incensed the Hyderabad authorities as Berar was still officially under the Nizam's sovereignty. At the end of May 1939, Sir Akbar Hydari requested 'that the attention of the Government of the Central Provinces and Berar ... be invited to the situation which had arisen as a result of the establishment at Pusad as a centre from which *jathas* were being dispatched into this State.' A detailed description followed of nine jathas (totally 1,044 volunteers), which had entered the State between 31 March and 22 May 1939 and a complaint that 'in none of these instances ... previous intimation [was] received from the authority of the Central Provinces ... and HEH's officers had to pick up information as best they could.' Sir Akbar did not entertain much hope that his request would produce effective results, however, as the Government of the

Central Provinces had always vigorously supported the satyagraha in Hyderabad. G.S. Gupta, Speaker of the Central Provinces Assembly, had been the plenipotentiary leader of the anti-Hyderabad agitation since May, while Shukla, the Prime Minister, had constantly turned a deaf ear to previous British appeals for moderation.[41]

At the all-India level, it had long been known to the Government of India that,

> apart from secret sympathy with a Hindu attack on a Muslim stronghold, Congress Governments were naturally unwilling, by taking active measures against agitation, to risk accusations of repression and in particular of aiding Muslim repression of Hindus.[42]

But, obviously, instructing British Governors of provinces to intervene forcibly on behalf of Hyderabad was a delicate matter and risked disrupting the provincial government experiment; there was, thus, little the British could or were prepared to do.

Not all governments in British India were unsympathetic to Hyderabad, however. The Premier of Punjab, Sir Sikander Hayat Khan, had issued appeals to the press not to publish any news from Hyderabad which might aggravate communal feelings, and later brought into force Section 4 to 7 of the Indian State (Protection) Act (*RHA* 1939, p. 308). In Madras, orders were passed, under Section 144 of the Criminal Procedure Code, 'forbidding meetings in Madras city in connection with the Hyderabad agitation' (*ibid*., p. 309).

On the other hand, the *RHA* (1939) reports that the Bombay Government had replied to a representation from the Nizam's Government:

> that they would allow the Press in their Province the same liberty of criticising the administration of Hyderabad State which the Press enjoyed in regard to the Bombay Government Administration; that incitement to, and preparation for, violence would be dealt with; and that the Government of Bombay would, if required, give the Nizam's Government such information as a friendly government was bound to give; but that they would not stop persons from proceeding to Hyderabad's territory with intentions which, if carried out in the State, might amount to a breach of Hyderabad State laws (*ibid*., p. 308).

The Central Provinces Government, refused 'even to keep the Nizam's Government informed of the development of the agitation in the Central Provinces, or of the possibility of despatch of jathas to the state' (*ibid*., p. 309).

Thus, the Hyderabad authorities received little or no help from neighbouring British India provinces. This uncooperative attitude, mainly on the part of the Bombay and Central Provinces Governments, allowed the proliferation of rallying points for agitators all round the State, with the tacit consent of the respective Congress ministries.[43]

Camps were thus started at Ahmednagar and Sholapur in the west, at Bezwada in the southeast, at Pusad in the north, and at Manmad in the northwest.[44] The reception of volunteers prior to their departure for Hyderabad was organised, while an increasingly strident anti-Hyderabad propaganda continued in British India. The alleged religious, social and economic disabilities of the Hindus in general, and of the Arya Samajists in particular, were emphasised. Muslims were condemned for this, and the administration of the Nizam compared to that of Aurangzeb. Statements were made that 'Hindustan belonged to the Hindus'; that 'the eight crores of Muslims should either be converted to Hinduism or drowned in the Arabian Sea or driven out of India'; that all mosques situated within 500 yards of any Hindu temple should be demolished; that for each Hindu killed in the Nizam's State three Muslims should be slain in British India, that the State of a tyrant like the Nizam should be destroyed, and so on.[45]

Processions were taken out (as in Bombay), sometimes accompanied by trucks provided with loudspeakers, shouting anti-Muslim and anti-Hyderabad slogans. Ballad songs were composed and magic lantern slide shows organised, 'disclosing' cases of oppression of Hindus and outrages on Hindu women. Booklets, handbills, newsletters and bulletins in different languages were printed and circulated at lectures, and substantial amounts of money were collected. It was reported, for instance, that,

> the 'Nizam Civil Resistance Fund' at Poona, out of a total of Rs. 72,795 had on the 15th June an unexpended balance of Rs. 483/-. Mahesha Krishna, the sixth 'dictator', collected about Rs. 75,000 from the Punjab and Delhi and of this Rs. 20,000 have already been sent to the Sholapur War Council.
>
> Some thirty odd branches of the Arya Samaj in the Punjab have promised to subscribe monthly to the central organisation sums varying from Rs. 5 to Rs. 550.[46]

Hindu newspapers, some out of sympathy and others for remuneration, were also joining in this campaign against the State—the *Kesari*, the *Lokamanya*, the *Riyasat* and the *Sarvadeshak* of Delhi being the most virulent.

In Hyderabad, Hindu response to agitation continued to be poor. By March, the effects of propaganda began to produce results in British India, however, as shown by the strength of jathas arriving in the State. Sixty-four persons, led by a Chand Karan Sarda of Ajmer, for instance, arrived from Sholapur early in the month. Later, 160—half of them from the Punjab—led by L. Kushal Chand (editor of the Lahore *Milap*) followed, also from the base at Sholapur.

Writing to the British Resident, Gidney, on 3 April 1939, Sir Akbar Hydari rued:

> Despite the lack of response from the residents of the State, and in spite of the suspension of Congress, there is no question that the Hindu Mahasabha and the Arya Samaj movements have rapidly gained momentum so far as the flow of volunteers from British India is concerned. As a result of meetings and extensive press propaganda organised all over India, increasing numbers of volunteers are being recruited and large sums of money collected. Many of the *satyagrahis* make no secret of the fact that they have been hired. They are now appearing in such places hitherto untouched as Raichur and Khammamet.

From April, this increase in the number of volunteers became markedly more dramatic. The Fortnightly Report mentions that on 22 April, a jatha of 528 was arrested at Gulbarga, another of 515 arrived at Umarkhed from Pusad in Berar on 5 May, and the largest ever jatha—782—arrived by train on 6 June; it was led by Punjabi ex-terrorist, Mahesha Krishna.

The despatch of large jathas was intended to disrupt the Hyderabad administration. It succeeded, as, for instance, in the case of the State jails, which had not been built to accommodate such numbers. The 8,000-odd satyagrahis behind bars by the end of June 1939 were put up, as well as could be, in existing penitentiaries and internment camps hastily built for the purpose. Meanwhile, rumours of bad treatment and of forcible conversion to Islam were rife. The condition of political prisoners was seized upon by the Arya Samaj and Hindu Mahasabha and became yet another item in the all-India anti-Hyderabad campaign. A 'Hyderabad Martyrs' Day' was decreed for 21 May, and representations were made on their behalf to British authorities. M. Sudhakar, Secretary of the International Aryan League sent lengthy telegrams to

Lord Zetland, Secretary of State for India, and to British MPs in London claiming

> total arrests Arya Satyagrahis alone ... exceed 10,000, majority belonging to State. Treatment of prisoners in Hyderabad jails extremely bad. Food and accommodation ... insufficient and unhealthy ... hard labour extorted in burning sun ... protests by prisoners resulted several *lathi* charges in jail causing large casualties .... Already ten prisoners have died.[47]

The report sent to the Secretary of State by the Superintendent (Political Branch), Hyderabad Residency for replying to Sudhakar, is worth quoting at some length as it throws light on many aspects of the satyagraha and most emphatically denies these charges:

> Total arrests from commencement in October to June 23rd are 7,989 and do not exceed 10,000 as stated. Further, this figure includes also *satyagrahis* of Hindu Mahasabha which is carrying on simultaneous campaign with Arya Samaj. Far from majority of *satyagrahis* coming from the State, the reverse is the case, the proportion of State subjects to total arrests being about 20%. This exposes ... the propaganda method of the Arya Samaj which has been endeavouring to keep up pretensions that the movement is mainly supported from within the State.
>
> Allegations regarding jails equally misleading .... Endeavours are being made to embarrass Government by overcrowding jails and then to make capital out of death and other incidents arising from indiscipline of prisoners .... *Jathas* contain some intellectuals but mainly consist of immature youths and members of labouring class completely ignorant of actual conditions in the State .... Untrue that *lathi* charges have been made on protesting prisoners. Nine deaths among prisoners is not abnormal for jail population of several thousand and time of year. Of these one had high fever on arrival, two were over sixty-five, and one was lunatic.
>
> Demand for intervention comes inappropriately from the aggressor party. Having recklessly used methods of propaganda, slogan shouting and mass *satyagraha* which have raised communal tension in many parts of India to dangerous pitch, it finds that it cannot shake the State and therefore misrepresents conditions in endeavour to involve paramount power. If demand for intervention is to be made at all, it should be by the State which ... has been subjected to form of invasion and campaign of vilification in press throughout India which with honourable exceptions have received no check from provincial governments (IOL, R/1/29/1921).

Representing the other point of view, the Council of Ministers, Central Provinces and Berar, sent a memorandum to the local British

Governor at the end of June 1939, asking for the intervention of the paramount power on the grounds that

> the contrast between British India and Hyderabad in the matter of religious and cultural liberty is so glaring as to call for speedy action by the paramount power ... before the situation deteriorates further, developing perhaps into a civil war between Hindus and Muslims in the Hyderabad State if not elsewhere.[48]

These allegations, too, were categorically refuted by the British Resident in Hyderabad who advised Sir R. Glancy, Political Adviser to the Crown Representative in a missive dated 12 July 1939:

> Had the contrast between religious and cultural liberty been so 'glaring' as the Arya Samajists and the Council of Ministers of the Central Provinces Government attempt to make out, I much doubt whether the State's Arya Samaj and Hindu subjects would have shown so much reluctance to participate in the struggle .... To speak therefore of ... the danger of civil war '*in* the Hyderabad State' is a misrepresentation of the real position. The agitation is from 'without' and not from 'within' the State and any danger that there might have at one time been of civil disturbance in the State was due to Muslim resentment against the Arya Samaj *jathas* which have been invading the State .... The danger of civil disturbance has now, I hope, been averted largely by reason of the refusal of the State's Hindu subjects to participate to any great extent in the agitation. There is I believe a strong feeling among not a few Hindus that the Arya Samaj attack on the State has been carried to extreme length and that it should be called off.

In fact, the *RHA* reports (p. 43) that by June 1939 there were signs that the agitation was flagging. The financing of the movement was becoming problematic and it was reported that 'Arya Samaj leaders were rather afraid that they might have to restrict the *satyagraha* or stop it altogether soon,' and that 'some of them emphasised the necessity of collecting men and money.'

Further, the Hindu Mahasabha—without consulting the Arya Samaj—had deputed Jagadguru Shankaracharya of Jyotirmath, Badrinath, one of their most orthodox pontiffs, to Hyderabad on a peace mission. During his visit, which had been authorised by the State Government, the Shankaracharya held discussions with various religious leaders and officials. As his feelings towards the (unorthodox) Arya Samaj were known to be anything but sympathetic, his visit was taken as the indication of an impending split among the leaders of the satyagraha. Indeed, the pontiff also sent a letter to the (surprised) Archbishop of Canterbury, in which his opinion of the Arya Samaj is clearly revealed. He wrote:

> Your Lordship ... as advisor to His Imperial Majesty for the maintenance of religious tolerance all over the Empire shall have to see that the prestige of the ancient Sanatana Dharma Hindu Religion [is] not in any way allowed to be invaded upon by the Non-Hindus (Muslims) or Un-Hindus (Arya Samajists) .... We learn that the [Hyderabad] Arya Samajists are sending some deputation to wait upon the [British] Premier. What for? We fail to understand .... Your Lordship knows that Arya Samajists are proslytizing [*sic*] people and they are for converting born Muslims and Christians into the Hindu fold which we Sanatanists have never allowed and would never allow ... the only remedy ... is that these Arya Samajists may be asked to return to India and present their grievances before the Hindus through the Hindu Ecclesiastical Committee of H.E.H. the Nizam, to which community they say they belong, instead of coming and worrying a Christian Government or a Muslim Government.[49]

The fact that Arya Samaj headquarters denied knowledge of any deputation going to England does not diminish the significance of this letter and it is obvious that the case of Arya Samajists in Hyderabad had lost the support of orthodox Hindus.

And there were other signs at hand. K.M. Munshi, Home Minister in the Bombay Congress ministry, who had earlier been reluctant to help the Nizam's Government, had now written a letter to Sir Akbar Hydari 'expressing his eagerness to act as intermediary'. Munshi presumably changed his attitude as he saw that enthusiasm for the Hyderabad satyagraha was waning; perhaps he was asked to do so by the Indian National Congress and accepted to intercede as an opportunity to acquire personal prestige. In view of his past attitude, however, his offer was declined.

The oncoming monsoon was another factor which was foreseen in both camps as likely to cause a lull in the agitation, as communications would become difficult. Pusad—the main base since the closure of Sholapur—would be unusable, as walking across the riverbed (Penganga), which was the usual mode of entry of jathas into Hyderabad State, would be impossible. Chanda and Basim (also in the Central Provinces) were now considered as alternative bases.[50]

By July, there were also indications that Muslim support for Hyderabad was growing in British India and that retaliation against

Hindus could occur at any moment. A deputation of Muslims from the North-West Frontier Province and Tribal Area actually travelled to Hyderabad in July 1939. They had met Arya Samajists in Lahore and Sudhakar, the Secretary of the International Aryan League, in Delhi. On both occasions, they had stated that 'if *satyagraha* against Hyderabad was not called off they would take their revenge on the three lakhs of Hindus inhabiting the Tribal Areas.' At this, they reported, 'the faces of the Arya Samaj leaders became white and no blood was left there'. The Nizam's Government, however, did not approve of such retaliation and dismissed the argument that, 'as the campaign was carried out by outsiders, it was just that the outsiders should suffer.' The deputation at any rate asserted that 'so far as they could judge from conditions prevailing in the North ... the *satyagraha* campaign would not last long. The Aryan organization was on its last legs'.[51]

The report of the Shankaracharya of Jyotirmath appeared in the *Bombay Chronicle* of 7 July 1939, and far from confirming the charges of religious oppression which he had come to investigate, he held:

> No serious case of defilement of [Hindu] temples or religious institutions were brought to our notice during the whole course of our journey, even though we had occasion to visit wayside villages .... We are pained to observe that in the reports in circulation under this head, there has been a little exaggeration .... If some of the Hindu institutions are not to be seen thriving as well as they ought to have been ... the fault is to be attributed not exclusively to the modern day religious apathy of the Hindus but to a great extent, to the stepmotherly attitude of the local officers [which] had much to do with it, in view of the numerous applications for repairs and renovations pending sanction for unreasonably long periods.
>
> We would emphatically refuse to attribute to Government, as the reports would have it, any overt acts of conversion in jails, etc. .... We have given our careful attention to the various *gashtis* relating to the conduct of festivals, processions, religious discourses, repairs, renovations and reconstruction of temples .... If narrow-minded subordinate officials of government have at any time misconstrued or misapplied the *gashtis*, Government as such could not be blamed for it.[52]

This unexpected public exoneration of the State Government's responsibility by the Hindu Mahasabha—the blame now being laid exclusively on misconduct of minor officials—was echoed in private parleys between the British and the leaders of the Arya Samaj satyagraha. On 21 July 1939, Sir R. Glancy, Political Adviser to the Crown

Representative, reported to C. H. Gidney, the British Resident in Hyderabad:

> Mr Gupta, the Speaker of the Central Provinces Assembly, who appears to be in some respects the leader of the Arya Samaj movement, admitted that the leaders of various religious movements, including the Arya Samaj, might have overstepped the mark in Hyderabad. And he said he was ready to believe that the higher authorities in Hyderabad were perfectly reasonable in their attitude: his complaint was that certain subordinate officials failed to carry out their duties properly.[53]

It was now evident therefore that the aim of both organisations was conciliation rather than pursuit of the agitation.

This deflection of the attack brought a possible solution within sight. It was long known that 'if the movement was called off the Nizam's Government was prepared to appoint a 'Religious Grievances Committee' to save the face of the Arya Samaj' (RHA 1939, p. 43). Now, the Shankaracharya was suggesting in the conclusion of his report that

> if the Ecclesiastical Portfolio is bifurcated into two, the Hindu and Muslim Ecclesiastical Portfolios, the former being manned by an experienced Hindu officer of high grade, with non-official committees with statutory status to help him at the centre, in the districts and in the *taluqs*, there will be no room left for any complaint by the Hindus, the communal tension will be immensely relieved and chances of friction between the two sister communities will completely disappear.[54]

On 19 July, the Nizam's Government announced reforms, including the setting up of a Religious Affairs Committee to which would be referred 'all important complaints, disabilities or restrictions in the performance of religious rites, arising from rules, regulations of administration'. In addition, this Committee was to be 'sufficiently representative of various communities, with equality of both official and non-official representations between its Hindu and Muslim members'.[55]

The next day, 20 July 1939, constitutional reforms were finally announced, albeit in a skeletal form. Extremist Muslims protested that the reforms were 'prejudicial to the powers of the Sovereign and of the Muslims of the Deccan',[56] but the Hindu agitation slackened and no further arrests in this connection were made.

Savarkar, the President of the All-India Hindu Mahasabha, wrote a conciliatory letter to Sir Akbar Hydari assuring him that the Mahasabha was ready to work 'any scheme of reforms which, however halting in relation to the final and full demands presented by the Hindu Mahasabha, were still sufficiently progressive to open out a channel to further peaceful and constitutional evolution' and that they would advise the Hindus to cooperate with the Government. K.M. Munshi, on the other hand, told the Viceroy personally that 'if their reasonable claims were met, the more moderate members of the Arya Samaj would lose interest' and that 'then, the Bombay Government might be able to act in helping the Nizam'.[57]

At all events, the Hindu Mahasabha resolved to suspend the civil disobedience campaign temporarily, as of 30 July 1939. The British Resident noted, however, that Savarkar had made the decision only on behalf of the Hindu Mahasabha.

The International Aryan League, for its part, was moving more slowly. It was reported that G.S. Gupta was in consultation with Gandhi and Rajagopalachari (Chief Minister, Madras Province) as well as Glancy in Delhi and Tasker (Revenue and Police Member) in Hyderabad. On 8 August 1939, a resolution was finally adopted by the International Aryan League to discontinue the satyagraha, 'in view of the spirit of conciliation ... and in deference to the opinions of highly placed friends and well-wishers'.[58] The State Government, for its part, agreed to make arrangements for the release of imprisoned satyagrahis and the payment of their railway fares home.

So ended the 1938–39 satyagraha.

At the end of this confrontation between the Nizam's Government and the Hyderabad State Congress, the Arya Samaj and the Hindu Mahasabha, it is clear that, in terms of net results, the State authorities had easily maintained the upper hand over their opponents. Hyderabad State Congressmen, who had demanded the 'immediate introduction of responsible government in the State', had not even obtained the lifting of the ban on their party, and had shown that they were divided and lacked mass support. The Arya Samaj and the Hindu Mahasabha, which had gone through considerable expense and hardship to 'redress Hindu grievances in Hyderabad State', now accepted that such grievances did not exist as they had described them, and declared themselves satisfied with the Government's face-saving proposal.

However, it is less clear that those, from within and outside the State, who had taken part in the 1938–39 agitation had really hoped for a shattering victory over the State authorities. Perhaps they were satisfied (in the context of a possible all-India Federation and of the growing Hindu–Muslim rift over the issue of Pakistan in British India) merely to have begun awakening the large Hindu population of Hyderabad State to its political potential.

But, whatever the original purpose of the satyagraha, the communal peace between the Hindu and Muslim communities, which had long been a traditional characteristic of the State, was seriously disturbed. Following the agitation, some Muslims overreacted to the new fear that the Hindu majority might not continue to accept their dominance as unquestioningly as they had done so far. They began organising their community on an aggressive political basis, without understanding, it seems, the intrinsic weaknesses of the Nizam's regime or of the Muslims' position in the State. In time, this mistake was to lead their whole community to political perdition.

In hindsight, therefore, the 1938–39 satyagraha accomplished a great deal more than could have been thought at the time of the agitation.

NOTES

1. Gashti No. 53, passed in 1929, superseded all previous orders and prohibited meetings of any nature without prior permission of the authorities.
2. The Constitutional Reforms Committee was chaired by a respected Hindu lawyer, S. Aravamudu Aiyangar (M.B.E., B.A., B.L.). Other members were G.M. Qureishi (Hyderabad Civil Service), Professor Qadir Husain Khan (M.A., Bar-at-law). The Secretary of the CRC was S. Yousuf Ali.
3. Among these five Muslims were S.H. Tirmizi, leader and President of the Hyderabad State Congress since September 1937, and Abul Hasan Syed Ali (later a prominent figure of the Ittihad-ul-Muslimeen!).
4. Until the Haripura session of the Congress there had been a

   > general tendency among the people of the India States to depend too much on the growing power of the Indian National Congress for a solution of their internal political problems. This is especially true of Hyderabad where the people had never made any real fight to assert their fundamental rights ... the Haripura session ... helped them to shake off the lingering remnants of their apathy.

   NMML, P. Naidu report to Gandhi, 1938 (hereafter Naidu 1938) Appendix IF, p. 2.
5. Naidu report to Gandhi, 1938, Appendix IF; In addition, the Public Safety Act limited the separation of the Judiciary and the Executive, IOL, R/1/29/1669, FR 2/8/38, 2.
6. These organisations were: Anglo-Indian and Domiciled European Association, Ittihad-ul-Muslimeen, Anjuman-i-Tabligh-i-Islam, Anjuman-i-Khaksaran, Arya Defence League, Shuddi Prachar, Hindu Subjects Committee, Seva Dal and Nizam Rashtra Maharashtra Parishad. IOL, FR 1/9/38, 3.
7. Mandumulu Narsing Rao, (b. 1896), an Andhra and a deshmukh, completed law in 1921 and practised until 1926; assistant-secretary to the Andhra Jana Sangh in 1921;

started the Nationalist (Urdu) newspaper, the *Raiyat*, in 1927 and worked as its editor; President of the Andhra Mahasabha in 1936; member of the Hyderabad Legislative Council (1938–42); participated in 'unity talks' in 1938–39 together with M. Hanumanth Rao, Bahadur Yar Jung and Akbar Ali Khan; appointed the Hindu spokesman for negotiating with Bahadur Yar Jung in 1939 (they nearly reached an agreement but Narsing Rao refused to sign it after meeting Gandhi at Wardha). He was regarded as the 'most sensible, moderate and the least communal of all the so-called Hindu leaders', IOL, L/P & S/13/1201, Intelligence Report, 3 June 1941 and Sen (1972, pp. 233–36).

8. Only two members of the Provisional Committee—Ramakrishna Rao and J.R. Desai —were in the new Committee of Action, Naidu (1938, p. 15). See also Salam (1941, pp. 40–44).
9. See 'Communal propaganda on the part of certain newspapers against the Hyderabad State', IOL, R/1/29/725 (1938). See also Ramesan (1966, p. 90).
10. From the religious point of view, the Sanathandharmists (Mahasabhaites) and the Arya Samajists are antithetical to each other, yet for political purposes, these arch-opponents march hand in hand as far as anti-Muslim activities are concerned (IOL, L/P & S/13/1200, *Deccan Times* (Madras), 22 May 1938).
11. IOL, R/1/29/1719, State Police Report, 14 April 1938; Through an extraordinary coincidence (?), the two young Muslims who were killed were both relations of Bahadur Yar Jung (one, a nephew); however, there is no evidence that this fact was exploited either by the Nawab himself or by the Muslim press.
12. The Resident reflected, 'The tradition of good relations and toleration existing between the two communities in Hyderabad received a shock from which it will not be easy to recover'. IOL, FR 1/4/38, 1.
13. IOL, R/1/29/1719, Hydari to Viceroy's Secretary, 19 April 1938.
14. IOL, FR 2/4/38, 3.
15. Naidu 1930, Appendix IH, pp.3–4.
16. IOL, FR 1/5/38, 1.
17. IOL, FR 2/8/38, 3.
18. IOL, FR 2/9/38, 2. The two sessions were finally held separately at Sholapur and Nagpur in December 1938.
19. IOL, FR 1/10/38, 3. Saxena was sentenced to three years imprisonment at Manamur jail, a special penitentiary for State prisoners interned by Executive orders.
20. 'The original founders of the State Congress consisted almost exclusively of men who had all been openly connected in some capacity or the other, either with definitely communal or else preponderately [*sic*] Hindu organisations', Naidu, (1938, p. 6); see also Salam (1941, pp. 53–58).
21. Naidu 1938, Appendix IJ, pp. 2–4; The Hindu Mahasabha demanded

    > (1) the right of the Hindus to educate children according to their requirements, i.e., in the mother tongue (2) the right of the Hindus to perform their religious rites and celebrate their religious festivals without any interference from the authorities (3) the right of the Hindus to form *akharas* [gymnasium and sports associations] (4) the right of the Hindus to full liberty of speech and association. (Naidu 1938, pp. 2–5).

22. IOL, FR 2/11/38, 3. Aurangabad was the place where the agitation was strongest at this stage (perhaps because it was an important Arya Samaj centre). By 10 December 1938, six batches totalling 42 persons were arrested there along with their 'dictators'.

23. IOL, FR 1/11/38, 2.
24. Already at Sholapur, the headquarters of the Hyderabad satyagraha, Muslims had begun organising counter-meetings and denouncing the anti-Hyderabad activities of the Arya Samaj. The situation was reported as tense. IOL, FR 1/12/38, 3.
25. Abul Kalam Azad is said to have assured Bahadur Yar Jung that as long as he was a member of the Congress Working Committee, there would be no attack on Hyderabad.
26. IOL, R/1/29/1734 (1938) Birla to Laithwaite, 18 December 1938.
27. IOL, FR 2/12/38, 2.
28. IOL, R/1/29/1803, Hydari to Gidney, 23 November 1938.

    > Under the Government of India Act, in the Federal Assembly out of 375 seats, 125 are alloted to the Indian States and 250 to British India out of which the total of general seats aggregates to 105 and the seats reserved for certain communities, commerce, industry, landholders and women aggregate to 62, not counting the Muhammadan seats which amount to 82. The Congress Party, on the most favourable estimate, cannot obtain more than 90 or 100 seats and, unless the Muhammadan group or the Indian States act with them, they can never be the predominant party or form a Government.

29. IOL, FR 2/12/38, 2.
30. *ibid*. As a gesture of goodwill, the Nizam's Government, shortly before Dr Hamid's visit, had appointed a special committee to consider the question of franchise, in the light of the recently submitted Aiyangar Committee Report on constitutional reforms; the committee was placed under Aiyangar's chairmanship and had four other members: two officials, and M. Narsing Rao and Bahadur Yar Jung.
31. *ibid*, 4. In the meantime, M. Narsing Rao reported the result of his 'unity talks' with Bahadur Yar Jung, and the agreements they had reached so far, to Gandhi, at Wardha: in the services, 75 per cent of posts to Muslims, 25 per cent to Hindus; in the local Assembly, 50 per cent Hindus and 50 per cent Muslims. No provision had been made for Christians and Parsis (one seat each) and both leaders had argued that their seats should be taken out of the quota of the opposite community. Neither Gandhi nor the other Congress leaders present apparently approved of these terms, Gandhi, for his part, asserting that the recommendation of the official Reforms Committee were better.
32. In his statement, K.R. Vaidya said: '*satyagraha* lasted for two months, and over 300 patriots are in jail .... The State Congress has tried to lay bare [its] intentions before the public oftentime and again seek in unmistakeable terms, but the Government have chosen to ignore it .... Under the circumstances, we feel as Congressmen that the only method of proving our *bona fides* before the Government is to suspend *satyagraha* for the time being and afford them an opportunity for introspection and searching of hearts .... We know that hostile propaganda will be made and that this suspension might be attributed to our weakness but no consideration except that of the ultimate good of the country ... has weighed with us in this matter. This momentous decision involving as it does the incarceration of all the patriots till their full terms of imprisonment and other various consequences, has been taken under the instructions of the Working Committee after mature decision and we are sure that it will receive the support of the youth of this State.' IOL, R/1/29/1803, p. 152.
33. IOL, FR 2/12/38, 2.

34. IOL, R/1/29/1803. Intercepted letter from Savarkar to Gupta, 22 July 1938.
35. Savarkar, who stated sarcastically in the above letter that 'the wonder is that the Congress Committees dare not utter a word of sympathy not to mention of protest, not even on the ground of civil liberty' later issued a statement in which he condemned Congress for 'interfering unnecessarily with the *satyagraha* movement', IOL, FR 1/12/38, 4.
36. IOL, R/1/29/1920, *RHA* compiled in the Intelligence Bureau H.D. (Delhi), April–May 1939, p. 27.
37. IOL, R/1/29/1921, Hydari to Gidney.
38. IOL, R/1/29/1920, 3rd April 1939.
39. IOL, L/P & S/13/1231, Bombay, Provincial Government Report, 2 June 1939.
40. IOL, R/1/29/1920, Hydari to Gidney, 26 May 1939.
41. Sir F. Wylie, Governor of the Central Provinces, reported to the Governor-General early in June 1939:

    > As you are aware, I have been pressing my ministry for months to stop residents from this province from interfering in neighbouring administrations .... I have completely failed .... In the case of Hyderabad, it is not Congress but Hindu Mahasabha and Arya Samaj who are sponsoring agitation, but agitation has almost certainly got secret sympathy of all my ministers. I doubt if Congress ... would dare to take effective line. I have exhausted every possible argument in the matter already on innumerable occasions and with every single member of my Council of Ministers and I have not been able to move them.

    IOL, R/1/28/1930, Government of Central Provinces to Governor-General, 4 June 1939.
42. IOL, L/P & S/13/1231. Telegram, Government of India to Secretary of State, (hereafter, Govt of I to S of S) 18 June 1939.
43. 'Bombay Province and Central Provinces, the home of the Maharashtrians, and the Punjab, the home of the Arya Samaj, are the principal recruiting areas: Sind, Delhi, UP, Calcutta and part of Madras contributed not a very large number.' IOL, R/1/29/1920, *RHA*, p. 32.
44. *ibid*., p. 28. Information was also given that: 'Volunteers [were] divided into two categories: those deputed to offer public demonstration and others deputed to travel secretly into the State to carry on subversive propaganda against the administration in villages'.
45. *ibid*. The 'Bombay Province Weekly Letter' No. 26 of 1 July 1939, also reports:

    > During the week ending July 1st ... 13 anti-Hyderabad meetings were held at nine of which resolutions were passed condemning alleged *lathi* charges against the undertrial prisoners at Aurangabad jail; criticising the action of the Madras Government in issuing prohibitory orders ... Mr Gandhi and the Congress for not supporting the agitation ... and suggesting that the Muslims should be driven out as the Jews had been from Germany'. IOL, R/1/29/1921.

46. IOL, L/P & S/12/1232, Govt of I to S of S, 5 July 1939.
47. IOL, R/1/29/1921. Copy of cablegram, M. Sudhakar to Col. Wedgewood, MP, and Lord Zetland, S of S for India (enclosed in letter No. 1580, 21 June 1939 from Sudhakar to Resident).
48. IOL, *ibid*., Gidney to Glancy, 12 July 1939.
49. IOL, R/1/29/1922, Shankaracharya of Jyotirmath to Archbishop of Canterbury, 5 July 1939.

50. IOL, L/P & S/13/231, FR (CP and Berar) 1/6/39, 2.
51. IOL, R/1/29/1921, Report of the meeting of Sahebzada Abdul Dawood and Abdul Aziz Chishti, members of the North-West Province deputation, with the Police Member and the Home Secretary, Hyderabad, 8 July 1939.
52. IOL, R/1/29/1922, *Extract from Bombay Chronicle*, 7 July 1939.
53. IOL, *ibid.*, Glancy to Gidney, 21 July 1939.
54. IOL, R/1/29/1922, *Bombay Chronicle.*
55. IOL, R/1/29/1921, Telegram, Crown Representative to S of S, 27 July 1939.
56. NAI, File No. 40(2)–P(5)/39. D.O. No. 1545-C.
57. IOL, R/1/29/1922. Crown Representative to S of S, 26 July 1939.
58. FR 1/8/39. Supplementary.

4

The Muslim Reaction: Bahadur Yar Jung and the Nizam, 1938–1944

The 1938–39 satyagraha and its developments took the Muslim community in Hyderabad State by surprise. They believed until then that they had little to fear from political stirrings among the Hindus and that the deterioration of Hyderabad's communal atmosphere was only a transient phenomenon, due to mounting tension in district areas where competitive conversion movements had taken place.

Satyagraha, demands for responsible government, clamours for civil and religious rights came, therefore, as an abrupt revelation that what was really at hand was a threat to the local political and communal status quo which was the very basis of Muslim hegemony over Hyderabad. Muslims were alarmed now, and realised the need to unite and get politically organised. The main outcome of this was the rapid rise of the Majlis-i-Ittihad-ul-Muslimeen to a position of political dominance over the Hyderabad Muslim community.

This success of the Ittihad-ul-Muslimeen can be ascribed to the energetic leadership of Nawab Bahadur Yar Jung, a local jagirdar and the first President of the organisation, who effectively channelled the anxieties of the Muslims towards political assertiveness. It was also helped by the obvious empathy between the Nizam and the Ittihad's leader. Indeed, had the Nizam not supported Bahadur Yar Jung, the Ittihad could not have developed as it did. But, while the Nizam's motive was, it seems, primarily to use Bahadur Yar Jung to voice his private political ambitions and grievances towards the British, Bahadur Yar Jung's goal was to draw the Nizam to commit himself openly to an 'independent' and 'Islamic' Hyderabad State. This, however (because of the British), the Nizam would not—or could not—do and, as a consequence, his relations with Bahadur Yar Jung and the Ittihad began to sour, in appearance at least. In fact, it is difficult to determine where conniving stopped and real disagreement began; for when, in 1943, the political extremism of Bahadur Yar Jung again drew sharp criticism from the Resident, the Nizam, instead of supporting the Muslim leader, ostensibly repudiated him. Whether in earnest or not, the Nizam's action damaged his standing with the Ittihad irretrievably, as Bahadur Yar Jung died in 1944 without the breach being healed. The Nizam thus unwittingly helped the transformation of the Ittihad-ul-Muslimeen from a political party altogether amenable to his influence to an increasingly unmanageable extremist organisation.

Until the late 1930s, the overwhelming majority of Muslims in the State showed not the slightest interest in politics. Being ruled by a Muslim, they did not feel the need to create a Muslim political party to defend their interests; besides, for the elite among them political strength through association with the lower socioeconomic classes was unthinkable. In addition, Sunni–Shia differences, allegiances to different sects and sub-sects, mulki–non-mulki susceptibilities, and even variations of spoken Urdu seemed to preclude the idea of political unity among the Muslims. Few among them in any case—the majority being illiterate—could understand the intricacies of the political scene in Hyderabad State. As for those who could, they merely observed the local political developments from a respectable distance, leaving it to the Nizam to take appropriate action. Congress politics held no attraction for them because, unlike Muslims in British India who at the time could think that they stood to gain as much as Hindus from the freedom struggle against the British, Hyderabadi Muslims knew that a Congress 'democratic agitation' in Hyderabad could only benefit the Hindus who represented the majority of the State's population (*Census of India* 1921, Part I, p. 174). As they also knew that the Nizam himself was opposed to Congress, they merely looked upon the ineffective attempts of some Hindus to create a local Congress party with distaste, but little apprehension.[1]

The actual Congress satyagraha and events of 1939, thus, shook the whole Muslim community. It was no longer mere assaults of rhetoric between some Hindus in the State and the Nizam's Government, but streams of political and communal militants converging from all over India to court arrest in Hyderabad. While some educated Muslims began to organise the defence of their community, all eyes turned to the Nizam.

Not unexpectedly, feelings of anxiety ran higher in district areas (the battlefields of conversion movements) where Muslims felt more isolated among the Hindu multitudes, than in the capital where they represented nearly half the population. This fear however, was somewhat lessened by the presence of Muslim government officials, police, and, when they lived in their estates, jagirdars. These, in general, modelled their attitude on that of the Nizam—who did not seem particularly perturbed by the satyagraha—and hoped this attitude would see them through the Hindu challenge.

The Nizam, for his part, relied ultimately on the British as he knew that, whatever reciprocal misgivings existed, the British would continue to support his rule rather than allow Hyderabad to fall prey to Congress. As it was, Congress itself was weak in the State and, without outside support, would be no match for the repressive machinery of his Government. In the Nizam's view, the other organisations involved in the agitation—the Arya Samaj and the Hindu Mahasabha—did not represent serious political threats. Judging by the increase in communal tension, their work with the Hindu masses cut both ways, since it strengthened Muslim cohesion and, in that sense, defeated its own purpose. Thus, feeling safe, the Nizam was watching the situation with interest, well-determined to keep control over all the political developments in the State, and ready to use the circumstances to his advantage. He had long resented the restrictions imposed on his powers by the British and their refusal to consider his pleas of 'independence'. Further afield, he also dreamt of the retrocession of Berar and other territories 'ceded' by his ancestors, and wanted the establishment of a port and a corridor to the sea. But he had, as yet, had no means of bargaining with the British. The emergence of the Ittihad-ul-Muslimeen on Hyderabad's political scene in 1938 was, therefore, undoubtedly for him an occasion of secret jubilation, and he set about working towards harnessing the new Muslim political energies to further his own ambitions.

From 1929, when it was created by a group of ulema, *masha-e-kheen* (religious leaders of Muslim sub-sects) and lawyers, the Ittihad-ul-Muslimeen had mainly three objectives:

(i) to unite and help the various Islamic sects for the solution of their common problems within the principles of Islam;

(ii) to protect the economic, social and educational interest of the Muslims;

(iii) to express loyalty to the land and to the ruler, and to respect the prevalent laws of the realm (R. Khan 1971, p. 786).

The Ittihad was, therefore, basically a religious and social organisation fulfilling among Muslims a function similar to that, say, of the Arya Samaj among Hindus. The main difference was in the statement of 'loyalty to the land and the ruler', but, at that stage, the Ittihad did not attempt to build itself into a mass political organisation 'because politics and political activities then were regarded as the State's concern' (M. A. Khan 1980, pp. 50–51). Thus, for about a decade, the Ittihad confined itself mainly to the religious field.

From the mid-1930s onwards, the rapid political developments in British India culminating in the Government of India Act of 1935 and the introduction of Congress governments in the provinces of British India all around Hyderabad, began to cause a stir among educated Muslims in the State. In February 1938, a meeting of the Ittihad was organised, at the initiative of Abdul Qadeer Siddiqui, the head of the Islamic Studies Department at the Osmania University, to consider adding a political clause to the constitution of the organisation (*ibid.*, p. 65). At this meeting, the Resident reported that the Hyderabadi Muslims decided to make the Ittihad into a Muslim organisation to organise the community and protect its rights—political, economic and social (*RHA* 1939, pp. 36–37).

Less than two months later, communal rioting occurred, in a rare instance in Hyderabad city itself, and brought the message of the Ittihad closer to the Muslim urban dwellers. At the same time, because the two casualties of the riot had been his relatives, Nawab Bahadur Yar Jung's calls for moderation at this difficult time brought added publicity and prestige both to him and the new Muslim political party.[2]

Until then, Nawab Bahadur Yar Jung was mainly known for his activities with the Tabligh and the Khaksar movements (see Mathur 1972; Shan 1973). Indeed, he had himself introduced the first in Hyderabad in 1927 (Allana 1969, p. 310) and promoted the second since its inception in British India in the early 1930s. In 1936, he could be seen 'parading daily with 100 uniformed men behind a flag' through the streets of Hyderabad, but in reality Bahadur Yar Jung does not seem to have devoted much energy to the Khaksar movement in Hyderabad, perhaps because he did not see eye to eye with Allama Mashriqui, the founder of the movement in British India.[3] On the whole, Bahadur Yar Jung at this stage was known more for his activities in the conversion (*tabligh*) field.

With an imposing figure, polished manners and a pious demeanour, Bahadur Yar Jung was cut out to be a popular hero. He was reputed for his sincerity and integrity and, although an aristocrat, he made himself easily accessible to the masses in a 'democratic posture' unknown in the Hyderabad class-conscious society. He is often said to have been the best Urdu speaker of his times and Jinnah himself, who had met Bahadur Yar Jung in Bombay in 1934 and whose Urdu was poor, often used him to translate his speeches and infuse them with his own style (Sayeed 1968, p. 199). But he could also quote Aristotle and Rousseau and was equally at ease in political discussions of state, national and international issues (M.A. Khan 1980, p. 19, 66, 68). An active worker of the All-India Muslim League, (Mathur 1972, p. 267) he was, above all, a religious preacher whose speeches had an Islamic vibrancy able to draw tears from the attending crowds. It is believed that the eyes of the Nizam himself flowed with such tears at an Ittihad meeting in 1930, and that following this, Mohammad Bahadur Khan was ennobled by firman to the title of Nawab Bahadur Yar Jung (Allana 1969, p. 309). In 1936, he was reported to have converted 550 harijans in a single tabligh tour of Osmanabad district[4] and in 1937, to have also been 'conspicuously successful' with the *Dhers* (semi-aboriginal cultivators) in the Warangal district.[5] By 1936, Bahadur Jar Yung's conversion campaigns were streamlined operations preceded by distribution of food and clothes and followed by the circulation of a printed Conversion Form which only required a signature.[6] A solid supporting network, with paid preachers and workers, was generally left behind to consolidate his work. For instance, seven branches of the tabligh movement and 15 Muslim preachers were established by 1937 in the Warangal district alone.[7] Bahadur Yar Jung made no secret of the fact that he planned an increase in the members of Muslim workers 'against the time when the State might be a federal unit surrounded by predominantly Hindu provinces'.[8] That Bahadur Yar Jung was a charismatic leader of exceptional organisational abilities is beyond doubt, and when the Ittihad turned to politics in 1938, the whole party naturally came to revolve around him. In 1939, he was elected President of the Ittihad, a position which he occupied without opposition until his death in 1944 (Allana 1969, p. 313).

The redirecting of the Ittihad towards political work brought rapid success to the organisation, not only because of Bahadur Yar Jung's leadership but because its timing coincided with a period of general anxiety among Muslims in the State. The Congress-backed Hindu agitation against the Nizam's regime, the increase in communal violence, the implications (for those who could understand them) of a future Indian Federation which the princely States were urged to join, and the successes of the Indian National Congress at the provincial elections—all such fears were further aggravated by the threat of a another World War and by the uncertainty it brought to the Indian subcontinent. Benefitting, in addition, from the covert blessing of the Nizam (a factor of superlative importance in a State where the ruler was the kingpin of local politics and the ultimate bestower of favour or repression), the Ittihad rapidly prospered. Its branches in Hyderabad city and district headquarters, a mere 58 in 1937, multiplied to 450 in 1944 (M.A. Khan 1980, p. 69).

The Ittihad's approach was broad-based and readily attracted the Muslim masses who were taken up by the idea of belonging to the same party as the State's ruling class. It appealed also to the Muslim mulki intelligentsia, at one with the party's aim of protecting Muslim supremacy in Hyderabad, and to the religious-minded who listened with favour to Bahadur Yar Jung's politico-religious speeches and agreed with the need to maintain an Islamic hold over the Deccan. Only the aristocracy and the large jagirdars initially kept aloof from the movement—probably out of mere conservatism—and Bahadur Yar Jung did not refrain from chastising them for their apathy (*ibid.*, p. 70); but, with time, they too, came to give at least some financial help to the party. Throughout, however, the main financial support to the Ittihad seems to have come from the broad membership itself and from large and small Muslim traders. Nothing is known of a possible contribution by the Nizam himself.

The Ittihad-ul-Muslimeen engaged in its first open political battle on the issue of constitutional reforms to be introduced in the State. The Aiyangar Reforms Committee had submitted its report to Government at the end of August 1938 and made recommendations on various topics of importance at State level: sovereignty, public services, civil rights, representation of economic interests, Legislative Council, religious grievances and so on.[9] Its salient suggestion was a parity of representation between the two main communities in a future Legislative Council. But, the idea of parity satisfied neither the Hindus nor the Muslims; the first, because justice would not be done to their proportion in the State's population; the second, because it gave away too much of their monopoly over governmental and administrative power. The Nizam, for his part, had 'not said much about the Reforms except to make sure that his hands were not tied over membership [of the Executive Council] ... and to keep [princely] budgets out of Assembly control.'[10]

'Unity talks' had begun immediately between Bahadur Yar Jung and M. Narsing Rao to try and find a possible compromise on reforms but Bahadur Yar Jung was adamant that reforms should not proceed so long as satyagraha was still in progress. He had been discussing the case of Hyderabad with the All-India Muslim League throughout 1939 and had obtained their support (see Zaidi 1978, pp. 157–8 and 172). In May 1939, at a Muslim League meeting in Sholapur, which Bahadur Yar Jung and 1600 followers had attended, a further resolution was passed stating that 'the Reforms should not be brought in [into] Hyderabad until a calmer atmosphere had been restored'.[11] With this, Bahadur Yar Jung suspended the 'unity talks' and strongly opposed the Reforms scheme. It was from that time that the Nizam began to see Bahadur Yar Jung regularly, presumably to convince him to pursue the talks rather than leave the reforms to be settled by the Executive Council. The British Resident reported:

> This contact [between the Nizam and Bahadur Yar Jung] first became noticeably close during the summer of 1939 when [the Ittihad] organised and led the strong Muslim opposition to the proposed scheme of Constitutional Reforms...

adding rather glibly,

> The Nizam allowed himself to be drawn into direct negotiations with the Ittihad and its President instead of leaving such negotiations entirely in the hands of the Executive Council.

He continues, however:

> It is not correct to say that I suspect the Nizam to be amenable to Bahadur Yar Jung's suggestion ... the Nizam is *not* under Bahadur Yar Jung's influence .... [He] is too strong a character and has too clear a sense of his own position as Ruler to allow himself to be put in such a position.[12]

And, indeed, anyone knowing the Nizam would be aware that, if he had 'allowed himself to be drawn into direct negotiations with the Ittihad', it was most probably with an ulterior motive and, in any case, with full self-possession and determination to keep himself politically abreast of the situation. As for Bahadur Yar Jung, he wanted the Nizam to commit himself to the cause of the Muslims (and to the Ittihad), no matter what the Executive Council or the British Resident thought of it. Thus began an intricate relationship which it is not always easy to elucidate. What is clear, however, is that, after these meetings, Bahadur Yar Jung began attacking both the British Resident regarding him as a foreigner who tutored the Nizam (see Yavar Jung 1949, p. 3) and the Executive Council, which, he charged, was disloyal and under British influence. Bahadur Yar Jung accused the ministers of having no conscience and of giving the Nizam wrong advice. Worse, he accused them of looking to the Resident rather than the Nizam, their Ruler (see M.A. Khan 1980, pp. 68–69).

The Executive Council, nevertheless, continued pressing the Nizam for an early announcement of reforms and the tug-of-war between the Ittihad and the State Government began in earnest. The Nizam, encouraged by Bahadur Yar Jung, wanted to make reference to Asaf Jah, 'the founder of the biggest Muslim State in India', in the firman announcing reforms, much to the consternation of the Resident. This mention of Asaf Jah, the Resident lamented, would be badly received as 'the last words of a message commending the new Constitution to 12½ million Hindu subjects'. Sir Akbar Hydari, the President of the Executive Council, also pleaded with the Nizam to avoid references to Hyderabad as an 'Islamic State'. After a long discussion, Hydari thought he had won the battle and even reported to the Resident that he had finally secured deletion.

Subsequent events showed, however, that Sir Akbar had not been as successful as he thought. The Nizam had kept Bahadur Yar Jung informed and shown him the substitute text proposed. Bahadur Yar Jung strenuously opposed the new text and, perhaps to help the Nizam refuse it, began organising a show of the Ittihad's strength.

As a result, when Sir Akbar returned from a visit to Bombay, on 14 June 1939, he was greeted with black-flag demonstrations throughout the city. The Nizam, then, gave him the copy of a letter outlining the Ittihad's views on reforms which he had received from Bahadur Yar Jung.

This letter, written 'on behalf of Hyderabad Muslims', set out clearly, for the first time, the political stand of the Ittihad. Three categorical demands were made:

(a) a statutory majority
(b) separate electorates
(c) ... no scheme which affected [the Muslim] 'traditional political supremacy'.

The letter continued:

> If radical changes in the scheme of Reforms are out of the question, at least there should be a reference to Hyderabad being an 'Islamic State' and the Muslims should be given 'statutory equality' in the Assembly.[13]

These demands, Bahadur Yar Jung stated, had now to be granted, as all his attempts to this end had so far failed; the responsibility for this failure rested 'entirely' with the President of the Executive Council; in view of this, and in the event of further non-compliance, Bahadur Yar Jung concluded, he would not be responsible, in the future, for 'any evil consequences'.

The members of the Executive Council took this letter very seriously, especially as they were advised that Bahadur Yar Jung's 'evil consequences' were to consist of satyagraha in batches of 500 daily, beginning on the day the Reforms were announced. They were also informed that 'this threat was a real one and not a bluff and that if carried out, it would lead to rioting and bloodshed.' With this, Reforms were postponed, 'pending further negotiations with the Nizam',[14] despite angry reactions on the part of the Hindus who charged that this postponement was an indication of the Nizam's partiality and amenability to Ittihad politics and Bahadur Yar Jung's influence.

The Nizam could not let the matter rest there, however, as, in the context, he also had to bring the continuing satyagraha to an end. It was known, at that stage, that Arya Samaj and Hindu Mahasabha leaders were ready to greet any announcement of reforms as a 'victory' marking the end of their agitation. Despite his Council's advice, the Nizam continued to see Bahadur Yar Jung through the end of June 1939 presumably to convince him to accept a compromise.[15]

Little is known of what passed between them at the time, but when reforms were finally announced on 20 July 1939, they still seemed to be opposed by the Ittihad and were, in fact, followed by a month of black-flag demonstrations by Muslims. Whether this had been orchestrated beforehand by the Nizam and Bahadur Yar Jung as a show of Muslim strength is a matter of conjecture. It is possible that the Nizam and Bahadur Yar Jung had not resolved their differences on the issues and that the Nizam, effecting a political volte-face with his usual fickleness, had forced his decision on Bahadur Yar Jung so as to end the Arya Samaj–Hindu Mahasabha satyagraha. In any event, Muslims in and outside the State were disappointed, as they had insisted that the announcement should be made only after the satyagraha had been called off.

In Hyderabad, following the Nizam's announcement, the newspaper the *Waqt*, the mouthpiece of the Ittihad, protested in virulently communal terms against the Nizam's decision, and was closed down by a Government order, upon which the Ittihad threatened once again to resort to 'direct action'.[16]

The Nizam was now in a delicate position. He could ill afford to lose the support of the Muslims and had somehow to defuse their discontent while at the same time keeping Bahadur Yar Jung's and the Ittihad's growing extremism in check. This he attempted to do in a number of ways.

In August 1939, for instance, on the occasion of his birthday celebrations—which were usually a rather modest affair—the Nizam sent invitations to a vast number of personalities, mostly Muslims, all over India. 'The unprecedented influx of guests for the Nizam's birthday,' remarked the Resident, 'was notable in itself and still more for the fact that practically all were leading lights of the Muslim League'.

But, said the Resident, 'the Nizam might make use of them to put some restraint on the Muslim extremists' and he concluded with a 'cautious hope that the Muslim agitation might take more constitutional channels'.[17]

The first consequence of the birthday celebrations, however, was broad contacts between the Ittihad and Muslim League leaders. Bahadur Yar Jung took this opportunity to organise political meetings, to draw as much advice as possible from seasoned politicians for the direction of his party, and to discuss the project of a union of Muslims in all princely States which he had been considering for some time and which he was shortly to create—the All-India States' Muslim League. The Resident reported, after the celebrations, that one of the visitors had claimed that Bahadur Yar Jung had been 'persuaded ... to confine his anti-Reforms activities to a demand for 'clarification',' but even this remained unconfirmed and proved later to have been incorrect.

Jinnah, who had also been invited but had excused himself 'on account of poor health', arrived in Hyderabad in September 1939. His visit had probably been deliberately postponed, as discussions between himself and the Nizam had been planned which would require more time than could be set aside during the birthday celebrations. Jinnah, indeed, had two long interviews with the Nizam (when all other guests had only had one), during which, it was reported, he seemed mainly to have been interested in strengthening the connections between the Muslim League and the Ittihad. The Nizam, for his part, talked about Bahadur Yar Jung—who was well known to Jinnah—and sought advice on ways to abate Muslim opposition to constitutional reforms.

The full content of these discussions was never made public but, shortly after Jinnah's departure, the rumour spread that concessions regarding the Reforms had been secured for Muslims and soon afterwards, early in October 1939, the Ittihad publicly declared that its threat of 'direct action' was withdrawn. It transpired subsequently that the Nizam, prompted by Jinnah, had made secret promises to Bahadur Yar Jung that he would not allow the introduction of Reforms which would give Muslims less than 51 per cent representation (all their numbers being put together) in the future Legislative Council. The Ittihad-ul-Muslimeen had scored its first political victory.

This success of the Ittihad in securing the Nizam's support against the parity of communal representation proposed by the Reforms Committee did much to enhance its stature. The fact that all-India figures such as Jinnah and the Nizam had personally discussed the issue with the Ittihad leader had also added to Bahadur Yar Jung's prestige and political weight.

Anxiety among Hyderabad Muslims persisted nonetheless, for, however favourable the terms obtained by Bahadur Yar Jung, constitutional reforms had been announced which still gave the Hindus unprecedented representation in the Legislative Council. The Resident commented:

> The introduction of the Reforms (or rather their announcement) was a great shock to the Muslims of Hyderabad who, until it was actually upon them, did not realise that it was a revolution in that other communities were to be taken into consultation on an equality with themselves. They were to get nothing, compared to their present position, whereas the rest were to get eight annas.[18]

This prospect caused much discontent and apprehension in Ittihad ranks, particularly as the contact with Muslim League leaders at the birthday celebrations had highlighted the difficulties which Muslims in British India were experiencing as a minority at the national level.

Even more determined to resist the Hindu offensive on Hyderabad which, if it succeeded, threatened to put the Muslims in the State in a similar minority predicament, the Ittihad redoubled its activities after

Jinnah's visit. Led on by Bahadur Yar Jung, the organisation spread to district areas. Branches were opened in most district headquarters (where Muslims were in general concentrated) and by 1940, the Ittihad was solidly established in Nander, Nizamabad, Osmanabad, Raichur, Bidar, Warangal, Medak, Parbhani and Bhir (M.A. Khan 1980, p. 70). In Hyderabad city, the Ittihad's many activities—Treasury, Theological Wing, Organisational Wing, Information and Developmental Wing, Students Hostel, Publication Division, Finance and Volunteers Organisation—were carried out from Darus Salam, a vast palace which the party had recently acquired as its headquarters. The party was increasingly prosperous through donations, subscriptions and membership fees, and district branches often owned their own properties; in general, they sponsored a local library, a gymnasium and sometimes a small scale industry, and thus attracted Muslims from different walks of life. The recruitment of volunteers, drilling exercises, uniforms (khaki shirt and pants and a black *fez*) also attracted those with military tastes and swelled the ranks of the Razakar organisation created by Bahadur Yar Jung in 1938. Much more will be said about the Razakars (literally 'volunteers') in the following chapters but, at this stage, their main function was to parade, to salute the Asaf Jahi flag, and sometimes to supervise law and order at Ittihad public meetings.

According to M.A. Khan, the creation of the Razakar organisation was inspired by Bahadur Yar Jung's feeling that 'no political system [could] succeed without a para-military wing attached to it' (*ibid.*, p. 93); but, no doubt, it was also prompted by his experience (and differences) with the Khaksar movement.

Bahadur Yar Jung's reputation as a pious Muslim had attracted the religious heads of the community who had influence over the masses. However, to assist him in running the Ittihad, the Nawab turned mainly to members with a solid secular education and in 1942, fifteen of the twenty top party executives were lawyers, half of them from the districts.

Tightly organised thus, the Ittihad lost no occasion to draw Muslims together. Annual conferences were organised on a grand scale and in January 1940, for instance, it developed into a three-day affair attended on an average by 12 to 15,000 people daily. In December the same year, Jinnah's birthday was celebrated for the first time in Hyderabad, and shortly after this a 'Deliverance Day' meeting was held and presided over by Bahadur Yar Jung to celebrate the resignation of Congress ministries in British India.

Not unexpectedly, the Ittihad's stand in defence of Muslim interest was growing more defiant as its sway over the Muslim population increased. After the 1940 annual conference, the Resident felt that

> there was a militant Muslim air about the whole proceedings which could not have failed to be very provocative to that 80 to 85 per cent of the population which is Hindu.[19]

It is at this conference that Bahadur Yar Jung, in his presidential address, revealed for the first time the full extent of the Ittihad's ambitions. In the first place, the Nizam should be made "King" as, Bahadur Yar Jung said,

> the history and treaties of Hyderabad show that His Exalted Highness the Nizam is not bound to seek anyone's permission or consent for the adoption of the ... title [of His Majesty] ... there is no reason why the Muslims of the Deccan, nay the Muslims of India, should not call him 'His Majesty' or 'Jalalat-ul-Mulk'.[20]

The whole assembly, thereupon, passed a resolution stating its 'strong and unswerving loyalty to its popular and august King' and prayed 'to preserve him and the Asaf Jahi Dynasty as the embodiment of the power of Muslims for ever'.

Second, the Ittihad rejected the notions of responsible government and of the constitution of a new Legislative Assembly in Hyderabad State as, with these, 'the administration of the country was liable to gradually pass into the hands of those who were not the well-wishers of the King and country'.

Third, the Ittihad reaffirmed its dedication to the socioeconomic interests of all Muslims in the State and demanded the protection of weavers—a significant proportion of who were Muslims—stating that 'the depression in the profession of weaving, or rather its stoppage, has thrown a considerable section of the population of the country into acute distress, poverty and unemployment'. The resolution on the matter urged the Government to institute an inquiry into their conditions, to revive the industry by appointing vocational teachers, and to give preference to unemployed weavers in the inferior services and in the leasing of uncultivated lands. In the meantime, it requested 'all Muslims to use, as far as possible, such articles in their daily life as are prepared by Muslim artisans and craftsmen [and to use] cloth woven only by Muslim weavers' (Resolution No. 5).

In addition, the Ittihad expressed its views on various issues. It declared its opposition to the participation of Hyderabad in the Chamber of Princes; to the employment, in high government office, of European officials who received 'about twice the normal scale of salary received by Indian officials of the same grade in addition to fat allowances' and who should be replaced by 'capable sons of the soil' (Resolutions 11 and 20); it recommended that 'the members of the Executive Council should be appointed for a period of five years only', and considered it

> essential to draw the attention of Government to the bad administration of the Police which was responsible for the unrest that has spread, the communal disturbances that have occurred, and the increase in crimes that has taken place in the country since the past few years [*sic*] and demands that Government should pay attention to reform the administration of this department and to pacify the country by entrusting the organ of the department to able and sincere individuals.

Finally, it was proposed that the Razakar district organisations

> should be so perfected as to be of utmost value to the King and country. Hence it [was] necessary to enlist all Muslims of no less than 15 and not more than 45 years as members of these organisations. This meeting expect[ed] that all persons ... [concerned would] join the volunteer organisations in their thousands.[21]

All these themes—the title of His Majesty for the Nizam, and opposition to responsible government, to constitutional reforms, to British-lent officers and so on—were to constitute the basis of the Ittihad's political work for years to come. As will be seen, the Ittihad grew increasingly assertive with time as the feeling of anxiety at the beginning slowly gave way to one of self-confidence, even bravado, as a result of party propaganda.

Thus, the Ittihad platform which had at first been formulated mainly to oppose the political and communal activities of the Hindus now included a fierce criticism of British influence over, and presence in, the State Government. This act of defiance, which in the public eye appeared merely as a defence of the 'Hyderabadi nationalism' professed by the Ittihad, seemed, however, to the Resident to have been inspired by the Nizam himself. He wrote:

> There is good reason to suppose [that] the attacks made at the conference [of the Ittihad] on the employment of British-lent officers ... were

> made with the Nizam's connivance or approval .... In fact, I am not sure that I cannot detect the 'hand' of the Nizam in parts of Bahadur Yar Jung's petition.[22]

And, indeed, the Nizam's subsequent attitude did little to allay British suspicions. Not only did he not condemn the anti-British feelings expressed by Bahadur Yar Jung, but he sought to present them as part of an inevitable evolution of Hyderabad's political atmosphere.

Immediately after the conference, of his own accord he sent a translation of Bahadur Yar Jung's presidential address to the Viceroy, then Lord Linlithgow, 'simply for your information', he said, 'so that you may see how the mentality of the people is gradually changing with the general spread of education and the process of time ... the conclusion is that nothing can be regarded as permanent or lasting ... unless it is in harmony with the feelings and sentiments of the people'.[23] The Nizam was thus expressing a tongue-in-cheek appreciation of the attack against the British in the State. He inflated the Ittihad much by presenting its stand as an inevitable change in the 'mentality of the people' when it was in reality only representative of a minority of Muslim extremists; and his conclusion, if the word 'people' is replaced by 'Muslim extremists', really meant that British presence could continue only with the latter's sanction. The fact that his own sporadic demands to successive Viceroys now coincided precisely with the 'feelings and sentiments of the people' as expressed by the Ittihad was not dwelt upon.

The British, however were not taken in. In reply to an enquiry from Delhi, the Resident wrote at length:

> There have been in the past, as you know, occasional murmurs in favour of 'sons of the soil' but no such open and public attack on the ability of British-lent officers. For this reason and also for the reason that I have been strongly suspicious ... that the Nizam has been using this conference as a means for the manufacture on a large scale of the 'public opinion' which he has quoted in his recent correspondence with the Viceroy, I thought it desirable to take up the matter ... with the Nizam. (2) I cannot say that my talk with the Nizam lessed [sic] my suspicion. He told me ... [t]hat he had warned Bahadur Yar Jung that if he did not show more restraint he would have to take action. He said that to that threat Bahadur Yar Jung had retorted that even if the Nizam took away his jagir he would not care .... [The Nizam] said that six months ago Bahadur Yar Jung would not have dared to make such a reply and added that even if he dealt with him, a dozen others would rise to take

> his place. His object was of course to show me that he had not the control over him that I supposed he had. Perhaps he has not, but that is ... his own fault because in dealing with Bahadur Yar Jung he foolishly refuses to work through his Council and is still, according to my information, in frequent correspondence with him.[24]

The threat of confiscation of jagir mentioned here was to materialise later but, even then, it is probable that it was pre-arranged between the Nizam and Bahadur Yar Jung. At this stage, however, the British could still argue that it was for the Nizam to control his jagirdars and it was presumably in order to pre-empt such pressure that the Nizam claimed helplessness: a confiscation of jagir was unlikely to silence Bahadur Yar Jung; and even if it did, it would not silence the Ittihad as 'a dozen others' (not necessarily jagirdars) could replace him.

The matter rested there for the time being but, as the Ittihad's propaganda (title of 'His Majesty' for the Nizam, criticism of British presence in the State) continued, the Nizam began to show displeasure overtly towards Bahadur Yar Jung. Whether it was merely to protect himself or again as part of a pre-planned strategy, the Nizam told Bahadur Yar Jung in July 1940 that he had to put right his relations with the British government. The advice was reiterated in an official communication from the Executive Council and, thus prompted, Bahadur Yar Jung, for the first time in his political life, requested an interview with the Resident. There, he was told that,

> Hyderabad was not a kingdom as Nepal was ..., had no international status like Iraq ... and was not independent as he claimed on the ground of the Nizam being the Faithful Ally of the British Government .... There was only one King—the King-Emperor—in the British Commonwealth of Nations and ... any attempt to place anyone else on a par with him would not be tolerated.... The attacks made on the lent British officers as well as on the Nizam's Government, Council and certain of his officers ... were unjustified. It was essential to do nothing in these difficult times to weaken the Nizam's Government which had to deal recently with many difficult situations .... If [the Ittihad] had representation to make to Government let them by all means be made, but in another and less dangerous way.[25]

But Bahadur Yar Jung was not moved. He did not comment on the issue of the title of His Majesty and, concerning his attacks on British-lent officers and other government officials, he said that the Ittihad would refrain from voicing its demands in public but would instead embody them in a memorandum which would be submitted to the Nizam's Government and would also form a reply to the official communication of the Executive Council (see Appendix X).

Given that this was his first official meeting with the British Resident—a man of very considerable power in Hyderabad State—Bahadur Yar Jung seems thus to have shown remarkable self-assurance. To the Resident he appeared as 'a fanatical Muslim ... with an exaggerated idea of his position as a member of the 'ruling class', as all the Muhammadans of the State are ... encouraged [by the Ittihad] to regard themselves'. The Resident commented further:

> For Bahadur Yar Jung, Hyderabad is a Muslim State and the Government is a Muslim government .... With this background to his character Bahadur Yar Jung is a man of hot temperament who had to be handled with care. It would be quite useless to attempt to threaten or browbeat him.[26]

After the interview, however, Bahadur Yar Jung did abstain for a while from direct attacks on the British and concentrated instead on propaganda work in British India on behalf of Hyderabad State and on his ongoing commitment with the Muslim League.

He went on a tour of south India in September 1940 and sought support for a proposal of retrocession of the Ceded Districts and part of the Northern Circars which, he said, was being examined by the Nizam and the British Governments. The 'news' of this proposal immediately provoked much heated debate between local Muslims (who came out in favour of the scheme) and Andhras (who vociferously opposed it). This potentially dangerous furore died down only when the Government of Madras intervened and categorically denied knowledge of any such intention of transfer.[27]

Bahadur Yar Jung then proceeded to Madras where he presided at a meeting of the Muslim Youth Conference of South India organised by the Muslim League on 21 September. There, he approved a resolution supporting the demands made by the Ittihad in their memorandum to the Nizam's Government. Particular stress was laid on the requests to establish a strong military force in Hyderabad, to increase the production of arms and ammunitions locally, to return the Ceded Districts, Northern Circars and Berar, and to grant complete independence to Hyderabad in a future Constitution of India. Bahadur Yar Jung, however, did not move the resolution himself but left it to a certain Bahamany who, it was reported, was 'in the secret pay of the Hyderabad authorities for propaganda [in south India] on behalf of Hyderabad State'.[28]

On 24 September, Bahadur Yar Jung spoke at Bandar, on the occasion of a Muslim League celebration, and repeated the Ittihad's territorial demands for Hyderabad. The next day he visited Ellore, where about 3,000 Muslims had gathered to hear him, and delivered 'a fervent speech' supporting Jinnah and the Pakistan scheme and condemning Maulana Abul Kalam Azad for joining the Indian National Congress. He concluded with an appeal to his audience 'to join the Muslim League, to pray regularly, [and] not to drink'.

Bahadur Yar Jung's tour of south India was widely criticised in the press in British India. *The States' People*, a magazine published in Bombay, stated in October 1940 that Bahadur Yar Jung's stand regarding territorial retrocessions to Hyderabad '[was] based upon no valid reasons whatever' and warned the Nizam, 'who [was] reported to be of personally amiable character [*sic*], not to walk unwarily into the traps now being laid for him by his over-zealous but under-discreet nobleman'. Bahadur Yar Jung was particularly taken to task for his 'wild speeches ... speaking of the Hindus as a conquered people and [of] the Muslims as a nation having a great destiny to fulfil'.

In Hyderabad, Bahadur Yar Jung, feeling perhaps that he had drawn too much public attention to himself, had delegated the direction of the Ittihad's propaganda machinery—the Information and Publication Departments at headquarters—to Syed Abdul Aziz (formerly a Minister in the Government of Bihar and President of the Provincial Muslim League, now Law Member in the Hyderabad Executive Council) who immediately applied his considerable skills to his new task. He was reported to have visited Patna in November 1940 with the 'chief object ... to initiate propaganda among local Muslims for the independence of Hyderabad', and to have appointed 'several paid propaganda agents'.[29] A few months later another report from Patna confirmed that

> propaganda to promote friendly Hindu feelings in support of the Nizam of Hyderabad is operating in this province ... through the well-directed efforts and influence of Mr Abdul Aziz and ... the help of paid agents, mostly young bhumihar Brahmins, to whom bulletins and propaganda literature are regularly sent. Prominent among these agents is one Ram Nandan Chaudhury, son of Ram Pd. Chaudhury, *zamindar* and banker of Gaya.[30]

Why these bhumihar brahmans worked, aside from remuneration, as propaganda agents for Hyderabad is not clear; but the contact between them and Aziz seems to have endured. Almost a year later, an intercepted letter (dated 12 September 1941) from Ram Nandan Chaudhury to Bahadur Yar Jung reported:

> My pro-Nizam campaign is continuing. I am getting the necessary leaflets and posters in Hindi printed again [in advance of Hindu festivals in the city in September] ... but that is not sufficient. Please send me also all kinds of English, Hindi, and Urdu pamphlets, leaflets and posters that the Information Department has for such occasions, and each ..., if available, in at least ten thousand copies.

All these activities, as well as the Ittihad's stand concerning the retrocession of ceded territories and the Pakistan issue, must have had the approval of the Nizam. Indeed, after Bahadur Yar Jung's interview with the Resident, he had said of the Nawab that he was 'level-headed and held sound views',[31] and there is little doubt that he had been kept informed of most, if not all, Ittihad plans.

Now, Bahadur Yar Jung and the Ittihad appealed to Muslims to gather en masse at mosques all over the State on 1 November 1940, to celebrate 'Hyderabad Day', commemorating the founding of Hyderabad. The appeal was widely answered, and seven such assemblies took place in Hyderabad city alone, the largest crowd (15,000) being attracted to Mecca Masjid, the principal mosque, where Bahadur Yar Jung was speaking.

In his address, Yar Jung touched on a number of topics—the War, Hyderabad in a future Dominion of India, treaties, ceded territories, responsible government. He repeated the theses, laid out in the Ittihad memorandum of August 1940, that the strength of the Nizam's army should be increased and arsenals established 'so as to help more effectively in the war effort'; that Hyderabad would return to being an independent State once India reached Dominion status; that fresh treaties would be signed with the new India once the State's former territories of the Northern Circars and Berar had been returned; and that responsible government was a domestic question which could be discussed later among Hyderabadis. The meeting ended with a resolution, proposed by Bahadur Yar Jung and passed unanimously, appealing to the British Government 'to help their old and tried Ally [*sic*], HEH the Nizam, to increase his army and to establish arsenals so that he may be in a position to help them more'. The resolution concluded, however, with the rather trenchant demand to the British 'not to interfere in the internal administration of Hyderabad's Government on the pretext of offering advice'.[32]

This time the Nizam himself felt that Bahadur Yar Jung had gone too far. But, firstly, he was anxious that British suspicions of connivance between himself and the Ittihad might have been revived and, on 18 November 1940, he resorted once again to writing to Lord Linlithgow, asserting rather lamely:

> ... I have personally had no connection, open or secret, with any of these matters. Far from it, I have occasionally had a warning conveyed to Bahadur Yar Jung through the Council to be more careful in future and not to stir up agitation needlessly in these critical times .... I told him ... that he should abstain ... from doing any act calculated to disturb the local peace and tranquility of the country; and that he should on the contrary co-operate as much as possible with the British Government as the Hyderabad Government itself was doing.[33]

The letter concluded with an eulogy he is reported to have made to Bahadur Yar Jung on the security enjoyed by Indian rulers thanks to British presence. Although this might appear to have been yet another feint on the part of the Nizam to prove his own loyalty to the paramount power, there is no doubt that, contained in this paragraph, were some of the Nizam's real feelings, as his attitude in later years was to prove. In this instance, he said:

> It must be remembered that if the British Government had not extended their benign protection to the Rulers in the past in spite of the many weaknesses and defects of the latter ... they would have been simply wiped off the surface of the earth by now. This fact ... was so obvious and self-evident that it did not require any proof. Therefore ... the duty of the 'Ruling class' was to discharge their duties conscientiously and carefully. Only in this way would they be able to face the future with a sense of security and ensure the continued existence of their dynasties and their States. Otherwise their future was full of danger and foreboded no good to them.

The thought that if the rulers—and the Nizam meant more particularly the Muslim rulers—were loyal to the British, they would be able to continue to exist in an independent India was a major flaw in the Nizam's political understanding of the situation. It was an unrealistic expectation, but one which he did not abandon even at the time, in

1947, when it had become a certainty that the British were to leave India and the rulers to sort out their differences between themselves, without particular concern for any former 'Faithful Ally'.

Back in 1940, however, the Political Department in New Delhi did not believe any of the Nizam's protests of loyalty. Indeed, his letter to the Viceroy only drew the dry comment that,

> in spite of the disclaimer contained in his letter ... the Nizam may be himself giving covert support to Nawab Bahadur Yar Jung's activities. This disclaimer may have been prompted by the fear that His Excellency would learn of that support.[34]

It was further recommended that the Resident should take up the matter with the Nizam and ascertain the course of action the latter proposed to take to control Bahadur Yar Jung's excesses.

The Nizam was thus in an increasingly difficult position. On one side, the British had to be pacified; on the other, regardless of what Bahadur Yar Jung did, he was loath to take too drastic a measure against him for fear of alienating the whole of the Ittihad and of losing prestige and authority with the Muslim population.

In addition, by 1940, Bahadur Yar Jung had grown less co-operative and amenable to the Nizam's influence. This was perhaps due to his continuous contact with the Muslim League and to his new responsibilities since March 1940 as the (unanimously elected) President of the All-India States' Muslim League, an organisation which he had formed in October 1939 after consultations with Jinnah. The All-India States' Muslim League was 'practically a 'one man show', Bahadur Yar Jung being [its] chief moving spirit and financial backer' (Mathur 1972, pp. 263–67) and, in real terms, it wielded little influence at the all-India level; but it broadened the Nawab's horizons and political views. By mid 1940, perhaps also because he had been altogether disappointed by the quality of the Nizam's support when in confrontation with the British, Bahadur Yar Jung began to move away from his previous stand of unconditional loyalty to the Nizam. He now came to consider that the relationship between the Muslim community in the State and the Ruler was not one of mere dependence but a symbiotic association. For, Bahadur Yar Jung argued, if the Muslims lost power in Hyderabad so would the Nizam, and reciprocally; thus, every Hyderabadi Muslim was invested with part of this sovereignty and could rightly claim 'Anal Malik' (I am King). By January 1941, this new approach was compounded by Bahadur Yar Jung into a *kalima* with which he could open all Ittihad functions, the congregation reciting after him:

> We are the Kings of the Deccan; the Throne and Crown of the Deccan are symbols of our own political and cultural sovereignty; His Exalted Highness is the soul of our Kingship and we form the body of his Kingship; if he ceases to exist, we cease to exist; and if we are no more, it will be no more.[35]

This kalima was rejected as heresy by some of the orthodox Muslims in the Ittihad (who considered that the Nizam did not owe his sovereignty to anything but the Divine will) and, by May 1941, it even caused a minor split within the organisation.[36]

Naturally, it was also not well received by the Nizam who felt that it was a pronouncement amounting to *less-majeste* which should not have been uttered at all, let alone by one of his jagirdars. He did not confront Bahadur Yar Jung directly, however, perhaps again for fear of creating an unbridgeable rift between them, but instructed the Executive Council to deal with the matter. There followed an official statement refuting the kalima at length. It was pointed out that when Bahadur Yar Jung had requested elucidation on the question of His Exalted Highness' sovereignty two years before (in the context of the constitutional reforms proposed by the Aiyangar Committee), it had clearly been stated that, regardless of any other factor, the Nizam 'always represented the people directly in his own person', that he was in possession of his sovereignty 'by natural right', and thus, that his status could never be dependent on one or the other of the communities in the State. The official statement concluded:

> His Exalted Highness and his Government have not found it possible to accept the theory of 'Responsible Government' for the same reasons as those which impel them to reject any doctrine, like that propounded by the Ittihad-ul-Muslimeen, which implies the division or diffusion of His Exalted Highness' sovereignty among 15 lakhs of his subjects.[37]

Having thus answered Bahadur Yar Jung, the Nizam proceeded to curb his activities, but this he did indirectly. He instructed the Executive Council to pass orders forbidding the participation of any *maashdar* (person holding a grant or allowance, *maash*, from government) in political activities. Henceforth, no maashdar would be allowed to make written or spoken statements 'capable of embarrassing the relation between Government and the people of Hyderabad or any section thereof or the relations between His Exalted Highness' Government and His Majesty's Government or the Government of India or the ruler of any State in India', and the warning was issued that,

> if any *maashdar* contravenes any of these Rules, Government ... with the sanction of His Exalted Highness will have the power to confiscate and resume the *maash* or exemptions or honour.[38]

Meanwhile, Bahadur Yar Jung had carried on with his activities, undaunted. In March 1941, he had organised the celebration of a 'Pakistan Day' in Secunderabad and had stated in one of his speeches that Hindus and Muslims could not be regarded as one nation as their culture and civilization differed and they had nothing in common; so far as British India was concerned, he continued 'Pakistan was the only solution for the problem.' This, as well as the statement he had made (in January) that he was opposed to any further negotiations for Hindu–Muslim unity in Hyderabad,[39] had caused the Nizam to send him a 'reprimand' in April. Now, in May 1941, he received yet again a 'warning' that the annual conference of the Ittihad-ul-Muslimeen, which was to be held later in the month, would be allowed only if its President ensured that 'nothing politically objectionable' would be discussed at the meetings.

The fact that Bahadur Yar Jung was permitted, with mere 'reprimands' and 'warnings', to pursue his political activities practically unhampered shows the extent to which the Nizam was prepared to compromise to keep the support of the Muslim leader and his party. But, despite all injunctions, and the new rules regarding maashdars, Bahadur Yar Jung wound up the annual conference of the Ittihad at the end of May with a speech reiterating 'in highly emotional tones' most of the arguments on sovereignty, Hindu–Muslim unity and Pakistan to which the State authorities had already objected.

Bahadur Yar Jung's speech received wide coverage in the local press and, urged by the Executive Council, the Nizam now found himself with no alternative but to order that Bahadur Yar Jung 'should be called upon to show cause why his *jagir*, title and maintenance should not be confiscated for his disobedience'. In appearance, thus, the relations between Bahadur Yar Jung and the Nizam were now at their lowest; in reality, close (even if strained) consultation continued, and, it seems, with the same concern to temporise. While Bahadur Yar Jung announced that, 'owing to throat trouble', he would be unable to address public meetings for the next two months, the Nizam intervened with the Executive Council—which had met to consider what action should be taken against Bahadur Yar Jung—and requested that nothing be done before Jinnah, whom he had invited to Hyderabad 'to curb Bahadur Yar Jung', arrived.[40] Jinnah's visit, incidentally, had been timed to coincide with the end of Sir Akbar Hydari's prime-ministership and his replacement by the Nawab of Chhatari[41] in August 1941, at a time when the Executive Council would be fully occupied with matters other than those relating to Bahadur Yar Jung. Jinnah arrived in Hyderabad on 29 August. He was met at the station by a delegation of Ittihad members, garlanded by Bahadur Yar Jung himself, and stayed in Hyderabad for a fortnight as a State guest. He left without giving any indication of what had passed between him and the Nizam on the subject of Bahadur Yar Jung. In any event, Bahadur Yar Jung shortly afterwards submitted an apology to the Nizam, which the latter accepted in an official firman, both texts being released to the press and provoking a favourable reaction among the Hindus. The British Resident remarked wryly, however:

> A much needed check has undoubtedly been given to the Nawab's activities. For how long this check will operate remains to be seen and a great deal may depend on the skill of the new President of the Council in handling this troublesome politician.[42]

In effect, Bahadur Yar Jung had been let off to pursue his political work, and he lost no time in making the Ittihad's stand on a variety of issues known to the new President of the Executive Council. At the annual conference of the Ittihad branch at Latur (Osmanabad District) on 6 September 1941, after praising the Nawab of Chhatari as an able administrator, Bahadur Yar Jung proceeded to list the 'expectations' of the Ittihad. It was hoped, Bahadur Yar Jung said, that the new President would:

(1) safeguard the powers of His Exalted Highness
(2) establish better relations between the British and the Hyderabad Governments
(3) make all endeavours to help the British Government in their present struggle
(4) modify the Reforms Scheme

(5) examine the State's finances
(6) consider the question of reducing the salaries of high officials
(7) ensure that appointments in the State service were given to educated young men of ability
(8) suppress bribery.[43]

It was, thus, altogether a moderate list of objectives, which most probably had the concurrence of the Nizam. The Nawab of Chhatari was not slow to single out the fourth point (on reforms) as the most significant demand and the one most likely to create difficulties with the Ittihad, as the Hindu leaders had, for their part, made representations for a speedy introduction of the reforms. The Nawab astutely struck a middle course, and moved the Executive Council to announce in October 1941 that the reforms would be introduced 'piecemeal', that is to say that the new Legislative Assembly would come into being only after the reformed district boards—which were to send their representatives to the Assembly—had begun to function.[44] The announcement was greeted with satisfaction by the Ittihad, but angrily rejected by Hindu leaders who declared that they would oppose the move. Bahadur Yar Jung was away on a State tour at the time, but Abul Hasan Syed Ali, his lieutenant and second-in-command of the Ittihad,[45] issued a press statement charging that Hindu leaders had effected 'a volte-face characteristic of Congress tactics'. It was they, he said, who had pressed for an early introduction of reforms and stated their willingness to work them. In the same press statement, he reasserted that the Ittihad considered responsible government of the British parliamentary type unsuited to India and that 'such a demand in Hyderabad, which [was] admittedly a Muslim state, [was] hardly understandable'.[46]

The issue of reforms and the political reactions of Hyderabadi Hindus will be examined in detail later; it is sufficient to say here that the matter remained unsettled at this stage, much to the gratification of the Ittihad.

Meanwhile Bahadur Yar Jung was busy spreading the same message on his tour of districts. At Gulbarga he asserted on 8 November 1941:

> Hyderabad does not need any democratic system of Government ... the Majlis-Ittihad-ul-Muslimeen is not prepared to accept any political or constitutional change .... The Majlis' policy is to keep the sovereignty of His Exalted Highness intact and to prevent Hindus from establishing supremacy over Muslims.

Elsewhere he said: 'All that was necessary for the State was to adopt a programme of rural reconstruction, to pay attention to the rights of the Depressed Classes, and protect the rights of the Muslims;' but if the Government introduced the reforms, 'the Muslims would be compelled to establish the Government of the Majlis-Ittihad-ul-Muslimeen'.[47]

After this, much to the consternation of the Executive Council, Bahadur Yar Jung and Abul Hasan Syed Ali were called in audience (on 22 November 1941) by the Nizam, and each presented with a set of jewelled buttons; the Nizam also issued a firman recognising 'the loyalty of Bahadur Yar Jung'. The Resident remarked that,

> the Nizam's actions just show how difficult it is for the members of the Executive Council to know where they stand when they have to deal with such fickle and unpredictable behaviour on the part of the Ruler.[48]

In fact, the Nizam's motives for bestowing such favours on Ittihad leaders at this time are difficult to determine. It appeared as if he approved of the threatening attitude adopted by the Ittihad but it could have been, on the contrary, that he was merely cajoling Bahadur Yar Jung and his lieutenant so as to make them more amenable to a reopening of the 'unity talks' on reforms which had been shelved since Sir Akbar Hydari's departure; or perhaps it was that he hoped to mollify their communal extremism and bring them more in line with his own recent press appeal for communal harmony. In any case, Bahadur Yar Jung, shortly after this, expressed his willingness to meet M. Narsing Rao anew, and Abul Hasan Syed Ali now stated that 'everyone would do their best to bring about communal harmony in the State'.[49]

Bahadur Yar Jung's prestige within the Ittihad was, by then, at its peak. At the end of December 1941, he was unanimously re-elected President of the party and in this capacity chaired its thirteenth Annual Conference on 31 December 1941 and 1 January 1942 at Jalna (Aurangabad district), attended that year by a record number of approximately 15,000 people. There, he again covered the familiar Ittihad topics and reiterated Hyderabad's claim to the Northern Circars, provoking yet another strong wave of opposition in the Hindu press in British India.[50] Immediately after this, he went on a tour of Malabar, Cochin and Travancore on behalf of the Muslim League.

When he returned at the end of January 1942, he found, however, that in Hyderabad, as in the rest of India, interest in local politics had receded into the background in view of alarming war reports. The Germans and the Japanese had been very unhappy with India for its participation in the War on the British side, and it was feared in Hyderabad that the Nizam's title of 'Faithful Ally of the British' would make the State a prime target for enemy attacks. A meeting of Hindu and Muslim leaders was hastily organised in February 1942 at which it was decided that political activities would be suspended for the time being and that all work should turn to the defence of the State. Bahadur Yar Jung and Abul Hasan Syed Ali, who attended the meeting, went on to call for the participation of all Ittihad members, as, they said, 'it was the duty of every Muslim to help the British Government at this critical time'.[51] Furthermore, the Resident reported that,

> On 2nd March ... Bahadur Yar Jung, K. Rao Vaidya and other Muslim and Hindu leaders met privately .... [They] decided that prominent Hindus and Muslims should form committees in every *mohalla* [suburb] in the city to suggest ways and means of securing Hindu–Muslim unity and advocated whole-hearted cooperation with the State Government in its civil defence measures.[52]

Reinforcing the feeling of alarm, refugees arrived from Burma with reports of the Japanese advance in the East, and some Marwaris and Komtis (money-lending castes) moved away from the State. Inhabitants of Hyderabad and Secunderbad, some 900 Hindus and Muslims, even began evacuating from the city to the districts. Meanwhile, Hindu and Muslim leaders continued to meet and discuss emergency measures. On 13 March 1942, about 3000 Hindus and Muslims attended a meeting presided by Bahadur Yar Jung, and resolutions urging inter-communal unity were unanimously passed. The suggestion was also made that a deputation should wait on the President of the Executive Council to ask that military forces be moved away from Hyderabad city.[53]

Friendly feelings between the communities seemed, thus, to have been re-established by March 1942, at the time of the visit to Hyderabad of the Cripps Mission. Sir Stafford and his delegation visited the State, as part of a tour of India to propose a future constitution of the country which would be satisfactory to all parties (and in the short term would convince the Indian National Congress to end its opposition to the War effort).

Sir Stafford met most leading Hindu and Muslim organisations and personalities in Hyderabad, but left the State without any assurance of a local consensus. The Resident wrote after the visit that Sir Stafford Cripps' Mission revealed clearly the long standing division of local opinion regarding the future of Hyderabad.

Extremist Hindus and Muslims had contradicted one another in their representations to the Mission, the former asserting that Hyderabad 'should be absorbed into greater and democratic India', the latter that it should 'retain its separate 'independent' entity'.[54] In this atmosphere, the communal harmony that had prevailed over the past few months quickly vanished. Now that the departure of the British from India had been broached, both Hindus and Muslims considered the future in terms of an impending showdown between the two communities. Ittihad branches in Hyderabad city began selling spears to their members 'for self protection' and, perhaps not to be outdone, Hindu leaders also urged their community to organise and collect arms. The Hyderabad State Hindu Praja Mandal (Hindu Mahasabha) held a meeting on 24 March 1942 and passed a resolution declaring itself the only organisation representing the Hindus of the State; at the same meeting two associations were created under the auspices of the Praja Mandal—the Hindu Basti Panchayat and the Praja Raksha Samiti—with the object of 'establishing *panchayats* in the city *mohallas* for mutual help in case of injury from enemy attacks [*sic*]' and akharas (gymnasiums) 'to train youth in first aid and self-protection in the event of Hindu–Muslim clashes'.[55]

Bahadur Yar Jung, for his part, exhorted his followers 'to make an effort to protect and maintain the Islamic State of Hyderabad with resolution and fortitude' stating that those who died protecting it would be true martyrs.

It is in such an atmosphere that a second serious communal outbreak occurred in the State, in a village in the Bidar district where ill-feelings were reported to exist for some time between Muslims and Arya Samajists. Communal violence had increased in Hyderabad after the 1938–39 satyagraha, but so far only one incident—in March 1940, also in Bidar— had been serious. On that occasion, the city's market had been burned down by Muslims and about a hundred shops mostly belonging to Hindus had been destroyed. Now, in May 1942, again 34 Hindu shops were reported to have been burned down, along with some houses, while armed mobs had fired at one another, injuring ten and killing one (a Hindu).[56]

While the Ittihad and the Arya Samaj mutually disputed the facts, recriminations and accusations only heightened communal tension and added weight to the call to arms of the leaders of both the communities. Guns, swords and spears were now made available at city and district branches of communal organisations, members being urged to protect themselves against what Bahadur Yar Jung described as 'internal dangers' and the Hindus as 'goondaism' (banditry). A Hindu pamphlet entitled 'Communal Riots and a Challenge for Civil War' was circulated in the State, accusing the Hyderabad Government of 'extreme bias against Hindus' and alleging that the State authorities 'secretly encouraged Muslims to commit atrocities on Hindus'. The pamphlet continued,

> Communal riots are staged for the purpose of training Muslims in the *Jehad*' [holy war] by which they propose to secure 'Pakistan' in the event of the war taking a bad turn.[57]

Chapter 5 reveals that this exploitation of the Bidar incident coincided with renewed Congress agitation in the State—the launching of a second satyagraha on the subject of reforms and civil liberties. Meanwhile the local Hindu press, particularly the weekly *Raiyat*, echoed the themes of the 'Quit India' movement launched in British India by the Indian National Congress and Gandhi.

Bahadur Yar Jung, who had only recently returned to Hyderabad from another extensive tour of India on behalf of the Muslim League and the All-India States' Muslim League, appealed to Muslims, students in particular, 'to keep aloof from the "Quit India" agitation'. On 13 August 1942, Bahadur Yar Jung organised a 'Hyderabad Independence Day' at which he claimed that, although 'his own genuine wish' was that 'the British should go' and that 'no Indian of real Indian blood and feeling wanted them to remain as rulers', he also did not wish to embarrass the British Government by pressing Hyderabad's demands at this stage. However, he insisted that

> at least a promise should be given now that after the war, Hyderabad would be granted its independence and regain its lost territories.[58]

Bahadur Yar Jung repeated this demand for Hyderabad's independence over and over again in all his district tours, conferences and meetings as, for example, in front of the gathering, variously reported as numbering between ten and 50,000, which attended the fourteenth annual session of the Ittihad in Hyderabad city in December 1942.

After stating that the Cripps' Mission had established a justification for Pakistan, Bahadur Yar Jung emphasised that 'if in future a Federal Government or Indian Union was formed, Hyderabad should hold the same independent position as any province'.[59]

Bahadur Yar Jung's appeal drew no official response from either the British or the Nizam. It seems, in fact, that relations between them were entering a new phase as the Muslim leader was increasingly impatient with the Ruler's indecisiveness in siding with the Ittihad. Despite Hyderabad's loyalty and contributions to the War, the British had not granted any of the Ittihad's demands. Bahadur Yar Jung probably felt the blame rested again with the Nizam's ever-ingratiating attitude towards the British. The relations between the Nizam and Bahadur Yar Jung were extremely important in the context of Hyderabadi Muslim politics; and any estrangement between them, as appeared likely by the end of 1942, could only have the most disastrous consequences, both in personal terms for Bahadur Yar Jung and in political terms for the Ittihad and the Nizam.

Bahadur Yar Jung (and the Ittihad) had long differed with the Nizam on the attitude to adopt with regard to the British presence in Hyderabad. Bahadur Yar Jung's main political thrust had been to attempt to force the British to consider Hyderabad State as separate from the rest of India. In this, his stand was similar to the Nizam's who had always insisted on the unique position of his State and on the distinction of the treaties and historical circumstances which linked it to the paramount power. But, whereas Bahadur Yar Jung 'demanded' recognition of the 'independent status' of Hyderabad, the Nizam never really forced the issue and, outside of secret parleys with Jinnah, seemed ready merely to wait until the end of the War. Then, he hoped, the British would at last reward his loyalty. In the meantime, as a rule, the Nizam stuck to the letter of his 'faithful alliance' and always responded to the British in the expected manner, at least officially.

Bahadur Yar Jung, on the other hand, was well accustomed to speaking his mind openly and often forcefully on all issues of concern to Muslims. That this licence was allowed covertly by the Nizam is beyond doubt, but, early in 1943, Bahadur Yar Jung's disrespect towards the British seems once again to have gone too far for the liking of the Nizam.

The point of issue, this time, was the title of GBE bestowed by the British on the Prince of Berar (the heir to the throne), a distinction which the Nizam had warmly welcomed, stating that the honour would 'strengthen the ties of friendship and unity that have always existed between the British Government and the house of Asaf Jah'.[60] Bahadur Yar Jung, for his part, denounced the award as 'a fresh seal on Hyderabad's subordination'. Intensely annoyed, the Nizam immediately demanded a public apology. But Bahadur Yar Jung, in consultation with the Working Committee of the Ittihad, tendered instead a letter justifying his action and, to add insult to injury, asserted that 'the Asaf Jahi flag was not a personal flag of the Asaf Jahi dynasty but ... an Islamic flag and a symbol of a great Islamic State', declaring that he would not lay down his life for a personal flag.

This was answered forthwith with a firman, issued on 22 March 1943, 'prohibiting Bahadur Yar Jung from making any public speeches or press statements in or outside the Hyderabad State for one year'.[61] Another firman was subsequently issued terming his declaration about the Asaf Jahi flag 'an act of impertinence and also of gross ingratitude for the honours and privileges he and his fore-fathers [had] enjoyed from the bearers of this flag'.[62]

Whether in earnest or in connivance with the Nizam, Bahadur Yar Jung took umbrage at this accusation and, on 10 April 1943, asked for permission to renounce his jagir, *mansab*, privileges and titles, and offer them as nazar to the Nizam.

Notwithstanding the tone of Bahadur Yar Jung's letter, which was judged 'sarcastic and almost insolent',[63] this voluntary relinquishment of privileges was accepted by a brief firman from the Nizam. Bahadur Yar Jung—or simply Bahadur Khan as he was henceforth to be called—acknowledged the firman in a second letter in which was noted the 'same ironical attitude', as well as the fact that, in addressing the Nizam, Bahadur Yar Jung had 'dropped all the usual fulsome form of address to His Exalted Highness such as *bandegan-i-ali*, *pir-o-murshid*, etc. and ... simply address[ed] him as "you" (*ap*)'.

Was the break between Bahadur Yar Jung and the Nizam a real one? The question might never be answered with certainty, but it is known that, aside from their official exchanges, 'there has been a good deal of passing of communications between King Kothi and Bahadur Yar Jung [*sic*]', and that the Nizam, in a telephonic conversation 'which lasted for 1½ hours', had 'tried to assure Bahadur Yar Jung that he would see that provision for a share to him of the *jagir* and *jamadari* would be made'.

In the 16 April 1943 issue of the Nizam Gazette appeared, in the space usually reserved for publication of firmans, a 'Notice issued from Nazari Bagh' that, 'the *nazar* offered by Bahadur Yar Jung, which has been accepted, is reserved for his family (i.e. for him) [*sic*]'.[64]

Thus, though accepting Bahadur Yar Jung's renunciation of title the Nizam added of his own accord a provision which, in the Resident's words, 'remove[d] any reality from the apparent punishment'.[65]

As to why the Nizam should have acted thus, Grigson said that 'HEH is afraid that he had gone too far and he is at least trying to keep Bahadur Yar Jung attached to him'.

In fact, this is possible, and could be seen as another instance of the Nizam's well-known fickle mind; but more might have been at hand, as is indicated by subsequent developments.

Bahadur Yar Jung left Hyderabad on 22 April 1943 for Delhi where he was due to attend meetings of the Muslim League and the All-India States' Muslim League. Once there, he sent a telegram to the Nizam asking for permission to address meetings, despite the Nizam's firman forbidding him to speak in or outside Hyderabad for a period of one year.

Surprisingly again, and much to the annoyance of the British Resident, Bahadur Yar Jung received a reply that

> 'while His Exalted Highness *for certain reasons* [underlined in the text] could not modify his *firman* prohibiting Bahadur Yar Jung speaking ... now that Bahadur Yar Jung had voluntarily resigned his honours, etc. in the State, he was a free man and no longer under the Nizam's orders, so that he could act as he thought fit'.[66]

The British Resident said:

> The Nizam while therefore conforming in the letter to our advice not to modify or withdraw his ban on Bahadur Yar Jung's public speaking, has double-crossed everyone by nullifying the likelihood of any practical effect resulting from that ban and by indicating to Bahadur Yar Jung that he is now free to do as he likes .... It is patent that the Nizam must have been mediating this plan of evading responsibility for some time ... otherwise why this remarkable eagerness to show the limit of his powers over his subjects outside his State? The whole incident serves to show clearly, if this were needed, the Nizam's fundamental untrustworthiness.[67]

From the Nizam's point of view, it had probably appeared urgent to proclaim official dissociation from Bahadur Yar Jung as the latter was, despite all threats and entreaties, growing more extremist and embarrassingly outspoken with time. Bahadur Yar Jung represented, among other things, Hyderabadi resistance to the influence of the paramount power, a point which the Nizam recognised with glee. But, as Bahadur Yar Jung was a jagirdar, the British would hold the Nizam responsible for his actions. After all, Bahadur Yar Jung 'owed his salt' to him and it was, therefore, for the Nizam to bring him to book. A convincing mode of evading this responsibility had thus to be found.

The Nizam, no doubt, 'must have been mediating this plan ... for some time' as it was difficult not to alienate Bahadur Yar Jung and Muslim opinion while 'conforming in the letter to British advice'. The voluntary relinquishment of his title and jagir would make Bahadur Yar Jung solely responsible for his actions (and liable to sanctions); while the provision that his estate would not be taken away from his family would hopefully merely indicate that the Nizam had freed Bahadur Yar Jung from political control.

Even though this was probably agreed upon between the Nizam and Bahadur Yar Jung,[68] the deviousness of the scheme did not endear the Ruler to the Muslims in the State. At the same time, it showed Bahadur Yar Jung that the Nizam would not be brought to adopt a stauncher and official 'independent Muslim' attitude; importantly, as it was to prove later, it also convinced Ittihad extremists that their party should distance itself further from blind loyalty to the throne.

Having returned from Delhi at the end of April 1943, Bahadur Yar Jung, for a while, circumvented the prohibitory order on his speeches by only giving 'private talks'; often, however, to gatherings of considerable size. He left to others—Abul Hasan Syed Ali or Abdur Rahman Rais, the editor of the *Waqt* and a prominent Ittihad member—the task of addressing Ittihad meetings, a duty which they discharged with even more fire than their leader. The Government retaliated, in July 1943, with orders prohibiting 'public or private entertainment of more than 50 persons at a time without prior permissions'.

Meanwhile, Bahadur Yar Jung—now a 'martyr' for the Muslim cause —enjoyed an even greater measure of popularity among Muslims.[69] He was again unanimously re-elected President of the Ittihad for the current *Fasli* year (6 October 1943 to 5 October 1944).[70]

At the expiry of the ban on his making speeches in March 1944, Bahadur Yar Jung organised a public meeting in Hyderabad city, which was attended by a record and enthusiastic crowd, and implied that his past misfortunes were to be blamed on the British rather than on the Nizam. He said:

> Brothers! It has happened in the past and may perhaps happen in future that in the interests of the protection and perpetuation of His Exalted Highness's Crown, I shall have to refrain from obeying orders which have not been given of [the Nizam's] free will but issued in his name owing to pressure from elsewhere. In such circumstances I will much prefer disobedience of these orders to their obedience.[71]

Despite the tone of this speech, the Nizam represented to the British that 'the wording of the speech implie[d] the speaker's regret', and proposed to return Bahadur Yar Jung's jagir and title by July. It was apparent that he was seeking a reconciliation with the Ittihad but by then the party was no longer as united as before. Indeed, there were signs within the Ittihad— as in Hindu organisations—of a split between its moderate and extremist groups. More will be said about this later, but the differences were so serious that at the fifteenth annual session of the Majlis-Ittihad-ul-Muslimeen, which was held at Warangal (24–26 May 1944), Bahadur Yar Jung announced that he would not accept the presidentship of the Ittihad the following year and that the selection of his successor should now be taken up.[72]

It is difficult to know what would have happened within the Ittihad had Bahadur Yar Jung remained alive. But he died suddenly, and in rather mysterious circumstances, on 25 June 1944, leaving both the Nizam and the Ittihad at a low ebb in their mutual relationship. According to one account (Allana 1969, pp. 321–22), Bahadur Yar Jung had felt unwell for a month before his death. He had travelled to Warangal on 24–25 May 1944, in spite of an exceptional heat wave, and had returned with a 'raging fever'. For the next few weeks, he had been 'almost bedridden' but had refused to rest. On 25 June 1944, he dictated letters as usual in the morning for about an hour, then addressed girl students at a local religious school and returned home for lunch with his wife, after which he retired for an afternoon nap. In the evening, he proceeded to the house of a friend, Justice Hashim Ali Khan, where he had been invited to dinner. Following the local custom, as soon as Bahadur Yar Jung was seated, a servant brought out a *hookah* (water pipe) and placed it respectfully before him. 'He just took one puff ... felt giddy, and was soon unconscious' (*ibid*., p. 322). He did not regain consciousness and died shortly afterwards at 9.10 p.m.[73] He was 39 years old.

It was said later that he had been poisoned by the mixture in the hookah. His widow, in particular, seems to have started the rumour but she did not allow a post-mortem to be carried out. The city police, for its part, issued an official communique stating natural death.[74] As for public reaction, M.A. Khan says that "many eyebrows were raised against the Government" (1980, p. 90). It is improbable, however, that the Government or the Nizam had any share in Bahadur Yar Jung's death; indeed, it is difficult to imagine that the Nizam could have conspired to eliminate Bahadur Yar Jung because, even if he had reservations about him, the Nizam knew, like many in Hyderabad, that 'while an extremist himself, Bahadur Yar Jung was able to control the extremism of others'. From the Nizam's point of view, Bahadur Yar Jung was probably the best man to lead the Ittihad and defend Muslim interests (and his) in Hyderabad. The British reaction to the news seems also to confirm that Bahadur Yar Jung's death could not have been anything but a loss to the Nizam, a fact that the latter could not have failed to appreciate himself. An illegibly initialled notation, handwritten in the margin of a letter from the Resident to someone in the Political Department at New Delhi, states, 'Fortunately, the Nizam may not find it easy to fill Bahadur Khan's place with one of equal oratorical effectiveness. His death is a relief'![75] Subsequent events would show how erroneous this judgment was. In any case, the Nizam also knew how difficult it was to keep a secret in Hyderabad, particularly one so important, and it is unlikely that he would have arranged Bahadur Yar Jung's death and thus taken the tremendous risk of being discovered. A revolt of Muslims could have followed with unforeseeable consequences for his person, his rule and his fortune. In fact, it was reported that the Nizam accompanied by the Nawab of Chhatari and several members of the Executive Council had joined the large crowds who paid condolence visits to Bahadur Yar Jung's widow.

With the death of 'the most outstanding Hyderabadi of the day',[76] the Ittihad had lost the exceptional figure who had led the party from obscurity in 1938 to the forefront of State politics by 1944. This he had achieved not only through his own genius at rallying the Muslim community behind the Ittihad flag but also through the support of the Nizam who, in contrast to his treatment of the Hyderabad State Congress, allowed the Muslim political organisation to develop practically unhampered by the Government.

The Ittihad had thus prospered rapidly but, in 1944, few in its ranks understood the precariousness of its position. The quality of Bahadur Yar Jung's leadership, the support of the Nizam, and the absence of any violent counter-attack by the Hindus had fostered an illusion of strength among Hyderabadi Muslims which even the changes in the political scene in British India at the end of the War did not dispel.

In fact, after Bahadur Yar Jung's death, the Ittihad's understanding of its own power became even more unrealistic as the party fell under a new and more extremist leadership. To quote a Muslim contemporary, 'With [Bahadur Yar Jung's] death, the restraining no less than the inciting influence disappeared' (Ali Yavar Jung 1949, p. 9), and the Nizam's close relationship with the party's leadership never resumed on the same personal footing. Soon, the consequences of these developments would weigh heavily on the future of Hyderabad State.

NOTES

1. Rare were the Muslims who differed from the mainstream, the most notable being S.H. Tirmizi who was elected President of the Hyderabad Congress Committee. Tirmizi, however, had no Muslim following. IOL, R/1/29/1531, FR 1/9/37, 2.
2. Bahadur Yar Jung had been 'miraculously effective' in calming the Muslim mob which had gathered after the incident (see M.A. Khan 1980, p. 65).
3. IOL, R/1/29/1311, FR 2/4/36, 6. Mashriqui was 'dictatorial in his thinking and his deeds' and Bahadur Yar Jung eventually severed his links with the Khaksar organisation in 1943 (see G. Allana, 1969, pp. 312–13).
4. IOL, FR 1/9/36, 1.
5. IOL, FR 2/5/37, 5.
6. IOL, FR 1/7/37, 1.
7. *ibid.*, 2/7/37, 2.
8. *ibid.*, 1/8/37, 1.
9. The Reforms Committee also made recommendations on Budgets, Central Advisory Boards and Committees, District Conferences, Judicial Benches, District Boards, Municipal and Urban Committees, and the Hyderabad Municipal Corporation.
10. IOL, R/1/29/2054, Gidney to Glancy, 28 June 1939.
11. IOL, R/1/29/1921, Hydari to Gidney, 19 June 1939.
12. IOL, R/1/29/2173, Gidney to Glancy, 30 September 1940.
13. IOL, R/1/29/2054, Gidney to Glancy, 28 June 1939.
14. *ibid.*, (letter).
15. IOL, FR 1/6/39/ Supplementary.
16. IOL, FR 1/8/39, 4. Similar action was taken against the *Deccan Chronicle* for 'unrestrained propaganda on behalf of the Arya Samaj agitation'.
17. IOL, FR 1/8/39, Supplementary. The Resident reflected later that the Nizam might also have had other ideas in inviting mostly Muslim League personalities.

'[The Nizam] may think [he wrote] that if after the war he has requests to make of the Paramount Power as a reward for [war] assistance, he may find the strong support of the Muslim League of no little advantage', IOL, R/11/29/1892, Gidney to Glancy, 26 September 1939.

18. IOL, R/1/29/2077, Secret Report, Tasker to Gidney, 16 March 1940. 'Eight annas' means 'a half' as one rupee was equal to sixteen annas.
19. IOL, R/1/29/2115, FR 2/1/40, 2.
20. IOL, R/1/29/2173, His Exalted Highness to Linlithgow, 29 January 1940. Appendix, 'Resolutions passed at the annual session of the [Ittihad-ul-Muslimeen] ... on 19, 20, 21 Isfandar 1349F'.
21. *ibid*., Resolutions No. 4, 13 and 24.
22. *ibid*., Gidney to Glancy, 29 April 1940.
23. *ibid*., His Exalted Highness to Linlithgow, 24 January 1940.
24. IOL, R/1/29/2173, Gidney to Glancy, 1 March 1940.
25. [In 1819 and 1820] it was the Governor-General who suggested that the Nizam might assume the title of 'His Majesty' ... the Nizam of the day was reported ... to view such a proposal with great distaste on account of his feeling of loyalty towards his nominal suzerain, the Moghul Emperor of Delhi. IOL, R/1/29/2842, Lothian to Griffin, 26 August 1944.
26. IOL, R/1/29/2173, Gidney to Glancy, 20 July 1940.
27. See *The Hindu* (Madras), 2 October 1940. *The States' Peoples Magazine* (Bombay) later attributed the rumour of the proposal announced by Bahadur Yar Jung to an alleged offer by the Nizam to buy back the ceded territories: 'Apparently the Court at Hyderabad is well aware of the needs of the British who are concentrating their war effort on the gathering of money .... The price of forty lakhs [4 million] of pounds ... which it is said His Exalted Highness is willing to pay ... will be a fabulous windfall to the British treasury in this time of their dire need. But the Andhra Desa is not a football ... to be kicked from one goal to the other. The proposed transfer by gift or purchase concerns the life and liberties ... of eighteen millions of Andhras. You cannot uproot them all in a day and transplant a whole sub-nation on a different soil that is ... barren of all democratic springs', IOL, R/1/29/2173, copy of article 'Self-Preservation or Self-Expansion?', from *The States' Peoples*, 17 October 1940.
28. IOL, R/1/29/2173, Madras CID Report No. 3942/C, 7 October 1940.
29. IOL, R/1/29/2173, Government of Bihar, FR 1/11/40.
30. IOL, R/1/29/2291, Report 2421-S.B. from Bihar Special Branch (Patna) to Intelligence Bureau (New Delhi), 26 February 1941.
31. IOL, R/1/29/2173, Government of Bihar, FR 2/11/40, Supplementary.
32. *ibid*., Report, Hyderabad Railway Police, 2 November 1940.
33. *ibid*., Nizam to Viceroy, 18 November 1940.
34. *ibid*., Herbert to Laithwaite, 5 December 1940.
35. IOL, R/1/29/2270, FR 1/1/40, Supplementary.
36. A new party was formed by two maulanas (Sayyid Badshah Husaini and Shaikani Ahmed Shukur); this 'Jamiat-Shaban-ul-Muslimeen' did not make much headway, however, 'mainly perhaps [said the Resident] owing to the belief that the Maulanas have been suborned by government', FR 1/5/41 and 2/5/41; for the maulanas, His Exalted Highness was *Mazher-e-Hukumat-e-Ilahi*, the representative of the Almighty on earth.

37. IOL, R/1/29/2302, Gazette Extraordinary, 7 May 1941.
38. *ibid*., 'Rules regarding Maashdars'.
39. A move for the renewal of the 'unity talks' which had broken down two years previously had been initiated by Sir A. Hydari at the instance of the Nizam. Preliminary discussions had begun on 7 January 1941.
40. IOL, FR 2/6/41, 1. This drew a sharp rebuke from the Executive Council to the Nizam that rules regarding maashdars should not have been issued if they were not to be applied against those contravening them.
41. Nawab of Chhatari (1889–1983). MBE (1918), KCIE (1928), KCSI (1933), GBE (1946). Member, UP Legislative Council 1920–25. Minister of Industries, UP, 1923–25. Home Member, UP, 1926–33. Acting Governor, UP June–August 1928. Member first and second RTC. Acting Governor, UP April–November 1933. President, Hyderabad Executive Council, August 1941–July 1946 and June–November 1947. Later Pro-Chancellor and Chancellor, Aligarh Muslim University (from W.P. Kabadi 1935, p. 131 and S.P. Sen 1972–74, pp. 308–9). The Nawab was basically a mild mannered moderate man who from the outset had difficulties with the responsibilities of his post in Hyderabad.
42. IOL, FR 1/9/41, 4.
43. *ibid*., 5.
44. IOL, FR 1/10/41, 3; The communiqué also emphasised that numerous other bodies were to be created or reconstructed, and cited, aside from the Assembly, 16 district boards, 12 jagir boards, 21 district municipalities, 92 town committees and 1000 *panchayats*.
45. Abul Hasan Syed Ali, born 1890 (Hyderabad), advocate in Hyderabad city:

    > Front rank leader of the Ittihad .... A prolific speaker ... came from fairly humble beginnings. After reading up to the Intermediate at Aligarh University he started life as a clerk in the Hyderabad Residency, then entered the legal profession and set up as a lawyer in the Hyderabad courts .... He now [1944] owns a considerable amount of land and house property, particularly in the Nizamabad district .... Associated with local Hindu political agitators during 1931–37 .... Revealed himself in his true colours in 1938 when he joined the Ittihad-ul-Muslimeen, threw off the mask of nationalism and toured districts delivering a series of spirited anti-Hindu speeches .... Elected Secretary of the Ittihad ... in December 1938. Presided over the annual meeting of the Ittihad ... at Gulbarga in June 1939 where he delivered a speech accusing the members of the Executive Council of disloyalty to His Exalted Highness and loyalty to the Paramount Power ... asserted that Hyderabad was an Islamic kingdom ... demanded retrocession of the Ceded Districts .... He is not trusted by many of his co-workers in the Ittihad ... who regard him as a political careerist.

    From IOL, R/1/29/2823, 'Notes on Abul Hasan Syed Ali' (Secret), September 1944.
46. IOL, FR 2/10/41, 4.
47. IOL, FR 2/11/41, 1.
48. *ibid*., Supplementary.
49. IOL, FR 1/12/41, 7.
50. *The Hindu* (Madras), 9 February 1942 published a resolution passed at a meting of the Masulipatam Journalists' Association stating that 'no portion of the territory in and outside the town of Masulipatam or forming part of ... the Northern Circars should be given over to ... the Nizam of Hyderabad as he had surrendered his sovereign rights ... by previous historical treaties and declarations'. This came as

a rejoinder to an article in the *Deccan Times* (Madras), 1 February 1942, which had reported that the British government was 'quite amenable to His Exalted Highness' demands' and that 'a notification confirming it would shortly be issued'. IOL, R/1/29/2518, Government of India, Bureau of Public Information, 11 February 1942.

51. IOL, FR 2/2/42, 6; and 5.
52. IOL, FR 1/3/42, 4. The Ittihad-ul-Muslimeen, the Depressed Classes Association, and the Hindu Praja Mandal also placed volunteers and services at the disposal of the State authorities.
53. IOL. FR 2/3/42, 4.
54. IOL, FR 1/4/42, 7.
55. IOL, FR 2/3/42, 6.
56. IOL, FR 2/7/40, 3 and IOL, FR 1/6/42, 7.
57. IOL, FR 2/7/42, 1.
58. IOL, FR 1/8/42, 2.
59. IOL, FR 2/12/42, 3.
60. IOL, R/1/29/2578, FR 1/1/43, 3.
61. The Nizam's firman stated, 'It is not infrequently observed that when Bahadur Yar Jung stands on the public platform ... he loses control of his tongue .... In view of this, I consider it necessary ... that Bahadur Yar Jung be henceforth forbidden to deliver any speeches either within or outside the Dominions for a period of one year', IRH, Judicial Police and General Dept., File No. 9/PA/52 (1943). This firman caused angry demonstrations by Muslims, one-day hartal of Muslim shops and violent statements in the press. IOL, FR 2/3/43, 3.
62. IOL, FR 1/4/43, 3.
63. IOL, R/1/29/2629, Grigson to Hawes, 20 April 1943. Grigson (Director-General of Police) underlines the 'rudeness' of Bahadur Yar Jung in couching the surrender of his honours and privileges in the form of a nazar, as it was a 'covert allusion to His Exalted Highness's well-known like for nazars'.
64. *ibid.*
65. IOL, R/1/29/2629, Lothian to Fitze, 25 April 1943.
66. *ibid.*
67. *ibid.*
68. It is probable that Jinnah was also consulted. Bahadur Yar Jung went to Bombay to visit him (31 May–9 June 1943) and the latter stated that he was in correspondence with the Nizam regarding the matter. IOL, FR 1/6/43, 4.
69. The following provides a good illustration of the fervour he commanded in Hyderabad. In August 1943, Bahadur Yar Jung went to Kashmir, to attend the Kashmir Muslim League Conference, but on arrival was served with an order prohibiting his entry and deported from the State. The news of his deportation was greeted in Hyderabad by a full hartal of Muslim shops, prayers in mosques for his safety and numerous protest meetings by the Ittihad (Fr 2/8/43, 5). When he returned to Hyderabad (early in September), Bahadur Yar Jung was greeted, immediately past the border of the State, by large crowds assembled at every railway station on the way (Kazipet, Jangaon, Aler, Bhongir and Secunderabad). At Hyderabad station, the train was decorated with flags and a crowd of about 5000 Muslims greeted him with shouts of 'Allah-o-Akbar', 'Quaid-e-Millat Zindabad', 'Sher-e-Islam Zindabad', and on alighting, Bahadur Yar Jung was profusely garlanded. Afterwards,

standing in a car, he thanked the crowds, gave an account of the treatment he had received in Kashmir, and condemned the 'arbitrary' action prohibiting him from participating in the Muslim Conference. After his speech, Bahadur Yar Jung was taken in procession to his house where many prominent personalities 'including a few Marwaris and other Hindus' called on him. (FR 1/9/43, 4).

70. IOL, FR 2/10/43, 4.
71. IOL, L/P & S/1202, 'Extract of Bahadur Khan's speech of March 18, 1944'.
72. IOL, FR 1/6/44, 5.
73. IOL, FR 2/6/44, 3.
74. IOL, FR 2/8/44, 9.
75. IOL, L/P & S/13/1203, Lothian to Griffin, 4 July 1944.
76. IOL, L/P & S/13/1209. Words used by W.W. Grigson, Director-General of Police, Hyderabad in his report of October 1944, p. 47.

5

1939–1946: The Determining Years

After its poor performance in the 1938–39 agitation, the Hyderabad State Congress was inactive and stood largely discredited with the younger (Left) sections of its membership. The efforts of Swami Ramanand Tirtha, a Congress leader who rose through the ranks in the satyagraha period, to revitalise the party and associate it more strongly with the Indian National Congress remained unrewarded throughout the 1940s. His attempts to launch a 'Quit India' agitation in Hyderabad on the INC model in 1942 only produced poor results as, once again, a policy of direct action drew little or no support from the older (Right) State Congress leadership and the population at large.

Meanwhile, the Communists were able to capture the lead of the Andhra Mahasabha and to foment a peasant agitation against landlords in the easternmost districts of Telengana.

The Ittihad-ul-Muslimeen, for its part, although its leadership was divided after the death of Bahadur Yar Jung, increasingly extended its influence over most sections of the Muslim community with strident assertions of strength at the local level and of 'independence' at the all-India level.

The Nizam's Government supported this notion of independence and, deluded by its 'alliance' with the British, continued to believe that Hyderabad's political future was ultimately to be settled from within, regardless of political developments beyond the State's borders.

When the ban on the HSC was finally lifted in 1946, it was more as a corollary to the action taken by the Government of India with regard to the INC than through the force of the Congress movement in the State.

Altogether, the period from 1939 to 1946 witnessed an increasing polarisation of the State's population. Divisions between moderate and extremist leadership became marked in all parties and organisations, while communalism and conflicting class interests permeated the society even more deeply. By 1946, little cohesion remained amongst Hyderabad's population, leaving the State helpless in the face of post-War political developments in the broad Indian context.

When, in December 1938, Gandhi intervened and called off the HSC satyagraha, it was much to the unhappiness of the young satyagrahis who were behind bars in the State's prisons.

As one of them, Swami Ramanand Tirth,[1] recalls in his *Memoirs*:

> We could not understand the propriety of this decision. Some of us were enraged at Mahatmaji for having given what we considered wrong advice. The State Congress would go to dogs [*sic*] and communal elements would get the upper hand. That was how we argued. But we were helpless and could do nothing except biding our time (1967, p. 107).

In the world outside, State Congress activities were at a standstill. Those of the leaders who were not in jail were reported to be 'remarkably secretive about future plans' but, the Resident thought it likely that their secretiveness was due to the fact that 'a decision about future plans lies in other hands than their own'. In fact, serious confusion and conflicts of opinion reigned within Congress ranks. Some of the members continued to favour negotiating with the Government for official recognition of the party and pursuing a non-violent campaign for constitutional reforms. Others—the younger and more extreme—opted for a resumption of agitation and repeatedly asked Gandhi for his approval. He withheld it, however, and advised the forty-odd HSC workers who had come to attend a Congress meeting at Wardha in February 1939, to devote themselves 'to awaken the rural population to political consciousness throughout the State'.[2]

Shortly afterwards (in March 1939), Gandhi took a formal stand against civil disobedience in the princely States, upon which some of the satyagrahis detained in Hyderabad were released. By 10 April 1939, all remaining Congress prisoners were freed and the HSC attempted to resume its activities.

The moderates, who still headed the party, again contemplated moves to get the ban on the party removed and, after a meeting at Manmad (Bombay Province) in September 1939, Kasinath Rao Vaidya, President of the tentative organisation, began correspondence with the State authorities. No change having occurred in the Government's stand, it was announced in December 1939 that the HSC had finally decided to change its name to Hyderabad State National Conference (hereafter the HSNC). Following this, the Working Committee of the HSNC issued a press statement announcing that the Nizam's Government had given an assurance that, provided its name was changed, no objection would be raised to the organisation functioning. And by 1940, despite the Ittihad's protests that the HSNC was still a communal organisation, all seemed set for renewed Congress activity in Hyderabad.[3]

In accordance with Gandhi's wishes, the HSNC would devote itself to 'constructive activities' such as the opening of national schools (*Vidyayak Karya Samitis*) and to the upliftment of the poorer classes, while at the same time building up mass support.

The HSNC, in fact, concentrated mainly on fresh enrolments. By the end of January 1940 it claimed to have recruited 15,000 members and hoped for 25,000 by the end of February. Where this influx of members came from is not clear, considering the previous record of the Hyderabad State Congress, but it can be presumed that some new members were gained from among the agrarian classes—owner-cultivators in particular. Congress workers had 'made attempts ... to persuade ryots to withhold land revenue in view of the hardships brought about by dry weather and the poor crops resulting'.[4] These attempts had been 'wholly unsuccessful', reported the Resident, but they had perhaps served to attract some ryot membership. It is doubtful, however, that the figures released by the HSNC were exact.

Another HSNC strategy was to attempt a unification of the three linguistic regional organisations—the Maharashtra Parishad, the Karnataka Parishad and the Andhra Mahasabha—which had been created in the 1920s and late 1930s. Since these regional 'Conferences' were allowed to function by Government, it was thought that no objection would be raised to their dissolution and merging with the HSNC. Thus, an appeal to the three organisations was put forward by Swami Ramanand Tirtha, then President of the Maharashtra Parishad, at the end of February 1940.

The fact that this was the initiative of the Maharashtra Parishad indicates that Marathwara was still the most actively pro-Congress region of the State. What is also particularly interesting is that it was the first open bid by Marathi-speakers to take the lead in a Statewide Congress movement. Indeed, since Marathi-speakers—Tirtha, Vaidya, Nanal[5] and others—were already at its helm, an amalgamation under the 'umbrella' of the HSNC would have meant in effect that the leadership of the Karnataka Parishad and the Andhra Mahasabha would pass to the Maharashtra Parishad. The move was also meant to give the HSNC a more convincing 'national' character, but it was in the end defeated, principally because of the strong opposition of the Andhra Mahasabha,[6] presaging the later irreconcilable political differences between Telugu and Marathi speakers in the State.

The State authorities, in the meantime, had been alarmed by the ambitions of the HSNC. Worried by developments in British India (between Congress and the Government of India) since the outbreak of World War II (September 1939), they had no intention of allowing the growth, whatever its name, of a Congress organisation in Hyderabad. Accordingly, they announced abruptly in March 1940 that, although the HSNC had so far been allowed to function, it had not actually been declared to be a legal association and had now to be dissolved.

In the confusion which followed, the HSNC split, as had the Hyderabad State Congress, between the moderates (inclined to comply with the Government order) and the extremists—infuriated by the prospect and advocating fighting the order with an immediate resumption of civil disobedience activities.

A party led by Tirtha went to consult Gandhi. He, however, only confirmed that the letter from the Nizam's Government which advised the HSC to change its name prior to any recognition did not, in fact, automatically imply *legal* recognition. His advice was, therefore, to comply with the order.

According to Tirtha,

> It was difficult ... to agree to [Gandhi's] proposition. There was a strong feeling that the Government had gone back upon their assurances, that they had committed a breach of faith .... After much heated discussion, it was decided to abide by the advice of Mahatma Gandhi. It was then expressly understood that this dissolution would lead to another struggle if the Government did not allow the National Conference to function (1967, pp. 112–13).

The HSNC was, thus, dissolved at the end of March 1940 amid much discontent in Congress ranks and rumours of a future satyagraha. The extremist sections of the Conference (students,[7] schoolteachers, lower government servants, small traders, factory workers, labourers) were particularly unhappy and despondent, as their efforts (and Tirtha's) to introduce political militancy in Hyderabad had been thwarted once again. It was reported that 'some leaders were contemplating joining the frankly communal State Hindu Praja Mandal [affiliated to the Hindu Mahasabha] while others ... preferred an organisation less avowedly communal'.[8]

Negotiations with the Government were, however, resumed and when, after a few months—during which the HSNC remained perforce inactive—it became clear that the State authorities would not lift the ban, a party of Congress workers returned to Wardha to obtain fresh advice from Gandhi. But Gandhi could not be swayed to support mass agitation. According to Tirtha:

> In the month of August 1940, some two dozen of us were huddled together in front of Mahatmaji in his hut at Sevagram. We placed before him our views and expressed a desire to allow us to resume the struggle. Having heard us patiently, he seemed to have relapsed into a contemplative mood .... He stated that there was no other course left open for us except resuming the struggle .... But this time he told us, the struggle would be more arduous .... We expressed our readiness to pay the price. But the Mahatma would not be satisfied with this assurance. 'Are you prepared for self-immolation? I will not write or negotiate with the Government for your release .... Have you the necessary strength?' And then came his last query 'Do you believe in non-violence as a creed?' We were taken aback by those interrogations .... We believed in non-violence as a policy. We had to admit it in all honesty. The younger section amongst us once again pleaded with him not to be too hard on them in imposing this condition. But Mahatmaji would not give in. 'I will only allow those to defy the ban who believe in non-violence as a creed. The rest should confine themselves to the constructive programme. Let there be two wings, one pursuing the constructive programme and the other defying the ban in vindication of the Hyderabad State Congress.' (1967, pp. 114–15)

It was obvious that Gandhi, pre-occupied by the delicate situation arising out of War developments and the fresh offers to the INC made by the British, could not properly think at this juncture of beginning a full scale agitation in a princely State such as Hyderabad (see Aggarwala 1965; Hutchins 1973). But, at the same time, he probably did not want to disappoint the most active elements of the State Congress. He thus astutely found the formula which would satisfy all; those of the most extreme trend would like the idea of action, be it 'self-immolation', even though this was to be done on an individual basis and without any hope of intervention by the Indian National

Congress. The less determined could also satisfy themselves with the 'constructive programme' and an open option to participate in non-violent satyagraha. This would keep them out of the way of the moderate Congress leaders who could then carry on with negotiations, an approach which naturally had their approval as well as that of the Nizam's Government.

Tirtha claims to have volunteered immediately and received first, Gandhi's sanction for individual satyagraha.[9] On his return from Wardha, Tirtha dispatched a letter to the state authorities stating that he felt 'compelled to offer civil disobedience owing to the attitude of uncompromising opposition of the Government of HEH [*sic*] towards the Hyderabad State Congress' (1967, p. 118). On 12 September 1940, he was arrested under the Defence of Hyderabad Rules and sentenced to three months imprisonment.[10] Further to this, Gandhi sent a letter to the Nizam's Government, declaring that he had advised the Hyderabad State Congress 'whose members [had] been acting under [his] general guidance' to begin an immediate form of direct action. But, said Gandhi, civil resistance would be 'confined to very few individuals who believe in non-violence not merely as a policy but as a creed'; only four individuals had been selected, 'this ... being the final and only list', without any 'public agitation behind the movement'.[11]

The four, all Hyderabadi Hindus, were sent by Gandhi to Aurangabad on 13 October 1940 and were arrested together two days later.[12]

Thus can be summed up Congress activity in the State through 1940 and 1941, as, following these arrests, there is no mention of any active incidents involving Congress for almost a year. There is also no evidence that the 'constructive programme' advocated by Gandhi was initiated. In fact, Congress as such seemed to have disappeared altogether from Hyderabad. Tirtha, who was himself in jail, explains that

> the cream of leading Marathwada Congressmen including G.M. Shroff were ... put under arrest and continued in detention for more than twenty-one months. Those who remained outside, in all the three regions, seem to have relapsed into regional activities working through the Provincial Conferences. The Hyderabad State Congress continued to exist in a symbolic manner with about half-a-dozen of Congressmen held in detention .... In fact, none [*sic*] outside seemed to attach much importance to the symbolic *satyagraha* which was offered to vindicate the existence of the State Congress (1967, pp. 121 and 123).

The apathy of Hyderabadis towards the State Congress seems also to have extended to the reverses of the INC in British India. The arrests of Nehru in November 1940 and of Rajagopalachari and Patel in December were merely marked by 'partial *hartals*' in Hyderabad city and Secunderabad but, the British Resident, reported little active interest.[13]

This general indifference can be attributed to factors inherent in the State party—lack of cohesion at the level of leadership and absence of mass support stemming from local factors outlined in Chapter 2. From 1940 onwards, other elements emerged to reinforce this attitude.

By mid-1940, preoccupation with the War overshadowed local issues all over India. The Germans seemed victorious on all fronts. Denmark, Holland and Belgium had fallen. Norway had been partially annexed and France had collapsed completely. Britain was in danger, and, after the Dunkirk disaster, was subjected to incessant air attacks. On 1 June 1940, Gandhi declared, 'We do not seek our Independence out of Britain's ruin' (Aggarwala 1965, p. 224). From Hyderabad, the Nizam telegraphed the King of England 'offering all his resources for the successful prosecution of the War'.[14] In July, although he had made various donations in cash and kind towards the war effort since the beginning of hostilities, he offered a further £50,000 and Rs 5 lakh from his own purse, a totally unprecedented gesture.[15]

This stand of the Nizam with regard to the War brought forth resolutions of loyalty to his Government, appeals to unity and recommendations to support the British. Not just the Jagirdars' Association, even the Arya Samaj issued a statement through Vinayak Rao Vidyalankar, one of its prominent local leaders, associating itself with the Government and praising England's part in the War. Britain was fighting for 'freedom of thought from Nazism' and, it was stated, the ideal of the Arya Samaj was also the same.[16] Local politicians such as Hanumantha Rao and M. Narsing Rao (moderate Congress wing of the Andhra Mahasabha), Mir Akbar Ali Khan (Union and Progress Party) and V.R. Vidyalankar (in his personal capacity) all came forward in support of Britain. The British Resident himself complimented the Nizam on the 'splendid lead which he [was] giving his subjects ... by [his] confidence in the victory of the Allies'.[17]

In such a situation, it is perhaps not surprising that the local population should have shown little interest in State Congress politics.

But there was another factor which reduced Congress influence more decisively in Hyderabad from 1940: the Andhra Mahasabha, the most important linguistic regional organisation in the State was falling increasingly under Communist control.

A feature of the Congress movement in Hyderabad was that its membership was generally drawn from the three linguistic regional organisations. At the time of the 1938 Congress satyagraha, the younger elements of these organisations were disgruntled by what they considered poor direction from their moderate leaders, and schisms had begun in the Maharashtra Parishad and the Andhra Mahasabha between extreme and moderate factions.

To digress for a moment, what the satyagraha had revealed within Congress was a conflict between the original leadership of highly educated, well-to-do and generally elderly figures, and the rising mass of active youth with their less influential, less educated and less wealthy leaders. The two had opposed one another on principles of policy—for or against 'direct action'—and this conflict, well illustrated in P. Naidu's communication to Gandhi (see Chapter 3), is confirmed by Tirtha in his *Memoirs*. Going back to 1937, he remembers:

> Prominent persons spoke in extremist language in private but they would be docile in public utterances and very mild in actual performance .... On studying the situation ... I realised that except for an individual or two ... there was none in the city of Hyderabad who would come forward and gather people's forces ... for the achievement of democratic freedom ... (1967, p. 68)

It is understandable that these 'prominent persons', being generally men of status and wealth, should have been more cautious over an involvement in actual agitation than ardent youngsters generally belonging to less affluent classes. But, as one reads on, the impression emerges that they were also disdainful of the mass following of the party and perhaps even scared of young aspiring leaders to whom they had no intention of relinquishing any part of their control over the party. This would be why they gave them a cold-shoulder rather than welcomed them, as Tirtha recalls:

> It was no easy matter to be with the leaders. In the first place, you would have to wait upon them at their leisure which was a late hour at night after they had completed every item of their daily work. I remember, one leader would keep me waiting till 10 p.m. and even after that he would find time only when he had disposed of all his clientele (1967, p. 81).

This unwillingness of the early leadership to associate with the younger elements of Congress became even more apparent when satyagraha was finally declared. To quote Tirtha again:

> Among those who were ready for action, there was hardly any person who could be considered elderly. To our good fortune, Govindrao Nanal, who was widely respected, came forward and gave the lead by being the first President of the Hyderabad State Congress .... His choice as the first President silenced all those who had derided the movement as children's pranks (1967, pp. 88–89).

The division appearing in State Congress ranks seems, thus, to have been between the 'old' moderates and the 'young' extremists, a common enough occurrence in the evolution of any party. But, here, disagreements over party policies were perhaps also an expression of conflicts between economic classes, 'the haves' and 'the have-nots', and their diverging interests. For the 'haves', it would not have done, in the case of an eventual Congress victory over the Nizam's regime, to be relegated to second place in the scramble for power. The wealthiest Hindu classes were thus consistently 'moderate' in the Congress agitation against the Nizam's regime. Hence one is led to think that the ideological purposes of 'the democratic movement' in Hyderabad were at least two-fold—'nationalist' in the extremist sections of Congress and 'provincial autonomist', so to speak, in the moderate camp. In time, this would be translated into adherence and opposition to the principle of Hyderabad's unification with the rest of the Indian Union.

In 1940, a similar type of conflict seems to have been occurring between 'extremists' and 'moderates' in the leadership of the Andhra Mahasabha. Here, however, it was even more marked than within the State Congress, as early leaders such as M. Hanumantha Rao and M. Narsing Rao who remained faithful to Congress were against men such as Ravi Narayan Reddy (the son of a Telengana landlord who had actively participated in the 1938 satyagraha) (see Ramesan 1966, p. 51 and Sen 1972 pp. 233–36) who inclined increasingly towards communism.

The schism within the Andhra Mahasabha began to be clear at the seventh Annual Session of the organisation held in April 1940 at Malkapur, when it was reported that 'misunderstandings between well-settled, elderly and educated workers and enthusiastic youngsters who had to struggle for their livelihood became serious' (Ramesan 1966, p. 51).

Discussions centred on constitutional reforms proposed by Government, and for the first time a resolution put forward by moderate leaders—that the reforms were inadequate but should still be worked—was defeated by a large majority and replaced by a statement that the reforms were totally unacceptable and should be rejected.[18] Within a year, Congress influence over the Andhra Mahasabha declined dramatically. At the eighth session of the Sabha held at Chilkapur (Nalgonda District) in 1941, Ravi Narayan Reddy who had the largest following in the ranks of the Andhra Mahasabha crossed the floor and 'a formidable force went over to the Communists' (Tirtha, 1967, p. 138).

After this, the 'anti-communist group' consisting of 'Congress-minded youths [*sic*], the bulk of whom were lawyers and middle-class gentry naturally led by landlords and jagirdars' completely lost ground. In the words of a chronicler, they 'had to be convinced to their amazement that they could not influence anything' (Ramesan 1966, p. 52). In 1943, the Resident commented:

> The growing strength of the communist section inside [the Andhra Mahasabha] is alarming the more moderate and 'propertied classes' leaders. The latter are ready enough to approve agitation against Government but do not appreciate agitation which reminds villagers of their economic rights as against the landlords and the propertied classes.[19]

At the eleventh session of the Sabha, at Bhongir (Nalgonda District) in 1944, this group saw no alternative but to secede altogether from the organisation and to create a separate association to be known as the Nationalist Andhra Mahasabha.

But dissensions in Congress ranks did not occur only in the Andhra Mahasabha. They also manifested themselves in the Maharashtra Parishad, as can be deduced from a development in mid-1940 at a time when the Ittihad-ul-Muslimeen was making renewed claims for the return of Berar and other ceded territories from the British. An opposing stand was adopted at a Maharashtra Unification Conference organised under the auspices of the INC at Poona on 24 May and attended by extremist HSC leaders, Y.D. Joshi and Raghavendra Rao Sharma in particular, who were using Poona as a base for agitation against Hyderabad State.[20] Several resolutions were passed at the Conference but the most important in regard to Hyderabad was that:

> the Marathi population in Native States and Marathwada from the Nizam's Dominions be annexed to a United Maharashtra at the time of a future reconstruction of the States.[21]

In Hyderabad, this was not well received by Congress moderates such as K.S. Vaidya (a founder member of the Maharashtra Parishad), Narsing Rao (of Congress Andhra Mahasabha) and 'other leading Hindus' who issued a statement in September that should Dominion status be granted to India,

> [it] shall not adversely affect the political status of Hyderabad or its chances of economic development .... No outside agency should be allowed to interfere with the internal administration of the State.[22]

Another factor further 'diluted' the impact of State Congress in Hyderabad. Communal relations which had begun deteriorating in the late 1930s worsened in the early 1940s perhaps as a reflection of the all-India atmosphere, but also largely as a result of the activities of both the Ittihad and the Hindu Mahasabha. The Arya Samaj, for its part, seems to have been growing more moderate and discriminating in its attacks against Muslims after its involvement in the 1938–39 satyagraha. For instance, at a meeting to commemorate the end of the satyagraha the previous year, Arya Samaj leaders had made speeches 'drawing a pointed contrast between the '*goondas*' [i.e. the Ittihad] and their generous and kind rulers, the Nizam and Hydari, both of whom [were] emphatically praised for last year's amnesty and the grant of religious rights'.[23] But the Arya Samaj went no further in its opposition to the Ittihad.

The virulence of the Hindu Mahasabha, on the other hand, had not abated, and it no doubt encouraged among Hindus the same defensive attitude that the Ittihad fostered among Muslims. Petty incidents now flared up frequently between the communities. Intentional desecrations of temples and mosques were becoming commonplace and trouble was most frequent during religious festivals, particularly in district areas. In 1940, Muharrum (February), passed off peacefully in Hyderabad city and, the Resident reported, 'both communities join[ed] in its celebration, the Hindu public taking part in large numbers'.[24] In district areas, however, the same festivities were marked by a series of minor clashes 'nowhere serious enough to be called riots' but, the Resident reported that communal friction was growing.[25] A month later, communal rioting in Hyderabad State reached an unprecedented height with an incident (already referred to in Chapter 4) which reverberated throughout India.

It happened in Bidar (Bidar district) on 23 March 1940, beginning with yet another petty altercation in the town's marketplace between a Hindu and a Muslim. The Hindu drew a gun, shot the Muslim dead, and ran away. When the police finally arrived on the scene, an angry crowd of Muslims was already on a rampage of the market, fires were lit and, in the end, the whole market was burned down. About a hundred shops, mostly belonging to Hindus, were destroyed, several lakhs of rupees were looted, and a few people were injured.[26] This episode, reported in the press in British India as the 'Bidar arson case', created a furore against the Hyderabad authorities as, it seems, 'the police did less than they should to check the mob' and as 'although the Nizam's government was well aware of this, it was unwilling at present to enquire'. In the Resident's view, 'an unfortunate handle [had been] given to the enemies of the State'. A self-appointed Hindu 'Committee of Enquiry' left Hyderabad for Bidar to investigate, following which Nehru himself made a pronouncement hostile to the State despite the fact that by then criminal cases against Muslims had been brought to court and money for reconstruction and compensation had been sanctioned by the Nizam's Government.[27]

Further communal incidents occurred in 1940. The Ganpati festival (15 September) led to a clash at Vijatpur (Aurangabad district) in which 15 persons were injured. Five days later, the celebration of the urs of a Muslim saint at Nander resulted in a riot in which two persons died and 15 were injured. The British Resident referred to it as 'a serious affair in which local Muhammadan hooliganism played a prominent part' and commented further:

> Thanks largely to the militancy of the Ittehad-ul-Muslimin [*sic*], Hindu–Muslim relations in Hyderabad State provide much food for anxious thought but the communal situation being what it is elsewhere in India, it would be idle to expect any improvement.[28]

Whether the increased communal tension in Hyderabad can be directly attributed to local rivalries or whether it was a result of an all-India phenomenon is difficult to say. However, it was in March 1940 that the demand for Pakistan and the Two-Nation Theory began to be strongly expounded by the Muslim League. Thus, when communalism decisively took hold of politics in British India, it is not surprising that in Hyderabad, too, it should have increasingly appeared in the political field.

The Hindu Mahasabha, taking for the first time a stand on a purely political issue, perhaps to counter the politics of the Ittihad measure for measure, pronounced itself in favour of the constitutional reforms which had been announced by the Government at the end of the 1938–39 satyagraha. The Ittihad had protested against the reforms but the Hindu Mahasabha passed a resolution, at the end of July 1940, that 'the Reforms be worked for what they were worth'. The effect, however, was unexpected. While the Ittihad made no response, Congress moderates complained in private that 'the grass [was] being cut from under their feet'. Narsing Rao, the editor of the local *Raiyat*, pointedly attacked the Hindu Mahasabha's initiative and warned his readers of 'the dangers of 'sub-Savarkars' and 'sub-Jinnahs' arising in the State',[29] the references being to B. Keskar (local secretary of the Hindu Mahasabha) and Bahadur Yar Jung (President of the Ittihad-ul-Muslimeen).

Soon after, perhaps to defuse the situation, the Nizam's Government initiated moves, in December 1940, for the renewal of the 'unity talks' previously abandoned by Narsing Rao and Bahadur Yar Jung (see Chapter 3). Again, the hope was expressed that a private understanding regarding constitutional reforms would be reached by leaders of the Hindu and Muslim communities. Sir Akbar Hydari would preside over discussions between Narsing Rao and Ramachari (State Congress, Karnataka Parishad) on the Hindu side, and Abdul Hasan Kaiser (of the State's Ecclesiastical Department) on the Muslim side.[30]

This choice of representatives was immediately attacked by the Ittihad which claimed that excepting itself and its president, 'no organisation or individual [was] entitled to negotiate on behalf of the Hyderabadi's Mussulmans [*sic*]'. The Hindu Mahasabha similarly stated that 'the Hindu community [would] not be bound by any understanding which [Hindu representatives] may reach with the Muslims .... [The Hindu Mahasabha] which represent[ed] the Hyderabadi Hindus [was] alone entitled to carry on any negotations on behalf of the Hindus'. At that, the hitherto politically-silent Depressed Classes Association issued a rejoinder stating that 'Hindu leaders [could] not speak for the Depressed Classes who form a separate community for themselves'.[31]

Thus, by an ironic twist, the 'unity talks' merely contributed further to a polarisation of communities in Hyderabad State. In this atmosphere, it is perhaps not surprising that the State Congress satyagraha taken up in October 1940 by a few individuals should have provoked little more than general indifference. Through the rest of 1940 and during the troubled 1941, little was heard of the Hyderabad State

Congress. In fact, it was not before mid 1942 and under instructions from Gandhi, in the context of the All-India Congress 'Quit India' movement, that Tirtha and a handful of others attempted once again to launch agitation in Hyderabad State.

Tirtha and the half-dozen satyagrahis who had been imprisoned in September 1940 were finally released by the State authorities on 16 December 1941 (Aggarwala 1965, p. 227).

The very next day, Tirtha, faithful to Gandhi's initial directives, issued a statement that 'since Government had not removed the restrictions imposed on the State Congress, there would be no change in the party's policy of agitation'.[32] He then proceeded to Wardha to seek Gandhi's approval but, by December 1941, Gandhi and the Indian National Congress Working Committee no longer agreed on the party's agitational policies. Gandhi still favoured the programme of individual satyagraha, while the Working Committee, concerned by the danger to India of Japan's entry into the War against the Allies, considered it more urgent to begin preparing for self-defence. The influence of the Working Committee prevailed in the end, and individual satyagraha was thus suspended in British India. Then, on 30 December 1941, Gandhi was relieved of the leadership of the Congress (Aggarwala 1965, p. 228; Coupland 1943, Part II, p. 265).

In Hyderabad, the news of Japanese successes early in 1942, the fall of Singapore (in February) and the invasion of Burma, greatly worried the population (Coupland 1943, p. 263–71). When the War moved closer to the State, with the Japanese air-raids on Vizagapatam (Visakhapatnam) and Cocanada (Kakinada) in April, this worry turned into frenzied alarm. Government began considering defence; local parties and organisations advocated the sinking of communal and political differences and pledged 'whole-hearted cooperation with the State government'. The Ittihad, the Depressed Classes Association, the Arya Samaj and the Hindu Mahasabha, in a spirit of 'national unity' (*sic*), all placed volunteers at the disposal of the State authorities.[33]

Meanwhile, the Cripps Mission had arrived in India (in March 1942) with fresh proposals to solve the Indian political impasse. What was now offered was the creation of a new 'Indian Union', with Dominion status, and a new Constitution, to be framed by the Indian people after the War. Indian States would be invited to join the Union and would be represented in proportion to their population. They would, however, be free to join the Union or not, and the British Government was ready to negotiate fresh treaties with the States if this was required in the new Constitution (see Coupland 1943 and Moore 1979).

The Cripps proposals, in effect, reversed the spirit of unity fostered in Hyderabad by the common anxiety over the War. Indeed, the question of the future of the State took precedence over the War issue, and revived all the communal and political divisions. In the main, moderate Hindus remained silent, but the extremists asserted that Hyderabad should be absorbed into 'greater and democratic India' while Ittihad Muslims demanded the retention of the State as a separate and 'independent' entity.[34]

Matters rested there for the time being and gradually as the Japanese threat receded, public attention returned to local issues. For the politically-minded, the revised constitutional reforms,[35] and for the population at large, high prices of grain and communal incidents,[36] regained importance.

Tirtha, in July 1942, received instructions from Gandhi to prepare a 'mass movement' in Hyderabad in tandem with a proposed country-wide anti-British movement. Following the lack of an agreement between Congress and the British Government with regard to the Cripps proposals, the Congress Working Committee passed a resolution at Wardha in July 1942 demanding the withdrawal of the British from India (Coupland 1943, pp. 283–88 and p. 291). This resolution was then adopted by the All-India Congress Committee at Bombay on 8 August 1942 and the so-called 'Quit India' agitation began forthwith. In Hyderabad, however, Tirtha was still unprepared. Workers of the Maharashtra Parishad had only just begun to recruit volunteers (mainly among students) and to instruct them about the features of the movement: they were to court arrest by shouting slogans such as 'the Resident should leave Hyderabad' and 'the Resident and Imperialism should go back',[37] but no overall strategy had been drawn.

To Tirtha's dismay, the organisation of a 'plan of action' proved impossible, once again on account of divisions within the State Congress. Most of the moderate (and most influential) Congress leaders were, at the time, members of the Hyderabad State War Defence Council which had been created in the wake of the Japanese alarm. They proved extremely reluctant to commit themselves too openly to a renewed agitation. They were 'playing for time and avoiding resigning from the Council as they anticipate[d] that if they resign[ed], they [would] immediately be arrested'.[38] In these circumstances, Tirtha had to confess to Gandhi that 'owing to various conflicting trends, Hyderabad may not act with one voice' and to ask if Gandhi would 'permit a few individuals to fall in line with the resolution and do their bit [*sic*]?' Gandhi replied that, 'Even if there were three persons in any State, they could join in the Revolution'. (Tirtha 1967, p. 129).

Tirtha claims that he sent a note to 'at least fifty prominent Congressmen' outlining the aim and methods of the 'Quit India' agitation in Hyderabad but that, when he asked three or four to meet him in Sholapur for discussions, none of them cared to do so. Only Govindrao Nanal, the ageing President of the State Congress, made the journey and agreed that the movement should be launched. Nanal, however, declined to participate as his health was deteriorating rapidly. Before returning to Hyderabad, he delegated in writing all his powers as President of the State Congress to Tirtha.

Now, as acting President of the Hyderabad State Congress, Tirtha despatched a letter to the State authorities early in August 1942 announcing his intention to launch a 'mass movement'. Returning by train from Sholapur, he was arrested upon alighting at Hyderabad's Nampally Station and jailed again, together with 16 of his comrades rounded up as a precautionary measure.

With the most prominent State Congressmen in jail or political hibernation, the conduct of the movement was left to a few students and the rank-and-file workers of the party. According to Tirtha:

> Everyone acted on their own initiative .... Whatever happened was all spontaneous .... So far as Hyderabad Congressmen were concerned almost all the active cadre was put under arrest. The movement did not grow as it was not nourished properly. The result was that after a short period it stopped altogether (1967, p. 135).

In fact, apart from a short flare-up following the arrest of Tirtha and his group, there was in reality no 'Quit India' agitation in Hyderabad for almost a month after the launching of the movement in British India.

On 10 August 1942, some college students of Secunderabad demanded a holiday to protest against the arrest of the Congress leaders. When this was refused, they proceeded, reported the Resident, 'to commit minor acts of hooliganism and to block one of the main thoroughfares of Secunderabad'. The police intervened, arrested five students, and dispersed the rest without the use of force.[39]

The authorities took no chances, however, and, when implementing the first stage of their City Riot Scheme, posted police pickets throughout the city. On the morning of 11 August, agitation began again and, although it remained confined to Secunderabad, it assumed somewhat larger proportions. The telegraphic report of the Resident details the only violence which occurred in the State in connection with the 'Quit India' movement:

> 11 August .... Disturbances developed to a more serious scale ... about noon Section 144 Criminal Procedure Code was promulgated and broadcast in town by loudspeaker vans. Mill workers from the Ramgopal Mills ... joined in stone throwing and rowdyism .... One crowd numbered over a thousand. Police had several times to charge and disperse crowds. During evening stone-throwing increased and tear gas was used. During day 75 persons were arrested but some were subsequently released only principal offenders being retained. 3 policemen were badly beaten up. Of the public only four persons were detained in hospital.
>
> 12 August. The situation eased except for some acts of hooliganism such as stoning of cars. A number of shops however remained closed. 50 of the 100 State police lent to Secunderabad were returned. Another 12 arrests were made. In Hyderabad [city] only incident was that ... a crowd of students had to be dispersed with tear gas. 12 arrests were also made here, 10 persons attempting to induce shopkeepers to close shops. The Ramgopal Mill workers returned to work.
>
> 13 August. Only incident in Secunderabad was some stone-throwing in some of the principal streets. A number of persons were temporarily detained by Police and there was no further disturbance. In Hyderabad, the sole incident was that of one man publicly offering *satyagraha*.
>
> 14 August. All quiet.[40]

The agitation, begun without strategy or leadership, was thus flagging after a mere few days.

In the following weeks, the few extremist Congress leaders who were still at large attempted to whip up some support. But they had to contend with the moderates who, now without opposition, controlled the Maharashtra Parishad—the main organ of the State Congress—and the weak Karnataka Parishad, 'the least organised during these days' (Tirtha 1967, p. 136).

The Andhra Mahasabha, under Communist control since the secession of Ravi Narayan Reddy from Congress, was uncooperative. No Congress leader had attempted to rally support for the agitation even from among those Mahasabhaites who might not have totally gone over to the Communists. Instead, moderates such as B. Ramakrishna

Rao and M. Narsing Rao were considering obtaining the support of some of the Ittihad Muslims who had declared themselves opposed to the agitation but who could perhaps be swayed because of their overall anti-British sentiments. Discreet discussion had begun, and soon rumours were rife that a joint Hindu–Muslim 'Quit India' campaign would resume on 9 September. Because of the alliance, the new slogans of the agitation would be 'Quit Hyderabad', 'Independence for Hyderabad', 'Hindu–Muslim Unity' and 'Shah Osman Zindabad'.[41] Moderate Congress opinion was divided, however, as some argued that agitation with such slogans would serve no other cause than that of Hyderabad's independence. The alliance between Congress and the Ittihad did not come through finally; but, by the time the agitation did resume, some of these slogans had already made inroads among—and were in fact used by—the less informed.

Congress extremists had made efforts to revive the movement by distributing leaflets and encouraging students to demonstrate on a large scale on 9 September.[42] However, it was reported, these efforts were 'practically abortive' on the day and led to the arrest of 'only 2 persons in Hyderabad city and 7 in the districts who had openly courted arrest'. The public, for its part, 'displayed little sympathy or excitement'.[43]

In the following months, agitation continued on a small scale, and sometimes humorously as when a donkey dressed up with hat and shoes and bearing labels 'Churchill', 'Resident' and 'Amery' was seized by the police in Hyderabad city. On the whole, however, agitation was poor and largely confined to the Marathi-speaking regions of the State. There is also an indication of participation by the Arya Samaj, but the number of arrests remained very low.

Thus, once again, Congress had failed to arouse widespread agitation in Hyderabad State. A mere 300 to 400 persons were arrested throughout the State in connection with the 'Quit India' movement,[44] and this mainly in Marathwara, while the agitation had been strongly opposed in many political quarters of the State.

After the failure of negotiations regarding joint anti-British action with moderate Congressmen, the Ittihad had been the first to ask its members to 'keep aloof from Congress agitation' and Hindus 'not to interfere with Muslim students and shopkeepers'. Bahadur Yar Jung had declared that

> Mr Gandhi's 'Quit India' resolution amounted to telling the British that they could only remain in India provided they transferred the political

administration of the country to the Congress .... the proposed mass-*satyagraha* was directed not only against the British but against the Muslims.[45]

Soon, other important local political bodies also took a stand towards the movement and, by the end of September 1942, it was clear that few, if any, fully supported the agitation. The Karnataka Parishad found that although it was in sympathy with the agitation, it was politically expedient to outwardly profess non-participation to prevent it being declared illegal; half-hearted support was expressed by the Arya Samaj which permitted individuals to participate provided they resigned their membership from the organisation. But many others stood frankly against participation as, for instance, the Depressed Classes Association which claimed that 'the HSC [did] not represent the aspiration of its communities', the Hindu Praja Mandal (Hindu Mahasabha) which followed the directives of its all-India parent organisation, and the Andhra Mahasabha, the Hyderabad Students' Union, and the Nizam's State Railway Employees' Union, which were under Communist control.[46]

The 'Quit India' agitation in Hyderabad, thus, survived mainly on the support of the extremist section of the Maharashtra Parishad and of that of some stragglers of the Karnataka Parishad and Andhra Mahasabha aided by individual Arya Samajists. By the beginning of 1943, the energies and interest behind the campaign had flagged, and its organisers had decided to wind up the movement. Overall, the State Congress lost rather than gained ground through their attempt to promote the 'Quit India' Movement. In fact, shortly after this, the headquarters of the organisation was transferred to Bombay.[47] Meanwhile the Communists, who had not been imprisoned, as had extremist Congress leaders, had taken the opportunity to strengthen their position in the Andhra Mahasabha and to thoroughly spread their influence in Telengana.

Under the growing influence of Ravi Narayan Reddy, the Andhra Mahasabha was now increasingly receiving guidance from the Comrades Association, the organisation representing the Communist Party of India (hereafter CPI) in Hyderabad. The CPI had consolidated its position in Hyderabad as in the rest of India after the Communist volte-face with regard to the War, when Germany attacked Russia in 1941. The Communists, considering that the War had changed from being an 'imperialist war' to a 'peoples' war', modified their political attitude and the CPI moved from opposition to support of the War effort (Coupland 1943, p. 35). Proscriptions on the CPI were lifted in British India, and Hyderabad followed suit. Since then, the standing of the CPI had vastly improved in British India and the Comrades Association of Hyderabad had become 'a definite link' in the all-India Communist network. The Association was in direct contact with the Bezwada branch of the CPI which supplied it with instructions and relevant literature.[48]

As the influence of the Comrades Association rose within the Andhra Mahasabha, that of Congress—represented by moderates, most Congress extremists being in jail—declined. By 1944, the routing of these Congress moderates was so complete that, in April, rather than attend the election of office bearers to the forthcoming eleventh session of the Andhra Mahasabha which they knew would be a Congress debacle, those who held office resigned. This gave the Communists 'a walk-over' and Ravi Narayan Reddy was elected President of the Andhra Mahasabha without opposition.[49]

Swami Ramanand Tirtha attempted to persuade Congressmen to attend the eleventh session which was to be held at Bhongir (Nalgonda district) in May 1944, but in vain. Congressmen being 'prominent by their absence', the Resident reported, they left 'the field clear for the Communist section to run the Conference on Communist lines'.[50] Numerous Communist party members of the Andhra region (in British India) had been invited (Regani 1972, p. 182) and, not unpredictably, the day turned into a Communist triumph. According to K. V. Narayana Rao, an eye-witness,

> Ravi Narayan Reddi [*sic*], the President, and his band of young workers took control of the Conference. The pictures of Russian Communist leaders were exhibited. Their success in organising the peasants was evident. The Conference was attended by about ten thousand people .... About one hundred Communists from Vijayawada attended the Conference. The Working Committee, constituted at the Conference, consisted mostly of Communists. It appeared to the public to be a Conference sponsored by the Communists among the Telengana Andhras to establish and stabilise their leadership and to spread their ideology (1973, p. 275).

Congressmen, who now realised that their boycott of the Andhra Mahasabha could quickly lead to complete loss of influence in all of Telengana, began to take steps to remedy the situation. Moderate leaders such as M. Ramchandra Rao, M. Narsing Rao and B. Ramakrishna Rao plunged into 'social and educational' work. They created an Andhra Literary Academy, set up *Gram Seva Sanghs* (Village Aid Societies), and upgraded some existing schools and libraries. Congress workers also toured rural areas extensively, spreading the word that 'the Communists [were] ... working on secret orders from Bezwada with no regard for the interests of the Andhras of Hyderabad' and appealing for unity against Communism but, it seems, with little effect.[51]

The Communists counter-attacked by reducing the enrolment fee to the Andhra Mahasabha from 4 annas to 1 anna. They encouraged the participation of the poor and the landless, and, by early 1945, claimed that the membership rose from twenty to 'about 90,000'. Simultaneously they began a campaign against landlordism in Nalgonda district. At this stage, the agitation was conducted mainly through the distribution of leaflets 'vehemently attacking' local landlords and accusing them of 'tyranny and oppression of *ryots*'.[52]

According to B. Pavier, the Communists attempted to institute the practice that 'members from landlord families should first organise against landlords in their own village before being allowed to engage in any other work' (1981, p. 110). Nalgonda was chosen because it was a district more affected than others by oppressive landlordism,[53] as also the closest to the Andhra CPI headquarters in Bezwada. The agitation, set in motion as a vote-gathering manoeuvre, was intense from the start. It can be held that an objective of the agitation was to intimidate landlords and to compel financial support for the Andhra Mahasabha but, the Resident said,

> many of the grievances are reported to be genuine or to be based on fact but the methods adopted have incited the ryots in some areas to such an extent that a breach of the peace was feared and the State Police have had to take preventive action.[54]

By then, it had become evident to Congressmen that alliance with the Communists in the Andhra Mahasabha—and more conclusively regaining the leadership—was impossible. Independent elections of office-bearers were organised and at the end of February 1945, a new organisation— the Nationalist Andhra Mahasabha—duly began functioning with M. Narsing Rao as President. In effect, with this formal separation, Congress was never to regain its grip over Telengana.

While the Communists were thus coming to prominence in the Andhra Mahasabha, little was heard of the Hyderabad State Congress.

The conduct of the party now rested exclusively with the Maharashtra Parishad but, there too, divisions between 'left' and 'right' factions were increasing. In November 1942, as the lacklustre 'Quit India' campaign in Hyderabad was winding up, the Resident reported that the rank-and-file of the Parishad had rejected its moderate leadership. He wrote:

> The [Maharashtra] Parishad has not been sufficiently forceful ... to satisfy the left wing and the younger members of the Congress who ... have now taken charge of the *satyagraha* campaign.[55]

But, with most of the leadership behind bars and without the support of the influential moderates, there was little substantial action which the young extremists could carry out. The 'Quit India' agitation ended by the beginning of 1943 and, with it, all HSC activity. The next attempt at reviving the party came in June 1943 when Maharashtra Parishad extremists resurrected the idea of uniting all active Congress elements in the State to agitate for responsible government.

A Conference was organised at Aurangabad announcing a resumption of the struggle for responsible government and urging Statewide participation. Although the Conference was officially a Maharashtra Parishad affair, 'little was done to disguise the fact that the meeting was in reality a State Congress meeting'. Proceedings led by extremists were 'extremely provocative and objectionable',[56] but produced little result. Representatives from all three linguistic regions attended, but as the pro-Congress Andhras were representatives of the (moderate) losing faction of the Andhra Mahasabha and the Karnatakas present had practically no following, the Conference was no conspicuous show of Congress strength and unity. One month later, formal discussions regarding an amalgamation of all three district organisations were begun in which the Maharashtra Parishad again took the lead and pledged to serve Congress interests but, as in 1940, the bid at unification was unsuccessful. It was now apparent that the dissension between extremist and moderate Congressmen was also one regarding allegiance to the Indian National Congress. Responsible government in Hyderabad was regarded as a desirable aim by both factions but the moderates, already opposed to the use of force in agitation and the disruption of law and order in general, were little interested in the notion of an integrated India. Whether 'federated' or 'united', the new India would retain considerable power at the Centre at the expense of the State's freedom of action, a freedom which the (well-to-do) moderates looked forward to enjoying once responsible government was established in Hyderabad. The left (extremist), by contrast, considered the introduction of responsible government as a preliminary to the merging of the State with India. They favoured doing away with the 'artificial borders' of Hyderabad and subscribed to the INC platform of a reorganisation of provinces along linguistic lines. This was expressed at the Maharashtra Unification Conference of June 1940, endorsed at the Andhra Provincial League meeting of November, and still constituted the basic left-wing approach in July 1943.

The State Congress, in such a situation, remained ineffective. For instance, an appeal to revive agitation one year, day for day, after the INC 'Quit India' Resolution (8 August 1943) 'failed to produce any real demonstrations anywhere in the State'.[57] In October, Gandhi's *Jayanti* (birthday) which was to be marked by mass processions in Hyderabad city, only attracted about 250 Hindus, most of them students and youths who had had been informed of it in advance, and led to only three arrests.[58]

The same month, Congress also failed in its attempt to exploit the problems of food shortage and high prices resulting from the War and local conditions. Crops had been poor in the State both in 1941–42 and 1942–43 (Qureshi 1947, p. 304) and the food situation, aggravated by the Japanese occupation of South-East Asia which had cut off the customary importation of Burmese rice, was the greatest preoccupation among the masses. The Congress, however, sought to exploit the food problem politically because the State authorities stringently enforced war-time measures to manage food supply.

At the beginning of the war, a 'Food Procurement Scheme' similar to that introduced in British India was promulgated in Hyderabad State and a special Committee was created to supervise price control and regulation of movement of essential commodities such as wheat, sugar, kerosene, paper, matches, and so on (*ibid.*, p. 303). It was hoped, at first, that fixed maximum prices of food grains reached through informal agreement between producers and traders would be accepted by all concerned but, instead, there was widespread hoarding and concealment of real crop figures. In addition, as prices in British India were fixed higher than in Hyderabad, large scale smuggling across the border became a serious problem.

Local prices rose so sharply as a consequence that Government cancelled the price control policy in the hope of bringing concealed stock on the open market, but in vain. Price controls were thus reintroduced (in 1943), this time bolstered by a 'Foodgrain Collective Levy Order'. A Supply Department was created to which a new government concern—the Hyderabad Commercial Corporation Ltd. —was appended to act as direct purchaser of grain. Food rationing was introduced in district areas[59] and special police flying squads and some army units were assigned to control smuggling. These measures were not immediately successful, however, due to the magnitude of the task and to the inexperience of the governmental bodies set up to tackle it and, at least until mid 1944, the food problem remained acute in Hyderabad State.

By and large, however, these measures were well received by local political parties and organisations. In October 1943, the Depressed Classes Association passed a resolution unanimously thanking the Nizam's Government for the proposed scheme. The same month, the Andhra Mahasabha also declared its support of Government and, in January 1944, some of its leaders, together with representatives of the Comrades Association, even attended an Ittihad 'Food Situation Meeting' at the end of which it was 'unanimously agreed that Government intentions and food policy were good and must be supported'.[60]

The Congress, however, tried to make capital out of the difficulties of the population in obtaining food and essentials. Most of these difficulties, the Congress argued, were caused by government policies which had precipitated exploitation and profiteering; such policies were not necessary and were introduced only because the Nizam's Government had aligned with the Government of India at an All-India Food Conference in Delhi.[61] The Congress, 'in defence of all those who suffered', began campaigning in district areas against the grain levies and food rationing with the help of recently released *satyagrahis* from the Maharashtra Parishad.[62]

The *modus operandi* was to approach small cultivators who were most affected by the scheme, the poorer classes who could no longer obtain essential commodities, and to organise village meetings. Parishad workers would express their views on price controls, food rationing and grain levies after which a petition of protest would be circulated among the audience.

The Nizam's Government reacted sharply to these activities. In January 1944, two workers of the Maharashtra Parishad were prosecuted for their involvement in 'directly instigating cultivators not to offer their grain to government' and in April, eight members of the

Parishad were confined to their villages for similar reasons. When the Maharashtra Parishad refused to discontinue its campaign, the Nizam's Government prohibited the annual meeting of the organisation from being held in May.[63]

By mid 1944, the Congress had thus gained some ground, albeit only in Marathwara which had always been its stronghold in the State. Part of this moderate success can be ascribed to the work on the food issue by grassroot workers but, no doubt, the release of all Congress satyagrahis and leaders—including Tirtha—by December 1943 also helped.

Indeed, since his release, Tirtha had actively involved himself at many levels. His first action was to make fresh demands to the State authorities for the cancellation of orders banning the HSC and to call, in Marathi and English leaflets, for the participation of 'all progressive and democratic elements in the State' in political work.[64] Unity and the propagation of Congress ideals seemed foremost in Tirtha's mind and, in March 1944, he attempted to form a nucleus of proselytising workers by launching a fortnightly Congress propaganda class. He had time only to instruct a first batch of forty volunteers when Government stepped in and closed the class (Tirtha 1967, p. 145).

Tirtha also attempted to re-install Congress in Telengana by calling for a reconciliation between Communists and 'nationalists' in the Andhra Mahasabha. But each faction stuck to its position and blamed the other for the split. The Communists were unhappy that the moderate section refused to cooperate with the left wing. One of the consequences of the continuing rift was that, of the first forty propaganda workers trained by Tirtha, 'the majority of trainees were Maharashtrians, the remainder Karnatakas, no Andhra followers [taking] part'.[65]

Undaunted, Tirtha sought again to bring about an amalgamation of the three linguistic district organisations, this time with the creation of the Joint Controlling Committee. Although the Committee was created, Tirtha did not obtain the confidence of the moderates dominating it, who were opposed to his left-wing influence in the HSC and the Maharashtra Parishad. In fact, since his attempts at conciliation with the Communists, Tirtha was regarded by the moderates with even more suspicion than before, particularly as it was now evident that he was personally well liked by the Andhra Mahasabha leadership. At the important Bhongir session of the Mahasabha in May 1944, the Communists had even expressed 'regret at the restrictions imposed on certain Maharashtra Parishad workers', criticised Government for the ban of the Parishad's annual conference, and requested the State to remove the ban on the HSC. Despite Tirtha's advocacy, the Joint Controlling Committee refused to consider any action against the ban of the Maharashtra Parishad conference and decided, instead, merely to appeal to the President of the Executive Council through a deputation (of moderates).[66]

Tirtha then explored other avenues which could possibly gather support for the HSC. He proposed, for instance, that a campaign in favour of the mother-tongue as the medium of instruction in schools be launched anew. But, his request for help from moderate leaders of the Maharashtra Parishad was met with a rebuff.

Thus rejected by the moderates of the Maharashtra Parishad, Tirtha turned to the Communists of the Andhra Mahasabha. In May 1945, he attended their twelfth annual conference at Khammam (Warangal District) at which Communists from Bezwada were prominent. He made a speech once again deploring the split within the Mahasabha, advocating responsible government in the State, and calling for a removal of the ban on State Congress. Responsible government was then adopted as the ultimate goal in a resolution of the conference, but the provision was made that for the time being a representative form of government comprising delegates of the three Hindu regional organisations and of the Ittihad would be preferred.[67]

The following month, Tirtha looked to British India and attempted to gain the support of the All-India States' People's Conference (AISPC). When P. Sitaramayya, Vice-President of the AISPC, passed through the State, Tirtha sought his advice on the question of the HSC. Sitaramayya is reported to have replied that Hyderabad lagged behind other princely States and that he was himself prepared to court imprisonment in the State 'if others like Kasinath Rao Vaidya cooperated with him'.[68] This was a pointed remark which revealed that the AISPC was well aware of the differences between moderates like K.R. Vaidya and Tirtha and his followers within the State Congress. An HSC petition was nevertheless sent to Nehru (President of the AISPC) and Sitaramayya, asking them to involve the AISPC more closely in existing agitations in Indian States. The same point was raised again at the AISPC session in Kashmir in August 1945 which both Tirtha and Vaidya attended, which merely drew a reply from Nehru that 'once the deadlock in British India was solved, everything would be possible for the people of Indian States'.[69]

Tirtha and Vaidya also attended AISPC meetings at Jaipur in October 1945 and at Udaipur in January 1946, where Tirtha was nominated a member of the AISPC's Standing Committee. On that occasion, Nehru made his first public statement on Hyderabad, describing it as 'the premier State in India ... not only in size but in the denial of all civil and democratic liberties'.[70]

By then, the political situation in British India had evolved considerably. The Wavell plan to solve the Indian political deadlock was announced in June 1945. The legality of the All-India Congress Working Committee and of the AICC was recognised, all Congress leaders were released, and a general conference of representatives from all important Indian parties and organisations was called at Simla to examine the new British proposal.

In Hyderabad, the Nizam's Goverment, following the pace of events in British India, announced in November 1945 that the ban on the HSC would be considered afresh. However, the following conditions were laid down:

1. The name of the association should be changed to one bearing no resemblance to that of the All-India National Congress, and should be approved by Government.
2. Its constitution should embody a provision that there shall be no affiliation with any political association outside the State.
3. No office-bearer of the association may be an office-bearer of any political association outside the State.
4. Every member of the association must affirm his personal allegiance and loyalty to the Ruler.
5. Membership of the association was restricted to persons domiciled in the State.
6. Such grievances and aspirations of the Ruler's subjects as the association may wish to express should be in a peaceful and constitutional manner (Tirtha 1967, p. 152).

For Congress leaders, it was now a question of obtaining consensus in the response to be given to Government. But, as ever, Congress remained divided, the moderates led by Vaidya inclined to accept Government conditions, the extremists under Tirtha expressing reservations particularly in regard to the implication of condition no. 6. According to Tirtha:

> The opinions among us were divided. Some of us were quite clear in our minds .... We were part and parcel of the AISPC ... a change in

> the name would not be difficult ... but the condition that we had to work in a constitutional manner was unacceptable. I argued that we would accept the word legitimate in the place of constitutional ... the object of the Government ... was evidently to rule out *satyagraha* as a method of achieving the goal [of Responsible Government] .... I could not reconcile myself to this right being given up (1967, p. 153).

Nehru, consulted in March 1946, sided with the Congress extremists and advised that the name of the Hyderabad State Congress should not be changed. A resolution adopted at a later meeting of the Standing Committee of the AISPC at Delhi—attended by representatives of Hyderabad's Maharashtra Parishad, (Nationalist) Andhra Mahasabha, and Karnataka Parishad—confirmed the new hard line of the AISPC. It issued an ultimatum to the Nizam's Government:

> In the event of the ban on the State Congress continuing and other civil liberties being denied, it will be the right of the State Congress to function in spite of the ban.[71]

As stated by Tirtha, 'all-India forces were now behind the freedom struggle in Hyderabad' (1967, p. 153). He himself had been named in the resolution as the future President of the forthcoming Hyderabad State Congress (Regani 1972, p. 197) and, presumably following elation at the meeting, the representatives of the State's linguistic organisations agreed both to the nomination and to the affiliation of their organisations to the general council of the AISPC.[72]

In July 1946, the Nizam's government, under this and, as will be seen presently, other pressures, agreed to lift the ban on the HSC without restrictions. The State Congress had finally obtained the official recognition it had been seeking since 1938. But, this was largely as a result of outside pressure on the Nizam's Government rather than that of purely local compulsions.

For all its newly acquired legality, the HSC had not rid itself of factionalism, however, and when Tirtha was, by a narrow margin, elected its President in August 1946, he had still not obtained the support of the moderates. It is thus at the head of a divided party that Tirtha began the final stages of confrontation with the Nizam's Government and the Ittihad-ul-Muslimeen.

With the death of Bahadur Yar Jung in May 1944, the Ittihad had lost its most dashing, but also most moderating, figure.

By-elections for the presidentship of the party were held in July 1944 and resulted in the victory of Abul Hasan Syed Ali, formerly

Bahadur Yar Jung's right-hand man. He defeated Fazle Husain, a young lawyer from Warangal. Husain had the support of the most extreme faction of the Ittihad led by Abdur Rahman Rais, the editor of the virulently communal newspaper, *Waqt*, (the mouthpiece of the Ittihad) and was said to be the man whom Bahadur Yar Jung wanted as his successor.[73] Abul Hasan Syed Ali, a 'moderate', was unpopular in most Ittihad circles. He was seen by many as 'a political careerist ready at any time to abandon his principles if offered some high government appointment such as membership of the Executive Council'.[74] Moreover, Bahadur Yar Jung, shortly before his death, had not recommended his name among those he proposed for the Ittihad's Working Committee the following year, although Abul Hasan Syed Ali had hitherto been his closest lieutenant. However, due perhaps to a fear of the unbridled extremism of the Rais group, Abul Hasan Syed Ali had been preferred to Fazle Husain, but it was very much a lacklustre president who succeeded Bahadur Yar Jung at the head of the Ittihad.

In the context of the period, this change of leadership created anxiety in the Muslim ranks. The Nizam's Government—itself influenced by the news that the end of the War was at hand and that sweeping changes were considered for British India—was again reconsidering the question of introducing constitutional reforms. This had been the main focus of political conflict between Hindus and Muslims in the State since 1938–39 and, in 1944, the extremists of the Ittihad were no more prepared for concessions than they had been earlier. They were, therefore, much concerned that a 'moderate' such as Abul Hasan Syed Ali had been elected to the most important position in the Ittihad. They wanted from him a clear commitment that Muslim supremacy in the State would be preserved at all costs. Instead, Abul Hasan Syed Ali affirmed, in one of his first official statements, a 'preparedness to renew discussions with Hindus' and an 'anxiety to bring about Hindu–Muslim unity'.[75] In the months that followed, Abul Hasan Syed Ali advocated the formulation of an entirely new reforms scheme and toned down his conciliatory approach to the Hindus. But opposition to his leadership continued within the Ittihad. In December 1944 however, Abul Hasan Syed Ali was confirmed as President of the party for 1945 by 106 votes to 31.[76] With the end of the War, the Muslims (as well as the Hindus) turned to speculation about the future. Abul Hasan Syed Ali, for his part, concentrated his efforts on demands and petitions to the Government of India in support of the Nizam's requests for restoration of the port of Masulipatam (Masulipatnam) to Hyderabad and for an 'honourable position' in future India (see Aitchison 1929, pp. 21 and 72).

A resolution recapitulating these demands was passed by the Advisory Committee of the Ittihad in September 1945. Perhaps because of his stand on these issues (as well as perhaps a lack of alternative candidates), Abul Hasan Syed Ali was, shortly after this, re-elected to the presidentship of the party.[77]

Hindu demands for constitutional reforms had, meanwhile, become more strident but, despite the pressures of the post-War Indian situation, the Nizam's Government still procrastinated. This was in part due to the reluctance of the President of the Executive Council, then the Nawab of Chhatari, who, well aware of the difficulties of implementing the reforms scheme, was 'not inclined to grasp nettles'.[78] It was also due to the Nizam himself who, as ever, looked upon any relinquishment of power with undisguised dislike. However, after a visit to Delhi in October 1945, Chhatari reported to the Nizam that the British regarded the introduction of constitutional reforms in Hyderabad as a pre-requisite to the removal of restrictions on his powers imposed in 1926 (see Chapter 2). The Nizam was taken aback, as he had expected the restrictions to be automatically lifted in appreciation of his war services. Now, advised to the contrary, he finally consented to issue a firman ordering the Executive Council to deal with the question of reforms urgently.

Work then began for the introduction of reforms in Hyderabad, but as the scheme under consideration was still the one originally recommended by the Aiyangar Committee, vigorous protestations from both Hindus and Muslims broke out at once. As reported in a secret British report:

> The objections of the Hindus were fundamental as they took exception to all the main features of the original scheme, e.g., to parity between the Muslims and other sections of the community, to functional representation, to the limitations of the powers and functions of the Assembly, to the lack of responsibility of the Cabinet to the Legislature, and to the franchise order which gave a vote to less than 1% of the population. In short, they stigmatised the Reforms as obsolete and incompatible with post-war political developments, and eventually, when their views had hardened, they demanded that the form of government should be 'nothing less than a responsible government under the aegis of HEH the Nizam and that his status should be that of

> a constitutional monarch with privileges and prerogatives similar to those of the king of England'.
>
> The Ittehad-ul-Muslimin [*sic*] were equally critical of the inadequacy of the Reforms, but declared themselves against 'responsible government' and its introduction in Hyderabad 'however much Englishmen or Hindus might desire it'.[79]

A stalemate was, thus, reached, which the British Resident attempted to solve in December 1945. He suggested to the Nawab of Chhatari that the demand for the replacement of functional representation by territorial representation might be met by increasing the number of seats in the urban constituencies, as this would enable more of the intending candidates (who lived mostly in towns) to stand for election. The Resident, at the same time, approached Abul Hasan Syed Ali, and emphasised to him 'the unwisdom from the Muslim point of view of demanding a completely new scheme of Reforms, as in the present political conditions of India they could never expect to obtain conditions more favourable to themselves than those in the present scheme'.[80]

Whether it is this argument alone which convinced Abul Hasan Syed Ali is not known, but shortly after his interview with the Resident, he is reported to have approached moderate Congress leaders K.R. Vaidya and Ramachari and, without taking the Executive of the Ittihad into his confidence, discussed a compromise over the Reforms (Khan 1980, p. 91). This was mainly in the form of amendments to include representation on territorial basis, extension of franchise and direct elections. He later outlined the substance of his negotiations with Congress in an address to the Ittihad, but Abdur Rahman Rais, in the *Waqt*, immediately rejected the proposed amendments, arguing that these would 'bring the Reforms very near to Responsible Government ... compromise Muslim supremacy in the State [and] whittle down the Royal prerogatives'.[81]

A campaign of vilification against Abul Hasan Syed Ali, now accused of having 'conspired' with Hindu leaders, began, following which the President of the Ittihad offered to resign. At the end of January 1946, a general meeting of the party took place at which Abul Hasan Syed Ali's resignation was accepted and an announcement made that new presidential elections would be held the next month. The 'agreement of moderates' had thus failed, and, it appears in hindsight, with Abul Hasan Syed Ali's departure, that the last chance of preserving Hyderabad's fabric through a negotiated compromise between the two major communities disappeared.

Factionalism within the Ittihad threatened the very existence of the organisation as Abul Hasan Syed Ali was now opposed to the extremist group. With the help of a certain Kasim Razvi, a lawyer and the President of the Latur district branch of the Ittihad, he formed an association known as *Majlis-e-Islah Nazm-o-Nasq*. This was ostensibly to bring about reforms in the State administration but, presumably, to create an independent following and draw political influence away from the Ittihad.[82]

By the time of the party's presidential elections in February 1946, however, Abul Hasan Syed Ali and Kasim Razvi had not quite gathered enough support to defeat Maulana Mazher Ali Kamil, a pious Muslim who had agreed to represent the extremist group to prevent the organisation from splitting apart. Kasim Razvi, Abul Hasan Syed Ali's nominee, lost; but, according to the Resident, the election of a new president did not solve the differences between the two rival groups. Indeed, the new President's term was to be a short one as he resigned barely a month later, following a tremendous (and utterly disgraceful) fracas in Hyderabad city.

Throughout February 1946, Abdur Rahman Rais and the extremist section of the Ittihad had strongly protested to the State Government that a hut which was used as a mosque at the Dichpalli leprosy colony (Nizamabad district) had been demolished—reportedly for sanitary reasons—by the colony's authorities. The Ittihad had asked for the immediate reconstruction of the 'mosque' and threatened to resort to direct action if the demand was not met. A 'Committee of Enquiry' had also been appointed and, on 13 March 1946, a public protest meeting was organised in Hyderabad city when highly emotional speeches were made. The assertion by one speaker that 'if the Dichpalli mosque could not be built, *Shah Manzil* [the official residence of the President of the Executive Council, then the Nawab of Chhatari] should not be allowed to stand' caught the imagination of the crowd.[83] About 5,000 persons began to move towards Shah Manzil, their numbers increasing on the way to 10,000 by the time the destination was reached. What followed is best described in the Resident's report:

> Mobs disregarded shouts of their nominal leaders that the dispute had been settled and many of them carried tins of kerosene and petrol ... [they] assaulted the President and Mr Grigson [Revenue and Police

> Member] and gave themselves over to acts of arson and wanton destruction. After setting fire to Shah Manzil, the mob proceeded to the residence of [Mr Grigson] which they also burnt. Chhatari received blows on the head and the body; Grigson a cut on the head and several blows; none of the rioters was injured as they melted away on appearance of the State forces .... All Chhatari and Grigson's personal possessions were burned except the clothes they stand in.[84]

As will be seen, the political consequences of this incident were many. For the present, it was evident that, although it was ostensibly a quarrel between the Ittihad and the State Government—as the demolition of the mosque had been approved by the Taluqdar (revenue official) of Nizamabad (a Muslim, however)—it was in reality a show of strength by the extremist faction of the Ittihad. It was staged for the edification of the moderates within the party, the State Government and the Hindus, at a time when the shape of future constitutional reforms was being decided. But, its immediate consequence was to create pandemonium within the Ittihad itself. Moderates angrily dissociated themselves from the incident. Qazi Hameeduddin (the President of the important Aurangabad district Ittihad branch), for instance, blamed Abdur Rahman Rais for inciting violence and suggested that the Ittihad distance itself from the incident while holding him responsible for it. Others, like Kasim Razvi, informed the Ittihad's secretary that they intended to table a no-confidence motion against its President and the Working Committee for 'mishandling the Dichpalli mosque agitation'. Kamil, thereupon, resigned and the two factions of the Ittihad prepared once again for a contest at the presidential elections.[85]

Altogether, the burning of Shah Manzil and Grigson's house indicated a fundamental change within the Ittihad. For the first time, violence and outrage had been used by the party in defiance of all authority. The fact that it was not immediately followed by the severest sanctions appeared to condone it as a viable means of political action. It was a precedent which gave the most vociferous section of the Ittihad a lever with which to intimidate the party's leadership and bring it to adopt extremist tactics. It would also affect the entire membership of the party whose expectations of a leader would necessarily be changed. It shattered any notions of the Ittihad's willingness to compromise on constitutional reforms. The feeling of bravado which might have followed the burning of Shah Manzil was, however, soon to give way to anxiety once again as the introduction of reforms seemed increasingly and unavoidably certain in the rapid changes which occurred within and outside the State over the next few months.

The Nawab of Chhatari, who saw the Shah Manzil incident as confirmation that he should personally have as little to do with reforms as possible, convinced the Nizam that the responsibility of finding a formula acceptable to both Congress Hindus and Ittihad Muslims be passed on to an ad hoc Member for Reforms Work. The State's Political Secretary, Nawab Moin Nawaz Jung, was chosen for the job.

As Moin Nawaz Jung was reputed to be in favour with the Ittihad, Chhatari hoped that its opposition to reforms would be somewhat lessened. Thus, it is probably with some relief that he left Hyderabad, in April 1946, at the head of the State's delegation (which included Ali Yavar Jung of the Finance Department) to the Cabinet Mission which had by then arrived in Delhi from England.

Hyderabad's proposals to the Cabinet Mission are outlined in the following chapter but it is important to note that, in the scheme proposed by the Cabinet Mission, British paramountcy would neither be retained by the Crown nor transferred to the new government of independent India and that the princely States were expected—and had agreed—to cooperate in the building up of a new constitutional structure. Hyderabad had not followed the lead of other States in that regard,[86] but, in the changed Indian context, it was obviously not possible to delay the introduction of constitutional reforms in the State very much further. Chhatari, on his return, was thus instructed to make the formal announcement of reforms, outstanding points having been settled in the meantime by Moin Nawaz Jung. The Nawab, however, who knew that his term in Hyderabad was coming to an end (in September 1946) refused to do so. The British Resident argued with him of 'the obvious unfairness of landing his successor with the task of making the Reforms announcement when he had nothing to do with the preparation of the scheme'[87] but in vain. The Nawab of Chhatari, still reluctant to be at the centre of a possible storm in Hyderabad, left the State early in July 1946 without discharging the order, and never returned. In the meantime, Sir Mirza Ismail, former Dewan of Mysore (1926–41) and Jaipur (1942–46) who had been selected to replace Chhatari, had informed the Nizam that he would not come to Hyderabad until the announcement about the reforms had been made. The task was, therefore, left to Nawab Mehdi Yar Jung, formerly of the Finance and Education Department and now head of the 'caretaker Government' set up to cover the brief interim period, and reforms were accordingly announced through an official communication on 27 July 1946. The Ittihad had thus been unable to prevent the introduction of constitutional reforms in Hyderabad, although it had opposed this since 1939. It had also hastened the departure of the mild Nawab of Chhatari only to see him replaced by Sir Mirza Ismail, a politician whom the Nizam himself saw as 'pro-Hindu and even pro-Congress and ... inimical to Muslim interests'.[88]

By 1946, the Muslims of Hyderabad had, therefore, many reasons to be anxious. At the local level, the introduction of reforms, however modified, represented a sizeable loss of effective Muslim control over the State, and the change at the head of the Nizam's Executive Council was, in all likelihood, not going to be to their best communal and political interests.

There was also the worry of the obvious Hindu political gain following the removal of the ban on the HSC at a time when the ascendancy of the Indian National Congress was reaching its zenith at the all-India level. Hyderabad Muslims now felt isolated as the Muslim challenge to Congress in British India had only led to a demand for Pakistan, itself irrelevant to Hyderabad territory.[89]

In the circumstances, the Ittihad's stance merely hardened. Kasim Razvi and Abdur Rahman Rais were locked in an electoral contest for the presidentship of the party but the extremism of their campaigning speeches had now become identical.

Not unexpectedly, communal rioting (which had abated perhaps on account of war conditions and the difficulties of food supply affecting both communities) dramatically increased. For now, in addition to purely religious antagonism, any manifestation of Congress sympathy was taken by Muslims as a Hindu challenge. In August 1946, for instance, a riot erupted near Warangal town when the Congress flag was hoisted over an ancient fort by Hindus shouting Congress slogans. Muslims attacked the demonstrators, killing one and injuring thirty. In October, at Kundalwadi (Nander district), a party of about ten Congress workers were confronted by a Muslim crowd and, after some reciprocal shouting of slogans, the Congressmen were attacked with swords and lathis; one Hindu died and another was injured.[90] But the motive could also be religious as in Kamalpur (Gulbarga district), where a Hindu *palki* (palanquin) procession passed a mosque, thereby 'provoking' Muslims. Stones were thrown and, in the scuffle which followed, firearms were deployed by both sides killing one (Muslim) and injuring twelve (seven Muslims and five Hindus). A few days later in the same district, the palki of another Hindu procession was burnt by Muslims, together with a few Hindu shops in the vicinity.[91] Conversely, in December, at Jogipet (Medak district) stones were thrown at a Muslim procession observing Muharrum while it was passing an Arya Samaj temple. Muslims retaliated by forcibly entering the temple, pulling down the Arya Samaj flag, and burning temple records and furniture. Two days later at Lallaguda (a suburb of Secunderabad), a Hindu was killed in the clash during a Muslim procession. Sometimes, rioting even occurred for no real reason, as in Umri, when a 'petty dispute between two Muslims and a Hindu over the purchase of a box of matches' led to a general melee and the use of firearms. One Hindu was killed, and nine Muslims and three Hindus were injured.[92]

It was in this atmosphere of political and communal tension that the Ittihad was preparing to elect its president. Competition between the Rais group and the supporters of Razvi had been fierce, although, the Resident reported that, 'the saner elements [in the Ittihad] ... [did] not approve of either candidate'.[93]

In the elections held on 27 December 1946, Kasim Razvi, however, defeated Abdur Rahman Rais and ascended to the presidentship of the party.[94] Razvi, a 44-year-old graduate from Aligarh and a lawyer by profession, was to remain at the head of the Ittihad until the integration of Hyderabad. He can arguably be considered to have been the political figure whose influence and unrealistic vision proved the most detrimental to the interests of the State in the crucial years of 1947–48. What is certain is that, with his becoming President of the Ittihad, began what Rasheeduddin Khan has termed the 'downfall of the organisation'.

> Gone were the days of the benign Bahadur Yar Jung's leadership, whose grace and culture had helped to partially conceal the 'fascistic' overtone of [the Ittihad's] doctrine of the Muslim minority's divine and historic right to rule in Hyderabad State (1971, p. 788).

Overall, the divisions within Hyderabad's population which appeared in the period 1939 to 1946 appear to have been more complex than those arising merely from communal disharmony. Naturally, the Hindu–Muslim division appears the most important as it was linked to the very tenet of traditional Muslim minority rule over the Hindu majority. But, in effect, the Hindu challenge helped Muslim cohesion. Because of it, the Ittihad was able with increasing success to convince most Muslims, including those of the poorest classes, that they were the 'ruling race' in Hyderabad and, thus, that they necessarily stood to lose should power pass to the Hindus. What the Ittihad apparently failed to grasp was that, by 1946, the dice had already been cast and that communal propaganda was no substitute for *realpolitik*.

But divisions occurred also within the communities themselves, and particularly among the Hindus who, by 1946 and in contrast to the Muslims, could well expect a brighter future. In their case, however, the crucial question was who among them would actually inherit power in a reformed Hyderabad. The landed and the well-to-do had long realised that sudden democratisation in the State could be inimical to their interests. It was important from their point of view, to retain the leadership of the 'popular' agitation exclusively within their socio-economic group. A Muslim writer even suggested, after the 1938–39 satyagraha, that agitation in Hyderabad State was, in part, a movement 'started by ... Hindu capitalists who sought to perpetuate the exploitation of the masses in the name of Congress', and that '[those] who professed to have the welfare of the masses at heart had no programme to benefit them' (Salam 1941, 136).

Meanwhile, some elements of those Hindu masses were ready for 'direct action', in the belief that the struggle for responsible government was a struggle to end all the frustrations of the current order. For the landless peasant or tenant, democracy would right the wrongs of landlordism; for the factory worker or labourer, it would do away with labour exploitation; for the student, opportunities would open for all; for the small trader, monopolies would disappear, and so on. What escaped them, in the euphoria of ideological dreams, was that the State economy was mainly controlled by a select Hindu group and that nothing short of its disappearance along with the Muslim regime would make political gains effective.

When this began to be understood, after the 1938–39 satyagraha, some, following Ravi Narayan Reddy's lead, deserted Congress and joined the Communist party and the fight against landlordism. Others like Tirtha attempted to fight within Congress and to reverse the political hold of those Hindu magnates. They denounced them to Gandhi and adhered faithfully to INC and AISPC directives in the hope, if one is to credit them strictly with their proclaimed self-effacement, that democracy would in time dawn equally over Hyderabad and the rest of India.

Gandhi understood the dilemma well. To side with the 'extremists' and help the Hyderabad State Congress towards 'direct action' could perhaps have hastened political results. But, in addition to being inopportune in the context of the all-India policies of the Indian National Congress, it would have alienated the support of the most influential Hyderabadi Hindus whose financial help the Congress movement could not afford to lose. On the other hand, to side with the 'moderates' would have made a mockery of the popular stand of the INC. In the event, Gandhi, with his usual genius, found a compromise which was neither of the alternatives. It certainly did not do away with the moderate leadership of the HSC and it simultaneously preserved the broader interest of the INC.

Had Gandhi's support for Tirtha and his followers been more forthcoming, it is almost certain that the record of the HSC between 1939 and 1946 would have compared more favourably with the success of the Communists.

NOTES

1. Swami Ramanand Tirtha (1903–1973). From a poor Gulbarga (Karnataka) family; became a *sadhu* (religious ascetic) as a young man. Student at Northcote High School (Sholapur) during World War I. Gandhian from the start. Left the government school for 'national' school after Indian National Congress non-cooperation resolution (Calcutta). Preached Hindu–Muslim unity during Khilafat agitation. Resumed studies in 1921 at Amalner National College in east Kandesh. Moved to Poona (1923–26) where he studied at Tilak Maharashtra Vidyapith. Obtained MA with thesis on the 'Evolution of Democracy'. Joined N.M. Joshi, 'the father of the Labour movement in India' in 1926 and worked with him as a trade-unionist. Was imprisoned at Sholapur for organising a strike. Became headmaster of the Hipparga National High School (Osmanabad district) in 1929. Moved to Mominabad (Bhir district) in 1935. Came in contact with W. Naik and K.R. Vaidya. Gained recognition for his dedication to political work at the Hyderabad State Educational Conference in 1937. Pledged himself to the 'liberation of Hyderabad State' in 1938. First dictator of Congress satyagraha (1938). Participated in individual satyagraha movement of 1940. Detained for 14 months (to December 1942). Participated in 'Quit India' movement 1942, and was again imprisoned. Was elected President of the Hyderabad State Congress in 1946; arrested in 1947. Liberated in 1948. Was inactive 1948–51. Member of Congress Working Committee 1951–54. President of Hyderabad State Congress Committee 1952–54. Chairman of the Reception Committee at the 58th Session of the Indian National Congress in 1956. Retired in 1962. Details drawn from Tirtha's *Memoirs of Hyderabad Freedom Struggle*; *Our Legislators* (Hyderabad, Dept. of Information, 1952); S.P. Sen, *Dictionary of National Biography*, and various files.
2. IOL, R/1/29/2018, FR 1/1/39, 2, and IOL, FR 2/2/39, 7.

3. IOL, FR 2/12/39, 2, and IOL, R/1/29/2116. FR 1/1/40, 1.
4. By then, the Government had already conceded Rs. 15.5 lakh on land revenue and implemented various relief measures. IOL, FR 2/11/39, 2.
5. IOL, FR 2/1/40, 2.

   Govindrao Nanal, an elderly and prominent lawyer of Parbhani (Aurangabad district). One of the founder-members of the Maharashtra Parishad.
6. IOL, R/1/29/2270, FR 2/10/41, 5.
7. IOL, FR 2/3/40, 5.

   Students were prime recruits in agitational politics, perhaps because their youth made them more prone to rash action as was exemplified by the *Vande Mataram* incident of Osmania University in 1938 (see Chapter 3). In 1940 they were involved again in a disturbance which, this time, was nothing short of outlandish. It occurred on 26 and 27 August 1940 and began with the refusal of seven students to pay the train fare back from Osmania University to Hyderabad city, although they later admitted to have had sufficient money. They were referred to the City Police by the railway authorities but gave false names and addresses and, as this was immediately discovered, they were arrested and searched. A crowd of students gathered, claiming that an 'insult to their uniform' had been committed, and attacked the police station where their friends were detained but were easily dispersed by the police. The next morning, a hundred students attacked the particular policemen involved in the arrests and when the Superintendent of the Railway Police and his deputy attempted to rescue them, they were also beaten up and had to retreat. Some students then boarded a train to a small wayside station (near the University) which they thoroughly vandalised, stopped a train and smashed its windows, removed a level-crossing gate and placed it together with a heavy iron bench across the track. Meanwhile 500 to 600 students proceeded to the house of the President of the Executive Council (Sir A. Hydari) and invaded its lower part. The Director-General of Police (Mr Hollins) and his deputy (Mr Anderson) who were present told them that Sir Akbar was sick and that they had to leave. At this, they were attacked, kicked and beaten up with sticks (Hollins had to have three stitches on the head). Hearing the fracas, Sir Akbar came out and, promising an inquiry, succeeded in making them leave; he also refused a forceful dispersal by the police and, instead, provided bus transport back to the University. The students, however, used the buses to drive around the city, shouting slogans and demonstrating. Surprisingly, the State authorities took a very lenient line and did not prosecute. (IOL, FR 2/8/40, 1).
8. IOL, FR 2/3/40, 5.
9. Gandhi had specified that one could offer satyagraha only after receiving his personal sanction. In November 1940, Gandhi launched individual satyagraha at the all-India level on the same basis of non-violence.
10. IOL, FR 1/9/40, 2. He was sent to Nizamabad jail where he spent, in fact, 14 months (Tirtha 1967, p. 119).
11. IOL, R/1/29/2077, Gandhi to Hydari, 10 October 1940; copy sent by Gidney to Herbert, 18 October 1940.
12. IOL, FR 1/10/40, 2; Tirtha explains (1967, p. 119), '[Gandhi's] idea was that these [four] were to continue *satyagraha* repeatedly even after their release'.
13. IOL, FR 1/11/40, 5 and 1/12/40, 2.
14. IOL, FR 1/6/40, 1.

15. 'When it is remembered [said the Resident] that all the wellknown contributions from the Nizam, whether to Universities in British India, to individuals or to the war, have for years consistently and invariably been charged to the State budget and that private gifts of more than about Rs 50 or Rs 100 have been exceedingly rare, the significance of this gesture, which was so far as I am aware entirely spontaneous, can be appreciated', IOL, FR 1/7/40, 3.
16. IOL, FR 1/5/40, 4.
17. IOL, FR 2/6/40, Supplementary.
18. IOL, FR 2/4/40, 4.
19. IOL, R/1/29/1922.
20. IOL, FR 1/6/40, 5. R.R. Sharma made a speech stating that it was 'Muslims [who had] hatred for Maharashtra because it was Maharashtra that destroyed the Moghul Empire'.
21. *ibid.* A similar claim was made at Bezwada in November 1940 by an 'Andhra Provincial League' which asked the British 'to restore the Andhra districts in Hyderabad to their rightful owners, i.e. the Andhras of the neighbouring Madras districts, after the war'. IOL, FR 2/11/40, 3.
22. IOL, FR 2/9/40, 6.
23. IOL, FR 1/7/40, 5.
24. IOL, FR 2/2/40, 3.
25. IOL, FR 1/3/40, 1.
26. IOL, FR 2/3/40, 3.
27. IOL, FR 1/4/40, 1 and IOL, FR 2/5/40, 2. The sums allocated were Rs 50,000 for reconstruction and Rs 20,000 for goods.
28. IOL, FR 2/10/40, 1.
29. IOL, FR 1/8/40, 1.
30. IOL, L/P & S/13/1201, Gidney to Fitze, 3 June 1941.
31. IOL, R/1/29/2270, FR 1/1/41, 1 and IOL, FR 2/1/41, 1.
32. IOL, FR 2/12/41, 5.
33. IOL, R/1/29/2426, FR 1/3/42, 4.
34. IOL, FR 1/4/42, 7.
35. The Constitutional Reforms Scheme had been appreciably modified in an attempt to meet some of the demands of the State Congress and the Ittihad-ul-Muslimeen:

    > Owners and tenants of lands and buildings in urban areas were given 20 new seats, the number of seats for *pattedars* and *kashtkars* [owner-cultivators and official tenants of agricultural land] was increased from 16 to 32 and the number of nominated members raised from 33 to 43. There would, therefore, now be 76 elected members as against 43 nominated members, 10 members of the Executive Council and 3 *Sarf-e-Khas* [Nizam's private estate] excluding the President who would also be President of the Assembly, in the Legislative Assembly .... The powers and functions of the Assembly were also enlarged by increasing the power of the Assembly to discuss and move resolutions on the Budget .... The franchise qualifications for *pattedars* and *kashtkars* had in addition been lowered from Rs 200/- land revenue to Rs 100/-, while all persons owning land and buildings or paying rental values of Rs 5/- per mensem were to be enfranchised .... The numbers of voters had, by this means, been increased from, 89,000 in the old scheme to 1,50,000 in the new. (From *Hyderabad Political Notebook* (Secret), IOL, Mss Eur F144/10.)

36. Production of rice in 1941–42 was down by 75 per cent and of wheat by 20 per cent, IOL, FR 2/1/42, 10. Another riot had occurred at Bidar on 29 May in which

34 shops had been set ablaze, one person died and ten were injured, IOL, FR 1/6/42, 7.

37. IOL, FR 1/7/42, ?3 and IOL, FR 2/7/42, 7
38. IOL, R/1/29/2439, Gidney to Polindia, New Delhi, 31 August 1942.
39. IOL, R/1/29/2439, Telegram, Gidney to Polindia, 13 August 1942.
40. IOL, R/1/29/2439, Summary of telegrams, Thompson to Christie, 15 August 1942.
41. IOL, R/1/29/24/39, Gidney to Polindia, 7 September 1942.
42. The leaflets often gave precise instructions on the ways in which civil disobedience could be carried out. 'Azad Bulletin No. 1, Mahatma Gandhi's Message to Free India', for instance, advises:

> Every man is to go to the fullest extent through 'Ahimsa' complete deadlock through strike and other possible means. (1) Acknowledge no authority save that of the people. (2) All Factories, Mills, Colleges, Markets, etc., must remain closed till freedom is won. (3) Do not cooperate with the Government. (4) Persuade the Police to disobey the orders. (5) Destroy the Telegraphic and Telephonic connections. (6) Disconnect the Train and Bus services. (7) Dislocate the Government Machinery. (8) Picket on Government Offices and request the workers not to attend the Offices. (9) Circulate by all means papers such as this in every part of the country against the Government. (10) Capture the College premises and take charge of the administration and close until India is free from the British. (11) Join the Meetings and rise in rebellion. Please circulate this among your friends after taking copies, (IOL, R/1/292439, Appendix, Gidney to Polindia, 31 August 1942).

43. IOL, R/1/29/2439, Gidney to Polindia, 14 September 1942.
44. Four hundred would be maximum as it is the figure claimed by Tirtha himself (p. 133). (IOL, R/1/29/2439, Gidney to Polindia, 26 October 1942.) The Resident reported: 'Agitation has been kept alive in the four Marathwada districts of ... Nander, Parbhani, Osmanabad and Aurangabad where the technique has been to persuade ... unemployed youths to offer occasional *satyagraha* .... there are no signs of this activity in any other part of the state'.
45. IOL, FR 1/8/42, 2.
46. IOL, FR 2/9/42, 2. For an indication of the Hindu Mahasabha reaction to Congress agitation in British India, see Coupland (1943, Part II, p. 267).
47. IOL, R/1/29/2578, FR 1/143, 2, and IOL, FR 2/1/43, 2.
48. IOL, R/1/29/2715, FR 1/2/44, 1, and IOL, FR 2/5/44, 15.
49. IOL, FR 1/4/44, 7.
50. IOL, FR 1/6/44, 3.
51. IOL, FR 1/8/44, 4, and IOL, FR 2/10/44, ?5.
52. IOL, L/P & S/13/1203, FR 1/145, 5, and IOL, FR 2/12/44, 5.
53. See P. Sundarayya (1972, p. 15); Nalgonda is said to have been the home of a particularly ruthless deshmukh who owned 40,000 acres and property in forty villages.
54. IOL, FR 1/1/45, 5.
55. IOL, FR 1/11/42, 2.
56. IOL, FR 2/6/43, 8.
57. IOL, FR 1/8/43, 2.
58. IOL, FR 1/10/43, 3.
59. Food rationing was introduced in Hyderabad city and Secunderabad in May 1944. IOL, FR 2/5/44, 1.
60. IOL, FR 1/11/43, 1 and IOL, FR 1/1/44, 2.

61. IOL, FR 2/10/43, 1. Hyderabad had attended the Fourth All-India Food Conference (October 1943), following which grain levies were introduced in the State. (See also Qureshi 1947, p. 314).
62. In 1943, 40 of the 45 convicted satyagrahis were released. Tirtha and four others remained in jail and were released in December 1943. IOL, FR 2/12/43, 2.
63. IOL, FR 1/1/44, 2, and IOL, FR 2/4/44, 1.
64. IOL, FR 2/1/44, 4.
65. IOL, FR 1/4/44, 3.
66. IOL, FR 1/6/44, 4 and IOL, FR 1/5/44, 4.
67. IOL, FR 1/5/45, 3.
68. IOL, FR 1/6/45, 5.
69. Vaidya attended presumably so as not to leave it to Tirtha alone to represent Hyderabad. The 'deadlock' Nehru referred to was between the Indian National Congress and the Muslim league over the question of Pakistan (Aggarwala 1965, pp. 238–42). See also IOL, FR 2/9/45, 3.
70. IOL, L/P & S/13/1203, FR 1/1/46, 3 and 4.
71. IOL, FR 2/3/46, 2 and IOL, FR 1/6/46, 5.
72. In September 1946, the three organisations finally merged into the Hyderabad State Congress. IOL, R/1/29/3127, Lothian to Griffin, 3 September 1946.
73. IOL, L/P & S/13/1209, W.W. Grigson's Report, October 1944, p. 47.
74. IOL, L/P & S/13/1203, Supplementary (Secret) to FR 1/7/44.
75. IOL, FR 2/7/44, 2.
76. IOL, FR 1/12/44, 5.
77. IOL, FR 2/9/45, 4.
78. *Hyderabad Political Notebook* (Secret), IOL, Mss. Eur F 144/10.
79. IOL, Mss. Eur. F 144/10.
80. *ibid.*
81. IOL, FR 2/12/45, 8. This agreement was also hotly rejected by the extremist faction of the Hyderabad State Congress.
82. IOL, FR 2/2/46, 5.
83. IOL, FR 2/3/46, 7.
84. *ibid.* Fourteen persons were later arrested but the case against them was finally withdrawn, IOL, R/1/29/3081, Herbert to Griffin, 8 February 1947.
85. IOL, FR 1/4/46, 6.
86. IOL, Mss. Eur F 144/10. In a communication to the Nawab of Bhopal, the President of the Chamber of Princes, the Nizam stated, 'Each State has got [*sic*] separate status .... Since Hyderabad is not a member of the Princes' Chamber, so its affairs will not be like those of other States', IOL, R/2 Temp. File No. 78/146, Telegram, HEH to Bhopal 23 May 1946.
87. IOL, Mss. Eur F 144/10.
88. IOL, R/1/29/3176, HEH to Herbert, 5 May 1947. Jinnah who visited Hyderabad in July 1946 had for his part disapproved of Sir Mirza's appointment and branded him as 'anti-Pakistan'. Sir Mirza, he said, would be 'a calamitous choice' (IOL, R/1/26/86, Correspondence May 1946, Appendix I). A colourful account of Jinnah's visit to Hyderabad is given by Sir Mirza Ismail in his *My Public Life* (1954) and confirmed by British sources (IOL, Mss Eur F 144/10). The humorous tone of the account must not detract from the consequences of Jinnah's visit which were not only to make the new President even less acceptable to State Muslims but

also to seriously affect subsequent relations between the Nizam's Government and the Muslim League. Sir Mirza wrote:

> When Jinnah came to know ... that I was being appointed, he rushed to Hyderabad to see the Nizam and made a determined effort to stop him from proceeding further .... Jinnah entered the room smoking a cigar, and seated himself in the chair in front of the Nizam with his legs outstretched. Immediately there was an explosion. His Exalted Highness exclaimed, 'Do you know who I am? Is this the way you behave towards the Nizam of Hyderabad?' The attack was so sudden and unexpected that the visitor was completely flabbergasted; he withdrew his legs, threw away the offending cigar and apologised. But the storm having burst, apology did not ease the situation. The Nizam swamped him with angry questions. 'What do you want? What do you want to tell me?' and so on and so forth. Jinnah sought to say something against the appointment, but before he could utter a few words, the Nizam cried—'I do not want any outside interference in my affairs. I can take care of the interest of my own people. I do not wish to discuss the matter with you' .... In between the explosions, Jinnah somehow managed to play his last card by uttering the warning that the Muslim League would never extend any support to Hyderabad, either in internal affairs or in the Constituent Assembly, if his advice was disregarded. That only made matters worse. 'What do I care? You were never helpful. I am not going to ask for your help.' Jinnah then said something about Constitutional Reforms. The Nizam cut him short: 'I am a fussy person, Mr Jinnah, I cannot go into details with you. If you wish to discuss the reforms, please go and see the minister in charge. Anything more? No? Then good-bye' (Ismail 1954, pp. 98–9).

Perhaps, the Nizam wanted to avoid interference by British Indian politicians, as following Jinnah's there could have been Congress intervention.

89. In the 1930s, the idea of an 'Usmanistan' (Hyderabad) had been floated. One would need to know more about the reality of the Nizam–Jinnah relations to understand why the idea of a 'triple alliance' between Pakistan, Bang-i-Islam (Bengal) and Usmanistan did not appear on the Muslim League platform. Perhaps, apart from the added geographical difficulties, neither the Nizam nor Jinnah was prepared to compromise on central control?
90. IOL, FR 1/8/46, 2 and IOL, FR 2/10/46, 2.
91. IOL, FR 2/9/46, 2.
92. IOL, FR 1/12/46, 1.
93. IOL, FR 1/11/46, 4.
94. IOL, R/1/29/3127, Summary of Reports, 31 December 1946.

6

1947: Independence or Accession?

Part 1
The First Negotiations with the Government of India: July–August 1947

The end of the War and the feverish anticipation of political changes in British India had little effect on the Hyderabad Government's stand towards internal political developments. A contemporary reflected:

> It is surprising that in 1945 few in Hyderabad realised what was coming to them. The Nizam was honoured by the King-Emperor for his service during the War; his nobles received their share in the shape of knighthoods and orders of the British Empire. The Nizam's Dominions were still a patch of yellow on the map of India. The sense of security was so deep that the government had drawn up plans for post-war development! (S. A. Khan 1959, p. 21.)

In fact, in the period leading to 1947, the Nizam's Government paid more attention to events in British India than to those occurring at home, in the belief, perhaps, that the latter were of little import in the planning of the State's future whereas the evolution of the all-India political situation would necessarily affect the status of Hyderabad in the forthcoming independent India. The Cabinet Mission visited India in 1946 and raised many questions regarding the princely States which remained unanswered (Coupland 1943, Part II, pp. 263–86; Aggarwala 1965, pp. 243–52). The Nizam, however, persisted in thinking that because of his status as 'Faithful Ally of the British Government', his treaties, and the substantial contribution he had made to the War effort, his State would eventually receive special consideration from the British before power was transferred to Indian hands.

At the end of the War, the Nizam had proposed that Hyderabad should not join any Union or Dominion which might be formed, but should remain independent, if possible in direct relationship with the British Government. His proposal hinged on the argument that

> the arrangement between His Majesty's Government and the Nizam's Government would not be a one-sided liability for the former, as friendly connections with so large a country in the heart of India willing to make any provision desired for British troops or air force, would be a valuable imperial asset.[1]

But the idea had failed to evoke favour with the British. Moreover, the Nizam's willingness to accept foreign military presence in his territories even after Indian independence probably alarmed the INC leadership and provided another reason to resist Hyderabad's bid for independence. It was later charged that the notion of an independent Hyderabad in direct relationship with the British Crown was first suggested to the Nizam by the British themselves, possibly by Sir Arthur Lothian, then the British Resident at Hyderabad. Sir Conrad Corfield, the Political Adviser to the Crown Representative, was reported to be its 'active sponsor' (Munshi 1957, p. 34).

While this is possible, as Sir Conrad and the Political Department were undoubtedly in sympathy with the princes, it is certain, however, that the idea was rejected by His Majesty's Government (Corfield 1970, p. 531, and 1975). Documents indicate that the Viceroy informed Sir Arthur Lothian in October 1945 that

> the policy suggested by the Nizam's Government in isolation from the rest of India and the maintenance of treaty relationship solely with the British Crown would be quite impracticable.[2]

By the time the Cabinet Mission arrived, the Nizam was still adamant, however, and stated that Hyderabad would continue to press for independent status within the Empire.

Sir Walter Monckton, Constitutional Adviser to Hyderabad State (and by all accounts a brilliant lawyer and negotiator), was called in from England to help plead the State's case with the Mission (see Birkenhead 1969; Munshi 1957; Campbell-Johnson 1951). His recommendations, after unofficial discussions with members of the Cabinet Mission, were far from encouraging, however, and were, in fact, for some form of federation with India.

On 20 April 1946, Sir Walter advised the Nizam's Government in the following terms:

> An Executive Centre was likely to be established, dealing with basic and all-India matters like Defence and Foreign Affairs. Bearing in mind, therefore, the impracticability of the Crown in the United Kingdom agreeing to maintain a direct separate connection with the State, and the perils of isolation, the wiser course would be for the State to agree to federate at the top, provided it was allowed to do so as a separate unit.[3]

Sir Walter also emphasised the necessity of obtaining an assurance from the British, in accordance with Treaty Rights,[4] that Hyderabad would be given access to the sea and that Berar would join Hyderabad and not any other unit in British India (failing which Berar should be used as quid pro quo in other cases). He also recommended, however, that the State's political situation be stabilised by administrative and constitutional reforms in order to preempt accusation of bias against the Hindus.

Sir Walter's recommendations were not all favourably received by the Nizam, in particular the suggestion regarding Berar[5] but, in the main, they formed the basis of the official memorandum submitted to the Cabinet Mission in May 1946.[6] The subject of Defence was taken up personally by the Nawab of Chhatari and Sir Walter Monckton in special interviews with the members of the Mission and later with the Viceroy—then Lord Wavell. An additional private memorandum was addressed to Lord Wavell stressing that, should the British army be removed from the State, the cantonments occupied by them should be handed back to Hyderabad and not to India as,

> whatever the State's arrangements with the proposed Union in regard to Defence, maintenance of internal order would not be a Union function ... the State would not entrust that obligation to the Union, nor allow the Union Army to be stationed in [Hyderabad].[7]

The Viceroy retained the memorandum to which, he said, 'a reply would be sent in due course', and ignored the spate of telegrams and letters he received from the Nizam in which the latter vented his feelings towards the coming of independence to India. The Nizam warned that handing power over to those who were unfit to hold it would mean producing chaos and turmoil, thereby jeopardising the peace and tranquility of India. So far as the State was concerned, the Nizam said, 'A British Resident [was] always necessary at Hyderabad'.[8]

The Viceroy replied that he appreciated the 'frankness with which His Exalted Highness had expressed his opinion' but referred him back to Sir Stafford Cripps' statement of 16 May 1946 in which it was made clear that negotiations were now to be made between the States and British India (see V.P. Menon 1957, pp. 482–86). It was thus becoming increasingly clear that the British would not commit themselves to securing preferential treatment for Hyderabad. Indeed, in the subsequent failure of the Cabinet Mission, Hyderabad was left to negotiate on its own, as were all the other princely States, with whatever new regime would emerge later.

Great resentment was expressed in local Muslim circles against the 'betrayal of Hyderabad' by the British. The Cabinet Mission proposals had envisaged the retention of the whole of India as a single 'Union', in some part of which Muslims would predominate and in others Hindus. The British felt, therefore, that the Nizam could at that stage still be persuaded to accept the scheme under some loose agreement and in spite of extreme local Muslim opinion which pressed for outright independence.[9]

But the possibility of Hyderabad joining an Indian Union became more and more remote in subsequent developments. Indeed, the arrival of Lord Mountbatten in India in March 1947, his lack of sympathy towards the princely States, and the announcement in June that the British had accepted the partitioning of the subcontinent into two Dominions after 15 August 1947, placed the Nizam in an extremely difficult position (Corfield 1975; Das 1982; Wakefield 1966). Hindus now clamoured for accession to India, while extreme Muslims insisted on an assumption of independence or for joining Pakistan.

When the Nizam finally announced, on 11 June 1947, that Hyderabad would join neither India nor Pakistan but would assume independence, it was, thus, partly an expression of old ambitions and partly a statement dictated by local circumstances. Accession to Pakistan would have been unrealistic in view of the State's geographical position, but accession to India would have in all probability provoked a violent Muslim reaction in Hyderabad—with possible repercussions in the whole of south India. The Nizam himself may have been threatened as he would have been considered a 'traitor' to the cause of 'Azad Hyderabad' (Independent Hyderabad).

It was clear, however, that Hyderabad's independence was more easily demanded than obtained, as the State was now in a position of inferiority on two counts. Its case was difficult to argue not only because of the inescapable geographical handicap but also because Sir Conrad Corfield's influence with the Government of India (under Mountbatten) had waned considerably while that of Congress had increased.

Despite its size and status, Hyderabad had no means to pressurise the Government of India. Sir Walter Monckton remained optimistic, nevertheless, that a plan could be evolved which would be acceptable both to Indian negotiators and to Hyderabad's Hindu and Muslim communities. Shirking the term 'accession', he proposed late in June 1947 that the State should agree to enter into a treaty with the Union of India by which in return for certain concessions, the Government of the latter would be allowed to conduct the State's foreign relations and defence against external aggression and to be responsible for its communications.[10]

While it was not yet exactly clear what concessions Hyderabad would demand, it was considered that this plan, which received the approval of the Nizam, had a reasonable chance of being accepted by both Muslims and Hindus, as it did not suggest accession of Hyderabad to India, but did imply close relations with the new Union.

It was with this initial brief that a first Hyderabad delegation was sent to Delhi, in July 1947, to begin negotiations with the Government of India and the States Department newly created under Sardar Patel in June 1947 (see V.P. Menon 1961, pp. 83–87 and 89).

The first round of negotiations between the Hyderabad delegation consisting of the Nawab of Chhatari (then President of the Hyderabad Executive Council), Sir W. Monckton, Nawab Ali Yavar Jung (Home Minister), Pingle Venkatrama Reddy and Abdur Rahim (members of the Executive Council)[11] and Lord Mountbatten, Sir Conrad Corfield and V.P. Menon (representing the States Department) began on 11 July 1947 and centred on three topics: the grant of Dominion Status to Hyderabad; the rendition of Berar to the Nizam; and the accession of the State to the Indian Union.[12] It soon became apparent, however, that the two delegations were at loggerheads on all the issues, and the Hyderabad negotiators returned home, at the end of July 1947, without any progress having been made.

On 8 August, the Nizam reopened the discussion with a letter to Mountbatten informing him that he was not contemplating joining either of the Dominions and that he was prepared to enter into a treaty with the Indian Union on Communications, Defence and External Affairs. This would only be with regard to standardisation of railways and interchange facilities, contribution of troops to the defence of India, and conduct of Hyderabad's external affairs 'in general conformity with the foreign policy of India'. In addition, he reserved the right to remain neutral in the event of a war between India and Pakistan, to appoint agents-general at his Government's discretion, and to be at liberty to reconsider the State's position should India secede from the British Commonwealth of Nations.

These terms were considered quite unacceptable in Delhi and it appeared certain, then, that a settlement with Hyderabad would not be reached prior to 15 August 1947, the deadline imposed by the States Department on all the rulers. The States Department had also made it known to them that

> the Instrument of Accession in the present form might not be available to them after 15 August and that they would then have to negotiate with the Government of India for terms which would probably be less favourable (V.P. Menon 1961, p. 115).

This argument had been compelling and had led to the unconditional accession of most States contiguous to India. By 15 August, out of the 565-odd Indian States, only Hyderabad, Kashmir, Junagadh, and two small states in Kathiawar (Manavadar and Mangral)—all Muslim majority States or States under Muslim rulers—remained yet to accede.

The Government of India in time settled the case of all the 'stragglers' (Kashmir excepted) with varying ease (see Handa 1968, pp. 329–38). With regard to Hyderabad, however, Lord Mountbatten informed the Nizam on 12 August that 'in view of its special position and peculiar problems ... the offer of accession would remain open ... for a further period of two months' (V.P. Menon 1961, p. 115).

On 17 August, the Nawab of Chhatari advised Mountbatten that the Hyderabad delegation was ready to resume negotiations.

Part 2
Local Reactions to the First Phase of Negotiations

The Nizam's firman of June 1947 in which he declared Hyderabad's intention to remain independent was variously received by the political organisations in the State.

The Hyderabad State Congress immediately counter-attacked on 16 June (at its first open session since official recognition) with the statement that 'the right to determine the relationship of the State with the Indian Union belonged to the people and not the Nizam'.[13]

Hyderabadis were urged 'to resist any attempt at the imposition of an autocratic regime isolated from the rest of India' (Tirtha 1967, p. 175). The HSC, it was declared, would only be satisfied with an immediate introduction of responsible government and accession to India.

At the end of the session, Tirtha, the elected president of the organisation since May 1947, asked for a 'plan of action' against the Nizam's firman to be devised forthwith. But, once again, the deep divisions within the party came to the fore. Referring to that period, S. Regani (1972, p. 199) writes that there was a rift in the State Congress between the groups led respectively by Swami Ramanand Tirtha and B. Ramakrishna Rao.

The first represented the extreme faction—the 'progressive element' comprising mainly high school and university students, teachers, petty bureaucrats; the second, the conservative elements of well-to-do businessmen and landowners, lawyers, bankers, professionals. Not unexpectedly, the two groups could not agree on the form of the opposition to the Nizam's Government. According to Regani:

> Two points of view emerged. One was to carry on a non-violent *satyagraha* by courting arrest, cutting of Sendi and toddy trees, ... no-tax campaign, defying of forest and excise laws, ... of rules ... regarding public meetings and by sabotaging communications .... The second view was to remain underground to fight the Nizam's Government .... The moderate sections ... opted for the non-violent *satyagraha* movement while the younger sections ... went underground to carry on a struggle on the lines of the 1942 movement conducted by Jayaprakash Narayan (p. 200).

In mid 1947, Jayaprakash Narayan was still popular as the hero of the 1942 underground resistance movement who had firmly condoned the use of violence to subvert British rule. His methods, favoured by the extremists in the State Congress, were not likely to receive the approval or the financial support of the moderates;[14] but Tirtha went ahead with a plan which would involve both satyagraha and an underground movement.

In brief, the agitation was to begin in Hyderabad city with the celebration of a 'Join Indian Union Day' on 7 August 1947. This would mark the launching of a satyagraha expected to spread Statewide under the direction of a Committee of Action composed of Tirtha's closest associates. The agitation would be directed from a central office in Bombay as well as 'zonal offices' in Bezwada and Gadag, and would thus be controlled from outside (Tirtha 1967, p. 177).

Tirtha did not admit that violence might be resorted to, as 'the State Congress could not officially call for a departure from its pattern of non-violent resistance',[15] but this did not convince the moderates.[16] Tirtha states that he consulted Nehru for the formulation of the final strategy and that, once it was settled, it was the AISPC which 'gave the signal to march' (1967, p. 172). It must be noted, however, that no finance was made available to him either by the INC, the AISPC (see Ghose 1973, p. 347) or the Congress moderates.

> The problem of finance stared us in the face in an awful way ... the few whom I had contacted in the State were not yet in a mood to pay .... I tried to tap some Congressmen who promised to do something but even this did not come in good time (Tirtha 1967, p. 179).

In the meantime, however, the Committee of Action had had close contact with Jayaprakash Narayan in Bombay and it is from the Socialist Party (the Congress Socialist Party until a few months before) that help was finally secured. Tirtha himself admits that

> the Central office of the Committee of Action was enabled to start functioning with financial help secured through Shri Jai Prakash Narain [*sic*] ... with whom the Committee of Action had long discussions about the conduct of the struggle .... Shri Jai Prakash gave them the necessary guidance and help whenever it was sought (1967, p. 179).

In contrast to the preparations for agitation made by the HSC, the Ittihad under Kasim Razvi's leadership staunchly affirmed its support of the Nizam's '*firman* of independence' and its opposition to any agreement with India. In a pattern which was to be often repeated later, the organisation took to the streets and staged demonstrations of strength and defiance, generally a parading of volunteers and noisy propaganda campaigns. Intelligence sources reported that:

> [Ittihad] banners and handbills are everywhere. "Long Live King Usman", "Free Hyderabad for Hyderabadis", "No pact with Indian union" etc. Lorry loads of volunteers, some from the bazaar and others from the college classroom, parade the thoroughfares of towns and make excursions through the rural area shouting their slogans and firing shots in the Arab manner.[17]

The Ittihad, in addition, worked to discredit the members of the Hyderabad delegation (particularly those who were non-mulkis)

Nizam Mir Osman Ali Khan Bahadur in 1937

Hyderabad: Principal Entrance Street and Charminar, 1891

Nawab Bahadur Yar Jung

Syed Kasim Razvi, 1948

Signing of the Hyderabad–India Standstill Agreement in Delhi, 1947

Nizam Mir Osman Ali Khan and Sardar Patel, after 'Police Action' in February 1949

J.N. Choudhury, K.M. Munshi and Swami R.N. Tirtha, 1948

Jawaharlal Nehru, the Nizam and Major-General Chaudhury in 1949

throughout the first phase of negotiations. As Chhatari, Monckton and Ali Yavar Jung were to discover on their return to Hyderabad in July 1947, a campaign of vilification had been conducted in the local Muslim press during their absence. They were alleged to have conspired against the State, to have held secret meetings with Pandit Jawaharlal Nehru, to have sold themselves to Sardar Patel (Yavar Jung 1949, p. 20). Only Rahim (sympathiser of the Ittihad) and Reddy, an elderly Hindu of no influence, were spared, and considered, in fact, 'to have saved the State' and prevented the issue of a letter conveying 'terms of surrender' (Yavar Jung 1949, p. 20).

Chhatari, Monckton and Ali Yavar Jung, thereupon, submitted their resignations and withdrew them only at Mountbatten's and the Nizam's insistence. But it was clear that the influence of the Ittihad was rapidly increasing.

This was not only due to the fact that the Ittihad continued to be seen as enjoying the Nizam's support but also because Muslims in ever-growing numbers came to consider that the Ittihad was the ultimate bulwark of independent Hyderabad. Only a minority of educated Muslims disapproved of Razvi and his extremism but were unwilling to say so publicly; for the rest, they enthusiastically responded to Razvi's calls for counter-preparations to Hindu agitation and for mass enlistment in the Razakars' corps. The Razakars had originally been organised by Bahadur Yar Jung on the model of the Khaksar movement in British India, but by July 1947, they had been reorganised on military lines by Kasim Razvi who had assumed the title of their 'Field Marshal' (Yavar Jung 1949, p. 28).

Interestingly, the Razakars also attracted a number of Untouchables of the Depressed Classes Association. B.S. Venkat Rao, a local businessman (later a member of the Hyderabad Legislative Assembly), had welcomed the Nizam's firman of independence and appealed to the members, at a Depressed Classes Conference at Aurangabad in June 1947, 'to join hands with the Muslims ... for maintaining their political power .... The Depressed Classes were prepared to make any kind of sacrifice with them for the achievement of their goal' (Venkataswamy 1955, p. 386).

Shyamsunder Subbiah, the president of the Conference, also declared on that day that

> the time had now come when the [the Depressed Classes] should declare an open revolt against caste Hindus and join hands with Muslims

> for the betterment of their condition. The Muslims are the only nation who [*sic*] can deliver their goods because they profess a religion which teaches them equality, liberty and fraternity among human beings (*ibid.*, p. 387).

Venkat Rao and Shyamsunder Subbiah were widely decried in Congress circles both inside and outside Hyderabad as uninfluential and unfit to speak in the name of the Depressed Classes, and it does appear that the Untouchable community was split by opposing allegiances. But the ranks of the Razakars were swelling in any case, and by mid 1947 they represented a new political force in the State. Their reputation soon spread India-wide, although, as will be seen presently, their strength, armament and numbers were at the time vastly overrated.

The Communist Party, which had been spearheading an anti-landlord agitation in Telengana since 1944, also reacted to the Nizam's firman and entered the fray. By that time, the Communists had so successfully infiltrated the Andhra Mahasabha (up to 1940 the oldest organisation of Congress-minded Hindus) that they had gained the leadership of the organisation.

Communist activity in Telengana has its chroniclers and historians, and it is not the aim here to retrace the work already done or to debate the ideologies underlying the party's struggle from 1944 to 1948. The object, rather, is to draw out those aspects of the Communist agitation which influenced the evolution of the political situation in Hyderabad State and to determine whether the Telengana struggle was an indigenous agitation against the Nizam's regime or a movement which owed its inspiration and its means to outside influence, that of the Andhra Communists in the Madras Presidency in particular.

In this regard, P. Sundarayya (1972, p. 55) a frontline participant himself, states:

> It was to the credit of our Party, to our Andhra unit, that it guided the Telengana anti-feudal and anti-Nizam struggle from 1940 ... and converted the Andhra Mahasabha into a united mass organisation .... It provided shelter and help to the cadre and people under the Nizam's attacks, in the coastal areas. It made the coastal districts the rear of this Telengana people's movement.[18]

After Ravi Narayan Reddy's election to the presidentship of the Andhra Mahasabha, campaigns against the subjection of lower castes and against the power of landlords in rural Telengana began. According to Sundarayya:

> From the beginning of 1944, the Andhra Mahasabha under the leadership of the Communist party conducted many militant struggles against *zamin*dars and *deshmukhs*, against the practice of *vetti* (*begar*-forced labour), against illegal exactions, and against evictions of cultivators from their lands (*ibid.*, p. 28).

These early 'militant struggles' consisted generally in encouraging low-caste cultivators and labourers (often of Lambadi tribal origin) not to perform free service, a traditional obligation of their castes. They were to resist the attempts of local landlords to appropriate their harvests, or even the marginal lands over which they had tenancy rights by usage, because of arrears of payment of loans or on any other pretext. Encouragement was also given to oppose the Government's food procurement schemes and grain levies, to demand permanent *patta*s, and/or reduced rents, and so on.

Landlords retaliated in most cases by attempting to overpower the recalcitrant peasants with the help of the local police patels or that of hired rowdies, or goondas as they are known. But, in the ensuing clashes between the goondas and the mobs of peasants of both sexes—the men armed with slings and lathis, the women with chilli powder, stones and boiling water—numerical superiority determined the outcome, and the peasants, even if only temporarily, were often victorious.

The Andhra Mahasabha at that stage contributed lathi-wielding 'peasant defence squads' and acclaimed these successes as part of the revolutionary struggle against landlordism. The idea of 'Vishalandhra' (Greater Andhra), a union of all Andhras in a Telugu-speaking province, was now introduced (*ibid.*, pp. 39–50).

By 1946, the agitation had spread to all areas of eastern Telengana (Nalgonda, Warangal and Khammam districts), and the State Government had resorted to sending the army and police—sometimes aided by local Razakars—to quell it. Repression escalated as a result, and the hunting of Communist leaders, the burning of rebellious villages, lootings, severe beatings and imprisonments became common; but, the use of firearms was still not common on both sides because it was not encouraged by the Communist leadership and thus called for no retort by the troops and police.

Towards the end of 1946, however, the high command of the Indian Communist Party, in the face of the severe repression of their party cadres in Telengana and the Madras province (then under the Prakasam ministry), authorised the formation of 'self-defence' squads trained in the use of firearms. Sundarayya writes:

> In those struggles of 1945–1946 ... the peasant squads were not trained to take up firearms .... Large numbers of country guns—muzzle-loaders—were available .... But the Party instructed the volunteer squads not to take recourse to them as it would transform the struggle into an entirely new stage and would have all-India repercussions. It was only under the incessant armed police attacks, ... that the Party, with the sanction of the Politbureau, allowed our cadre to arm themselves ... and to go in for armed self-defence. It was only then [that] some elementary field craft, use of explosives for mining and bomb-making, and tactics to attack enemy targets, etc. were taught to a limited cadre (*ibid.*, p. 40).

The Nizam's Government reacted sharply to this development. The Communist Party was banned in December 1946 and its leaders were relentlessly hunted out by the police and army.[19] But, by early 1947, the Communist Party had firmly established itself in the Telengana region. As some leaders were arrested, others took their place and the Communist upsurge in Hyderabad began to assume all the trappings of a successful mass movement. This was not fully appreciated at the time even by the CPI's leadership, as 'backward Telengana' seemed hardly likely to be the cradle from which an all-India 'People's Democratic Revolution' could spring. 'Our party had not understood the depth of the Revolutionary upsurge of the masses', Sundarayya admitted (1972, p. 52) and, in 1946, little capital was made of the Telengana struggle at the all-India level. It is important to realise at this stage that Indian communists favoured the formation of linguistic provinces in India, and, as Sundarayya shows, the Communist Party in Andhra was the first to advocate the notion of the united Telugu-speaking province, Vishalandhra (*ibid.*, p. 53).

The broad aim of Communists in Telengana was, thus, to bring about a dissolution of Hyderabad State and a merging of its territories with neighbouring linguistic provinces; but this was anticipated to be a slow process.

Thus, a broad similarity of purposes existed between the Communist Party and the Hyderabad State Congress inasmuch as they were both staunchly opposed to Hyderabad's independence.

Although the Indian National Congress nurtured no friendly feelings towards the Communist Party in the rest of India,[20] an ad hoc alliance—the 'United Front'—was struck in the State between the two parties.

In June 1947, the HSC had passed a resolution opposing Hyderabad's independence and announced that the State Congress would not accept anything short of accession to the Indian Union and the establishment of responsible government. In September, the *People's Age* (Bezwada) carried a declaration:

> The call [of the Hyderabad State Congress] has been supported in a statement issued by Narayan Reddy ... on behalf of the Communist Party of Hyderabad and the State Andhra Mahasabha (Communist) .... The flag of the Indian Union is also the flag of the Hyderabad people .... The Communist Party of Hyderabad and the State Andhra Mahasabha (Communist) are also taking part in the struggle for joining the Indian Union .... The Communist Party ... pledges all-out efforts to make this struggle a success.[21]

Congress-oriented historians and contemporary writers have since charged that the so-called Hyderabad State Congress–Communist Party 'United Front' was merely a ploy of the Communists 'to ride the wave of Congress popularity' on the eve of Independence, gather support for their own party (tarnished by its pro-British policy during the War) and eventually to gain control over the Hyderabad State Congress (Regani 1972, pp. 86–87 and 90–91).

Tirtha, for his part, even denies that the 'United Front' ever existed and affirms:

> The Committee of Action ... conducted the movement entirely on its own and never sought alliance with the Communists or any other section (1967, p. 196).

An Intelligence Report states, however, that:

> [When] the Congress launched its *satyagraha* ... the Communists aligned themselves with the 'progressive forces' which were pledged to end the days of 'feudal oppression'. Swami Ramanand Tirtha, the Congress leader, denies that common cause was made with communism but the Police Minister commenting on this, quotes Dr. Subbarayan, the Home Minister of Madras, as publicly declaring that there is no practical difference between the two.[22]

In fact, despite Tirtha's statement, it is hard not to think that, from his point of view, an alliance with the Communists, with their strong organisation in Telengana and their armed squads, could have appeared as anything but a welcome adjunct to the Congress plans of satyagraha and disruption of the administration. The alliance would have not only encouraged agitation in all areas at once, it would have also allowed Congress a re-entry in the eastern districts which had been practically closed to its influence since 1941.

It is against this background that the plan of action of the HSC was put into operation.

'Join Indian Union Day', 7 August 1947, sparked off the satyagraha. From the early hours of the morning, Congress supporters wearing 'Join Indian Union' badges and carrying Congress flags had gathered in the heart of Hyderabad city. Tirtha, after touring the Central Provinces, Maharashtra and Berar to garner support, duly re-entered the State on the day and led a procession to the Sultan Bazaar area where the flags were unfurled.

It seems however that, as in 1938 and 1942, Congress agitation had started on a damp fuse. The public did not join the demonstrators as had been anticipated and the police, although present, did not even proceed with arrests. Tirtha believes (1967, pp. 179–80) that the authorities did not expect the function to be held as early as it was held. However, except for a lathi charge, the police did not react in the evening either when the demonstration was repeated. A few volunteers were arrested and were let off some hours later.

Perhaps, as Tirtha suggests, 'the Government was still waiting for something more to happen' (*ibid.*, p. 181). Perhaps the Nizam had also decided that, till 15 August when he would assume 'independence', it was better politics to show some tolerance towards Congress activity in the State.

And, indeed, on 15 August 1947, the State authorities stopped being lenient. Repeated demonstrations of flag hoisting and processions were met with mass arrests and an active search for Congress leaders. Tirtha himself was arrested in the early hours of the morning, along with another prominent Congress worker—Dr G.S. Melkote (*ibid.*, p. 182). With this, the second phase of the strategy planned by HSC was put into operation.

Civil disobedience and defiance of State laws began. Toddy trees, a source of excise revenue for the government, were cut and burnt in large numbers (Campbell-Johnson 1951, p. 446).

> Students boycotted their schools and colleges, village *patels* resigned their jobs and refused to carry out the Nizam's orders, village records were burnt, and customs outposts were burnt or raided.[23]

Whole villages on the outer limits of the State were encouraged to claim that they had acceded to India. And according to one account, border camps at Bezwada, Sholapur, Manmad, Chanda and Adilabad were ready to provide arms to villagers to confront the Nizam's forces (Regani 1972, p. 201).

Meanwhile, the alliance between State Congress and the Communist Party seemed to be paying off handsomely, at least in the initial weeks. According to Sundarayya:

> Joint meetings and demonstrations were held with the national and red flags fluttering together. Whatever programme the Congress chalked out, we made it a huge mass affair .... If the Congress called for a demonstration or picketing by a limited number of *satyagrahis* we used to make it a huge mass demonstration or mass picketing.
>
> When the Congress gave the call for boycotting colleges and schools and courts, we again made it a mass affair ....
>
> The Congress gave the slogan of breaking the customs barriers between the Indian Union and Nizam's territory, resignation of *patels* and *patwaris*. Our Party and the Andhra Mahasabha converted it into destroying all the records of these posts.
>
> The Congress gave a call for cutting toddy-yielding sheaths of palm and date trees and called for boycott of toddy shops to deprive the Nizam's State of one of its main sources of revenue .... We converted it .. into large scale destruction of date and palmyra trees and also physically preventing toddy-tappers from making toddy ....[24]

The Nizam's Government acted promptly and despatched army and police units to the disturbed areas, Razakars of local Ittihad branches often taking part in the offensive. By then, the agitation was considered to be primarily led by Communists rather than Congressmen, and this was causing some serious concern in Delhi. It is at this chaotic point of time that negotiations were pursued with India.

Part 3
Negotiations to Standstill Agreement: August to November 1947

In hindsight, negotiations between the Government of India and Hyderabad State had little chance ever to arrive at a compromise which would be acceptable to both parties. Patel, on the one side, was insistent that nothing but the accession of Hyderabad would satisfy India while, on the other, the Nizam, despite all handicaps, was adamant that he would go no further than a 'treaty'.

The Nizam, moreover, had not empowered the Hyderabad delegation to finalise any agreement without his approval. As a result, Chhatari's and Monckton's best efforts were generally in vain. Consequently, the State's last chances of preserving its independence came to nought.

After August 1947, the situation became rapidly complicated by realities in Hyderabad and in India—internal agitation and disorder in the State, communal massacres in Punjab, and hostilities in Kashmir. There were, in addition, rumours in Delhi that the Nizam was making surreptitious moves to import arms and ammunition from abroad. Likewise, in Hyderabad, hearsay from the States Department corridors reported that an economic blockade of the State was in preparation.

The delegations continued to meet, nevertheless, with remarkable zeal on both sides; but debates often concerned points of detail or principle, the discussion of which did little to hasten a possible settlement. Suggestions to clear the impasse were occasionally proposed by one party or the other—the 'Instrument of Accession' should be renamed 'Articles of Association' or 'Heads of Agreement' (Monckton); a referendum should be held in Hyderabad (Patel)—but to no avail.

Three months after Independence, negotiations had failed to produce any result. V. P. Menon (1961, p. 311) says, 'It was clear that we had reached a stalemate in our negotiations .... There was no advance in the respective positions of the Government of India and the Nizam.'

However, by October 1947, the anxiety of a possible war with Pakistan on the issue of Junagadh (see Hodson 1969, pp. 426–440) and the disquietening news of developments in Kashmir seems to have frayed Menon's nerves.[25] For it was he, at that time, who suggested that India should come to 'an agreement' with Hyderabad, although accession, the usual prerequisite for any agreement with the princely States, had not been secured. Menon says:

> With this idea in my mind I went to see the Sardar. I expressed my personal belief that in view of the existing political and communal situation in the country, as well as the commitments of the Army, it was necessary to purchase peace in the South .... I suggested therefore that if we could get from Hyderabad the substance of accession by an

agreement, this would at least give us some breathing-time (V. P. Menon 1961, p. 311).

Menon's idea was that Hyderabad should propose a 'Standstill Agreement' conceding the substance of accession which, he told Sir Walter Monckton, he hoped he would be able to bring Nehru and Patel to accept. Thus, while the initiative towards a Standstill Agreement was India's, the onus of presenting an acceptable compromise was left to Hyderabad.

After much discussion and difficulty at home, the Hyderabad delegation eventually (on 16 October 1947) presented a draft Standstill Agreement and a draft collateral letter from the Nizam, but both these were found unacceptable in Delhi. Indeed, Patel stated 'emphatically' that he would rather break off negotiations than accept the agreement as drafted by Hyderabad (V. P. Menon 1961, p. 312).

To avert another crisis, Mountbatten intervened and suggested that Menon himself should re-write both documents. When this was done, and after some changes introduced by Sir Walter Monckton, Menon's texts for the Standstill Agreement and the collateral letter were finally approved by Patel, Nehru and Mountbatten. All that remained to be done now was to obtain the Nizam's signature ...

The documents were taken back to Hyderabad on 22 October with the undertaking by the delegation that they would be returned to Delhi, duly signed by the Nizam, by 27 October. A strange incident in Hyderabad, however, was to upset all plans and seriously affect future negotiations between the State and India.

The documents brought back by the delegation were passed on to the Executive Council for deliberation. After three days of careful examination (23, 24 and 25 October), the Executive Council recommended by six votes to three that the Standstill Agreement should be accepted and signed by the Nizam.

Advised of this decision in the evening of 25 October, the Nizam postponed signing the documents that night. This was perhaps because he was still 'preparing two collateral letters' himself (Campbell-Johnson 1951, p. 232), but also most probably because he was waiting to hear from the Ittihad which had sent emissaries to Karachi to consult Jinnah.[26]

The following evening, the delegation called for the documents, as they were to depart for Delhi early the next morning. Again the Nizam postponed signing, this time 'without explanation' (Campbell-Johnson 1951, p. 232). But it was still expected that the delegation would leave for Delhi as planned. This, however, was not to be. That same evening, the Ittihad emissaries returned from Karachi, presumably with advice from Jinnah[27] that the Agreement was not to be forwarded to Delhi in its present form. The simplest way to achieve this was to prevent the delegation from leaving Hyderabad and the Ittihad applied itself to the task immediately. At daybreak the next day, the delegation, as Ali Yavar Jung put it, 'found that it was the victim of a *coup d'etat*' (Yavar Jung 1949, p. 25).

Campbell-Johnson, Mountbatten's attache recorded in his diary:

> At three o'clock in the morning, a crowd estimated at about twenty-thousand swarmed around the three adjacent houses occupied by Chhatari, Monckton, and Sir Sultan Ahmed. There were loudspeakers in the crowd telling them to remain orderly and to create no disturbance beyond preventing the delegation from leaving. No Hyderabad police were seen at the time and the Ittihad publicly took credit for this militant challenge (1951, p. 232).

Laik (1962, p. 73) also describes how

> tens of thousands of people ... covered every inch of the roads around the houses of the delegates. By daybreak, miles and miles of roads in the vicinity were simply covered with a seathing [*sic*] mass of humanity.

The delegates were eventually freed by the army (at about 5.00 a.m.) and the Nizam, for the first time ever (Yavar Jung 1949, p. 25), summoned his Executive Council to King Kothi, his residence, where angry scenes followed:

> Sir Walter Monckton rebuked the Commissioner of Police for his inaction only to get the reply that the Police, if ordered to intervene, would have refused to resist the Muslim crowds. If that was so, would the Army also have refused? If not, why was no preparation made? Did the Police not know at all? Was no report made to Moin Nawaz Jung, the Police Minister, or to the Police Commissioner himself, by the Intelligence Department? Was the Police in league? (Ali Yavar Jung, 1949, p. 25.)

At 8 a.m., the Nizam sent a message to Mountbatten that the delegates could not return to Delhi that day as planned, owing to 'unforeseen circumstances'. The Nizam blamed the Ittihad for the disturbances, and reiterated his concurrence with the Council's advice to sign the

Standstill Agreement, adding that he would force Kasim Razvi to accept the decision (Campbell-Johnson 1951, p. 232).

This, however, he apparently proved unable to do. According to Campbell-Johnson's account,

> The next morning, at a second interview with the delegation, the Nizam called Razvi in, but far from converting him it was Razvi who dominated the Nizam, spoke of the Agreement as meaning the death of Hyderabad, and pleaded for a chance to reopen negotiations in what he regarded as more favourable conditions arising from the Indian Government's preoccupations with troubles elsewhere (*ibid.*).

Razvi argued that, 'the Indian Union is fully occupied with the trouble in the North. If we insist ... they cannot do anything to us' and, in order to press Hyderabad's case more forcefully, he asked for the constitution of a new delegation.

As the Nizam seemed to waver and disregarded the delegation's opinion that Razvi's proposed course of action would be 'illusory and disastrous' (V. P. Menon 1961, p. 314), Monckton, Chhatari and Sultan Ahmed tendered their resignations which the Nizam, this time, accepted. In all appearances, the Ittihad had prevailed over the Nizam himself.

However, because the Nizam's behaviour in this instance was very uncharacteristic of his usual reaction whenever his authority was challenged, it is necessary to estimate whether, by this stage, the Ittihad had grown, as it has been suggested, into a 'Frankenstein' whose strength had now overpowered its patron. Or was there, in fact, collusion between the Ruler and the extreme Muslim party, with the former still very much in control?

There are no textual documents which could provide an accurate answer to this question. Although it has since been considered that the first premise is the correct one,[28] it must remain doubtful, considering the State's position and the political options open to the Nizam at the time. Besides, simply underestimating the Nizam's strength will not do, particularly in the light of testimonies such as Campbell-Johnson's, who visited Hyderabad much later (in May 1948)—when the Ittihad's sway over the State had grown even more—and Claude Scott's, then Director of Information, Hyderabad and a 'shrewd journalist', who stated that, 'there was no doubt ... that the Nizam was the master of the State and that Razvi would be quite unable to call Moslems into any conflict involving disloyalty to the Nizam' (Campbell-Johnson 1951, p. 334).

As for Campbell-Johnson, V.P. Menon recorded that '[Campbell-Johnson's] impressions were that the Nizam was the key man in the situation and that, with regard to the main issue of the relations with the Indian Union, nothing was being done without his approval' (1961, p. 341).

It is therefore possible that, contrary to Ali Yavar Jung's (and others) opinions, there was no real '*coup d'etat*' in Hyderabad when the delegation was forcefully prevented from leaving for Delhi. The Nizam, it was known, favoured independence. To him as well as to the Ittihad, the text of the Agreement—which established that the State would have no authority over External Affairs, Defence and Communications and that India in future would assume some of the prerogatives which had been those of the paramount power up to 15 August 1947—was utter anathema. Signing the Agreement was ratifying the subjection of Hyderabad to India and opening the door to accession and responsible government, an objective which the States Department had proclaimed and never abandoned. Once the Agreement was signed, who would come to Hyderabad's help? The British had been non-committal throughout and had now departed, and it was clear that no safeguard could be entertained from Mountbatten.

To heighten the Nizam's anxiety, there was also the sombre forecast made with a great deal of insight by Sir Walter Monckton who warned the Executive Council that the chances of India accepting a treaty on a basis other than accession were 'remote':

> The Council should ... assume that there will be a breakdown in negotiations .... Hyderabad must be prepared to meet ...
>
> (a) a violent propaganda campaign against the State inside India and in England and the U.S.;
>
> (b) a recrudescence of trouble from the State Congress who are likely to get financial help from the Congress Party (not of course from the Dominion Government as such);
>
> (c) a great deal of covert economic, financial and business pressure and obstacles.
>
> There is moreover the fear that at a later stage, if it becomes necessary to deal severely with hostile Hindu elements in the State, the Dominion government might find an excuse (however specious) to say they cannot stand by and see the Hindus oppressed and ill-treated in the State,

> which is wholly within their borders: they might then ultimately intervene by force. Or again if there were interruptions in railway, telegraphic or telephone communications in the State, the Dominion might make an opportunity to intervene on the ground that these are through communications vital to the security of the Dominion.[29]

Faced with such bleak prospects, the Nizam had turned to Karachi for advice. Although what passed between the emissaries of the Ittihad and Jinnah remained a well-kept secret, it can be supposed that Jinnah, waiting on the outcome of developments in Kashmir, welcomed the opportunity to render the life of Indian leaders a little more difficult. He may have advised Hyderabad 'not to give an inch' until at least the Kashmir issue had been settled.

The Nizam, then, probably agreed with Razvi that the Agreement was not to be signed for the time being. But how was this to be possible? Not only had a final text been drawn up—after long and tedious negotiations and much effort to convince New Delhi that the Nizam was genuinely prepared to accept a compromise—but the agreement had been approved officially by the Executive Council.

If the Standstill Agreement was somehow to be stalled, only Razvi could do it, and it is therefore possible that he was entrusted with the task by the Nizam. However, a method had to be found which would involve neither violence nor the State Government. Hence the '*coup d'etat*' in which the orderliness of the crowds of Muslims that morning was exemplary, no harm was done to the delegates (unlike during the Shah Manzil incident), police intelligence was 'lacking' and the army was 'unprepared'.

Naturally, the Nawab of Chhatari and Sir Walter Monckton, who had been involved personally in the drafting of the Standstill Agreement, could hardly be expected to renege on their commitments in Delhi. As such they had become liabilities to the State and had to be removed. This would explain the subsequent public encounter between the Nizam and Razvi and the former's backing down. It would also explain the Nizam's acquiescence in the calls for a new delegation which, as was probably expected, brought about resignations, the most important being that of the Nawab of Chhatari (Monckton himself would come back later). This not only freed the way for future negotiations, but also allowed the formation of a new Cabinet in which, as will be seen, the Ittihad found more than due representation.

Thus, after all, the Nizam might not have been the victim of any 'Frankenstein' and it is not at all clear that the Ittihad had 'proclaimed to the world that the will of the Nizam counted for nothing' (Yavar Jung 1949, p. 25).

However, if the Nizam connived to that extent with the Ittihad—even as a calculated risk dictated by a conviction that hardcore Muslims in the State and outside were the only true well-wishers of his regime—he gave his 'allies' enormous influence over the future conduct of State politics, and his foes a decisive weapon with which to bring his rule to an end.

A new Hyderabad delegation consisting of Moin Nawaz Jung, Abdur Rahim and Pingle Venkatrama Reddy, thus arrived in Delhi on 31 October 1947. They were thus described by V. P. Menon:

> The first two were among the three members of the Nizam's Executive Council who had voted against the acceptance of the Standstill Agreement. Abdur Rahim, a communalist fanatic of little or no ability, was a prominent member of the Ittihad. Nawab Moin Nawaz Jung, the leader of the delegation, was at that time Hyderabad's Minister for Police and Information .... and he fully subscribed to the doctrines of independence for the State .... Pingle Venkatrama Reddy was selected probably only because he was a respectable old Hindu; he had no political following nor had he any opinion of his own (1961, p. 314).

Not unexpectedly, Mountbatten and the States Department were disgruntled by this change. It was made clear at the outset of their discussions with the new delegation (2 November 1947) that there would be no question of re-examining the terms of the Standstill Agreement which had been formulated after much tiresome negotiation with the previous delegation, particularly as those terms had already been accepted by the State's Executive Council and the Nizam himself.

Moin Nawaz Jung pleaded, nevertheless, that discussions be re-opened on the basis of the original draft agreement proposed by Hyderabad but this was indignantly refused (*ibid.*, p. 315). It seems, however, since the Kashmir situation had not yet been resolved, that the Hyderabad delegation was merely using delaying tactics in the hope of gaining some advantage should the Kashmir situation worsen for India.

The Nizam also played his part, by asking in November 1947, for negotiations to be postponed until Mountbatten had returned from a visit to London (7–22 November; *ibid.*, p. 317). This was granted on the condition that a settlement be reached by the end of the month.

The final meeting between the Hyderabad delegation and the States Department and Mountbatten took place on 25 November 1947. On that day, perhaps because no advantage could be hoped for any longer with regard to Kashmir (where the military situation had become increasingly favourable to India), the Hyderabad delegation agreed to take the Standstill Agreement back to the Nizam practically without any modifications. On 29 November 1947, the Nizam signed it.[30]

Thus, the Nizam's gamble in backing the Ittihad had not paid off. He had waited in vain for dividends to accrue from their assurance that a better deal could be extracted from an India weakened by defeat in Kashmir. As Campbell-Johnson said, 'the Nizam has succeeded only in completely forfeiting whatever reserve of confidence the Government of India—and Patel in particular—had in him' (1951, p. 231).

He concluded, however, that, 'For all that, the Standstill Agreement allow[ed] a breathing space for a year for heads to cool and hearts to soften' (*ibid.*, p. 245).

But the future would soon show that these were mere pious wishes, as the atmosphere of mutual suspicion prevailing between India and Hyderabad as well as the internal situation in the State showed no signs of improvement.

NOTES

1. IOL, Mss. Eur. F 144/10 (1956), 'Visit of the Cabinet Mission to India', p. 1.
2. IOL, Mss. Eur. F 144/10. *op. cit.*
3. IOL, Mss. Eur. F 144/10, *op. cit.*, p. 5.
4. The British were bound to leave Hyderabad in an economically secure position should treaties be terminated.
5. '[The Nizam] stated categorically that he would *never* [*sic*] agree to any interchange of territory ... as he felt that Berar formed an integral part of Hyderabad. He even expressed his intention, if the matter could not be settled satisfactorily in this country, to go to England and to pursue the case there', IOL, Mss. Eur. F 144/10, *op. cit.*, p. 4.
6. Hyderabad's memorandum to the Cabinet Mission repeated that His Exalted Highness would prefer to maintain his relations with the British Crown and for India to remain within the British Commonwealth; that, should the British not be in a position to implement their treaty obligations, Hyderabad be left with the prospect of a reasonably secure future; that Berar, the Northern Circars and the

Ceded Districts could not be transferred to India and that Hyderabad should, without dispute, have the use of a free port. IOL, Mss. Eur. F 144/10, pp. 5–6.
7. IOL, Mss. Eur. F 144/10, p. 7.
8. *ibid.*, p. 5.
9. IOL, L/P & S/13/1203, Herbert to Griffin, 28 July 1947.
10. IOL, L/P & S/13/1203, *op. cit.*, p. 4.
The States Department under Sardar Patel was created in June 1947; see V. P. Menon (1961, pp. 83–87, 89).
11. Sir Sultan Ahmed, a jagirdar of the State, was added to the delegation in September 1947.
12. The brief account of negotiations which follows is mainly drawn from V. P. Menon (1961, Chapters 17, 18 and 19). For Corfield's part in the negotiations, see Philips and Wainwright, (1970); also M. Edwardes, (1963, pp. 186–90 and L. Mosley (1961, pp. 158–175).
13. *The Hyderabad Problem: The Next Step* (Hyderabad, Socialist Party Struggle Committee, 1948), p. 59 (hereafter *Hyderabad Problem*).
14. Jayaprakash Narayan was to change his stance the following year and revert from socialism to 'Gandhism', see S. Ghose (1973, pp. 414–16). But in January 1946, the Congress Socialist Party had opposed a resolution of the Congress Working Committee in which faith in non-violence was reaffirmed. See *ibid.*, pp. 414–15.
15. *Hyderabad Problem*, p. 61.
16. Yet Gandhi's own stand towards violence in Hyderabad seems to have been flexible (see Tirtha 1967, p. 191).
17. IOL, L/P & S/13/1204, Squire to Gordon-Walker, 25 March 1948. Secret Report, p. 145.
18. C. R. Rao (1972, p. 12) also wrote, 'Since the beginning of the Communist movement in Telengana, the Andhra Provincial Committee of the CPI kept in close contact with the Telengana party unit and helped it with all its might .... The two units acted almost as one and the Andhra area practically became the supply base of the Telengana struggle'.
19. 'In the earlier part of 1947 ... combined operations were conducted by the Military and Police, 25 villages were combed and more than 900 communists arrested', IOL, L/P & S/13/1204, *op. cit.*, p. 149.
20. In 1944, Gandhi had expelled all Communists from the Indian National Congress, and had not relented even at the prospect of independence. The Communist Party of India for its part denied (at Delhi, June 1947) that the 'Mountbatten Award' was real independence and stated that it was rather 'the culmination of a double-face imperial policy which sets in motion disruptive and reactionary forces to disrupt the popular upsurge'. In December, the CPI further characterised the Nehru government as 'a government of the Indian big bourgeoisie which had entered into an agreement with British imperialism and formed an alliance with the Indian princes and landlords'. See Sinha (1968, pp. 41–42).
21. Quoted in *Hyderabad Problem*, pp. 72–3.
22. IOL, L/P & S/13/1204, *op. cit.*, p. 149.
23. *Hyderabad Problem*, p. 60.
24. P. Sundarayya, (1972, pp. 56–57). Sundarayya adds that the Communist Party quickly understood that 'toddy tappers, a large percentage of the rural poor, were losing by this programme their occupation and livelihood ... the Party corrected

this error ... and gave a call "Tap the toddy, give it clean and cheap to the people. But do not pay taxes"' (p. 57). The alliance had begun to crack.

25. It is also possible, although V. P. Menon remains silent about it, that far from losing his nerve, he saw the capital which could be made out of the Communist agitation in Hyderabad State and suggested a standstill which would not only give India 'some breathing time' but would possibly allow the internal situation in Hyderabad to deteriorate further, with help from outside if necessary.
26. Ali Yavar Jung, (1949, p. 25) and V.P. Menon (1961, p. 314) claim respectively that three and two men were sent to Pakistan.
27. Jinnah denied it, see Campbell-Johnson, 1951, p. 233.
28. Ali Yavar Jung wrote for instance (1949, p. 26) that after October 1947 'Hyderabad had a Victor Emmanuel and a Mussolini'.
29. This recommendation by Sir W. Monckton was found in a document bearing page number 97 (XIII.97) rescued along with other papers from a pile of material destined to a bonfire at the Andhra Pradesh State Archives, Tarnaka. The pages following the document were missing but p. 105 (XIII.105) bears the date of 22 September 1947 and records the minutes of a 'Meeting of the Governor-General with the Hyderabad Delegation, Confidential Copy No. 11'. A report of this meeting is found almost verbatim in V.P. Menon 1961, pp. 308–09. Other documents retrieved were Minutes of the meetings on 10 October 1947 and 19 October 1947, of the final text (22 October 1947), and of the Nizam's collateral letter. These documents have now been donated to the University of Western Australia, Reid Library.
30. The Standstill Agreement was signed for a period of one year and read as follows:

29 November 1947

HYDERABAD STANDSTILL AGREEMENT

Agreement made this Twenty-ninth day of November Nineteen Hundred and Forty-seven between the dominion of India and the Nizam of Hyderabad and Berar.

WHEREAS it is the aim and policy of the Dominion of India and the Nizam of Hyderabad and Berar to work together in close association and amity for the mutual benefit of both, but a final agreement as to the form and nature of the relationship between them had not yet been reached;

AND WHEREAS it is to the advantage of both parties that existing agreements and administrative arrangements in matters of common concern should, pending such final agreements as aforesaid, be continued;

NOW, THEREFORE, it is agreed as follows:

Article 1

Until new agreements in this behalf are made, all agreements and administrative arrangements as to matters of common concern, including External Affairs, Defence, and Communications, which were existing between the Crown and the Nizam immediately before the 15 August 1947, shall, in so far as may be appropriate, continue as between the Dominion of India (or any part thereof) and the Nizam.

Nothing herein contained shall impose any obligation or confer any right on the Dominion

(i) to send troops to assist the Nizam in the maintenance of internal order;

(ii) to station troops in Hyderabad territory except in time of war and with the consent of the Nizam which will not be unreasonably withheld; any troops so stationed to be withdrawn from Hyderabad territory within 6 months of the termination of hostilities.

Article 2

The Government of India and the Nizam agree for the better execution of the purposes of this Agreement to appoint Agents in Hyderabad and Delhi respectively, and to give every facility to them for the discharge of their functions.

Article 3

(i) Nothing herein contained shall include or introduce paramountcy functions or create any paramountcy relationship.

(ii) Nothing herein contained and nothing done in pursuance hereof shall be deemed to create in favour of either party any right continuing after the date of termination of this Agreement, and nothing herein contained and nothing done in pursuance hereof shall be deemed to derogate from any right which, but for this Agreement, would have been exercisable by either party to it after the date of termination hereof.

Article 4

Any dispute arising out of this Agreement or out of agreements or arrangements hereby continued shall be referred to the arbitration of two arbitrators, one appointed by each of the parties, and an umpire appointed by those arbitrators.

Article 5

This agreement shall come into force at once and shall remain in force for a period of one year. In confirmation whereof the Governor-General of India and the Nizam of Hyderabad and Berar have appended their signatures.

MIR OSMAN ALI KHAN
Nizam of Hyderabad and Berar

MOUNTBATTEN OF BURMA
Governor-General of India

7

The Ultimate Phase: Police Action

Part 1
Developments after the Standstill Agreement

Following the resignation of the Nawab of Chhatari on 29 October 1947, Mehdi Yar Jung, an elderly minister, was appointed acting premier. Then, on 28 November, Mir Laik Ali, a business magnate of the State and a patron of the Ittihad, was made prime minister of an 'Interim Government' which was planned to last one year and to prepare the way for the introduction of 'wide ranging Constitutional Reforms'.

Ali Yavar Jung states that

> [Mir Laik Ali] had been recommended by the Ittihad as the one acceptable Mulki and, since Mr Gulam Mahomed,[1] Pakistan's Finance Minister (who was the first choice of the Ittihad) was unable to accept the offer, the Nizam agreed that Mir Laik Ali should be approached. He accepted it after a good deal of hesitation and not without first obtaining Mr Jinnah's permission which was firm for the limited period of a year[2] .... Neither politics nor administration was his *metier* and in both he took counsel from Moin Nawaz Jung who combined administrative ability with narrowness of political outlook and imagination. He exercised great influence over Mir Laik Ali; in fact it was said that the Prime Minister was keeping his seat warm for his brother-in-law to take over when the moment was propitious. That is why none of his senior colleagues in the Council ... was taken into the new Government which Mir Laik Ali announced in January [1948] (1949, p. 27).

In November 1947, the Nizam had invited the participation of the Hyderabad State Congress in the new government. The differences between the State and the party were to be settled, the *Dawn* reported (26 November 1947), by admitting the principles of responsible government 'provided it [was] accepted that Hyderabad will be for Hyderabadis', of parity between Hindus and Muslims in the Executive and the Legislature, of a new Constitution for the State (the Interim Government to indicate the composition and terms of reference of a Constitution Committee).

In the meantime, it was proposed that the Interim Government be composed of:

a) Muslims—Four (all representing the Ittihad-ul-Muslimeen)
b) Hindus—Four (the Hyderabad State Congress could nominate any three, the fourth one being a representative of the Scheduled Castes to be nominated from the present legislature)
c) The Nizam's nominees—Four (one of these will be a Hindu)

and that 'the first Prime Minister will be a Muslim in which case the vice-premier will be a Hindu and vice-versa' (*ibid.*).

Mir Laik Ali himself, upon taking up office, attempted to woo the HSC by announcing on 30 November that 'all political prisoners in the State would be released immediately, except those who [had] been convicted of grave offences' and that

> the release of political prisoners would be unconditional. There would be no insistence on the Congress formally withdrawing the satyagraha movement as a condition precedent to the release, and he [Laik Ali] would spare no effort to see that the principal political elements were represented [in the Interim Government] as the first step in the constitutional advance of the State (*Dawn* 2, December 1947).

Various offers and declarations of goodwill were thus made to encourage Congress participation in the Interim Government, but Swami Ramanand Tirtha, apprised of government proposals while still in jail, refused all overtures (Tirtha 1967, pp. 184–85). Well aware of the divisions within the HSC, Laik Ali and Moin Nawaz Jung continued nevertheless to cajole the party through its conservative group which, they thought, would be more amenable to offers of high government office than the extremists. They knew too that Tirtha's faction was considered not to be of true Congress colours in Delhi and that Patel himself, who was particularly weary of 'the communist menace in India', would prefer the power within the HSC to revert to its conservative section. This purpose would be served if 'right' rather than 'left' Congressmen accepted the ministerships offered.

Tirtha, released from jail on 30 November 1947, declared that 'there [was] no basis for compromise between the State Congress and the Nizam's Government' and that 'the recent Standstill Agreement between the Government of India and the Nizam's Government did not bind the State Congress to come to terms with the Nizam'.[3] Meanwhile, parleys continued in Hyderabad between Government officials and the 'right' section of the Hyderabad State Congress. The *Dawn* also reported (16 December 1947) that 'the Congress High Command in Delhi [had] advised Swami Ramanand Tirtha, President of State Congress, to send representatives to the proposed Interim Government'.

The outcome of these various manoeuvres was not very successful, however, as Congress conservatives did not seem to welcome being openly associated with the Nizam's Government at this stage. Finally, only one prominent Congress 'right' member, G. Ramachar, accepted a ministership. As a result, the Laik Ali government, announced in January 1948, failed in its attempt to be truly representative of all the political parties in the State.[4] It was said, indeed, that 'the entire Cabinet [wore] the complexion of the Ittihad',[5] a cheerless inference for Congressmen—both in Delhi and Hyderabad—who looked upon the extreme Muslim party as the arch-enemy.

Theoretically, the announcement of a State Cabinet more openly committed to the Ittihad than any previous one should have closed the ranks of the forces opposing the Nizam's regime, and in particular reinforced the bonds between the HSC and its allies of the 'United Front'. In practice, this did not occur, however, as both Socialists and Communists soon became disgruntled with the alliance for their own reasons.

From June 1947, the Socialists had begun to vigorously implement the plan of civil disobedience set out by the State Congress Committee of Action. To their resentment, however, the Government of India had in the meantime pursued, and then concluded, negotiations for a Standstill Agreement with Hyderabad. It had, in addition, generally been hostile to the Socialist anti-Nizam agitators operating from bases in the border areas.

The reasons for this hostility seem to have been two-fold. Firstly, the Socialist Party–Hyderabad State Congress alliance had never been viewed with great enthusiasm in Delhi because of the antagonism (already mentioned) which existed between the Indian National Congress and the Socialist Party at the all-India level. Secondly, right-wing Congressmen inside and outside the State feared that the influence of the Socialists would permeate the whole of the HSC and further strengthen Tirtha's left leadership which had long been anathema to them.

As the agitation began, the Government of India also came to look on the Socialists as an embarrassment—and possibly a national danger. This was because the Socialists were now encouraging villages on the borders of Hyderabad to accede to India and press the Indian government to recognise their de facto accession. This put Delhi in a delicate position, as such piecemeal accessions were not welcome at the very juncture when a Standstill Agreement with Hyderabad was being sought. Moreover, as these amounted to unilateral declarations of rebellion against the State's central authority, others could be inspired to do the same—the Communists in Telengana, for example—with unpredictable consequences.

Thus, when such villages declared that they had freed themselves from the Nizam's regime, the Government of India gave them no support. Instead, events were left to follow their own course much to the resentment of the militant Socialists who claimed later (in mid 1948) that

> if the Indian Union had encouraged these free zones and accepted their accession ... as they rose up in revolt, Hyderabad would have already been a proud province of the Indian Union.
>
> As it was, these free zones merely became battle fronts where bitter and deadly struggles flared up from time to time .... However, till the conclusion of the Standstill Agreement, the struggle was expanding its sweep in all sectors.[6]

The Socialists were opposed to the notion of a Standstill Agreement with Hyderabad as it implied the paramountcy of the Nizam and viewed its signing as evidence of the weakness of the Government of India; but they were still prepared to continue the struggle until its original objects had been secured. In December 1947, Tirtha had repeated that 'the movement launched on 15 August 1947 ... would not be terminated unless the issue of accession and the objective of responsible government were achieved' (Tirtha 1967, p. 187). By then, however, the Government of India's attitude towards the Congress–Socialist alliance in Hyderabad had changed from caution to increasing irritation, especially as the right-wing elements had not reconciled with Tirtha and in fact 'intensified their whisper campaign saying that "the movement was slipping from the hands of the Congress"' (Gour *et al*, 1973, p. 111).

Tirtha reports (1967, p. 192) that he had a meeting with Sardar Patel in Bombay at which the latter seemed 'rather impatient'. It is probable that Patel remonstrated with him about border incidents resulting from the declaration of 'free zones'.

Thereupon came a shattering pronouncement by the President of the HSC. According to Socialist sources:

> Under the pressure of ... outside influences Swami Ramanand Tirtha made a rather unfortunate statement of policy: 'the border incidents had nothing to do with the State Congress. They were not included in the programme of the State Congress ... Our movement is strictly non-violent' (Gour *et al* 1973, p. 80).

After this,

> Congress Ministers and Congress workers in the border regions tried to split up the unity of the Hyderabad people's resistance forces by invidious distinctions between Socialists and the State Congress workers .... Promises of aid were conveniently forgotten and action was threatened against some who were actively building up the Hyderabad peasants' resistance power (*ibid*., p. 62–63).

Indeed, at a conference of Premiers (of Bombay, Central Provinces and Madras) held in Delhi in February 1948 under the auspices of the States Department, the Premier of Bombay had stated that 'some Socialists and Congressmen operating from the Bombay side of the border were using firearms' (V. P. Menon 1961, p. 326) and it had been decided that 'whoever was using firearms on our side should be disarmed' (*ibid*.).

The Socialists bemoaned the fact that:

> The opposition of Congress Government even took the form of arresting some Socialists for alleged possession of arms [*sic*]. Such policies created confusion and ... a distinct sense of pessimism among the workers of the State Congress (Gour *et al* 1973, p. 81).

The Congress–Socialist alliance in Hyderabad thus lost its initial impetus, although it was to be briefly revived later. While border incidents engineered by State Congress continued to occur, they were sporadic and desultory, for, without the Socialists, the fighting capacity of the HSC as well as its means were practically nil.

Altogether, right-wing forces had won a battle over left tendencies in the State but there still remained the strong communist agitation in Telengana. Although it paid lip service to the 'United Front' for a while, it followed an independent and escalating course and could not be undermined from within, as had been the Congress–Socialist alliance.

In the 'United Front', despite early Communist pronouncements of allegiance to Congress policy, the atmosphere between the two parties had been marred from the start. Congress had been suspicious of the real motives of the Communists. There were, moreover, differences in regard to the character of the armed struggle to be waged against the Nizam's regime:

> The cooperation that had existed in the initial stages of the merger movement between the Congress and the Andhra Mahasabha cadre evaporated within a few weeks. The sweep of the anti-feudal and anti-landlord movement and the character of the anti-Nizam movement ... cooled the ardour of the Congress leadership. Further, with their having no stomach for such a radical programme, with no roots among the toiling people, their squads degenerated into raiding and launching attacks against the people and in support of the existing landlords.
>
> Our squads had to act and disarm many of these Congress squads (Sundarayya 1972, p. 59).

What seems to have happened—which Sundarayya does not make clear in the above passage—is that although a common plan of action had been evolved in principle, Communist and Congress squads continued to follow two different objectives. For the Communists, the agitation was primarily an anti-landlord, anti-feudal, agrarian movement aiming at what they considered a more equitable distribution of land in Telengana. Their locally recruited squads accordingly attacked and dispossessed landlords, occupied government wastelands and organised armed protection to groups. For the Congress squads, often hailing from regions other than Telengana, the aim was to disrupt the State administration through civil disobedience and defiance of State laws. They enforced it, when necessary, by action against recalcitrant villagers. Moreover, as they did not have a stake in the region, landlords obviously showed greater readiness to abide by Congress directives. Clashes of allegiance between the squads led to Congress forces, less numerous and organised than those of the Communists, often losing the day.

The Communists began to make various accusations against the Congress squads. They complained, for instance, that 'when the Nizam sought to suppress the people's movement with all his might ... [the Congress squads] retreated to the borders where they carried on some armed actions' (C. R. Rao 1972, p. 14). Meanwhile, the Communists said, Congress leaders 'were fighting a 'ferocious' battle in the press from luxurious hotels like the Taj in Bombay, Woodlands in Madras, etc'. (Sundarayya 1972, p. 150).

At the same time, the Communists were upset at the continuing negotiations between the Government of India (the Indian National Congress leadership) and Hyderabad, notwithstanding the 'people's struggle' in the State:

> In spite of the fact that the people of Hyderabad were engaged in a life and death struggle and facing a terrific repression, in spite of the fact that the people were demanding a stop to these talks and insisting on unconditional accession to Indian union ... Government of India States Ministry continued the talks only too eager to give the Nizam a breathing space (Gour *et al*, 1973, p. 45).

Like the Socialists, the Communists were thus accusing the Government of India of weakness towards Hyderabad and, not surprisingly, when the Standstill Agreement was finally signed in November 1947, they too protested that Delhi had accepted that the Nizam 'could do whatever he liked with the lives of the people' (C.R. Rao 1972, p. 9).

They viewed the Standstill Agreement as a stab in the back, a betrayal by the Congress leaders, and 'a surrender to the Nizam', (*ibid*., p. 11–17)

In December 1947, the leadership of the Communist Party of India passed from the hands of the P.C. Joshi, a reformist, to those of the radical B.T. Ranadive. Whereas under Joshi the CPI had judged Nehru 'worthy of left wing support' and was prepared to play the role of 'loyal opposition in free India', with Ranadive this approach was reversed. Nehru was seen as a 'reactionary bourgeois leader' whose policies were leading to 'subservience to the imperialist camp', and the CPI was called to an 'uncompromising struggle against the government' (Overstreet and Windmiller 1959, pp. 252–75).

At the Second Congress of the Communist Party of India in Calcutta—28 February to 6 March 1948—a new 'Political Thesis' was put forward. Besides scathing attacks on the INC leadership and its policies, the Mountbatten Award, the princes, the Socialist party and the bourgeoisie and capitalists, Telengana was cited as an example of successful 'armed insurrection of the people against the government' through which revolution could be brought to the whole of India.[7]

Having thus assumed national importance for the CPI, the Communist struggle in Telengana reached new heights.

An Intelligence Report of March 1948 reads:

> The incidents now occurring [in Telengana] are not sporadic outbursts but betray a carefully laid plan which is usually executed with ease and impunity. Communist bands numbering anything from 500 to 2,000 and armed not only with guns and rifles but with automatic weapons have in several instances emerged victorious from their encounters with the police and are emboldened in consequence .... They have been seizing arms and ammunition from village officials and from police outposts, wrecking motor buses and, since February, committing sabotage on the Nizam State Railway. The CID reports commonly contain the account of atrocities such as burying alive, torture, the blinding and maiming of victims .... Along the borders the most common target is naturally the Customs outposts many of which have been destroyed, whilst in the interior ... the grain which has been stored by officials performing the levy is looted, the cattle belonging to those who have contributed their quota is lifted and their agricultural implements broken. The gangs operating are well equipped and the conclusion is irresistible that supporters on Indian soil have been supplying the modern weapons used.[8]

The Communist agitation in Telengana was thus intensifying. Incidents were now occurring not only in the easternmost districts of Nalgonda and Warangal but also in some areas of Karimnagar, Medak and Adilabad, and, in one instance on 2 March 1948, as close as 46 miles from Hyderabad city itself.

Despite the obvious difficulties of the State Government in stemming the agitation and the avowed intentions of the CPI to spread the insurrection to the rest of the country, the Government of India did not come to Hyderabad's rescue. On the contrary, the Nizam's repeated pleas to the States Department to honour the provisions of the Mountbatten Award regarding the supply of arms and ammunition to the State were ignored. In fact, support to communist activity in the border region of the Madras province continued.[9]

An intelligence officer wrote:

> It would be an exaggeration to say that the Hyderabad administration had broken down in the districts in which the Communists are operating,

> but it is true to say that the administration is facing great difficulties, particularly as the Communists seem to enjoy a good deal of immunity in Madras territory .... Madras police officers have told Hyderabad officers privately that they do not interfere because the raiders are the proteges of the Provincial Ministry.[10]

On the face of it, it seems illogical that the Government of Madras should have given aid to the Communists who were the avowed enemies of the INC and that the Government of India should have turned a blind eye to this 'anomaly'.

The compelling explanation, however, is that it was known in Delhi that the HSC by itself—divided and weak as it was—could not do much to embarrass the State authorities, and that the Communist activity in Telengana was therefore the only alternative means left to weaken the Nizam's regime.[11]

Besides, the Indian Union could not divert troops from Kashmir to Madras (Menon 1961, p. 326) and such Communist agitation as existed on the border and in the State had to be condoned for the time being, even if it meant that greater efforts would have to be made to uproot it later, once the accession of Hyderabad to the Indian Union had been secured.

State Congress went along fully with this approach, in the knowledge that if, after accession, measures had to be taken against the Communists, the Government of India would be there to fight the battle for them. By March 1948, the 'United Front' had thus practically collapsed, but the situation in the State had not improved. In fact, the Laik Ali Ministry was facing serious difficulties as India hardened its attitude in the negotiations and demanded a disbandment of the Razakars whose depredations were given wide publicity. This threatened to deprive the Hyderabad Government of its staunchest supporters and it was clear that Laik Ali had to take some action.

Laik Ali cleverly utilised the hostility of the CPI towards the Nehru Government and the resentment of local Communists towards the Standstill Agreement. He began to send feelers to the Telengana Communist leaders, representing to them the advantages of an alliance against their common Indian enemy who was reported to be preparing for military intervention. Makhdoom Mohiuddin and Ravi Narayan Reddy, two leading Communist figures who were underground, were contacted. Although the Communist ranks were divided on the issue, the deal was struck and on 4 May 1948, the Nizam's

Government lifted the ban on the Communist party in Hyderabad (see K. V. Narayana Rao 1973, p. 276; Munshi 1957, p. 153; D. Das (ed.) 1973, vol 7, p. 199).

Following this,

> the Hyderabad City Committee [Communist] ... issued a press statement that the Indian Government, being a bourgeois-landlord government, was allied with British imperialism, that we should oppose the Indian army's entry into Hyderabad and raise the slogan of 'Azad Hyderabad' (Sundarayya 1972, p. 179).

Sundarayya later hotly denied that this alliance actually occurred but a Madras Intelligence Report of May 1948 states:

> The Communists are now alleged to be acting with the connivance and sometimes in actual association with the Razakars and the Nizam's police. Whether this is true or not, it is quite conceivable that the Communists have taken advantage of the lifting of the ban on their party within the Nizam's Dominions to make Hyderabad territory the base for their operations in Indian territory. It is also possible that the Government of Madras are responsible for the serious situation that has arisen by their own past toleration of Communist activity in this area so long as these activities were directed against Hyderabad.[12]

More precise was the report by A. Kaleshwara Rao, an Andhra Congress leader to the Government of India at the beginning of June 1948:

> The Hyderabad government have lifted the ban on the Communist Party and withdrawn all warrants of arrest against Communist leaders. A pact is said to have been entered into between the Communists and the Ittihad-ul-Muslimeen .... The Nizam government encourages the occupation of Munagala and Lingagiri[13] by the Communists and when the Communists retire into the neighbouring Nizam area and into the hills therein, when superior forces come to Mungala, the Nizam Govt. [*sic*] will allow them to do so without any arrests or obstruction (D. Das (ed.) 1973, vol. 7, pp. 214–15).

The tables had thus been turned, and it was India which was now hampered in its fight against the Communists of the Madras region by Hyderabad State.

There is no doubt that this turn of events weighed adversely in the conduct of negotiations between Hyderabad and India, especially as the Ittihad and its Razakars were reported to have an increasingly free reign over the State.

With the appointment of the Mir Laik Ali Cabinet in January 1948, the Ittihad rose to the zenith of its power.

The party was now able to exert covert influence at all levels of State affairs, externally with the control of the negotiating delegation, and internally through sympathetic officials occupying key positions in the government and administration.

This was not only due to the clever political manoeuvring of Kasim Razvi who, as has been seen, had been able to oust the Chhatari Government at the end of October 1947; it was also more generally the reflection of the extent of the fears of the Muslims in the State in the increasingly alarming realities of the Indian context.

Indeed, had the Muslims not supported the Ittihad, it would not have been able to achieve such a meteoric rise. But, with a hostile Government of India, a Pakistan naturally hesitant to commit itself to a rescue of Hyderabad in case of aggression, and the disappointing attitude of Mountbatten towards the old 'Faithful Ally', the Ittihad represented the only consolation to the feeling of isolation and insecurity gripping the minority community.

For long, Ittihad propaganda had been most successful with the young and lower-class Muslims intoxicated by the politico-religious theory of a collective Muslim sovereignty in the Deccan while, in general, the upper classes had turned up their noses at the extreme Muslim movement. Now, however, the real dangers looming over the State and the fact that the Ittihad had reached such heights of power made party politics more acceptable and seemingly more relevant to all Muslim classes. India had shown in the (admittedly smaller) case of Junagadh that it was prepared to use both fair and foul means to achieve its ends. Already, only months after the signing of the Standstill Agreement, the effects of an insidious economic blockade (denied in the official circles of Delhi) could be felt in the State. What would follow was unknown and it is this uncertainty that the Ittihad exploited.

In July 1947 Razvi had advocated resistance and ultimately martyrdom as the best defence of the State. A call for more volunteers to join the Razakars, a body which he now planned to transform into a fully effective armed contingent, met with very good response (Regani 1972, p. 206).

The Razakars had been organised originally as local defence squads designed 'to assist the State police' depleted by the War effort and 'to help in the maintenance of peace and stability in Hyderabad'

(M.A. Khan 1980, p. 93). The Razakars were also meant to boost the prestige of the Ittihad in district areas. In practical terms, their duties were then to inspire awe in the local population by displays of strength and, if disturbances occurred, to join the police in applying '*lathi*-force' to recalcitrant State subjects. In Bahadur Yar Jung's days, Razvi himself had been the deputy commander-in-chief of the Razakars for the Marathwara area (*ibid.*, p. 114) and thus he had first-hand knowledge of the strengths and shortcomings of the organisation. For instance, although the dedication of its members was beyond doubt, their members, estimated (by Munshi 1957, p. 37) at 30,000 by January 1948, were vastly insufficient in Razvi's new scheme. Also, their armament—some muzzle-loading guns, swords, daggers, spears and lathis—was hardly impressive or adequate for an effective para-military body.

Razvi's first objective—to increase the membership of the Ittihad and the number of Razakars—was made easier to attain by the ready response of the local Muslim population, and of the faction of Untouchables led by B. S. Venkat Rao, (Minister for Education in the new Cabinet (see Venkataswamy 1955). There was also the influx of Indian Muslim refugees who, when it was announced that India would be partitioned on communal lines, began to flock to Hyderabad in response to a persuasive propaganda campaign by the Ittihad.[14]

By March 1948, the total membership of the Ittihad-ul-Muslimeen was reported to be 900,000 with 52 centres in the State, each under a *salar* or area commander (Khan 1980, p. 94). Razvi claimed that the Razakars numbered 200,000 although this figure was estimated by British sources to be about half that amount.[15]

To join the Razakar organisation, volunteers were required to take this oath:

> I, ..., volunteer to the Razakar corps of the Ittihad-ul-Muslimeen, do hereby solemnly pledge myself to dedicate my life to the cause of the party to which I belong and to Hyderabad when called upon by my leader. In the name of Allah, I will fight to the last to maintain the supremacy of Muslim power in the Deccan (Regani 1972, p. 206).

After this a 'uniform' would be supplied (khaki military shirt, or coat if an officer, khaki pants, leather belt, and a black fez cap) and 'military' training would follow with physical exercise, marches and drills.

The Nizam denied that the Razakars were armed with government support. But Razvi is believed to have had access to obsolete army and police equipment, mainly muzzle-loading guns, which were allegedly made available to the Ittihad from government stores for Rs. 25/- each, thanks to ministerial cooperation (Gour *et al*, 1973, pp. 84–85). It is difficult, however, to be clear whether the State government did or did not contribute materially to the party. M. A. Khan (1980, p. 95) maintains that the Razakars were 'financed through voluntary and forcible contributions, careerist politicians, party funds and semi-government agencies'. Ali Yavar Jung, however, believes that the

> supply of rations, uniforms, firearms and training, and payment of allowances to such a large number of men was beyond the capacity of the Ittihad despite all the assistance given by the more enthusiastic Muslim industrialists (1949, p. 28).

K.M. Munshi, for his part, claims that

> the Razakars had almost unlimited means at their disposal and who but the Nizam's Government could have built them up? They used several three-ton lorries and dozens of jeeps and one-ton trucks. They demanded free transport from the Nizam's State Railways and the Road Transport Service of the State and in spite of petrol being in short supply, had plentiful supplies from the Government depots (1957, p. 38).

In reality, it is doubtful that the Ittihad obtained any free supplies from the Government, but certainly administrative red tape presented no problems to the party, thanks to the help given by all echelons of State bureaucracy.

Thus organised, the Razakars became a force to be reckoned with at the local level.

Increasingly, they were sent either alone or together with police and army units to district areas affected by Congress or Communist activities. It was said in some regions that Razakars reigned by day while Communists were *cheekati doralu* or kings at night (Sundarayya 1972, pp. 113–4). This led to the allegation in India that Communist activity in Telengana was increasing as a response to Razakar violence in the region (Munshi 1957, p. 91) but, as will be seen presently, there was little evidence to support it.

The Razakars were also used in punitive actions against political opponents, groups or individuals, whom they hunted out and sometimes pursued even on the Indian side of the border, and in missions of espionage, arms smuggling, propaganda as well as more conventional party work. Soon they were feared not only by the local Hindu population but became unpopular even among some sections of Muslims (M.A. Khan 1980, p. 96) because of their fearful reputation—cultivated by Razvi—and of real or fabricated reports of violence marking their activities.

According to Ali Yavar Jung (1949, p. 28),

> Where the commanders and section commanders were good, the force was well disciplined. Otherwise, they broke loose and combined patriotism with loot and arson. Occasionally they also indulged in murder and rape. Sometimes they came into conflict with the Police and Army, but the Police whenever it intervened was either suppressed or discouraged and few atrocities were punished.[16]

Razakar depredations attracted countrywide attention, particularly as their 'atrocities' were often wildly exaggerated in the Indian press which conveyed the impression that law and order had completely broken down in Hyderabad. Credence to this was particularly boosted in February 1948 when G. Ramachar, the Congress leader who had agreed to participate in the Laik Ali Cabinet, resigned with the alarming declaration that in Hyderabad,

> arson, loot and murder formed the normal events of the day .... Village after village was burnt down .... There has been no security of life and property in the State .... Do or die *jehad* [holy war] has been proclaimed against everyone who opposes [the Ittihad's] goal of the establishment of an Islamic State (Munshi 1957, p. 77).

It is doubtful, however, that G. Ramachar's statement was wholly accurate. R. Stimson, a respected journalist and the BBC representative in Delhi, visited Hyderabad for ten days barely a month after Ramachar's resignation. His lengthy confidential report to the British High Commission throws quite a different light on the Razakar organisation and their real strength in the State:

> Razvi told me that the Razakars number two hundred thousand and would soon be three hundred thousand. When I pretended that I had misheard these figures, he brought the present figure down to one hundred thousand. It is possible, I think, that one hundred thousand young Muslims throughout the State have expressed their willingness

> to become Razakars ... but I doubt whether the effective strength of the Razakars at this moment is more than thirty thousand to fifty thousand. Razvi himself admitted that the whole volunteer army had not more than three thousand to four thousand muzzle-loaders, together with a few 12-bores and sporting rifles.
>
> Kasim Razvi organised a Razakar parade for me in Hyderabad city and told me that it would be a big show. I expected at least three thousand Razakars to attend the parade since there is a majority of Muslims in Hyderabad city and since Hyderabad city is Razvi's own headquarters. I counted fewer than four hundred of whom twenty or thirty were children under ten years of age. At the other end of the scale there were one or two graybeards. The rest were youths of seventeen to twenty. Most of them had a rudimentary kind of uniform—a khaki bush-jacket or a tin hat or a fur cap or a leather belt. There were about fifty weapons on parade, practically all muzzle-loaders; for the rest there were half-a-dozen 12-bores, two revolvers, and an assortment of steel-tipped lances, bamboo poles and canes.
>
> Kasim Razvi was wearing a pale grey uniform ... and a green beret. The two smartest units were personal bodyguards of Kasim Razvi's, each ten strong. One unit was dressed in black and Kasim Razvi referred to them as his Black Guards. The parade consisted of very sloppy marching, sloppier arms drill and P.T. All in all, it was a sorry exhibition. When the parade was over three truck loads of volunteers ... drove off firing blanks into the air. Others marched off behind a drum-and-fife band.
>
> In the villages I visited, two dozen in all, there was a Razakar unit in each of six villages. Here it was the same story. A couple of dozen young Muslims with one or two muzzle-loaders between them, and a few spears and bamboo poles shambled around bovinely, out of step and looking utterly pathetic.[17]

It is therefore difficult to believe that the Razakars were as formidable a force as Razvi or Congressmen liked to present them. Communist writers also testify to the weakness and military inefficiency of the Razakars (C.R. Rao 1972, p. 15). Whatever their real strength may have been, the mere presence of Razakars in Hyderabad was decisively to affect the whole State. Indeed, the acquiescing attitude of the Nizam's Government towards such a communal organisation provided the Government of India with a ready justification for continued economic and political pressure on Hyderabad, and eventually for breaking off negotiations towards a permanent and amicable settlement with the State.

Part 2
The Last Phase of Negotiations: Breakdown and Police Action

The Standstill Agreement had, in the meantime, brought no amelioration in the relations between Hyderabad and the Indian Union.

The Nizam continued to consider that his State was independent, save on the three subjects of External Affairs, Defence and Communications, agreed to be devolved to India in the provision of the Standstill Agreement. His concern, overall, seems to have been to impress on India that his stand was to be taken in earnest and that he would not be bullied into accession.

The Government of India, on the other hand, relinquished none of the demands made before the Standstill Agreement and, in fact, insisted on their being accepted before the end of the agreement period.

After the events of October 1947, Sardar Patel showed even less faith than before in the bona fides of the Hyderabad Government, but V. P. Menon assured him that within a year of the Standstill Agreement, the Nizam would be brought to agree to accession or to grant responsible government. 'If he refused,' Menon said, 'the Government of India would have to reconsider the very basis of their approach to the Hyderabad problem' (V. P. Menon 1961, p. 321).

Thus, towards the end of December 1947, what was to be the last phase of negotiations towards a settlement of the future relationship between Hyderabad and India began in an atmosphere of deep mutual suspicion. In June 1948, the Government of India declared that it did not propose to pursue the talks any further. The last few months of negotiations were not only unfruitful, they were mostly tedious and undignified and have been aptly described as

> a story of allegations and counter-allegations, of breaches of the Standstill Agreement, of subversive or unbecoming propaganda, of raids into one another's territory, of a loan to Pakistan and a discriminating Currency Ordinance on the one side and an economic blockade on the other (Yavar Jung 1949, p. 29).

These developments need little detailed comment, as they were all nullified by subsequent events. The Currency Ordinance was one of the two economic measures taken by the Hyderabad Government in August 1947 which the Government of India claimed (in December) were breaches of the Standstill Agreement (V. P. Menon 1961, p. 322). It promulgated a restriction on the use of the Indian rupee for ordinary transactions in the State. The other was a concomitant declaration that the export of gold, jewellery and precious stones to India was prohibited.[18]

It is difficult to ascertain what exactly the Nizam's Government intended to achieve through these measures. The professed justifications were that the Currency Ordinance was passed in order to popularise the use of Hyderabad's own currency and that the ban on the transfer of precious metals and stones dated back to 1943.[19] However, it is probable that they were meant to stress that Hyderabad would neither relinquish the prerogatives of an independent State in internal affairs nor meekly accept the dictates of the Government of India in future negotiations. This was particularly important in the context of a tightening economic blockade and of State Congress raids on Hyderabad's borders which, it was known, India supported covertly (Campbell-Johnson 1951, p. 288).

It is to be noted that the Standstill Agreement had recognised 'the sovereign right of Hyderabad in regard to currency and coinage' (specified in the Collateral Letter) and therefore, strictly speaking, the Currency Ordinance was in order; as for precious metals and stones, no provision had been made in the Standstill Agreement which guaranteed that they would continue to circulate freely between Hyderabad and India.

The loan to Pakistan of Rs 20 crore (approximately £15,0000,000) in Government of India securities was also considered a breach of the clause regarding External Affairs in the Agreement. Hyderabad, however, protested that it was purely an economic matter in the nature of an investment devoid of political significance (V. P. Menon 1961, pp. 324, 326–27) and agreed later to ask the Government of Pakistan not to sell the securities before the end of the Standstill Agreement (30 November 1948).[20]

The Nizam's Government, for its part, countered that the Government of India was preventing the delivery of imports from abroad to Hyderabad and that arms and ammunitions had not been supplied as agreed in the Collateral Letter. But the Government of India made no reply, although the non-supply of arms was itself a definite breach of the Standstill Agreement.

In the intervening months, the emphasis of the Government of India's complaints about Hyderabad shifted from the provisions of the Standstill Agreement to an increasing state of domestic unrest which was by then widely reported in the Indian press.

The Ittihad and Kasim Razvi, in particular, had become major targets of criticism and pressure was applied on the Hyderabad Government to prohibit Razakars from assisting the police in maintaining law and order. According to a statement made by Sardar Patel, Razakars were 'terrorizing the Hindu population of the State' (V. P. Menon 1961, p. 325) and Laik Ali was urged to ban the organisation immediately. Laik Ali retorted, however, that the Razakars had come into being 'because of the apprehensions of Muslims in Hyderabad that their lives were in danger' (*ibid.*, p. 328) and refused to comply.

In March 1948, the Government of India summed up the situation in a lengthy letter to the Nizam's Executive Council, and officially requested the Hyderabad Government to take 'prompt and definite steps to fulfil their obligations arising out of the Standstill Agreement and to ban the Ittihad' (Poplai (ed.) 1959, vol. 1, pp. 306–17).

Sir Walter Monckton (who had been recalled from England early in March) and Laik Ali, in turn, alleged, on 5 April, that the economic blockade against the State had been tightened, that a 'propaganda war' against Hyderabad was being carried on 'at full blast', and that Indian troops were reported to have been concentrated on the borders of the State. In conclusion, referring to Article IV of the Standstill Agreement, they asked for the dispute with India to be settled by independent arbitration.

The Nizam, in the meantime, complained to Mountbatten that the letter of the States Department 'was in the nature of an ultimatum to be regarded as an open breach of friendly relations' and reiterated the request for arbitration (Poplai (ed.) 1959, vol. 1, p. 333).

Sir Walter Monckton also took up the question of the economic blockade personally with Nehru who, according to V. P. Menon, made the following reply on 7 April:

> Nehru said that he was not aware of any orders issued by the Government of India for the economic blockade of Hyderabad. It might be that the merchants themselves had decided not to send any goods to Hyderabad because of the uncertain political situation there, but he had impressed on all the provincial governments the desirability of letting ordinary goods go through. It was of course difficult in the circumstances to allow warlike stores to be imported to Hyderabad and there might have been a measure of confusion on the part of local officials between warlike and other stores .... He promised to take up the matter with the

> provincial governments and other authorities once again (V. P. Menon 1961, p. 335).

But this promise remained unfulfilled.

Significantly, Nehru, on the same day (7 April), also assured Sir Walter Monckton that the Government of India did not intend to invade Hyderabad. There is evidence, however, that by March 1948, plans for 'Operation Polo', the code name for the armed invasion of Hyderabad, were already finalised. Mountbatten states that he knew nothing of it before 16 March, when Lieutenant-Colonel E.N. Goddard, who was the Commanding Officer, Southern Command, asked him what he thought of 'Operation Polo'.

'This was the first indication which I received [he said] that a military plan had been prepared for the movement of troops into Hyderabad' (Hodson 1969, p. 486). Nehru, who was immediately consulted, 'expressed surprise that [Mountbatten] did not know about the plan and that [he] should be so upset about it' (*ibid.*, p. 489).

Yet, when Sir Walter and Laik Ali raised the question again with Nehru, on 14 April, as 'the statements of various Indian Congress leaders had given rise to a feeling that an armed invasion of Hyderabad was imminent' (V. P. Menon 1961, p. 336), the latter stated that 'the speeches made in India were the result of mounting anger against Hyderabad' and that 'the talk of a showdown was altogether absurd' (*ibid.*, p. 336). Five days later, however, Nehru sent Sardar Baldev Singh, then the Indian Defence Minister, a letter which, in Mountbatten's words, 'was in effect an order that certain troops, including the Indian Armoured Division, should be moved to concentration areas around Hyderabad' and 'on 25 April ... the move started—though slowly and to the Poona area rather than direct to concentration areas' (Hodson 1969, p. 491).

On the same day, Indian newspapers reported, under headlines such as 'War or Accession', that Nehru had said, at a Bombay meeting of the All-India Congress Committee held on 24 April:

> There are two courses now open to Hyderabad—war or accession. War is a prolonged affair, and if we resort to it, many new problems may arise. We have therefore been trying to solve this problem by negotiation, but that does not mean we are afraid of following the path of war (*ibid.*, 1969, p. 490).[21]

These belligerent intentions of the Indian Union were not only proclaimed outside Hyderabad, they were also spread within the State by

K.M. Munshi, former Home Minister of the Bombay Province. In January 1948, he had been appointed India's Agent-General in Hyderabad in accordance with Article 2 of the Standstill Agreement.

The choice of Munshi for this delicate post was in itself ominous as it was known that Munshi was Patel's man and, in fact, that he had accepted the Hyderabad appointment at Patel's personal request (Munshi 1957, pp. 1–3), despite the fact that he had not been popular in Hyderabad since 1938.

Munshi himself states:

> I knew that my presence in Hyderabad as Agent-General was not going to be hailed with joy.
>
> Ten years earlier, when I was Home Minister of Bombay, I had declined to oblige the Nizam by taking action against the Arya Samajists who were halting in Sholapur on their way to Hyderabad to offer *satyagraha*, (*ibid*., p. 4).

When Munshi undertook his appointment early in January 1948, he immediately ran foul of local feelings both through his actions and his utterances. Indeed, a dispute flared up with the Nizam's Government the moment he set foot in the State on the issue of his accommodation. Munshi apparently expected one of the former British residencies to be available to him until 'Deccan House' belonging to the Government of India was made ready for him and his staff.[22]

The Nizam at once took umbrage and protested to Mountbatten that Munshi's request was unconstitutional and part of a 'sinister plot to revive paramountcy' (Campbell-Johnson 1951, p. 288).

Razvi, meanwhile, threatened that, 'if Munshi occupies the Residency, he will not only be resisted but the bricks of the building will be thrown into the river Musi' (Munshi 1957, p. 8).

As a personal favour to Mountbatten, the Nizam agreed in the end to allow the use of the Hyderabad residency at Bolarum for the eleven days it would take to get 'Deccan House' ready. The local Muslim hostility had not abated by Munshi's next step either, which was to chip the words 'Deccan House' from the stone gate-posts of his new residence and to have them re-chiseled with the equivalent in Sanskrit—'Dakshina Sadan'.[23] The Indian Union flag was also hoisted over the building.

Once installed, Munshi began travelling frequently to India, addressing meetings and generally keeping Hyderabad affairs in the limelight.

It was reported, for instance, that, at a formal function in Bezwada, Munshi stated that 'India was the third greatest military power in the world' and said 'Hyderabad is India, bone of its bones and flesh of its flesh ... the people of both are one and indivisible'.[24]

Munshi himself makes no mention of such statements in his book of reminiscences on Hyderabad, but gives ample account of the difficulties of his life in the State without explaining that, by March 1948, he was 'openly hinting' at the probability of an Indian military intervention in the State and even 'naming various dates for 'D' day' (Hodson 1969, p. 483).

Sir Walter Monckton complained about it personally to Mountbatten on 7 April but the latter, although he clearly knew otherwise, assured him that India had never contemplated resorting to military intervention.

It is recorded, however, that Munshi at a meeting on 6 March with Mountbatten advocated sending the Indian Police to restrain the activities of the Razakars, an act which, according to his legal interpretation, would 'come within the terms of the Standstill Agreement' (Campbell-Johnson 1951, p. 195). Mountbatten apparently told him that '[his] proposal for police action was absolutely wrong' and spoke firmly of 'India's need to adopt an ethical and correct behaviour towards Hyderabad and to act in such a way as could be defended before the bar of world opinion' (*ibid.*). Mountbatten is also reported to have later told Campbell-Johnson that

> while he [had] no doubt about Munshi's drive and ability, he [was] far from happy whether his temperament or political outlook fit[ted] him for this particularly delicate stage in the handling of the Nizam, which call[ed] for unusual diplomatic patience and non-communal objectivity (*ibid.*).

Were those in the Government of India—and Patel, in particular—really concerned about handling the Nizam with tact at that stage?

Indeed, the choice of K.M. Munshi for the post would indicate no such concern. It was in sharp contrast with that of Nawab Zain Yar Jung, Hyderabad's Agent-General in New Delhi, who, by all accounts, did his best to defuse feelings (*ibid.*, p. 323) and quickly earned the reputation of being sensible and reliable (Hodson 1969, p. 481), even with V.P. Menon himself.[25]

Thus, the exchange of Agents-General did little to mitigate the relations between the two parties. In fact, the Government of India, alarmed by Munshi's highly coloured reports and increasingly convinced that the Nizam and his delegation were merely playing for time while equipping Hyderabad for a military showdown, placed little faith in the value of continuing negotiations.

But Mountbatten (who was due to leave India on 21 June 1948) and Sir Walter Monckton knew that only an agreement with India—whatever the terms—would save Hyderabad from worse fate, and they continued genuinely to work towards a permanent settlement between Hyderabad and India.[26]

In mid April 1948, Sir Walter put forward a four-point plan which had the approval of Mountbatten, Patel and Nehru. In essence, it proposed a change of government and an early introduction of responsible government in Hyderabad. But the Nizam rejected the offer (by firman on 23 April) and merely expressed willingness to associate all unrepresented political parties in a remodelled Cabinet (see V. P. Menon 1961, p. 340; Munshi 1957, p. 149).

Mountbatten then invited the Nizam to Delhi for personal consultation but the latter declined and proposed instead that Mountbatten should visit Hyderabad. Mountbatten, however, equally wary to avoid inferences of weakness, decided to depute his Press Attache, Alan Campbell-Johnson.

The impressions gathered by Mountbatten's envoy during his three day stay in Hyderabad (15–18 May 1948) were far from encouraging. He reported:

> The Nizam is the key man in the situation. As regards ... relations with the Indian Union, nothing is being done without his approval or connivance ... any agreement he finally enters into will be honoured, in the sense that his regime is strong enough to withstand opposition from any quarter.[27]
>
> He is in a mood of aggressive fatalism, and ... is ready ... to try to perform a 'Samson Act' on the Government of India; in other words, if he goes under, full preparations have been made to ensure that the political and social structure of the State should go under with him. On the other hand, the Nizam is searching furtively and anxiously for an honourable settlement. He is a ruler of the old school; he has no liking for the trappings of the Constitutional Monarch and will put up the same kind of resistance to that status as Queen Victoria did. The tighter the corner, the more he will fall back on prerogatives. I do not believe that he will voluntarily accept an accession solution which makes him anything other than the official fountain-head of law and custom inside his own state, (Campbell-Johnson 1951, pp. 338–39).

But Mountbatten considered that the Nizam may have been deliberately 'giving the works' (*ibid.*, p. 340) to his envoy and continued to press for a settlement. On 25 May, in the longest meeting of his entire Indian Mission—five hours in all—he belaboured Laik Ali on all issues, but the latter remained as firm in his rejection of accession as his master.

Campbell-Johnson reports:

> Mountbatten began by giving him with brutal frankness a picture of what would happen if no settlement was reached .... If after his departure in a few weeks India were to decide upon armed intervention, what could be done by the Hyderabad army? Laik Ali said he fully appreciated the military position but that he considered accession ten times worse than paramountcy (*ibid.*).

Mountbatten's gloomy forecasts must have made an impression on Laik Ali, nevertheless; following the interview, he is reported to have requested Menon for a meeting on the night of the 25th and to have carried on discussions with him until the early hours of the 26th (V. P. Menon 1961, p. 342). By the morning, Menon had produced a completely redrafted proposal of settlement, carefully named Heads of Agreement. In effect, this document was to be the Government of India's last attempt towards a negotiated solution to the 'Hyderabad problem'.

The Heads of Agreement devised by Menon listed eleven points which Hyderabad had to accept as a prerequisite for an amicable settlement with India (*ibid.*, pp. 342–43).

It was a clever piece of work and a credit to Menon's acumen as it contained, in its fine print, many implications and avenues for later interpretations which would have served India's interests well. But, in the atmosphere of suspicion reigning at the time, it collapsed quickly under Hyderabad's scrutiny, and objection after objection was raised by the Nizam, much to the impatience and irritation of the States Department in Delhi.

Patel then wrote to Nehru:

> I must frankly say that I was sorely disappointed that after so much profitless discussion with so many Hyderabad delegations, we are still thinking of producing formulas for their acceptance .... I feel very strongly that a stage has come when we should tell them quite frankly that nothing short of unqualified acceptance of accession and of introduction of undiluted responsible government would be acceptable to us .... I would not, therefore, like to waste any more time on devising formulas

> but would present the delegation with a brief letter containing the above-mentioned conclusions on behalf of the Government of India (D. Das (ed.) 1973, p. 212).

At this stage, however, Hyderabad's objections appear to have been raised mainly in sheer self-preservation. The Nizam objected, for instance, to a clause in the first Head of Agreement, which stipulated that, in respect of Defence, External Affairs and Communications, the Hyderabad Government would pass 'such legislation as the Government of India might request them to enact'. The Nizam demanded the self-explanatory amendment that 'the Government of India would request to pass legislation on the three subjects only when that legislation was similar to the legislation in force in India'. Another point raised was that the words 'under section 102 of the Government of India Act, 1935' should be added to the clause stating that 'The Government of India would not station their armed forces in the Hyderabad State except on the declaration of a state of emergency'. Under section 102, a state of emergency could only be declared when the security of India was threatened either by war or by internal disturbance (V. P. Menon 1961, p. 347) and thus, by demanding the addition, the Nizam was merely pre-empting any discriminatory move by India against Hyderabad.

Hyderabad demanded many other alterations—gradual rather than immediate disbandment of the Razakars, retention of 8,000 irregulars in addition to 20,000 troops, and so on. Menon painstakingly listed them in his effort to emphasise the conciliatory attitude of the Government of India and the lack of good faith of the Hyderabad party (*ibid.*, pp. 342–51). Read dispassionately, Hyderabad's demands appear in fact to have been prompted by a legitimate—and, in the circumstances, justified—fear in respect to the various terms offered. In any case, the Government of India never compromised on its fundamental demands, and acceptance of the substance of accession as well as the introduction of responsible government remained to the end the basis of the proposed settlement.

It is curious, that in Menon's otherwise detailed report, there is no mention that a plebiscite on the issue of accession had also been planned and agreed to by both parties. The Nizam's firman accompanying the settlement was to say specifically:

> I have now decided to consult the will of my people upon the question whether Hyderabad should accede to India. I shall therefore take a

> plebiscite in Hyderabad on the basis of adult franchise. In order to ensure that the plebiscite is fairly conducted, I shall arrange for it to be held under the supervision of some impartial and independent body. I shall accept the result of the plebiscite whatever it may be (Poplai (ed.) 1959, p. 322).

According to one opinion, the provision of a plebiscite and of a speedy introduction of responsible government shows that India agreed, up to a point, to accommodate Hyderabad's demands for technical changes.

> No doubt they calculated that eventual responsible government and a plebiscite on accession would achieve all they wanted ... their conciliatory attitude shows that at this stage at least they were content to wait patiently for the ripe plum to drop (Hodson 1969, p. 486).

It appears, however, that when Hyderabad insisted, among other things, on the inclusion of an arbitration clause overriding all Heads of Agreement as in the Standstill Agreement, India refused to move any further. The Heads of Agreement had been carefully drafted to preserve the practical paramountcy of the Indian Union over Hyderabad affairs. The introduction of an arbitration clause would have, therefore, undone all the advantages of the settlement as, in international law, a provision of arbitration between States implied an equality of status of the two parties, an admission which India was not prepared to make. But, as K.M. Munshi himself pointed out to Patel, according to the same canon, India was unable to prove that Hyderabad was a dependent State. In his legal capacity, Munshi advised that the best policy in the circumstances was 'to say nothing' (D. Das (ed.) 1973, p. 322).

Patel was thus made aware that a plebiscite would no longer guarantee India's interests, if the proposal of an overriding arbitration clause were also accepted. He had agreed to the idea at the time, although he knew that a plebiscite would not automatically lead to accession (Campbell-Johnson 1951, p. 343), because he was relying then on the implications of the Heads of Agreement (unfettered by an arbitration clause) to achieve the substance of India's goals. This, perhaps, explains why the Government of India insisted on the stringent wording of the Heads of Agreement. Ali Yavar Jung wrote:

> [the Heads of Agreement] conceded the substance of accession without the advantages of accession. Instead there was a strong odour of paramountcy ... the question arises: where was the hurry and what was the

> necessity for introducing paramountcy and achieving the substance of accession for the short period between the lapse of the Standstill Agreement and the holding of the plebiscite? (1949, p. 31.)

The answer to the question is obvious and poignantly important in the light of subsequent events: it was because India had serious doubts that the population of Hyderabad would decide in favour of accession. In fact, Swami Ramanand Tirtha himself, the chief supporter of the idea of Hyderabad's accession, now said:

> During the negotiations, the Government of India seems to have put forward a suggestion for a plebiscite to ascertain the will of the people. I was opposed to such a suggestion fundamentally. What was the necessity for it? (Tirtha 1967, p. 189.)

This is an astounding question, indeed, from someone who had consistently clamoured for the accession of the State 'in the name of the people'.

To conclude this point, the Nizam could perhaps have avoided accession through a plebiscite drawing on the support of the Muslim population, of the Untouchables of the Venkat Rao faction, most probably on that of the Communists (as the lifting of the ban on their party in May 1948 could indicate), and on that of those Hindus who had a stake in the State. There was also the force of subjectivity; in that respect, a reflection made by one of the rulers on another subject comes to mind:

> If a ruler were to seek support from village to village, he would be able to rally the masses behind him more readily than the most influential political leader and get 90 per cent support ... the 90 per cent are the ignorant masses who are blindly loyal to old institutions, including Kingship .... Politically, the masses are raw material liable to throw their weight more from prejudice than from reason.[28]

For anyone familiar with the Indian context, the assertion does not seem overly exaggerated. However, the Nizam would not be allowed to find out. In subsequent developments, India never consulted the State's population and this is perhaps why Menon did not elaborate on the subject of the plebiscite in his later account.

On 15 June 1948, the final text of a settlement was communicated to the Nizam,[29] and although it had been re-drafted three times since 26 May, largely through the intercession and personal influence of Mountbatten, (Hodson 1969, p. 486, fn 1) the Nizam still refused to sign.

Mountbatten attempted an eleventh-hour miracle with a long letter basically urging the Nizam to place trust in the Government of India, and by deputing Sir Walter Monckton to read it out personally (V. P. Menon 1961, pp. 348–50). Monckton arrived at Hyderabad at 6.30 a.m. on 17 June and at 1.15 p.m. sent a telephone message of a single word to Mountbatten: "Lost" (Hodson 1969, p. 487). The Nizam still insisted on arbitration, among other things, and this was the end of the road.

On the evening of 17 June, Nehru told a press conference in the course of a lengthy address:

> So far as we are concerned, these terms [draft Heads of Agreement] are the utmost limit to which we can go .... If the Hyderabad Government is prepared to accept them, it can accept them still, but obviously the situation is not a static one .... We are not going to rush into anything till we are convinced that nothing else remains. If these terms are acceptable still, well and good; but these terms are not to be varied. That is the position (D. Das (ed.) 1973, p. 333; see also pp. 327–35).

It was a forceful ultimatum which was immediately answered from Hyderabad. Repudiating the responsibility for the breakdown of negotiations, the Nizam's Government stated, and it is worth quoting it at length:

> In response to the oft-repeated suggestion made to the Nizam by the Government of India, [the Nizam had] agreed to leave it to the people of his State to decide whether Hyderabad should remain independent or accede to India .... In order that this verdict might be free and impartial, the Nizam offered to conduct the plebiscite under the supervision of a neutral and impartial body such as the United Nations or the International Court of Justice. The final choice having been left to the popular will, it was expected that interim arrangements to last until the verdict was announced would present no difficulty. This was not to be. The Government of India demanded that the substance of accession should be conceded immediately, irrespective of what the decision of the plebiscite might be. This was obviously unfair and amounting to prejudicing the popular will ....[30]

Turning to other issues, the statement continued:

> Although internal arrangements in Hyderabad are no concern of the Government of India ... in this sphere also the Government of India

> proposed radical changes in the interim period .... As regards Hyderabad's other demands the Government of India would not agree to give any assurance that the State would have economic and fiscal freedom and freedom of overseas trade. They would not even accept these freedoms in principle. It is clear that what the Government of India wanted was that Hyderabad should concede all their demands because of India's superior position .... India's attitude throughout the long negotiations was one of dictation and coercion.

Then, listing Hyderabad's grievances, the Nizam's Government complained that

> the promises made by the Government of India when the Standstill Agreement was signed with regard to the removal of restrictions on the flow of goods and essential commodities into Hyderabad had not been fulfilled. Vital necessary supplies of arms and ammunition were withheld while subversive activities on the borders increased. To-day, Hyderabad is facing a total blockade, and the necessities of life, including salt and medical supplies, are being denied to its people. An organised propaganda campaign had been launched against the State, while repeated requests made by the State to remove the difficulties by arbitration under the terms of the Standstill Agreement have been refused by the Government of India.

The statement ended with the assurance that

> in spite of this ... Hyderabad is anxious to forge friendly ties with the Indian Union and is prepared for an honourable settlement with the Dominion.

In the context of the preparations for confrontation which continued on both sides, it was obvious, however, that neither really contemplated any longer that "an honourable settlement" could feasibly be reached.

Now that the veil had dropped, events moved swiftly.

Mountbatten left India on 21 June 1948,[31] probably relieved that the whole volatile case had not exploded before his departure, and with the assurance given him by Nehru both in public and in private that

> orders would not be given for operations to start unless there really was an event, such as the wholesale massacre of Hindus within the State, which would patently justify in the eyes of the whole world action by the Government of India (Hodson 1969, p. 493).

It appears, however, that on the very day of his departure, Patel wrote (to N. V. Gadgil, a minister in the Nehru Cabinet) that the time had come

> [to] take firm and definite action ... [to] go ahead with determination and vigour in applying the economic sanctions as well as dealing effectively with border and other incidents [and to] put [the] military in a state of preparedness for all eventualities (D. Das (ed.) 1973, p. 217).

A few days later, in a telephonic conversation with K.M. Munshi who was conveying to him the hopes expressed by Zahir Ahmad (Secretary of the External Affairs Department, Hyderabad Government) that the last settlement offered by India could still be worked, Patel apparently said 'jocosely':

> 'Settlement! .... What settlement?'
> 'The Mountbatten Settlement' [Munshi said.]
> 'Tell him that the Settlement has gone to England', [Patel] replied caustically and laughed (Munshi 1957, p. 177).

Thus, no settlement, tightened economic blockade and stepped-up military preparations were now India's strategies.

By early July, the international press reported a series of economic measures taken by the Government of India against Hyderabad: Indian air services crossing Hyderabad would not in future touch down at any aerodromes in the State and the licence of a local airline—Deccan Airways—was suspended; trains passing through Hyderabad were reduced to one a day and this under escort by Indian troops; the transfer to Hyderabad of Government of India securities was restricted by a new ordinance and the export to Hyderabad of gold, jewellery, precious stones, coins and foreign exchange was banned; all agency arrangements between the Imperial Bank of India and the Hyderabad State Bank were suspended 'with immediate effect'. At the same time, the Reserve Bank of India carried a notification advising that payments of debts from Indians to Hyderabadis were to be made to blocked accounts at the Reserve Bank.[32]

On 21 July, following earlier reports that 'a mysterious four-engine aircraft' was regularly landing at night at Bidar (50 miles west of Hyderabad city) from a base in the Sind desert, the Government of India forwarded an official complaint to the British Government that direct flights between Hyderabad and Pakistan were made by a certain

Sydney Cotton, an Australian employed by a British firm. This was said to be in defiance of the Indian Civil Aviation Department ruling that an aircraft must land at an intermediate point in Indian territory for customs clearance (*The Times* (London) 23 June and 21 July 1948).

The inference was that gun-running was taking place, although Cotton himself claimed that this was a 'mercy plane' laden with medical supplies unavailable to Hyderabad hospitals since the economic blockade. The Hyderabad Government declared that it regarded Cotton's activities as 'an unsolicited gesture of sympathy'. However, it complained, in turn, that industrial machinery from Britain was stranded in Indian ports, petrol supply had been cut off, and no salt for the population, no medicine for hospitals, and no chlorine for the purification of water were available in the State (*ibid*., 23 July 1948).

Meanwhile, tension escalated with an armed clash between Razakars and Indian troops near the village of Nanaj on 24 July 1948 when, according to Munshi's report,

> a large number of Razakars and some Pathans ... cleared Nanaj of the villagers ... and laid an ambush in a fortlike house. When a party of Indian troops was moving from Sholapur to Barsi [an Indian enclave in Hyderabad] on normal patrol duty, they were fired upon by the Razakars and Pathans from this house. Six men were killed and six wounded. The army immediately deployed, captured the village after a bitter fight and occupied it (Munshi 1957, p. 182).

This occupation of Nanaj by Indian troops was seen as a prelude to a full attack by India; the Nizam's Government protested to Delhi that 'a grave and flagrant violation of Hyderabad's territorial integrity' had taken place and requested the immediate withdrawal of Indian troops. At the same time, steps were taken to reinforce the Air Raid Protection units (disbanded since the end of the War, but reorganised in June 1948) 'to meet any eventual possibility of air raids' (*The Times* (London) 27 July 1948).

Meanwhile, Nehru said at a meeting in Madras on July 25:

> How can we deal with a government that is practically run by gangster elements? .... If and when necessary, we shall have military operations against Hyderabad .... In no circumstances whatsoever is the independence of Hyderabad going to be accepted .... Hyderabad must and will become a full member of the Indian Union (*ibid*.).

On the same day, the Nizam took the decision to refer the dispute to the United Nations and wrote personal letters to the King of England and British Prime Minister Attlee expounding at length the Hyderabad case and dwelling on his former status of 'Faithfull Ally'. He appealed to the monarch 'to use his personal influence to see that Hyderabad gets a fair hearing' and to Britain to help find an amicable solution (*ibid*., 25 July 1948).

The fate of these attempts will be examined later but, by the end of July 1948, the most fantastic rumours spread throughout India when P. V. Joshi, the (Congress) Commerce and Industries minister in the Laik Ali Cabinet resigned with a sensational report that the most basic safety of life and property had disappeared in some regions of the State. Joshi's account was given wide publicity in the Indian press thanks to Munshi's efforts, although he was later to say that Joshi had resigned when 'the ship was sinking' (Munshi 1957, pp. 178–79). At the time, however, he made all possible capital out of the resignation. V. P. Menon, while admitting that, in the atmosphere of 'mutual suspicion and excitement' then prevailing in Hyderabad, 'it was only natural that many incidents should be exaggerated and that rumours should often be given evidence without justification' (V. P. Menon 1961, p. 352), does not hesitate to use Joshi's report as evidence of the deterioration of internal conditions in Hyderabad.

Following allegations that 'the police had joined the Razakars in looting, murder, arson, and rape', Menon quotes Joshi's words:

> A complete reign of terror prevail[ed] in Parbhani and Nander districts .... Brahmins were killed and their eyes taken out. Women had been raped, houses had been burned down in large numbers .... Government ... [was] powerless to prevent these heart-rending atrocities (*ibid*., p. 353).

This, and further clashes between Razakars and Indian troops in August 1948,[33] coupled with reports of Razakar activities in border areas and allegations of incursions in Indian Union territory (D. Das (ed.) 1973, pp. 227–29), led finally to an official communication from the Government of India by the new Governor-General, C. Rajagopalachari, to the Nizam on 31 August 1948:

> Allowing for all exaggeration, there is no doubt that the unrestrained activities of private armies ... have created a state of terror for the vast majority of the people in Hyderabad and on the borders thereof. There

> has rapidly grown a feeling of utter insecurity among all classes of people and demand of intervention by the Indian Union.[34] It is morally impossible for the people of India to ignore the conditions prevailing in Hyderabad and affecting its people, as well as endangering the peace of South India.
>
> It is not possible to allow this sense of terror and insecurity to continue .... Your Exalted Highness should ban the Razakars and ... invite the re-posting of an adequate military force of the Government of India at Secunderabad so that there may be no doubts left in the public mind in Hyderabad and outside as to the security of person and property .... I see no other effective way of restoring security and confidence (V. P. Menon 1961, pp. 229–31).

The Nizam replied by telegram on 5 September 1948:

> I have received Your Excellency's letter dated 31 August .... It appears ... that a very wrong impression of insecurity of life, honours, and property in Hyderabad prevails at your end .... Please let me say that the matter of allowing Indian troops to remain in my territory is out of the question. My own troops are able to satisfactorily safeguard the life and property of my own subjects and are fully capable of dealing with the situation (*ibid.*, p. 232).

Thus, a final stalemate had been reached. India demanded to be allowed to station her troops in Hyderabad and the Nizam refused. Despite the wide disproportion in military capacities, he was prepared to resist, perhaps in the hope that the United Nations Organisation which had been approached would, in the end, intervene in the dispute.

The Times (London) reported on 9 August 1948, the rumour that the Hyderabad army had been strengthened to 40,000, that supplies of arms including anti-tank guns had been received by air, that defensive positions on the main roads had been prepared, and that many bridges were planned to be demolished. Laik Ali was also quoted as having said:

> If the Indian government takes any action against Hyderabad, 100,000 men are ready to join our army. We also have a hundred bombers in South Arabia ready to bomb Bombay (V. P. Menon 1961, p. 160).

This rumour of a so-called 'Peacock Airborne Division' as well as all other canards which were given credence at the time contrast sharply with the estimate of the State's armed forces given only a few months earlier in a British intelligence report. In March 1948, according to that report, the Hyderabad army numbered 24,000 but,

> of fully equipped and trained troops there [were] perhaps no more than five or six thousand. The army [had] no tanks and no aircraft. They [had] some obsolete Staghound armoured cars ... without their firing mechanism ... and an undisclosed number of Bren gun-carriers.
>
> The Hyderabad army commander, Major-General El Edroos (an Arab with thirty-two years service in the Hyderabad army) ... said that ... India ... 'can walk into Hyderabad whenever she wants to' .... In the average Hyderabad village perhaps two to five per cent of the population is Muslim. With the first appearance of an Indian uniform the villagers would surrender, partly because the Hindus of Hyderabad are Hindus first and Hyderabadis second, partly because the average villager is afraid of being involved with the military or the police, and partly because it is the Hindu tradition not to resist invasion. The State authorities would have to try to make a stand on Hyderabad city, Aurangabad and Gulbarga, the three largest cities of Hyderabad ... these cities might hold out for a few days.[35]

It is perhaps because of this that Sir Mirza Ismail, former Prime Minister of Hyderabad, was requested by the Nizam early in August 1948 to intercede on his behalf in a last attempt at settlement with the Indian Union. Discussions were held between Sir Mirza and C. Rajagopalachari and Nehru in Delhi during the first week of August, but the mediation of a pro-Congress Muslim was violently opposed by the Ittihad at home, and the mission ended in failure (Ismail 1954). On 8 August, Sir Mirza declared in a press statement that his efforts to bring about agreement had been 'nullified by the influence of extremist elements in Hyderabad, more particularly by the Ittihad-ul-Muslimeen (Moslem Unity party) members of the Council, who prevailed on the Nizam to reject my advice'.[36]

On 19 August 1948, Laik Ali announced officially that the State would place the dispute with India before the United Nations. On 24 August, it was announced from Lake Success that Hyderabad had formally asked the Secretary General of the Security Council, under article 32 of the Charter, to consider 'the grave dispute which, unless settled in accordance with international law and justice, [was] likely to endanger the maintenance of international peace and security'.[37]

Menon, in the meantime, advised the Hyderabad Government that the States Department of the Government of India regarded the dispute with Hyderabad as a 'purely domestic issue' and did not consider that Hyderabad had 'any right in international law to seek the intervention of the United Nations Organisation or any other outside body for the settlement of the issue' (V. P. Menon 1961, p. 356).

The invocation of international law to settle the dispute was a point which India was particularly anxious to avoid, as it raised again the clause of outside arbitration which had been refused in June. As has been said, India knew that within the legal international definition of the term, it could not prove effectively either that Hyderabad was a 'dependent state' or that its dispute with Hyderabad was really 'purely domestic'. Furthermore, the intervention would have tied Indian hands by bringing the issue into international limelight. It would have thus ultimately prevented the Government of India from using its main advantage—superior armed force—in its confrontation with Hyderabad.

In the State, it was considered in some circles that an appeal to the UNO amounted to suicide (Yavar Jung 1949, p. 42) as it was certain to precipitate India's armed intervention. Mir Laik Ali went ahead, and announced to the Hyderabad Legislative Assembly (on 4 September 1948) that a delegation headed by Moin Nawaz Jung, would proceed to Lake Success. He ended his address with the statement that 'even should the United Nations turn down Hyderabad's appeal, the State would not give up its claim to independence'.[38]

In the meantime, the King of England and Prime Minister Attlee had responded to the Nizam's calls for help, the first with 'hope and prayer that a peaceful solution ... may be found', the second with 'regret that [the British Government ... could not] accede to [Hyderabad's] request'.[39] The Nizam had the support of the Conservative Party in England, nevertheless, as is clear from the frequent attacks made by Churchill against the Attlee Government on the subject of Hyderabad[40] and by the spate of letters received by members of Parliament expressing support to Hyderabad. One of these stated:

> We should have had the good grace and decency to see that her [Hyderabad's] RIGHTS [*sic*] were respected by a foreign Indian government whose members, far from being the good friend the Nizam was, were ready to stab us in the back during the War. It would appear that Britain gives better treatment to her enemies than to her friends ...[41]

In Hyderabad, the Muslims put the blame on Mountbatten who they said had been 'far more concerned with scoring a dazzling if superficial triumph than with ensuring the maximum of justice for all', and on the British in general for not fulfilling the obligations of their treaties and promises:

> Whatever the rights and wrongs, it is nevertheless disconcerting and embarrassing for an Englishman visiting Hyderabad to hear from all Muslims and some Hindus that the British government and a British Viceroy ... are guilty of unforgettable perfidy.[42]

When Indian intervention became imminent, the Nizam was again to ask the British and the King for 'immediate intervention from your side', but by then, as an internal report reveals, the British Prime Minister had decided 'not to send any reply to these telegrams and ... suggested that the King should likewise take no action'.[43]

Thus, Hyderabad State could not expect any support from the British. It was still hoped, perhaps, that should India begin hostilities, Pakistan and other Muslim countries of the world would come to its rescue or that the Security Council of the UNO would look at its case sympathetically. Whatever it was, the tone of its communications with India remained unchastised. When Nehru told the Indian Parliament, on 7 September 1948, that the Government of India had 'asked the Nizam for the last time to disband the Razakars immediately and ... to facilitate the return of [Indian] troops to Secunderabad ... to restore law and order' (D. Das (ed.) 1973, p. 431; see also pp. 338–42), P. V. Reddy, Hyderabad's Deputy Prime Minister, addressed the Hyderabad Legislative Assembly the same evening and answered:

> In spite of sporadic ... breaches of law and order, the situation in the State has, on the whole, remained peaceful and is completely under control .... The Government of India have no right to interfere with the administration of the State, and under the Standstill Agreement, are not entitled to send any troops to or to station them at Secunderabad .... If the Government of India decide ... to resort to aggression, [the] responsibility for the consequences ... will rest entirely with them.[44]

On 10 September, Laik Ali, characterising the Indian demand as 'extraordinary', repeated in a letter to Nehru that the despatch of Indian troops would be regarded by Hyderabad as 'a gross infringement of its territorial sovereignty and integrity' and would have 'very serious consequences'.[45]

Razvi, for his part, was reported in the *Dawn* (10 September 1948) as saying:

> Hyderabad can take it ... [the people] are determined to shed their last drop of blood to safeguard the honour, integrity and independence of their country.

The next day, the Government of India answered Laik Ali's letter, in what was to be the last communication between the Indian Union and 'independent' Hyderabad, with the declaration that

> [as] the Nizam's government appeared determined to regard facts not as they were but as they wished others to believe them to be [and as] the only law that now prevailed in the State was the law of the jungle by which the Razakars and their allies preyed upon a large majority of helpless citizens ... [t]he Government of India regarded themselves as free to take such action as they considered necessary (V. P. Menon 1961, pp. 357–58).

There the matter briefly rested; and at 4 a.m. on 13 September 1948, 'Operation Polo' was set in motion. Indian Union troops marched into the State from all cardinal points and five days later, at 5 p.m. on 17 September, the Nizam, asking for a ceasefire with immediate effect, surrendered. Any notion of Hyderabad State's 'honour, integrity and independence' had ceased to exist.

NOTES

1. Mir Laik Ali was the director of eight major concerns in Hyderabad State among which were the Hyderabad State Bank, Deccan Airways Ltd., the Singareni Collieries Co., the Hyderabad Construction Co., the Nizam Sugar Factory Ltd., and the Hyderabad Roller Flour Mills Ltd. (See *The Hyderabad Problem: the Next Step* (hereafter *Hyderabad Problem*, Appendix II). Gulam Mahomed was the former Finance Minister of Hyderabad State, later to be Governor-General of Pakistan (see Munshi 1957, p. 75).
2. Mir Laik Ali was at the time the delegate of Pakistan at the United Nations Organisation (see Ali Yavar Jung 1949, p. 21; Munshi 1957, p. 69).
3. Letter to Moin Nawaz Jung, 13 December 1947 in *Dawn* (Karachi), 15 December 1947.
4. The new government comprised of six nominated members (Mir Laik Ali, Prime Minister; Pingle Venkatrama Reddy, Deputy Prime Minister; Nawab Moin Nawaz Jung, Finance and External Affairs; Abdul Hameed Khan, Police and Customs; Raj Mahal Lal, Law and Judicial; Nawab Fazal Nawaz Jung, Revenue), four representatives of the Ittihad-ul-Muslimeen (Mohd. Yamin Zuberi, Local Government and

Labour; Abdul Rauf, PWD; Mohd. Abdur Rahim, Railway and Communications; Mohd. Ikramullah, Planning and Development), and one representative each of the Lingayats, the Congress Right, and the Depressed Classes, respectively Mallikarjunappa (Public Health and Medicine), G. Ramachar (Commerce and Industries)—later replaced by P. V. Joshi—and B. S. Venkat Rao (Education). IOL, L/P & S/13/1204, Squire to Gordon-Walker, 25 March 1948, p. 142.

5. *ibid.*, p. 143.
6. *Hyderabad Problem*, p. 61. This last assertion is correct only if activity in Telengana, in which Congress and the Socialists had little part, is included.
7. For Congress comments see Munshi 1957, p. 127. For the full text of the 'Political Thesis' see M. B. Rao (ed.) 1976, pp. 1–118. P. Sundarayya, C. R. Rao and Ravi Narayan Reddy were, among others, members of the discussing panel at the Communist Party of India Second Congress, *ibid.*, p. 216.
8. IOL, L/P & S/13/1204, *op. cit.*, pp. 149–50. For a Communist account of incidents see Sundarayya 1972.
9. In other parts of India, the CPI had come under severe repression, (see Masani 1954). CPI leaders had been arrested in Madras city but not in regions bordering Hyderabad.
10. IOL, L/P & S/13/1204, *op. cit.*, p. 160.
11. Munshi (1957, p. 133) claims that 'it was difficult for the Madras government to suppress the Communist activities in the Telugu-speaking districts of their own province, for the people, including the Congressmen, sympathised, and not necessarily passively, with the Communist resistance in Hyderabad'.
12. IOL, L/P & S/13/1204, Madras Weekly Report, 10–18 May 1948, 19.
13. Munagala and Lingagiri were Indian enclaves in Hyderabad State territory.
14. IOL, L/P & S/13/1204, *op. cit.*, p. 151. 'Into the Razakar organisation were brought quite a number of Muslim "refugees" from outside the State, while many thousands of Hindus, dismayed or terrified by the Razakar regime, fled to the neighbouring provinces. One of the wild ideas in Razvi's mind, following the immense exchange of population in the Punjab in 1947, may possibly have been that Hyderabad could become a Muslim state in population also by attracting the Muslim minority from India and eventually driving out or outnumbering the local non-Muslims' (Smith 1950, p. 45).
15. IOL, L/P & S/13/1204, *op. cit.*, pp. 144 and 162.
16. Razvi himself admitted in March 1948 that 'looting and murder were proceeding on a large scale' but claimed that 'such incidents were always started by Hindus' (Martin 1948, pp. 230–31).
17. IOL, L/P & S/13/1204, Squire to Gordon-Walker, 25 March 1948, Appendix II.
18. See *Keesing's Contemporary Archives*, vol. VI, 1946–48 (Bristol, Keesing's Publications Ltd.), p. 9422.
19. *Keesing's Contemporary Archives*, *ibid.*
20. The loan to Pakistan was particularly irritating to India but its Government was itself withholding 55 crore of assets from Pakistan despite an agreement made at the time of Partition. It was to take a fast by Gandhi for India finally to relent (see Campbell-Johnson 1951, p. 289).
21. Apparently, when Mountbatten asked Nehru whether he had been quoted correctly, Nehru replied that he had been 'completely mis-reported' and that 'the error was due to the fact that he had been speaking in Hindustani and ... not been

properly understood by the Madrassi stenographer who was taking down the report'. But, as Hodson remarks, 'it is difficult to accept Pandit Nehru's explanation. So gross a distortion of what he said on a matter of vital importance would plainly have called for an immediate sharp denial, without any prodding or delay. The Madrassi stenographer does not make a convincing scapegoat' (Hodson 1969, p. 491).

22. There were two British residencies in the State: one in Chaderghat in Hyderabad city, the other at Bolarum, some 17 km away from the capital.
23. IOL, L/P & S/13/1204, *op. cit.*, p. 157.
24. IOL, L/P & S/13/1204, Bombay Weekly Political Report No. 2/48, 18–24 January 1948. Munshi's brief seems to have been to embitter rather than smooth relations with Hyderabad (see Munshi 1957, p. 146).
25. Campbell-Johnson (1951, p. 341) says 'V. P. [Menon] spoke in the most fervent and emotional terms of his esteem for Zain Yar Jung ... the understanding that clearly exists between the two men is encouraging'. Nawab Zain Yar Jung was a nobleman of Hyderabad and a civil engineer by profession. The uncle of the former home minister and then delegate of Hyderabad, Nawab Ali Yavar Jung, Zain Yar Jung was a moderate who was later to fell out of favour with the Ittihad (see S. A. Khan 1959).
26. Mountbatten knew that action against Hyderabad would not occur while he was still in India but would probably be launched after the monsoon (see Campbell-Johnson 1951, pp. 493 and 342).
27. Note that the Nizam's regime was reported by India to be tottering on account of internal difficulties.
28. Statement made by the Rajsaheb of Dhrangadhara on the subject of a confederation of States as an alternative to Partition, NML, AICC, File No. 2, Doc. No. STS/1–5, 8 April 1947.
29. For the full text of the proposed settlement see D. Das (ed.) (1973, pp. 321–25).
30. *Keesing's Contemporary Archives*, *op. cit.*, p. 9421. This is perhaps also why V. P. Menon avoided the whole subject of the plebiscite. (The passages quoted below are from this same document.)
31. Mountbatten was replaced as Governor-General of India by C. Rajagopalachari, former Premier of Madras, who had not been unsympathetic to Hyderabad in 1938–39.
32. *The Times* (London), "Undeclared War Threatened", 2 July 1948.
33. Notably at Yelsangi, an Indian enclave in Hyderabad territory, on 5 August 1948, when Indian forces went into action 'with full fire-power' against Razakars who were 'besieging the village'; 25 Razakars were reported killed. On 26–27 August, another 17 Razakars were killed in the Indian village of Khaimer, *Keesing's Contemporary Archives*, *op. cit.*, p. 9522.
34. The notion that 'all classes of the people' of Hyderabad asked for the intervention of the Indian Union is an important claim which is not evidenced outside Congress literature.
35. IOL, L/P & S/1204, *op. cit.*, p. 161.
36. *Keesing's Contemporary Archives*, *op. cit.*, p. 9522.
37. *ibid.*, p. 9523.
38. *ibid.*
39. IOL, L/P & S/13/1242, Commonwealth Relations Office, 20 July 1948.

40. On 31 July 1948, Churchill told Attlee's ministers that in view of past pledges 'they had a personal obligation ... not to allow a state, which they had declared a sovereign state, to be strangled, starved out or actually overborne by violence. To sit after all they had said and let that happen ... would be an act of shame with which their names would be burdened for generations which otherwise might not have paid attention to them', *The Times*, 31 July 1948.
41. IOL, L/P & S/13/1243, A.H. Saunders to E. Bevin, M.P., 8 August 1948.
42. IOL, L/P & S/13/1204, *op. cit.*, p. 166.
43. IOL, L/P & S/13/1244, Doc. No. 3532/48.
44. *Keesing's Contemporary Archives*, *op. cit.*, p. 9524.
45. *ibid.*

8

The Aftermath of Police Action

The victory of the Indian troops[1] over the Nizam's forces was greeted in the state, not unexpectedly, with elation by Hindus and gloom by Muslims. Fareed Mirza, a revenue collector in Hyderabad State (1941–1945) who had resigned in protest against the 'subversive activities of the Ittihad' and the government's one-sided policy, recalls:

> On the morning of 18th September ... I went around some of the main bazaars of the city. The Indian Army had not yet arrived. But it had become known that Hyderabad had been defeated and it was a matter of some hours when the Indian Army would enter the capital.
>
> Thousands and thousands of Hindus young and old were roaming the streets of the city in a very jubilant mood. They were carrying tri-colour flags in their hands, or [on their] bicycles, rickshaws, motor cars and other vehicles. They were shouting 'Jawaharlal Nehru Ki Jai, Sardar Vallabhbhai Patel Ki Jai, State Congress Zindabad' and other such slogans. The Muslims were very depressed and grieved. They had never expected that such a thing would happen. Their leaders had said to them that the time had come when they would march towards Delhi and hoist the Asafia flag on the Red Fort .... Within five days everything had been changed. I felt sorry for them (1976, p. 34–35).

Later the same day, Major-General J.N. Chaudhury, the commanding officer of the Indian troops, accepted the formal surrender of the Hyderabad army from General El-Edroos and entered the capital.

Mir Laik Ali and the members of his Cabinet were immediately put under house arrest, Kasim Razvi was imprisoned,[2] but the Nizam was left free and reported to be staying in his palace. Later, he would, of course, cease to be an autocratic ruler and would be equal in status to any other prince who had acceded to India. However, although the

Indian Union now placed Hyderabad State under military rule—with Major-General Chaudhury as Military Governor—it was understood that there was no intention of deposing the Nizam or ending his dynasty.[3]

It must be said that, once defeated, the Nizam showed utter compliance to his victors' wishes. On 23 September 1948, for instance, he spoke over the radio (the speech was most likely written for him):

> In November last, a small group which had organised a quasimilitary organisation surrounded the homes of my Prime Minister, the Nawab of Chhatari, in whose wisdom I had complete confidence, and of Sir Walter Monckton, my Constitutional Adviser, by duress compelled the Nawab and my other trusted ministers to resign and forced the Laik Ali Ministry on me. This group headed by Kasim Razvi had no stake in the country or any record of service behind it. By methods reminiscent of Hitlerite Germany it took possession of the State, spread terror ... committed arson and looting on a large scale ... and rendered me completely helpless. I was anxious to come to an honourable settlement with India but this group ... got me to reject the offers made by the Government of India from time to time. I am a Moslem and I am proud to be a Moslem. But I know that Hyderabad cannot remain apart from India .... In the very nature of things, Hyderabad, 86 per cent of whose people are Hindus, cannot possibly become an Islamic State.[4]

The same day, the Nizam also sent a telegram to the United Nations Security Council at Lake Success withdrawing Hyderabad's complaint against India. Following this, the Hyderabad question was adjourned sine die on 28 September 1948.[5]

The Nizam, although he was soon to lose a great deal of property including his private estate (the so-called *Sarf-e-Khas* of 7,000 square miles), had a better deal than his compatriots. Other Muslims in the State were not so lucky. Indeed, with the entry of the Indian army, retaliation against Muslims began. There was a State-wide purge of the government and administration, as also bloody attacks by Hindus in district areas.

Few facts were allowed to transpire outside Hyderabad at the time and detailed accounts of what happened off the battlefield during and after the so-called 'police action' are hard to come by. But one report from a reliable source states categorically that,

> the Muslim community fell before a massive and brutal blow, the devastation of which left those who did survive reeling in bewildered

fear. Thousands upon thousands were slaughtered; many hundreds of thousands uprooted. The instrument of their disaster was, of course, vengeance. Particularly in the Marathwara section of the state, and to a less but still terrible extent in most other areas, the story of the days after 'police action' is grim ...

It is widely believed that the figure ... of Muslims massacred is 50,000. Other estimates ... run as high as 200,000 [the *Dawn*, 13 October 1948] and by some of the Muslims themselves still higher. The lowest estimates, even those offered privately by apologists of the military government, come to at least ten times the number of murders with which previously the Razakars were officially accused.[6]

Responsibility for the massacres and the accompanying terror is not easy to fix. The behaviour of invading troops is seldom pretty; and in this instance the military personnel were emotionally involved in the communalism .... In some instances it was charged that the invading army looked on while civilian reprisals took place .... The damage seems to have been done in the crucial days that elapsed between the invasion and the setting-up of martial law. In some areas it was a matter of two or three days; in more outlying parts, control was re-effected only after a considerable period ... in this interval the populace widely rose against the local Muslim petty officials, against individual Muslims who had been browbeating them, or just against Muslims as Muslims, and wreaked agonising vengeance. In some areas, all the men were stood in a line and done to death. Of the total Muslim community in Hyderabad, it would seem that somewhere between one in five of the adult males may have lost their lives in those few days. In addition to killing, there was widespread rape, arson, looting, and expropriation. A very large percentage of the entire Muslim population of the districts fled in destitution to the capital or other cities (Smith 1950, pp. 64–67).

According to Sundarayya,

the ordinary Muslim people ... were pounced upon and untold miseries were inflicted on them. The Hindu people ... rescued such ordinary Muslims to the extent possible, gave shelter to them in their houses and rescued thousands of Muslim families from the campaign of rape and murder indulged in by the Union armies (1972, p. 189).

Thus, the first local consequence of police action, far from being the genocide of Hindus by Razakars, which was feared in some Indian quarters (Munshi 1957, p. 233) was the total upheaval in the fortunes of Muslims, entailing not only a loss of livelihood and status but often of life, honour and property.

Meanwhile, it was announced that the Nizam's regime would be 'liberalised' and that an interim government, 'consisting of representatives of public opinion', would be installed 'as soon as possible'. At the same time, the preparation of electoral rolls on the basis of adult franchise would proceed at top speed to allow the election of a Constituent Assembly by the middle of 1949. Because Swami Ramanand Tirtha had declared upon his release from jail that the future of the State would be decided 'by the free will of the people in a plebiscite',[7] it was also believed that the military government (and the flow of outsiders which had followed it) would not remain in the State for too long.

In immediate terms, a thorough reshuffle of the entire administrative machinery in the State was undertaken. A great number of government employees—both Hindus and Muslims, but mainly Muslims— were summarily dismissed or retired and replaced exclusively by Indian Union personnel. On 20 September 1948, D.S. Bakhle and D.R. Pardhan, formerly of the Bombay Government, were respectively appointed Chief and Additional Chief Civil Administrators, A. V. Patro from the Madras Police was made Inspector-General of Police, and the *Dawn* and *The Times* (London) of 20 September 1948 both reported that all the Collectors of the sixteen districts of the State were to be replaced by nominees of the Indian Union government.

These changes were at first generally looked upon as the necessary evils of a transitional period. It was expected that a new government would soon replace military rule and that a plebiscite would be held to ascertain the popular will in regard to the State's future.

As weeks went by, however, it appeared that these expectations were quite off the mark. No interim government could be introduced, the Indian Union now claimed, because of ongoing disturbed conditions in Telengana where Communists were still fighting and because pockets of Razakars' resistance were reported to exist. In these conditions, it was decided, the military government would gradually hand over charge of the pacified areas to an Indian Governor (civil) rather than to a locally recruited interim government. There would, therefore, be no interim government before the general elections of a Constituent Assembly, and it was also made clear that any talk of a plebiscite on the question of accession was now ruled out as 'superfluous'.[8]

This cavalier treatment of democratic procedure and the blatant exclusion of local elements from employment in the new administration soon provoked the dissastifaction of Hyderabadi Hindus. Far from opening new opportunities, the worst characteristics of an exploitative regime imposed from outside were becoming evident. Reporting the Hindu discontent to Patel, a Hyderabadi Congressman pointed out that the argument that the State did not possess sufficiently qualified personnel 'used to be put forward by the Britisher before the Indian' and claimed, 'Hyderabad may not have many or all A-1s but surely Hyderabad can at once produce sufficient B-1s to soberly discharge these responsibilities—at most with some assistance here and there from India' (D. Das (ed.) 1973, p. 295).

He also warned that

> unless the local element is included adequately in the administration, whatever the administrative set-up, it is least likely to command the ... confidence and co-operation of Hyderabadis in general (*ibid.*).

But this warning was not heeded and, as time went by increasing numbers of Hindus in the State began openly to voice their dissatisfaction with the Indian treatment of Hyderabad (see Appendix 11 and Tirtha 1967, p. 231). But this was of no avail; despite its knowledge of local discontent, the Government of India showed no intention of loosening its grip over Hyderabad and absolute domination continued in effect until 1952.

As has been seen, the official reason—and, no doubt, there was some truth in it—was that the Indian Union could find no locally adequate substitutes for the vast number of officials of the previous regime who had hastily and indiscriminately been dismissed; administrators in Hyderabad State had generally been Muslims and not many local Hindus had been trained to shoulder administrative responsibilities. In these conditions, the handing over of the State's administration to those insufficiently qualified Hindus—merely because they were Hindus—was not justifiable. The Indian Union Government, therefore, preferred to carry the burden on its own, even if it could ill afford to do so at the time (D. Das (ed.) 1973, pp. 321–23).

However, this argument still did not explain why even Hindus were not employed—although the States Department fully knew of the poor quality of its own staff. Clearly, another and more important reason was at play. Indeed, it appears in hindsight that the Indian Union was reluctant to devolve any measure of authority to persons whose allegiance to its government and policies had not been established beyond doubt. State Congressmen would have been the natural candidates had their party been unified and conservative. But the HSC was, in fact, even more divided than before the police action (D. Das (ed.) 1973, pp. 283–96 and pp. 320–67). Its leader was the radical Swami Ramanand Tirtha who had reasserted his position over the party by expelling, shortly after his release from jail, hundreds of members of the (conservative) B. Ramakrisha Rao faction (Munshi 1957, p. 247). It will be recalled that Patel had shown no sympathy towards the radical faction of the HSC because of their Socialist connections, some even said pro-Communist bias (Tirtha 1967, p. 227), and he had certainly no intention of handing power over to them, particularly as the Communists were still active in Telengana.[9] Patel also feared perhaps that radical Congressmen and Communists would be in agreement on many aspects of the State's future: land reforms and the removal of the Nizam; and the division of Hyderabad into separate linguistic units and a merger of these units with re-organised co-linguistic provinces of India.

The question of a reorganisation of India along linguistic lines—the principle of which the INC had long endorsed[10] had been examined from November 1947 by the Linguistic Provinces Commission (the so-called Dhar Commission). However, its recommendations, presented to the Constituent Assembly in December 1948, were unfavourable. The Dhar Commission had 'strongly disapproved of the formation of States on a linguistic basis and warned that the unity of newly independent India would be jeopardised if the map of India were redrawn with linguistic affinity as the deciding factor' (Arora 1956, p. 27; see also Windmiller 1954 and 1956).

This conclusion was reiterated in the findings of another commission, the Linguistic Provinces Committee, set up in December 1948 in response to the widespread political opposition which had followed the publication of the Dhar Commission Report. As such, from mid 1949 onwards, although some concessions had been made to the principle of a separate Andhra State (Bondurant 1958, pp. 29–32), the INC was not prepared to countenance any further talks on the question.

As regards Hyderabad, therefore, Nehru and Patel opposed Tirtha's approach and favoured instead those conservative Congress leaders in the State who were prepared to wait and abide by the INC's decisions. However, as these conservative leaders were discredited in the State because they had not forcefully participated in the anti-Nizam movement, they could not be handed responsibility until they had regained some popularity. Thus, while 'efforts were made to put the progressive section led by Swami Ramanand Tirtha into the background and bring the liberal elements to the foreground in the State Congress' (C. R. Rao 1972, p. 20), the Indian Union continued to impose its official machinery over Hyderabad. General Chaudhuri's term as Military Governor ended in December 1949. He was replaced by M. K. Vellodi, ICS, Secretary of the Indian States Ministry who became Hyderabad's Chief Minister and retained the position until the general elections of 1952.[11] By then, Tirtha had been marginalised, and it was B. Ramakrishna Rao who succeeded Vellodi as Chief Minister until 1956, when the State was finally trifurcated and merged with adjoining linguistic regions (see K. V. Narayana Rao 1973, P. R. Rao 1978, and G. R. S. Rao 1975 for developments after 1956).

It is ironical that though the INC wished to postpone the reorganisation of India on a linguistic basis[12] and that Nehru himself opposed the idea of dismembering Hyderabad (Arora 1956, p. 28; Tirtha 1967, p. 232), the Government of India's treatment of Hyderabad served greatly to destroy the State's traditional cultural identity. Thus, it was easy for disintegrationist forces to take root.

According to Windmiller (1954, p. 305), 'Hyderabad [was] ... the keystone to the entire linguistic states movement in South India, for, the formation of united Maharashtra and united Karanataka as well as Vishalandhra depend[ed] upon its disintegration'.

The 'importation' of Indian officials—mainly from Andhra and Maharashtra—was reported in 1949 to be 'creating blocs in the services'.[13] In the absence of a strong unifying influence from within, this led in effect to the division of the State's population into factions owing their allegiance increasingly to the linguistic principle.

Maharashtra, Karnataka and Andhra Pradesh were eventually created; but whereas the Marathi and the Kannada speakers of the State accepted without demur the amalgamation of their respective regions with the co-linguistic areas of India, those speaking Telugu only consented to the merger of Telengana with Andhra after a 'Gentlemen's Agreement' outlining their guarantees in the new set-up was formulated. Was it, as has been said, that the people of Marathwara felt united with the Marathas of the adjoining Bombay district because of the pervading influence of the Arya Samaj and the Shivaji tradition? Had the people of Telengana no such common ground with their co-linguistic neighbours of the former Madras province and, indeed, did they fear that the 'well-placed coastal Andhras' would 'dominate them in every sphere'?[14]

In 1952, these fears of socioeconomic exploitation led to a mulki–non-mulki agitation and to the raising of the slogan 'Hyderabad for Hyderabadis', which was directed mainly against the Andhras who had infilterated into Hyderabad's administration. This agitation did not abate with the formation of a united Telugu-speaking State in 1956, nor with the passing of time, as is evidenced by the two bloody crises which rocked Andhra Pradesh in 1969 and 1972 (see Appendix 12).

In 1971, a participant wrote,

> It is indeed a tragedy for the Telugu People that, after 16 years of co-existence, emotional integration could not be achieved and both the regions [Andhra and Telengana] are now dead earnest to disintegrate the State (Venkat Rao 1973, p. v).

This tragedy cannot but be seen as one of the long-term outcomes of the disintegration of Hyderabad State.

Nizam Osman Ali died on 24 February 1967.

A contemporary reported:

> I have never seen such a vast crowd anywhere on any occasion and it was so touching after 10 years to hear 'Shah Osman Zindabad' .... People came from all the towns and villages of the old Hyderabad State and waited all night for the procession. Many wept, especially all the scheduled castes.[15]

NOTES

1. Five Indian army battalions had taken part in 'Operation Polo', including armour and air force. New Delhi later released the following figures of casualties: Razakars: 1,373 killed, 42 wounded, 1,911 captured; Hyderabad State's Army: 807 killed, 64 wounded, 1,647 captured; Communists, Pathans, Arabs and Rohillas: 43 killed, 4 wounded, 267 captured. No figure of Indian losses other than "10 killed" was given. (*Keesing's Contemporary Archives*, vol. VI, 1946–1948, p. 9606.)
2. Razvi was later condemned to seven years imprisonment at the end of which he went to Pakistan. Laik Ali escaped on 6 March 1949 and fled to Pakistan (D. Das (ed.) 1973, pp. 356–59; Laik Ali 1962).
3. This was perhaps due to the Nizam's 'voluntary surrender' and compliance which had been engineered by K.M. Munshi, earning the latter much criticism and disfavour in Indian political circles (see Munshi 1957, pp. 232–33).

4. *Keesing's Contemporary Archives, op. cit.*, p. 9606.
5. *ibid.*, pp. 9522 and 6. For information regarding the presentation of Hyderabad's case at the UNO Security Council see *United Nations Security Council Official Records*, 357th meeting, Document Nos. S/1000, S/1015, S/1029, S/1031; (see also Das (ed.) 1973, pp. 317 and 319.)
6. This is echoed in Mirza's account (1976, p. 38) 'All kinds of atrocities had ... been perpetuated [*sic*] on Hindus by the so-called Razakars. But no doubt what was done after police action was much more than what had been done before'.
7. *The Times* (London) 20 and 21 September 1948. Tirtha does not acknowledge this in his *Memoirs* (1967).
8. In fact, the Razakars had surrendered their arms to the Communists in several districts of Telengana (see *The Times* (London) 14 October 1948; Sundarayya 1972, p. 187).
9. The Communists resisted the Indian Union, arms in hand, until the end of 1951 (C. R. Rao, 1972).
10. For a genesis of the Indian National Congress' stand on the question of linguistic provinces, see the *Report of the States Reorganisation Commission.*
11. Mr Vellodi was assisted by seven ministers, four of whom were non-officials nomi-nated by the Hyderabad State Congress. All of them were conservatives (Tirtha 1967, p. 229).
12. A 'National Unity Party' dedicated to postponing the linguistic reorganisation of India for 25 years was created in Bombay in 1952 ostensibly with Nehru's endorsement (see Windmiller 1954, p. 310).
13. For an outline of the fears of the Telengana people see *The Telengana Movement: An Investigative Focus* (Papers presented at the Telengana University and College Teachers' Convention, 20 May 1969, Hyderabad; published by Anand Rao Thota, Hyderabad, July 1969); see also Venkat Rao P., *et al*, 1973, Part II, pp. iv–vii.
14. See *The Telengana Movement: An Investigative Focus,* p. 10.
15. IOL, Mss. Eur. D 798/21. Begum Hussan Yar Jung to Tasker, 10 March 1967; about half a million people attended the funeral procession, *The Times* (London), 27 February 1967.

9

Conclusion

Two major periods can be distinguished between 1938 and 1948 in the history of political developments in Hyderabad State: the first, between 1938 and 1946, when there was internal conflict (revolving around demands for, and resistance to, constitutional reforms) between a section of the State's population and forces supporting the prevailing regime; the second, between 1946 and 1948, when these forces entered into additional confrontation with the Government of India on the question of the State's future.

In subsequent writings, particularly those of Indian nationalist historians, these two periods are generally presented as a continuum. The intervention of the Indian army in 1948 is seen as the final episode in the struggle which Hyderabad's 'freedom fighters' waged against the Nizam's autocratic regime for at least a decade.

In hindsight, the impression emerges, however, that this correlation between the two periods is not so obvious. One feels, indeed, that the earlier political developments in Hyderabad State had become practically irrelevant in the post-War political atmosphere of India. By 1946, the Government of India was intent on obtaining the quick accession of all the princes whose territories lay within the new borders and on establishing the bases of a politically homogeneous India under (Congress) centralised control.

In this context, the wishes of the people of the State—in Hyderabad or elsewhere—had become secondary and it is probable that, regardless of their nature, the Government of India would have acted in no different a manner in the end.

The object here is not to conclude whether the Government of India was justified in acting as it did in Hyderabad. To ask whether police action was really motivated by a breakdown of law and order in the State or dictated by considerations of India's national interests are questions of little historical interest, so long after the irreversible fait accompli. However, because India's action in 1948 influenced the course of later regional politics, it is important to ask whether imposed accession corresponded effectively with the political aspirations of the Hyderabadis. It is known that the 'extremists' in the Hyderabad State Congress agreed with it and that the 'moderates' appeared ambivalent on the issue until the end, but what of Hyderabad's population at large? As no plebiscite took place after police action, it is difficult to make any statement with certainty. Politically, the majority—agrarian, rural and illiterate—of the population had remained unmoved by the appeals of State Congress leaders, whatever their leanings, and by the importation of Indian National Congress ideals from outside.

The 1938–39 satyagraha served to highlight this. It demonstrated that political propaganda conducted in urban centres was insufficient to rally the countryside to the fray. To an extent, the comparatively greater success of the Arya Samaj and the Hindu Mahasabha at this juncture showed that communalism acted more powerfully on the rural masses than mere political arguments. However, the influence of communalism waned considerably in the rural areas when satyagraha was discontinued and jathas from British India no longer entered Hyderabad. Nevertheless, communalism left an indelible imprint on State politics, both Hindu and Muslim. It was aggravated, as in the rest of India, by the demand for Pakistan in 1940, and remained latent in most aspects of the State's politics until the end.

As for the HSC, its unsuccessful attempts in 1942 to introduce the 'Quit India' agitation into Hyderabad and in 1947–48 to rouse the masses into rebellion against the Nizam's stand in the conflict with India demonstrated the utter political weakness of the organisation.

The main reason for this weakness was chiefly that (as outlined above) that the political platform of the urban, highly-educated and wealthy Hindus (who had taken the early lead in the Direct Conferences and then of the State Congress movement), elicited little response from the illiterate mass of rural Hindu population. Even the latent communal bias in the Congress platform which sought to present the Muslims as the privileged elite—which they were to an extent in urban areas—lost its impact in the countryside where the majority of rural Muslims were as poor and uneducated as their Hindu counterparts. Influence in the district areas rested not with Muslims as such but with large landlords and moneylenders who were rarely, if ever, attacked on the early Congress platform. In fact, most 'moderate' Congress leaders were landlords. It is significant that the only notably successful mass movement in Hyderabad was that launched by the Communists against landlordism and caste or class privilege in Telengana from 1940 onwards.

As is evident, the HSC did not draw support at the grassroots. Its second wave of leaders, the 'extremists' represented by Swami Ramanand Tirtha and his followers, attempted in the 1940s to reverse the trend by modifying the image of the party. Turning to the 'constructive programme' advocated by Gandhi and showing readiness for 'direct action' against the Nizam's regime, this new leadership attracted some membership from among the youth of the State, mainly students and teachers. But, again, the response from the countryside was poor. Admittedly, Telengana was by then firmly under Communist control and the HSC could not be expected to make great strides there. But, even in Marathwara–Karnataka and Hyderabad city, the party never gained much lasting strength, plagued as it was by internal dissensions. Tirtha's influence was opposed by the older generation of Congress leaders who looked with suspicion or antagonism at his steadfast allegiance to Gandhism and INC guidelines. It is extremely significant that when (in June 1947) Tirtha, President of the State Congress at the time, advocated agitation in favour of the accession of Hyderabad to the India Union, he received no help from these 'moderate' leaders. He was forced, as a result, to seek a 'United Front' with the Socialists and the Communists.

At that stage, it had become clear that the 'moderate' faction of the Congress favoured the introduction of responsible government as a means to winning a greater share in the administration for the local (Hindu) community which they claimed to represent. The 'extremists', on the other hand, subscribed broadly to the same political ideals but in the context of an eventual integration of the State with the Indian Union. These differences persisted because of basic differences in the class interests and economic aims of the respective leaderships: on the one hand, the 'moderates', well-established, well-educated Hindus who saw themselves as the natural heirs to the authority of a defeated Nizam's regime, and intended merely to replace the Muslim elite with elements from their own group; on the other, the 'extremists', less affluent, less educated Hindus who, like Tirtha, hoped to abolish class privileges and avail all the greater opportunities expected with Hyderabad's accession to democratic India.

Throughout the 1930s and 40s, popular acceptance of the prevailing political regime had remained high. Whatever the cause—sheer apathy, traditional self-effacement, or genuine contentment—the supporters of the Nizam's rule claimed that this was an indication of the insignificant degree of political dissatisfaction in Hyderabad. However, it could be argued that Nizam Osman Ali had throughout merely benefited from the reserves of communal goodwill which had accumulated in Hyderabad through centuries of peaceful Hindu–Muslim relations.

In contrast to British India, inter-communal relations in the State had not been affected at the popular level by the super-imposition of a third party—the British—or by the competition for concession or favour and the virulent caste antagonism which had followed. On the contrary, Muslims and Hindus had interacted directly with one another under the patronage of successive Nizams; loyalty to the Asaf Jahi dynasty, religious toleration, and a tacit understanding on employment and State resources had all evolved as a result.

To be sure, in economic terms, it was a capitalist system which gave the rich little cause, and the poor little scope, for complaint; but it was in that way not very different from that of British India or, indeed, from that of many parts of the world at the time.

Thus, the majority of Hyderabad's population—impoverished, illiterate and agrarian—lived under conditions similar to those of poor peasants throughout India. And, like them, they were often too ignorant and pathetically respectful of social, economic and religious traditions to protest. Unlike them, however, they remained impervious to Congress influence both because the State Congress movement remained on the whole as a distant urban phenomenon and because Congress leaders, in the initial period in particular, made little effort to translate political themes into concepts intelligible to them or to spread notions of rebellion against the established order among poor ryots. Some of Hyderabad's peasants proved, as in Telengana, that they could be spurred into political agitation on issues with which they could identify; but, aside from this section of the peasantry under Communist influence and of elements of the (scant) middle and lower classes under 'extremist' Congress influence, the majority of the population abstained from political activity and continued to live as peacefully as circumstances permitted. It is remarkable, for instance, that at the worst of communal massacres following the partition of India in 1947, and even though Muslim extremism was by then at its height in the State, Hyderabad remained unaffected. Some disturbances on what was by now communal grounds, occurred in border areas where the Congress–Socialist–Communist agitation was taking place. But they were few, and the population at large did not participate; in fact, many instances were reported of neighbours helping one another, regardless of community.

As for the wealthy classes—professionals, landowners, traders (whether Muslims or Hindus)—Hyderabad's economic and social system gave them various advantages, some of them unknown to their counterparts in British India: no income tax, a generally buoyant economy, an almost static social order which made it difficult for the lower classes to rise and challenge their position, secure commercial and professional contacts within the State, as well as a rule of law generally more flexible than in British-controlled India. As a result, the Congress stand against the Nizam's regime placed the rich Hindu classes in a dilemma, particularly after 1946. They favoured the reforms demanded by Congress, as these would have ultimately given them the upper hand over Muslims at the local level. At the same time, however, they were not eager to relinquish their economic advantages and the direction of State affairs to outsiders, as was likely to happen if Hyderabad acceded to India. This is, perhaps, why many 'moderate' members of Congress remained openly or secretly in favour of a compromise with the existing regime.

But, if such were the feelings of the upper and lower classes of the population, one wonders why there was so little popular resistance to the intervention of the Indian army in 1948. More to the point, why did the regime not capitalise on these favourable elements within the State to gather support and boost itself to a position of strength which would have rendered the Government of India's stand on accession more difficult?

Part of the answer could be related to the personality and idiosyncracies of the Nizam himself. In a princely set-up such as Hyderabad's, much depended on the Ruler and his prerogatives. The Nizam could veto any decision taken by any official in the State, impose new policies on his Executive Council, or override existing ones with firmans.

Excepting the British Resident who was more of a watchdog than an adviser, there were, in internal affairs, no moderating influences over the Nizam. The Ruler, therefore, tended to use his own counsel which was often guided by no more than fickle personal likes and dislikes and the mood of the moment. Had the Nizam been a man of progressive outlook, events in the State could probably have taken a different turn. But Nizam Osman Ali Khan, although a shrewd politician, was essentially a Ruler of the old school, jealous of ancestral prerogatives and imbued with the importance of his position. Access to him was difficult, not only because of courtly etiquette but also because, a man of frugal—some say, miserly—habits, he lived practically as a recluse in his palace. He kept himself well apprised of the minutest details of State affairs, nevertheless, and manipulated all kinds of intrigues from a distance, in a way reminiscent of bygone Mughal emperors. Unfortunately for him and his regime, however, he did not have much contact with the masses. He applied himself to his task as head of State with an almost obsessive notion that his role was to control political leaders and officials rather than to consult public opinion. In brief, his approach was altogether ill-adapted to the troubled political era of the 1930s and 40s in India which demanded vision and flexibility, particularly from the princely houses.

But despite the Nizam's idiosyncracies, his regime could have retained broad popularity with the masses had the Ruler's political behaviour not departed from the communal impartiality which had been the traditional stand of his ancestors.

In times of crisis, as in 1938–39 when communal politics made their entry into Hyderabad (and time and again after this), the Nizam appealed to communal harmony and repeated the old Hyderabadi maxim that 'Muslims and Hindus were the two eyes of the nation'; but it was very apparent that he was quite openly sympathetic to the Ittihad-ul-Muslimeen.

In the early stages (1938–39), when the Ittihad had just turned to politics with the obvious consent of the Nizam, his supporters could argue that he had merely allowed an avenue of expression to Muslim political feelings—while the Hindus themselves were engaged in agitation—but that the State Government still remained above party politics. Even the close relations between the Nizam and Bahadur Yar Jung up to 1944, could be defended as indicating that some official control was being exercised over the Muslim party in the interests of communal peace. Significantly, numerous 'unity talks' took place in the period between moderate Hindu and Muslim leaders; in fact, goodwill between political leaders seems to have survived to the end of 1945 and Abul Hasan Syed Ali's last attempts at compromise.

By 1946, however, the change in the Ittihad from moderate to extremist leadership seriously affected internal matters. A firm stand by the Nizam at that stage would have been welcomed in moderate quarters, particularly as events in British India heralded Indian independence and called for a sober and realist appraisal in all princely States.

But the personal relations between the Nizam and the Ittihad had, in the meantime, changed considerably. Since Bahadur Yar Jung's death in 1944, they were in fact quite strained; by the time the extremists seized power within the Ittihad, they had become frankly ungracious and the former deference shown by Muslim leaders to the Nizam had all but disappeared. Ittihad extremists, opposed to any concessions to Hindus within or without, resented the cautious stand adopted by the Nizam. They demanded that he should side more forcefully with their political interests and defend the 'Muslim status' of Hyderabad at the all-India level. But, by then, many worries weighed on the Nizam's mind. In 1945–46, he had been profoundly distressed by the unsympathetic attitude of the British towards him, their old 'Faithfully Ally', and by their unwillingness to help Hyderabad obtain special consideration in the plans concerning the future of the subcontinent. By June 1947, India was partitioned along communal lines, accession was imperiously demanded by the new government at New Delhi, and the Nizam, it appeared, finally lost his head. He let his fear of a Hindu India, obviously ill-disposed towards his regime, govern his better judgment and opened himself to the argument of Ittihad extremists that Hyderabadi Hindus would now certainly follow the change in the country's political wind; only the Muslims who stood for 'Azad Hyderabad' could be relied on to remain loyal.

The developments of October–November 1947, in which the Nizam could be suspected of having connived with the Ittihad to replace Hyderabad's respected delegation to New Delhi with less competent Muslims, and which resulted in the resignation of the moderate Nawab of Chhatari, did much to fuel disharmony. Indeed, these developments not only destroyed the credibility of the State Government, they also made a mockery of all the Nizam's previous claims of communal impartiality. He was now considered, inside and outside Hyderabad, at best to have been overpowered by the State's most extreme Muslim lobby and, at worst, to be actually in accord with them for communal or perhaps selfish motives. In any case, it was now impossible to refute convincingly the charges of governmental bias against Hindus which had long been publicised by Congressmen and the press throughout India.

Within the State, so far, the most potentially dangerous opposition to the regime had emerged from the extremist Congress faction, a body which had the support of neither the moderate and influential urban Hindus nor that of the rural masses. Now, however, even the moderate Hindus (as also the moderate Muslims, to be sure) who had long subscribed to the mulki feeling and to the notion of a 'Hyderabad for Hyderabadis, regardless of community' were alienated. In the countryside, the Razakars and their uncontrolled depredations—even if often petty and insignificant—confirmed the rumours (derived mainly from all-India journalistic exaggeration) that the rule of Muslim goondas had altogether replaced official authority. As already said, it is remarkable that, in the Indian context of communal massacres at the time, this did not lead to widespread rioting or retaliation against rural Muslims. There is no doubt, however, that it alarmed the rural folk and shook their implicit faith in the Nizam's regime.

Thus, at one fell swoop, through lack of moral fibre or actual duplicity, the Nizam had destroyed the prestige of his position and the credibility of his communal impartiality which were his very best assets in the State.

It could be said, therefore, that October and November 1947 were crucial moments in the history of the last years of Hyderabad State. In these months the Nizam committed a monumental political blunder which finally alienated most of the population. In the final analysis, it seems that the Nizam merely intended to use the Muslim extremists as an instrument for political bargaining rather than as a serious threat in the negotiations with the Government of India. But, whatever the motive, it was an ill-advised move which, forceful itself, called for force as an answer, at a time when all that remained in the State to oppose the Indian army was the hollow bombast of some isolated Muslims.

Having said this, it is most probable that, no matter how much popular support the Nizam's regime could still command in 1947–48, the Government of India would not have compromised its stand on the accession of Hyderabad. Because of this, the Nizam's political blunder in siding with Muslim extremists loses much of its importance. It even has the redeeming feature of having spared greater shedding of blood at the time of police action as it had discredited the regime and thus did not need sacrifice to defend it.

But, if it is easy to understand that it was fear—justified, as events proved—which drove the Muslim extremists and the Nizam to their desperate political posture of 1947, it is not as easy to understand the reasons which prompted the Government of India's dictatorial attitude towards princely States. After the departure of the British, India was in an overwhelmingly superior bargaining position, and the speed with which most accessions were obtained indicates that princes in general were well aware of it. By the end of 1947, Hyderabad remained the last princely State still outside the Indian Union. But what was the compulsion for the Government of India to press for immediate accession? Hyderabad could well have been allowed to survive as long as it could in the vastly different atmosphere of independent India. Sooner than later it is certain that the Nizam's Government would have found it impossible to continue resisting internal pressure for democratic reforms, and integration would have been only a matter of time.

The last agreement drafted between the State and the Indian Government shows, indeed, that by June 1948 the Nizam had reconciled himself to the inevitability of a gradual introduction of responsible government in Hyderabad. Why, then, was India so intent on obtaining a quick satisfaction of its demands on Hyderabad, even if it meant wrenching it by force? The *White Paper on Indian States* (p. 45) asserts that 'highly practical reasons ... rendered a real organic unification of India imperative'. But it is important to note that, of the reasons invoked—'geography', 'all-compelling defence and internal security requirements', 'basic economic needs of the country'—none takes account of the people's wishes, an argument hitherto exploited *ad nauseam* in Congress propaganda.

It would seem, therefore, that the Government of India's primary concern—to bring about a united and centrally-controlled India—absolutely overrode all other arguments, particularly in the context of developments in Kashmir. From the Indian National Congress point of view, the integration of the princely States was necessarily the next step in the implementation of Indian independence. If the people of the princely States were in agreement, all was well and good; if not, however, no alternative was envisaged and, whatever the means, their 'agreement' had to be obtained. Apologists for India, no doubt, will argue that the end—the substitution of democratic rule for the former princely autocracies—justified all means, even dubious, of obtaining it.

Various regional lobbies now began to expect that the linguistic reorganisation of India, which had figured prominently on the INC agenda since 1920, would be implemented. By 1948, however, according to the Linguistic Provinces Commission (or JVP Committee) Report, the INC had changed its stand and now confessed that

> when the Congress had given the seal of its approval to the general principle of linguistic provinces, it was not faced with the practical application of the principle and hence it had not considered all the implications and consequences that arose from this practical application (p. 2).

It was feared that, if the new Union were reorganised along linguistic (and ethnic) lines, 'fissiparous tendencies' might emerge and gradually encourage regional rather than national loyalties.

However, Telugu speakers in the coastal districts of Madras began agitating for an 'Andhra for the Telugus'. In October 1953, the Government of India was compelled by serious disturbances in south India to form an Andhra State occupying the northeast position of the former Madras province. The process could not be stopped after this precedent, and talks of an overall reorganisation of India along linguistic lines began in earnest.

In this scheme, Hyderabad State occupied a central position as it encompassed three regions—Marathwara, Karnataka and Telengana. A considerable body of opinion in Hyderabad was opposed to a dismemberment of the State on the grounds that its three linguistic areas had been integrated since the times of the Bahmanis, six centuries previously, and that the State had developed its own composite culture distinct from adjoining regions. Nehru himself was sympathetic to this appeal, but even he proved unable to resist the pressure of the advocates of trifurcation. Hyderabad State was thus split into three (with the States Reorganisation Bill of 1956) and each area respectively amalgamated with the linguistically-adjoining region of India.

Appendix 1

Average of areas under crops 1936–40
(Total area of Hyderabad State: 82,698 sq miles or 52,926,720 acres)

Crops	*'000 acres*	*Percentage of gross area sown*
FOOD CROPS		
Jowar	9237	32.67
Cereals and pulses	2846	10.00
Bajra	2040	7.20
Wheat	1276	4.50
Gram	1193	4.30
Rice	1043	3.80
Other food crops	402	2.60
Maize	645	2.28
Fruits and vegetables	615	2.17
Ragi	135	0.51
Sugarcane	45	0.16
Barley	16	0.06
Total	19493	70.25
NON-FOOD CROPS		
Linseed	447	1.72
Sesamum	541	1.92
Rape and mustard	14	0.05
Groundnut	1426	5.08
Castor	729	2.73
Other oilseeds	596	2.33
Cotton	3555	12.40
Sunn	59	0.21
Other fibres	43	0.15
Indigo	1	–
Tobacco	72	0.26
Fodder crops	736	2.60
Condiments and spices	522	1.80
Other non-food crops	409	0.13
Total	9150	31.38

Source: from Tables XXI and XXII, Qureshi 1947, pp. 40 and 42

Appendix 2

Facts and Figures about Hyderabad State

The Hyderabad State

Area and population

IS 82,698 square miles or 52,926,720 acres, is more than the area of England and Scotland put together, is the biggest State in India and the area exceeds the Provinces of Bengal before partition (77,422 square miles) and Bombay (76,443 square miles).

HAS a population of 16,338,534 as per 1941 census.

Cultivation and Irrigation: Live-stock and Forests

HAS 25,032,000 acres under cultivation including paddy (1,419,000), wheat (485,000), jowar (7,555,000), groundnut (2,936,000) and cotton (2,156,000).

HAS 1,794,000 acres under irrigation.

HAS 8,000 major and 25,000 minor tanks.

HAS 6,000 miles of channels including distributaries.

HAS 87 lakh of cattle.

HAS a total area of 9,466 sq miles of forests (i.e. 11.4%).

HAS 1,236,544 lakh of cattle grazing in government forests.

HAS nearly 7,100 acres under afforestation, 1,000 families engaged in afforesting waste belts of Marathwada Districts.

Industries: Large-scale

HAS 639 large industrial establishments employing on an average 75,165 persons.

HAS 6 cotton mills producing 168 lakh lb of cotton and 21,924,336 lb of yarn.

HAS an annual production of 10,95,831 tons of coal.

HAS a production of 16,372 tons of paper.

HAS a production of 150,070 tons of cement.

HAS a production of 3,22,060 gallons of power alcohol.

HAS a production of 14, 221 tons of glass.

HAS a production of 3,447,251,000 cigarettes.

HAS mica mines producing 95 cwt of finished mica and graphite mines yielding about 35 tons of crude graphite annually.

HAS a production of 39,926,161 units of electric power.

HAS electricity supplied to 10 cities and towns and 17,298 consumers of power and lighting.

HAS 209 Joint-stock Companies with authorised capital of O.S. Rs 406 million, issued capital of O.S. Rs 197 million and paid-up capital of O.S. Rs 104 million.

Industries: Small-scale and Cottage

HAS Cottage Industries of Yarn Spinning, Cloth Weaving, Paithan Industry of Gold Embroidery, Aurangabad Himru, Mashru, and Kamkhab, Blanket Making, Nawar Making, Cloth Dyeing and Printing, Silk Weaving, Wool Carpet, and Durry Making, Bidriware, Silver Filigree Work, Nirmal Toys Works, Hand-made Paper, Metal Industry, Tanning, Sword Stick, Button Industry, Toy

Making, Beedi Making, Soap Making, Cane Work, Brush Work, Mat Making, Tusser Work, Clay Works, Brass Industry, Brick and Tile Making, Carpentry, Smithy, Rattan Work, Biscuit Making, Fruit and Vegetable Processing, Furniture Works, Bangle Making, Masalah (Perfumery), Hosiery.

Trade

HAS an ascertained valued of rail-borne goods amounting to Rs 68 crore or 86 per cent of the total trade, while the value of goods passing through the Frontier was Rs 11.6 crore. The total value of imports and exports amounted to Rs 79.6 crore.

Currency

HAS the Hyderabad rupee as the standard coin equivalent to 3.2326 grams of fine gold and 25.86 U.S. cents.

HAS about Rs 600,000,000 (including notes and subsidiary coins) in circulation.

HAS begun the formation of the Reserve Bank of Hyderabad.

Government Finance

HAS an annual revenue of about Rs 250,000,000.

HAS about Rs 1,100,000,000 in different Reserves.

Communications

HAS 1,704 Hyderabad Post Offices (16 Head-Offices, 359 Sub-Offices and 1,329 Branch Offices) and 16 Indian Union Post Offices, 15 Indian Union Combined Post and Telegraph Offices, 127 Indian Union Postboxes in post offices and outside and
1 Indian Departmental Telegraph Office.

HAS 1,734 Telephone installations excluding extensions.

HAS its own Broadcasting Stations at Hyderabad City and Aurangabad City.

HAS 4,106 Radio licensees.

Transport

HAS a total length of 6,191 miles of roads including 1,560 miles of metalled roads.

HAS 1,607 miles of railways as follows:-

i. 1,172 miles within the State owned and worked by H.E.H. the Nizam's Government.
ii. 30 miles outside the State owned and worked by H.E.H. the Nizam's Government.
iii. 36 miles within the State owned by H.E.H. the Nizam's Government and worked by the Barsi Light Railway Company.
iv. 58 miles outside the State owned by the Government of India and worked by H.E.H. the Nizam's State Railway.
v. 211 miles within the State owned and worked by Foreign Railways.

HAS an import railway trade of 443,117 tons and an export trade of 1,020,036 tons.

Note: *This excludes the traffic imported and exported to and from stations on the foreign railways lying within the State and also all through traffic passing over the Nizam's State Railway System.*

HAS one Co-operative Credit Society serving the staff of the Railway and allied services with 10,835 members and Rs 1,70,350 as paid-up capital.
HAS one General Hospital with 116 beds and 9 dispensaries in the districts to cater for the staff of the Railway and allied services.
HAS 11 primary and 2 middle schools to provide for educational facilities to the children of employees of Railway and allied services.
HAS 4,597 route miles of the Road Transport Services.
HAS a Company named Deccan Airways Limited with an air mileage of 1,858.
HAS an aero club entirely subsidised by Government for training pupils.
HAS 9 aerodromes in the State.

Social Services
HAS 225 medical institutions, with 3,008 beds available.
HAS 17,627 Co-operative Societies with 1,341,079 members and Rs 1,81,62,090 as paid-up share capital.
HAS 8,389 educational institutions, with 18 Colleges, with 111 High Schools, 189 Middle Schools, 7,677 Upper and Lower Primary Schools, and 412 Special Schools.
HAS 5,79,053 Scholars studying.

For the Tourist
HAS the Ajanta and Ellora caves famous for their paintings all over the world (with the State Railway Hotel at Aurangabad nearby).
HAS the Bhadrachallam temple of Ramdas fame.
HAS the Pakal lake which has never known drought.
HAS the Darga of Khaja Bande Nawaz of all-India fame at Gulbarga.
HAS the reputed shrine of Thulja Bhavani at Thuljapur.
HAS the Holy Gurudwara of Guru Govind at Nanded.
HAS Kishkindha (a venue of *Ramayana*) in Anegondi bordering on the river Tungabhadra.
HAS ruins of the capital of the famous Hindu King Nala at Naldrug.
HAS the great fort and other ruins of the Kakatiyas at Warangal.

Source: *The Hyderabad Government Bulletin on Economic Affairs*, December 1948

Appendix 3

A. Revenue receipts and service expenditure, 1900–1951 (in crore rupees)

Year	Receipts	Expenditure	Year	Receipts	Expenditure
1900–01	4.17	4.11	1926–27	7.58	6.71
1901–02	3.87	4.04	1927–28	8.42	7.09
1902–03	4.34	4.16	1928–29	8.92	7.64
1903–04	4.69	4.49	1929–30	8.52	8.02
1904–05	5.04	4.28	1930–31	7.62	8.30
1905–06	4.64	4.14	1931–32	7.72	8.75
1906–07	5.48	4.65	1932–33	8.06	8.55
1907–08	4.84	3.82	1933–34	7.95	8.41
1908–09	4.92	4.79	1934–35	8.53	8.43
1909–10	4.85	3.76	1935–36	9.06	8.43
1910–11	5.22	3.94	1936–37	9.43	8.99
1911–12	5.03	4.36	1937–38	9.40	9.08
1912–13	5.52	4.53	1938–39	9.15	9.14
1913–14	5.92	5.17	1939–40	9.60	9.76
1914–15	6.05	5.19	1940–41	10.89	10.38
1915–16	6.30	5.58	1941–42	10.17	10.52
1916–17	6.04	5.69	1942–43	12.34	11.02
1917–18	6.11	6.08	1943–44	16.73	12.21
1918–19	5.84	6.01	1944–45	18.18	14.04
1919–20	7.06	5.98	1945–46	20.86	16.35
1920–21	6.48	6.40	1946–47	20.72	20.17
1921–22	7.11	6.69	1947–48	20.99	34.72
1922–23	7.14	6.57	1948–49	30.11	30.54
1923–24	7.57	6.57	1949–50 (R.E.		
1924–25	7.83	6.29	for six Months)	16.34	15.26
1925–26	8.16	6.46	1950–51 (B.E.)	29.89	30.01

Source: *A Review of Hyderabad Finance*, p. 90

B. Main heads of internal income and expenditure, 1884–85 and 1935–36

MAIN HEADS	Income		Expenditure	
	1884–85 (1294 F)	*1935–36 (1345 F)*	*1884–85 (1294 F)*	*1935–35 (1345 F)*
1. Land Revenue	1,86,70	3,35,57	29,84	67,45
2. Excise & Opium	35,86	1,96,19	1,78	36,90
3. Customs	48,25	1,04,67	5,15	20,74
4. Forests	1,93	14,08	54	10,15
5. Registration	..	3,32	..	1,76
6. Stamps	4,09	20,46	85	97

continues

	Income		Expenditure	
MAIN HEADS	*1884–85*	*(1935–36)*	*1884–85*	*(1935–35)*
	(1294 F)	*(1345 F)*	*(1294 F)*	*(1345 F)*
7. Post Office	1,17	13,27	2,45	13,96
8. Railways	13,31	1,04,00	25,01	1,57
9. Law & Justice	2,40	2,34	7,49	23,65
10. Police	99	2,26	24,78	65,75
11. Military	9	23	70,36	79,66
12. Education	8	4,93	2,44	1,03,76
13. Medical	..	92	2,03	28,17
14. Administration	..	1,01	12,81	42,00
15. Public Works	..	1,06	15,85	68,21
16. Municipalities	..	5,72	3,77	20,85
17. Agriculture	..	35	..	8,06
18. Veterinary	..	11	..	4,76
19. Co-operation	..	7	..	4,22
20. Industries	..	62	..	3,88
21. Mines	..	3,95	..	39

Source: *Some Economic Facts and Figures of H.E.H. the Nizam's Dominions*, p. 42.

Appendix 4

Hindu/Muslim Population figures in percentages, 1901–1951

Year	*1901*	*1911*	*1921*	*1931*	*1941*	*1951*
Total Population	11,141,142	13,374,676	12,471,770	14,436,148	16,338,534	18,655,108
Hindus	9,870,839	11,626,146	10,656,453	12,172,845	N.A.*	16,088,905
Percentage	88.59	86.92	85.44	84.32	N.A.	86.24
Muslims	1,155,750	1,380,990	1,298,277	1,534,665	N.A.	2,206,182
Percentage	10.37	10.32	10.40	10.63	N.A.	11.82

Source: *Census of India*

* N.A. = Not Available

Appendix 5

Selective survey of the occupational profiles of the Hindu and Muslim communities in Hyderabad (1911)

(Other main communities: Jains: 21,026; Sikhs: 4,726; Christians: 54,296; Parsis: 1,529; Animistic: 289,722)

Description	*Total number of workers and dependants*	*Hindus*	*Percentage of workers*	*Percentage of community*	*Muslims*	*Percentage of workers*	*Percentage of community*
HYDERABAD STATE	13,374,676	11,626,146	86.9	100	1,380,990	10.3	100
– Pasture and agriculture (ordinary cultivation) Total	7,619,505	6,699,604	87.9	57.6	652,361	11.67	47.2
– Income from rent of agricultural land	731,803	620,618	84.8	5.3	95,822	13.1	6.9
– Ordinary cultivation	4,064,950	3,573,266	87.9	30.7	336,342	8.3	24.3
– Agents, managers of landed estates (not planters), clerks, collectors	34,540	18,445	53.4	0.15	15,599	45.1	1.12
– Farm servants, field labourers	2,788,212	2,487,275	89.2	21.3	204,398	7.3	14.8
– Raising of farm stock	597,728	590,888	98.8	5	4,507	0.07	0.32
– Mines	15,325	14,031	91.5	0.12	909	5.9	0.06
– Textiles	517,750	469,166	90.6	4	55,172	10.6	4
– Trade: Bank managers, money lenders, exchange insurance agents, brokers	22,223	18,035	81.1	0.15	3,122 14	0.22	
– Trade in textiles	81,139	67,214	82.8	0.5	11,878	14.6	0.9
– Hotel managers and owners, cookshop sarais	261	59	22.6	–	124	47.5	–

Description	Total number of workers and dependants	Hindus	Percentage of workers	Percentage of community	Muslims	Percentage of workers	Percentage of community
– Public force							
– Army	68,750	27,356	39.7	0.23	37,961	55.2	2.7
– Police	35,135	9,823	27.9	0.08	24,912	70.9	1.8
– Village watchmen	60,513	56,206	92.8	0.5	4,116 6.8	0.3	
– Public Administration	346,184	249,272	72	2.1	92,461	26.7	6.7
– Village officials and servants other than watchmen	201,860	176,178	87.2	1.5	24,954	11.8	1.8
– Professions and Liberal arts							
– Lawyers of all kinds including vakils and law agents	6,835	3,922	57.4	0.03	2,821	41.2	0.2
– Medicine, medical practitioners, dentists, occulists, vet surgeons	23,760	18,666	78.5	0.16	4,951	20.8	0.35
– Professionals & teachers of all kinds, clerks and servants connected with education	23,574	14,018	59.4	0.12	8,314	35.2	0.6
– Domestice service	421,147	222,557	31.8	1.9	190,387	45.2	13.8
– Cooks, water carriers, doorkeepers, watchmen and other indoor servants	406,181	209,242	51.5	1.8	189,248	46.5	13.7
– Private grooms, coachmen, dogboys, etc.	14,966	13,315	89	0.11	1,139	7.6	0.08

Scurce: *Census of India* (1911), Vol. XIX, Part II, pp. 261–64.

Appendix 6

Literacy by religion: State summary

	Total	*Literate*	*Illiterate*	*Literacy in English*	*Literacy in Urdu*
All religions	14,436,148	595,633 4.1%	13,840,515 95.8%	72,846 0.5%	192,039 1.3%
Hindus (Brahmanic)	9,699,615	391,317 4%	9,308,298 95.9%	38,872 0.4%	78,418 0.8%
Adi-Hindus	2,473,230	13,880 0.5%	2,459,350 99.4%	1,174 0.04%	2,472 0.09%
Muslims	1,534,666	158,859 10.4%	1,375,807 89.6%	19,275 1.2%	104,980 6.8%

Source: *Census of India* (1931), Vol. XXIII, Part II, pp. 188–89

Appendix 7

State population classified according to size of rural and urban centres (Total State population (1931): 14,436,148)

		Percentage
Under 500 inhabitants	2,851,391	19.8
500–1000 "	3,819,128	26.4
1000–2000 "	3,843,747	26.6
2000–5000 "	2,440,955	16.9
5000–10000 "	422,849	2.9
10000–20000 "	343,042	2.4
20000–50000 "	186,023	1.3
50000–100000 "	62,119	0.4
100000 and over	446,894	3.1

Source: *Census of India* (1931), Vol. XXIII, Part II, p. 8

Appendix 8

Population in Hyderabad city and district headquarters (1931)

Place		*Population*
Hyderabad city	:	466,894
Warangal	:	62,119
Karimnagar	:	10,903
Adilabad	:	8,096
Medak	:	11,156
Nizamabad	:	18,809
Mahbubnagar	:	13,300
Nalgonda	:	9,711
Aurangabad	:	29,288
Nander	:	26,992
Bhir	:	14,840
Parbhani	:	16,830
Gulbarga	:	41,083
Osmanabad	:	11,266
Raichur	:	27,910
Bidar	:	15,198

Note: In some districts, the headquarter town was not the most populous—other centres, however, rarely exceeded 30,000.

Source: *Census of India* (1931), Vol. XXIII, Part II, pp. 258–59

Appendix 9

Memorandum
submitted by
The Working Committee
of the
Majlis-i-Ittihad-ul-Muslimeen
to
the President of the Executive Council
H.E.H. the Nizam's Government
on
1 August 1940

1. The war has brought the Muslims of Hyderabad face to face with problems of such grave import to the present and future of the State, that the Working Committee of the Majlis-i-Ittihad-ul-Muslimeen, the sole organisation of the Muslims of the State, desires to apprise the Government of Hyderabad of the views the Majlis holds in respect of those problems, and expects that Government will be pleased to give them their earnest consideration.
2. Government are aware that the Hyderabadis believe firmly that the grim struggle that Britain is carrying on against Hitlerism is as much in the interests of her freedom as of every one of her allies, and that on that account, they feel happy in the knowledge that Hyderabad has unstintedly placed whatever military and other resources it has at the disposal of her Ally. But their regret is that the help offered is not commensurate with her prestige.
3. It is true that Hyderabad is under no treaty obligation to restrict its military strength or her right to manufacture war material of any description. But the fact is that owing to the easy-going policy pursued in the past, Hyderabad has had to depend more and more for her defence on her British Ally, so much so, that to-day she is mortified to witness but a tiny army going out to the front in the name of Hyderabad, equipped, strange as it might seem, with material supplied entirely from abroad. The Majlis therefore is strongly of the opinion that it was high time that the military policy of the State was overhauled, and a number of State-owned factories set up immediately to supply to the State forces all the material they would need for modern warfare. For, unless this is done, it is obvious that the people of the State will not be in a position to make the maximum effort to throw every ounce of their energy into the fight or to participate in the war to the extent of their desire. The Majlis is further of opinion that all the financial help the Government and the people are capable of giving towards the prosecution of the War should hereafter be utilized in augmenting the State military forces and in the maintenance of the proposed war factories within the State.
4. Apart from providing men for extra army and hands for war factories, the Majlis-i-Ittihad-ul-Muslimeen is prepared even to supply the nesessary [*sic*] number of volunteers from amongst its own members not merely to maintain peace and order in the country, but also to serve as a war depot for the army in the field. The Majlis begs to make it clear that the Muslims of Hyderabad are anxious to make every sacrifices [*sic*] in their power to rehabilitate the military strength of this Muslim State in a way that might enable it to fulfil efficiently all its military obligations

to its great Ally at this hour, as well as to preserve peace in the land in times of internal disorder.

5. Another subject of no less importance engaging the thought of the Majlis is that of the sovereignty and integrity of the State. Hyderabad has been an independent sovereign State since 1724, when Nizam-ul-Mulk Asif Jah I declared his independence in the South. It is in that capacity that the sovereigns of Hyderabad had come to the rescue of Britain in the hours of her need, and formed an alliance with her. There is nothing in the treaties entred [*sic*] into between the contracting parties which reduces Hyderabad to the position it is reduced to at this moment, so derogatory to her prestige and so harmful to her integrity. The thought that the State should have reached this stage through the agency of a friendly power whom Hyderabad had always succoured in the past is indeed very painful to the present generation who cannot reconcile themselves to the inheritance left to them by the past, and who are anxious to see Hyderabad rejuvenated and free to enter upon a new life unencumbered by arbitrary conventions.
6. The march of events in British India should make the State authorities seriously think. The political status of that part of the country is undergoing a violent transformation, and it is soon to assume independence in terms at least of the Statute of Westminster. When England is going to that length in her treatment of British India which has persistently thwarted her rule over it, the least that a faithfuly Ally, such as Hyderabad, should expect from her is to be left alone to carve out her destiny on her own lines, and be free to live in friendly association with her neighbours, the coming Dominion Government.
7. It may be called to mind that Hyderabad's [*sic*] relationship with British India is governed by specific treaties entered into with the British Government. These treaties, which mainly relate to the defence and foreign commerce of Hyderabad, will in the opinion of the Majlis not hold good when Britain ceases to be directly responsible for the fulfilment of her own part of the contract. In other words, Hyderabad will return to the *status quo ante*, the moment British India assumes Dominion Status, and will be free to enter into fresh treaties with the Dominion Authority.
8. Such being the inevitable implication of the grant of Dominion Status to British India, the primary question which should engage the attention of the Government of Hyderabad is the return to the State of all the territories ceded to the British Government for the upkeep of the subsidiary force stationed for her purposes within the State. The circumstances of the State which obliged her in the past to hand over to the British Government the administration of certain parts of her territory in the interests of her defence do not exist at the present moment, as Hyderabad can administer them herself and maintain an extra army out of its revenue such as she might need now or in the days to come. Majlis therefore expect the Government to move in the matter full in advance of the grant of the Dominion Status to British India, and affect a satisfactory settlement.
9. To sum up:
   (A) The Majlis is anxious to see;
      (1) the augmentation of the State Forces, and
      (2) the establishment of War Factories,

   in order that Hyderabad might effectively help Britain in the War and be a source of strength to herself when that is over.

(B) The Majlis is equally anxious to urge upon the Government of Hyderabad the imperative need in the event of the grant of the Dominion Status to British India of negotiating with the British Government for:

(1) The withdrawal of the subsidiary forces stationed within the Dominions by the British Government and the consequent retrocession of the ceded territories

(2) A re-orientation of Hyderabad's alliance with Britain calculated to reassure herself of her independence, and integrity both internally and externally.

10. In conclusion the Majlis begs to emphasize that with the great political consciousness awakened among the Muslims of Hyderabad, as well as among the Muslims of the rest of India, who all look upon the Throne of Hyderabad as an embodiment of their political status in the country, and are intent on upholding its independence and integrity even to their utmost, it becomes the sacred duty of the present Government of Hyderabad to make every effort and every sacrifice to let the State regain her rightful position in India in the manner outlined above, and fervently prays that God might vouchsafe to them wisdom and strength to work zelously [*sic*] for the consummation which we all have in view. If, however, the opportunity is missed, or the Government fail to rise equal to the occasion, the Majlis is in no doubt that all the responsibility for the inevitable reaction among the Muslims of Hyderabad and of the rest of India will be laid at their door.

BAHADUR YAR JUNG,
President

HYDERABAD DECCAN
Jamadius Sani, 1359 H
1st August 1940

Appendix 10

The Last Draft Agreement between Hyderabad and India
Governor-General to Nizam

15 June 1948

It gives me very great pleasure to be able to write to you at last when the long and protracted negotiations between Hyderabad and India are drawing to their successful conclusion because Mr Laik Ali is taking down to you today the final papers which have been agreed up here, subject to Your Exalted Highness' ratification.

The situation has not been easy to hold here, and we are all agreed that the matter must be concluded today, Tuesday, without fail in the interest of good feeling and friendship.

I have only five days left in India, and they are very fully taken up indeed with meetings and farewell lunches, receptions and dinners. It will be difficult to find the time to come to Hyderabad, but I am so anxious to be able to express the goodwill of India in person to you before I go, that I will somehow find the time to get down even if it is only for two or three hours, for I should much like to renew our acquaintance before I leave.

I. (DRAFT) LETTER

From Prime Minister of India.
To Prime Minister of Hyderabad.

In connexion with the Agreement which has today been signed between the Government of India and the Government of Hyderabad, I have to state that:

(1) The Government of India will do their utmost to ensure that the flow of goods of all kinds at present held up between Hyderabad and India is resumed and maintained.

(2) The Government of India wish to collaborate on a joint basis in the economic development of Hyderabad, and to afford all facilities to this end.

(3) It is not the policy of the Government of India that there should be any unfair discrimination against Hyderabad in the working of the new Agreement.

(4) In the course of discussions the representatives of the Hyderabad Government raised the questions of:

 (a) Hyderabad having freedom of control over overseas export and import trade under its own authority, the transactions thereof being conducted through the Reserve Bank of India.

 (b) The question of Hyderabad becoming a member of some international organizations, i.e., Food Organization, Postal Union, Health Organization, International Monetary Fund.

These questions cannot be considered in isolation and have to be decided with reference to the constitution of these organizations and the Government of India's relations with them. The Government of India, however, is prepared to consider these matters sympathetically with the representatives of the Hyderabad Government.

II. (DRAFT) FIRMAN

(1) After protracted discussions between my Government and the Government of India, I am now in a position to announce the lines of my policy. I am most anxious to put an end to the uncertainties which prevail as to the nature of the relationship between Hyderabad and the Dominion of India. The views of the Dominion of India have been made clear to me and mine are well known to them. I have now decided to consult the will of my people upon the question whether Hyderabad should accede to India. I shall, therefore, take a plebiscite in Hyderabad on the basis of adult franchise. In order to ensure that the plebiscite is fairly conducted, I shall arrange for it to be held under the supervision of some impartial and independent body. I shall accept the result of the plebiscite whatever it may be.

(2) But I am satisfied that more is required than the holding of a plebiscite, in order to restore confidence and tranquillity. I have, therefore, decided to instruct my Government to proceed in accordance with the following principles. In doing so, they will appreciate that the re-establishment of goodwill between India and Hyderabad is the object of my policy and is of greater importance than the terms of any agreement which may be reached between India and Hyderabad in accordance with these principles.

- (i) It is my intention to introduce responsible Government in Hyderabad and to that end to establish a Constituent Assembly early in 1949.
- (ii) In the meantime, there should be a reconstitution of my Government as a result of which a new Interim Government will be formed, in consultation with the leaders of the major political parties.
- (iii) My Government has been able to reach agreement with the Government of India on the nature of the interim relationship between Hyderabad and India pending the holding of the plebiscite. This agreement, which involves some modification of the existing Standstill Agreement, has been embodied in a separate document signed by my Prime Minister.

III. (DRAFT) HEADS OF AGREEMENT

(1) The Nizam's Government agree that they will, on the request of the Government of India, pass legislation similar to the legislation of the Government of India on any matter enumerated in the schedule attached.

(2) If the Nizam's Government fail to pass the required legislation with due despatch, the Nizam himself will forthwith pass the necessary ordinance under his own powers.

Defence

(3) The Dominion Government agree to fix the strength of the Hyderabad Army at a figure not exceeding an overall strength of 20,000. The provisions of the Indian State Forces Scheme of 1939 will apply *mutatis mutandis* to these Forces and the Government of India undertake to supply arms, ammunition and equipment on the scale and conditions laid down in the Scheme. The Government of India will have the right of periodical inspection and the Nizam's Government will also give all facilities in regard to such inspection and furnish such information and returns as they may be requested to do by the Government of India from time to time.

(4) The Nizam's Government agree to limit their irregular forces to 8,000 in addition to ceremonial and household guards. The Hyderabad Government agree that all other formations of a military character shall be disbanded. Progressive steps will be taken for the disbandment of the *Razakars* within three months; rallies, parades, demonstrations and speeches by *Razakars* will cease forthwith.

(5) It is agreed that the Government of India will not station their armed forces inside Hyderabad State; if in an emergency the Government of India wish to station their forces inside the State for the period of a state of emergency declared in India by the Government of India Act, 1935, this will be agreed to by the Hyderabad Government. In such an event it is further agreed that the Government of India will be willing to pay to Hyderabad nominal compensation for the occupation of buildings in the State and for other services.

(6) If in any emergency as above, Indian Army units are stationed in the Hyderabad State they will be subject to the appropriate Dominion law governing the armed forces of the Dominion.

External Relations

(7) It is agreed that Hyderabad's external relations with any foreign country shall be conducted by the Government of India. Hyderabad will, however, have freedom to establish trade agencies in order to build up commercial, fiscal and economic relations with other countries; but these agencies will work under the general supervision of and in the closest co-operation with the Government of India. Hyderabad will not have any political relations with any country.

Continuance of Existing Agreements and Arrangements

(8) Subject to the above paragraphs, the existing agreements and administrative arrangements in regard to matters of common concern shall continue and will be given effect to by both sides. The said agreements and arrangements shall not cease to have effect on 29 November 1948, as

was provided in Article 5 of the Standstill Agreement of 29 November 1947.

....	....
On behalf of the Government of India	On behalf of the Government of Hyderabad

SCHEDULE

(a) Defence

(1) Any armed forces raised or maintained by Hyderabad whether within or without the State.
(2) Naval, military and air force works.
(3) Arms; firearms; ammunition.
(4) Explosives.

(b) External Affairs

(1) External affairs; the implementing of treaties and agreements with other countries; extradition.
(2) Admission into, and emigration and expulsion from, Hyderabad, including in relation thereto the regulation of the movements in Hyderabad of persons who are not Hyderabad subjects.
(3) Naturalization.

(c) Communications

(1) Posts and telegraphs, including telephones, wireless, broadcasting and other like forms of communication.
(2) Railways of the Government of India in the State; the regulation of the Nizam's State Railways in respect of safety, maximum and minimum rates and fares, station and service terminal charges, interchange of traffic and the responsibility of railway administrations as carriers of goods and passengers; the regulation of other railways in the State in respect of safety and the responsibility of the administrations of such railways as carriers of goods and passengers.
(3) Aircraft and air navigation; regulation and organization of air traffic and aerodromes; provisions for the safety of aircraft; carriage of passengers and goods by air.

Source: Poplai 1959, pp. 321–25

Appendix 11

'The Finish Up of Hyderabad'

What could not be accomplished in 1935 has now become a fait accompli by just a stroke of Sardar Patel's pen and under the stress of high sounding national slogans. To those who can dive beneath the surbace [*sic*] and know the reality of things, it is quite obvious that what is being witnessed in Hyderabad today has not been arrived at by any evolutionary process or by any progressive forces having been brought into action by any individuals, group, or parties within. It is simply a thrust from above with no support or prop of an indigenous make. The Indian Union Authorities have become ipso facto-masters of the situation and Hyderabad is no more the self-contained unit that it was. The foundations of the change were laid when J.N. Choudhry set his foot on Hyderabad soil as the Commander of the Indian Union Forces. The Nizam's rule as the Sovereign of Hyderabad ended that day and the rule of the Indian Union began and from that time onwards, the work of the Interim Administration has been to weaken the vestiges of Independence that were left and erect a structure of its own pattern on materials imported from outside. Hence we see a curious spectacle of Hyderabad being emasculated and the Hyderabad Administration that was working out by its own intelligentia [*sic*] destroyed by the representatives of the Indian Union with the full knowledge, connivance, and backing of the Indian Union Government and we are being asked in the name of the nation to submit to the rule of outsiders, whose only qualification is that they have been sent by a Government, whose head for the time being, happen to be Pandit Nehru and Sardar Vallabhbhai Patel. In the name of nationalism, democratic freedom, oneness of the whole Indian Continent, we have been made to pay this price. We have been disarmed from the Nizam downwards to the petty official and the general populace, all have been humiliated, one Department after another, has been done away with, under some pretext or another. Apart from suspensions, dismissals, retirements forced and voluntary of the officers and men of almost all the Departments, there has been an attempt to retrech [*sic*] in the name of efficiency, and because to aid the new personnel, instead of the Urdu knowing staff, persons with knowledge of English and the regional languages were required. And, further for the sake of the supposed maintenance of law and order, these people are given a blank cheque to arrest and detail [*sic*] any person or persons they desire without question from any quarter and to keep them without trial for months together, without the least compunction. It is humiliating to admit and it is a tragic fact for me to have to state that for the last year and a half since the Indian Union has tried to play the saviour's part, nothing has been left undone by the representatives of the Indian Union and by the Prime Minister and the Deputy Prime Minister to add insult to injury. The Hyderabadis who had looked up to the Leaders of the Indian Union had never expected that asking for help would ultimately mean the wiping away of Hyderabad in its entirely [*sic*]. Impelled by patriotism, with a view to maintain national solidarity and assert the national outlook they had wished and desired aid. They relied on the truth, honesty, patriotism of the people who had come into power and their assurances and never thought that they would play them—their own countrymen—false. Now they realize they were mistaken in thinking the Indian Union Leaders to be angels and not mere men as found elsewhere in the world, and that they would not be trampled underfoot by the very persons whose help they sought. And this is tragic, not only because in the process what was worthy of preservation and maintenance, both in substance and form has been destroyed, but because at every stage of the destructive process people who have brought about this destruction have done it all wantonly and without any regard to even ordinary decency. Everything has been topsy-turvied and intense suffering caused to people for which no parallel can be found anywhere in the world.

Despite the double doses of mastery, Hyderabad never lagged behind any part of India in the struggle for Independence and assertion of nationalistic ideals. Both the people and the administration were progressive-minded and yet it is the irony of the situation, that she is obliged to go down the steps humiliated and forlorn with frustration and disappointment facing her at every turn.

It was all done in a very crude manner. With the defeatist mentality on the part of the Muslims and with the Hindus already prepossessed in their favour on account of their suffering and frustration in the previous regime, it was considered perhaps, that there would be no opposition from any quarter, to anything that might be desired to be done and if per chance, there hadpaned [*sic*] to be any, the alternate use of the sweet words of Pandit Jawaharlal Nehru and Sardar Vallabhbhai Patel and the big stick would whittle it away. It was forgotten that facts would remain what they are, in spite of contrary versions of it and propaganda and would be a perennial reminder of what in reality is. For instance, this is a fact that till only a short while ago, prolonged negotiations have been conducted and the Indian Union was prepared to recognise the independent status of Hyderabad, which goes to prove that if, as it has unfortunately happened, Hyderabad had not declined the offer made by the Indian Union and created rifts amongst its own people, the position would not have been what we are witnessing today. But simply because events have taken a different course and the Indian Union has come to dominate the situation, it does not mean that the whole structure of the Hyderabad Administration was bad or not progressive enough to satisfy the aspirations of the people, or the tendencies of the times, and that on this assumption, the whole structure could be brought down by just a stroke of the pen, arbitrarily, as if none counted here and the people of Hyderabad were only a set of barbarians, kept in control by a few brilgands [*sic*] where there was neither culture, nor law nor order.

This would be big pill to swallow.

The truth however is, it was alright till the recent tussle. Hyderabad was a self-contained independent unit and its system of administration was well organised. The departments of the State function in quite a regular constitutional manner under the supervision of able efficient officers, who were imbued with the spirit of service. Everybody worked with an eye on improvement. Non-officials sat on the statutory Departmental Committees.

We had a Legislature, almost a fully elected body, an able and independent judiciary and the various Departments of the Police, Army, Communications, Railways, Irrigation and P.W.D., Excise, Revenue, Forests, Agriculture, Trade, Commerce and Industries, Co-operative Society and Banking, Finance, Education and a host of others, our own Mint and Currency, Accounts and Audit, and a network of Schools, Colleges and an University, which is the only one of its kind in India.

Despite the seemingly arbitrary nature of the sovereign, the administration was constitutional in character. The Nizam though personally was inclined that way and some times did behave in that manner causing injury to the interests of the State and individuals, supposed in the older sense to be the arbitrary ruler of the State, answerable to none, whose word was law, generally speaking, acted as the Constitutional Head of the State on the advice and counsel of his Cabinet which worked in a team spirit with joint responsibility.

The Sovereign's rights were exercised through only constituted bodies like the Judicial Committee and Atiyat Committee to serve as correctives in cases of injustice in judicial and revenue cases. With all this, the level of taxation was less, & the state had considerable reserves, nearly 80 crores!

It is only people who are lost with all this, to a sense of shame and self-respect and have become a lifeless mass of matter that can take pride in and gloat over the change that has brought them down from independence to subordination. If at all, it can be a matter of pleasure or profit only to those who have come to dominate. To those who have come to occupy a lesser position, who have been dominated, it can only mean humiliation, disaster and ruin. Of course, in this unnatural situation, there would be people of the dominated region to whom the reminants [*sic*] of the table may be given, for them to work as enthusiastic supporters of the new set up, so that they may play the part of appeasors against the antipathy that may naturally be felt by the people in having lost all their prestige, position and power and all that they had stood for and valued.

The immensity of the change that has been so ruthlessly brought about can be known from the mention of this bare fact, that since April 1, for which preparations have been going on ever since the Military administration started functioning on behalf of the Indian Union, the following Departments have ceased to be the Departments of H.E.H. the Nizam's Government or of the State of Hyderabad, and have been taken over in the direct charge and control of the Indian Union at the Centre over which neither the people nor the Government of Hyderabad have any sort of control in any shape or form, and for the working of which no aid, counsel or advice is sought from the people of the soil:

(1) The Army (2) Transport (3) Railway (4) Communications
(5) Aerodromes (6) Income-Tax (7) Post Office (8) Currency
(9) Mint (10) Audit (11) Radio-Broadcasting, Wireless installation, etc
(12) Telephones & Telegraphs

High Court has become a subordinate branch of the Indian Union Judiciary, with all that it implies. The Judicial Committee is finished.

What remains is just an unimportant, insignificant part of the administration, all the key Departments having been taken over.

The substance is gone, the shadow remains.

The part that gives dignity, prestige, power, predominance goes to the Indian Union. What is left is just there to keep the things going.

It is obvious henceforth the doors of these Departments would be closed up for the sons of the soil, who are already at a discount and opened wide for any Tom, Dick and Harry to come from outside and boss the show. The sons of the soil would have to play a second fiddle and sing to the tune of their new masters.

Another outstanding feature of the present change-over and the integration of the State with the Indian Union would be that instead of having its own income on the lines evolved hitherto, Hyderabad would have to depend on Subventions and doles from the Centre for carrying on, not only the day to day administration but also for its nation-building activities, if they happen to entertain such ambitions in future, but this being not a very trustworthy factor on account of not only the unsatisfactory conditions at the Centre, but also because there would be the psychological tendencies of the Ministers in charge of the Central establishment, there would be the need felt for immediately raising up revenue by resort to new taxation, which in other words, means that the people of Hyderabad would have to pay twenty times over according to the Indian Union standard.

The thing is so apparent that mere reference is enough to show how over burdened the people would be, with new taxation. This is the price we are paying for being recognised as a citizen of the Indian Union, in the new context. As a citizen of Hyderabad before, we hadn't to pay so heavily.

15th Oct. 1950

Source: Kishen 1952

Appendix 12

Political Crises [in Andhra Pradesh] Since 1956

Since its emergence in 1956, Andhra Pradesh was rocked by two serious violent political agitations in 1969 and 1972. The agitation of 1969 was popularly known as the 'Telengana agitation' and that of 1972 the 'Jai Andhra movement'. The Telengana agitation arose because of the feeling of the people of Telangana that the 'Gentlemen's Agreement' which had facilitated the formation of Andhra Pradesh had been violated by the leaders of the Andhra region. Some of their grievances were real but many of them were imaginary. Leaders of the Andhra region did nothing to remove the suspicions of the Telangana people. The 'Gentlemen's Agreement' was violated in 1956 itself when Sanjiva Reddy, the first Chief Minister of Andhra Pradesh, refused to name any Telangana minister as Deputy Chief Minister saying that the Deputy Chief Ministership is like the unwanted sixth finger of the hand. But when D. Sanjivayya became the Chief Minister, he named K.V. Ranga Reddi from Telangana as the Deputy Chief Minister.

The influx of the people of coastal Andhra into the city of Hyderabad had also created its own social tensions. Slowly the discontent spread to government officials and unemployed youth who got the feeling that they were neglected and exploited by the domineering officials of the Andhra region and the enterprising people of the Andhra area. In order to draw the attention of the government to their grievances, the people of Telangana began to organise protest meetings and observed 'Telangana Safeguard Day' as early as 10 July 1968. In the meeting held at Hyderabad city, Mahadev Singh, a prominent trade union leader, cautioned the government that if it failed to redress the grievances of the Telangana people, the latter may be compelled to demand a separation from Andhra Pradesh [*The Deccan Chronicle*, 7 July 1968].

One of the main causes of the dissatisfaction of the people of Telengana was that a large number of persons from the Andhra region were appointed to the posts in Telangana on the ground that qualified personnel from Telangana were not available. The acute discontent of the Telangana people manifested itself when a student of Khammam went on hunger strike in January 1969. By the middle of January the agitation spread to other districts. Students were in the vanguard of the movement. One section of the students wanted full implementation of safeguards while the other section demanded the separation of Telangana from Andhra Pradesh. The non-gazetted officers of Telangana joined the issue by threatening to launch direct action if the 6000 Andhras occupying Telangana posts were not repatriated to the Andhra region [*The Hindu*, 12 January 1969].

The agitation took a violent turn in certain areas. To prevent the spread of violence to other areas, the five opposition parties in the State legislature—Bharatiya Jana Sangh, Muslim Majlis, Samyukta Socialist Party (SSP), CPI and CPI(M)—warned the Chief Minister not to ignore the students in the struggle for the implementation of safeguards.

The Chief Minister convened a meeting of all the political party leaders of the State on 18 and 19 January 1969. The two important issues agitating the minds of the Telangana people, namely, the repatriation of Andhra officials from Telangana and the quantum of surplus revenues of Telangana were discussed at the meeting. The Chief Minister announced that all the party leaders agreed to the suggestion of appointing a senior officer to decide the quantum of Telangana surpluses. He also announced that Andhra officials in Telengana would be provided jobs in Andhra area. He appealed to the striking students to call off their agitation and restore a peaceful and cordial atmosphere in the State.

Unfortunately, on 20 January the police opened fire on the agitating students in Hyderabad. This incident provoked the students, and the appeal of the Chief Minister fell on deaf ears. When the students continued their agitation, government extended the 'Sankranti' vacation. On 22 January the agitation took an extremely violent turn all over Telangana resulting in heavy damage to railways and other public property. Communications were also disrupted. In order to defuse the situation the government announced that the Andhra personnel in Telangana would be repatriated by 28 February 1969. It also announced that the Comptroller and Auditor-General of India agreed to depute a senior official within a week to work out Telangana surpluses. These announcements did not quell the agitation.

While the people of both the regions were emotionally upset a rumour was spread that an Andhra official (a deputy surveyor) was burnt alive by Telangana agitators at Nalgonda. This led to a counter agitation in the Andhra area.

Meanwhile, the Telangana Student Action Committee on 9 March 1969 called upon the students of Telangana to abstain from classes till separate Telangana was formed. K.V. Ranga Reddi, former Deputy Chief Minister (under Sanjivayya's Ministry), joined the students stating that 'without separate statehood the injustices to Telangana cannot be rectified and prevented' [*Times of India*, 10 March 1969].

While the political situation was taking this turn for the worse, the Supreme Court granted an injunction on the Andhra Government order under which the non-mulkis employed in Telangana were to be relieved by 28 February 1969. Subsequently, the order was declared to be *ultra vires* of the Constitution [*The Hindu*, 29 March 1969].

The agitation took a new turn when eight Congress legislators from Telangana supported the students and demanded the formation of separate Telangana.

The Prime Minister who was watching the situation closely announced in the Lok Sabha on 11 April 1969 an Eight-Point Plan to resolve the tangle. Among them were (1) the appointment of a high powered committee under a retired or serving Supreme Court judge to determine the Telangana surpluses; (2) the constitution of a Telangana Development Committee with the Chief Minister as Chairman to review periodically the Telangana development programme; (3) the constitution of a committee of jurists to examine the feasibility of providing safeguards to Telangana people in matters of public employment, etc.

The Prime Minister's Eight-Point Plan did not find favour among the dissident Congress legislators and non-Congress parties. The student agitation now passed into the hands of politicians. These politicians formed themselves into what was called the Telangana Praja Samiti and began to organise the movement in a planned manner.

The Praja Samiti called upon the people to observe 1 May 1969 as the 'Telangana Demand Day'. The observance of Demand Day led to violence in some parts of Telangana and the police had to open fire. The Prime Minister invited Praja Samiti leaders for talks in New Delhi but 14 out of 15 invitees declined the invitation stating that 'the creation of a separate Telangana State is not negotiable'. The stalemate continued and on 4 June 1969, the situation in Hyderabad city became so violent that a 33-hour curfew was imposed. Many members of the Congress demanded the resignation of Chief Minister Brahmananda Reddi.

Meanwhile the Praja Samiti leader, Dr Chenna Reddy, and the students' agitation leader, Mallikarjun, were arrested but agitation continued even in October 1969. The dissident Congress legislators also felt that they could not oust Brahmananda Reddi. The Chief Minister was able to stick on to his position due to the firm support he received from the Prime Minister. She refused to be cowed down by agitations and violence. Slowly normalcy returned to the State. Brahmananda Reddi expanded his cabinet and made J.V. Narasinga Rao as the Deputy Chief Minister.

In September 1971, Brahmananda Reddi resigned his position to make room for a Telanganite to become the Chief Minister. On 25 September 1971, P.V. Narasimha Rao from Telangana was elected the leader of the Congress Legislature Party. The Telangana Praja Samiti members rejoined the Congress. A few days later P.V. Narasimha Rao formed his ministry. Andhra Pradesh got its first Chief Minister from Telangana.

During the Chief Ministership of P.V. Narasimha Rao, Andhra Pradesh witnessed another agitation—this time in the Andhra region. The agitation was the outcome of the Supreme Court's judgement on what was known as the 'mulki issue'.[1]

---

1. In 1919, the Nizam of Hyderabad issued a firman laying down that only mulkis were eligible for public appointments in the State. A mulki was one who was born in the State of Hyderabad or had resided there continuously for fifteen years and had given an affidavit that he had abandoned the idea of returning to his native place.

After the trifurcation of the Hyderabad State in 1956, the mulki rules continued to be in force in the Telangana region. As a result the people of the Andhra region found it difficult to enter into government service in Telangana. Some of the Andhra employees challenged the validity of these rules in the Andhra Pradesh High Court. On 14 February 1972, a full bench of five judges by a four–one majority held that mulki rules were not valid and operative after the formation of Andhra Pradesh [*Asian Recorder* 1972, p. 10663].

The High Court judgement came as a rude shock to the people of Telangana who continued to insist on the enforcement of the mulki rules. The Chief Minister, P.V. Narasimha Rao, in order to placate his fellow Telanganites, announced that the government would prefer an appeal to the Supreme Court against the ruling of the Andhra Pradesh High Court. Further, he announced that the government would go ahead with the regionalisation of services and take steps to safeguard the 'legitimate interests' of the Telangana people in the matter of employment opportunities [*ibid.*, p. 10664].

On 3 October 1972, the Supreme Court gave its verdict on the mulki rules stating that they were valid and were in force. This judgement created a great political crisis in the State. The people of the Andhra region felt that they were reduced to the status of second class citizens even in their own State capital. They felt that the only way to safeguard their dignity and honour was to sever their connections with Telangana.

The Government of India realising the intensity of the feelings of the people of both the Andhra and Telangana regions on the issue of mulki rules tried to arrive at a compromise by continuing the mulki rules in the twin cities of Hyderabad and Secunderabad until the end of 1977 and in the rest of the Telangana region until the end of 1980. Parliament passed a bill to this effect on 23 December 1972. The people of the Andhra region who wanted the immediate abolition of the mulki rules were taken aback. They felt that their dignity and honour could be safeguarded only in a separate State of their own. In order to achieve a separate Andhra State they started an agitation popularly known as the 'Jai Andhra Movement.'

On 31 December 1972, the Congressmen of the Andhra region met at a convention at Tirupati which was attended by a large number of Andhra Congress members of the Legislative Assembly, Council, and presidents of Zilla Parishads. B.V. Subba Reddi, who earlier resigned his position of Deputy Chief Minister of Andhra Pradesh, presided over it. The convention issued a call to the people of Andhra to 'paralyse the State Administration' by refusing to pay taxes to the government and by defying the prohibitory orders. To implement the decisions of the convention an 'Action Committee' was constituted with Subba Reddi as the President. The committee included six of the eight ministers who had resigned earlier over the mulki rules issue [*Asian Recorder* 1973, p. 11210].

The Jai Andhra agitation spread like wild fire and paralysed the administration. As a result, President's rule was enforced in the State on 18 January 1973. The State Assembly was kept in suspended animation. Meanwhile, the Congressmen of Telangana met at a convention on 21 January 1973 at Hyderabad under the Presidentship of Dr M. Chenna Reddy and resolved to fight for a separate Telangana State and converted itself into a 'Congress Forum for Telangana' [*ibid.* p. 11227].

Although the Jai Andhra movement enjoyed popular support it did not make much headway due to the lack of proper leadership. The one leader, Kakani Venkataratnam, who could have provided effective leadership died of a heart attack on 25 December 1972. B.V. Subba Reddi, partly due to his ill-health, could not rise to the occasion. The movement degenerated into a vulgar agitation. The Communist Party of India which was opposed to bifurcation of the State began to organise rallies to counteract the separatist movements in both regions.

Though the agitation continued for more than two months it failed to make any impact on the Central Government. The Andhra Congress leaders became restless and they met at Chittoor on 18 March 1973 to decide the future course of action. The meeting ended in confusion, as a large number of students forced the Congressmen to quit the Congress Party and form a regional party [*ibid.*, p. 11342].

After the imposition of the President's rule, the advisers to the Governor, especially H.C. Sarin began to act with vigour, even though the administration was almost paralysed due to the strike of the non-gazetted government officers [NGOs] of the Andhra region. On 25 March 1973, the NGOs called off their 108-day-old strike.

Meanwhile another twist was given to the agitation when the Andhra Pradesh High Court declared on 17 February 1973 that only people from outside the State who came to Telangana and settled there were mulkis and not those who were born and brought up in Telengana [*ibid.*, 11343]. As a result of this decision, the Telangana people lost even the small benefits they got by the Mulki Rules Act passed by Parliament in December 1972. Here it may be stated that when the Supreme Court upheld the validity of the mulki rules it did not express its opinion on the 'definition and applicability of the Mulki Rules' because these points were not raised before the Court. As a result a number of cases came before the Andhra Pradesh High Court challenging the definition of the word 'Mulki' in December 1972. On 11 July 1973, the Andhra Pradesh High Court gave another verdict that the mulki rules (both old and new) applied only for initial recruitment and not for subsequent stages of promotion, seniority, reversion, retrenchment or ousting from service whether temporary or permanent [*ibid.*, p. 11458].

As a result of these developments and gradual loss of public support, the Congressmen both in Andhra and Telangana regions their demand for a bifurcation of the State was futile. They wanted a face-saving formula to call off the agitation. Sensing the changed mood of the people the Central Government held discussions with the leaders of both the regions and evolved what is known as the 'Six-Point formula' [*ibid.*, p. 11705–06] which was endorsed by the leaders of both the regions, with minor changes. The six points were:

1. Abolition of Mulki Rules and Telengana Regional Committee.
2. Local candidates were to be preferred for direct recruitment to non-gazetted posts and Assistant Surgeons.
3. Creation of a high-powered tribunal to deal with the grievances of the government employees.
4. Creation of a State level planning board with sub-committees for different backward areas.
5. Establishment of a Central University at Hyderabad to augment education facilities, and
6. Amendment of the Constitution to implement the above five points.

The Andhra Congress Action Committee accepted all six points on 1 October 1973, and gave up its ten-month-old agitation for the creation of a separate Andhra State. On 18 December 1973, the Lok Sabha passed the Constitution (33rd Amendment) Bill to give effect to the Six-Point formula. The voting was 311 for and 8 against. Simultaneously, the mulki rules which had become 'unnecessary' with the acceptance of the Six-Point formula were repealed [*ibid.* pp. 11800–01]. The Telangana Regional Committee which had been constituted in 1958 was abolished from 1 January 1974 under a Presidential order. On 10 December 1973, President's rule in Andhra Pradesh was revoked and a 15-member popular ministry was formed with J. Vengal Rao as the Chief Minister. With the advent of the popular ministry, normalcy returned and the State enjoyed political stability.

In the general elections to the Andhra Pradesh Legislative Assembly held in February 1978, the Congress Party led by Indira Gandhi, former Prime Minister of India, swept the polls by winning 175 out of the 294 seats. Dr M. Chenna Reddy, who had spearheaded the movement for a separate Telangana State in 1969, was elected Leader of the Congress (I) Legislative Party. Dr Reddy, known for his dynamism and administrative skill, became the sixth Chief Minister of Andhra Pradesh and assumed office on 6 March 1978. He announced that the bifurcation of the State is no longer an issue and that he wants the continuance of Andhra Pradesh as an integrated State.

Economic activity in Andhra Pradesh has picked up and the State had in the recent past made great progress in agricultural development. Activity on the industrial front is also picking up. In an atmosphere of political stability and dedicated work there is no doubt that Andhra Pradesh will make progress in all directions and become one of the leading States of the country.

Source. P.R. Rao 1978, pp. 119–26

Bibliography

PRIMARY SOURCES

A. Unpublished

Andhra Pradesh State Archives, Hyderabad (Tarnaka and Secretariat Repositories)

HEH, the Nizam's Government. Relevant Files in English from:

Political Secretariat (1846–1945)
Finance Secretariat (1859–1947)
Constitutional Affairs Secretariat (1928–1950)
Education Secretariat (1863–1952)
Local Government Secretariat (1939–1948)
Labour and Social Welfare Secretariat (1945–1948)
Rural Reconstruction Secretariat (1937–1948)
Industries Department (1889–1950)
Judicial, Police and General Department (1937–1952)
Political Department (1921–1935)
Home and Health Department (1937–1956)

National Archives of India, New Delhi

Government of India

Foreign and Political Department

Reforms Branch (1920–1922, 1928–1934)
Aitchison Treaties Branch (1933)
Special Branch (1930–1931)
Internal Branch (1882–1936)
[In 1937 the Foreign and Political Department was bifurcated into separate departments: (1) External Affairs Department (2) Political Department. The functions of the Internal Branch were placed under the latter.]
General Section (1937–1949)
Political Section (1939–1946)

Federation Branch (1935–1936)
Special Representatives' (SR) Papers (1936–1937)
Internal Section A (1937–1949)
Hyderabad Branch (1947–1954)
Crown Representative Records, Hyderabad (1930–1947)

Nehru Memorial Museum and Library, New Delhi

1. *General (All India)*

Papers of the All-India Congress Committee (1917–1969)
Papers of the All-India States' People's Conference (1937–1949)
Papers of the All-India Hindu Mahasabha

2. *AICC files and correspondence dealing specifically with Indian States or Hyderabad*

Correspondence relating to the policy of Congress towards the Indian States (1934–1935)
Correspondence between Nehru and Hardikar regarding Congress attitude towards the Indian States (1936)
Pamphlets on the 'Popular Rule' Movement in the Indian States and resistance against State's repression (1937–39)
Correspondence with Andhra PCC (1937–38)
General Correspondence files on contact with Muslim masses (1937–1941)
Files on political movements in Indian States (1937–38).
Files on democratic movements in Indian States (1938)
Files on landlords' movements (1938)
Files on Muslim satyagrahis (1940)
File on Affairs of the Indian States, mainly Hyderabad and Datia-Jhansi, and the movements for popular rule (1946)
Leaflets, resolutions and letters to Nehru regarding misgovernment in Indian States, correspondence of Nehru with the States (1947)
Leaflets dealing with dissensions in Hyderabad State Congress, correspondence with Swami Ramanand Tirtha (1948)
Correspondence with Dr Pattabhi Sitaramayya on the question of the merger of the Indian States with the Union (1948–50)

3. *Private papers*

Sir Harcourt Butler
Ms Padmaja Naidu
Sir Mirza Ismail

India Office Library and Records, London

1. *India Office Records, Political and Secret Department*

Political and Secret Separate (or Subject) Files 1902–1931, L/P & S/10
Political and Secret Annual Files, 1912–1930, L/P & S/11
Political (Internal) / Indian States Files and Collections, 1931–1950, L/P & S/13

2. *Crown Representative Records, Foreign and Political Department, Government of India.*

Accounts (A), R/1/1
Internal A (Int. A or I.A.), 1885–1946, R/1/20
Political (P), 1922–1947, R/1/29
Special (S), 1930–1931, R/1/32
Miscellaneous, 1897–1947, R/1/36
Hyderabad Residency Records (1853–1947), R/2 Temp.

3. *Private Papers*

Keyes Collection, MSS. Eur. F131
Lothian Collection, MSS. Eur. F144
Tasker Collection, MSS. Eur. D798

B. Published

I. Official Publications

HEH the Nizam's Government

1. *Reports*

Administration Report of the District Jails (1901–1941)
Agricultural Statistics, Estimates of Area and Yield of Principal Crops in Hyderabad State (1925–1945)
Annual Administrative Report of the Agriculture Department of HEH the Nizam's Government (1914–1939)
Annual Report on the Administration of the Customs Department (1919–1946)
Annual Report on the Administration of the District Police (1893–1945)
Economic Investigations in the Hyderabad State (1929–1930)
Financial Statistics (1891–1949)
Report on Public Instruction (1816–1941)
Report on the Administration (annually, 1912–1948)
Report on the Administration of Hyderabad City Police (1935–1949)
Report on the Administration of Justice, HEH the Nizam's Government (1918–1940)
Report on the Working of the Department under the Director General of Revenue (1915–1927)
Some Economic Facts and Figures of HEH the Nizam's Dominions (Hyderabad-Deccan, Government Central Press, 1937)
Statistical Abstracts (1912–1934)
Statistical Year Books (1935–1945)
Trade Statistics (1933–1947)
Triennial Report ... on the Administration of the Department of Industries and Commerce (1918–1945)

2. *Government Publications (pre- and post-intervention)*

Memorandum of Treaties Obligations of British Crown in respect of 'Defence', 1930 (Hyderabad, Government Central Press)
Agricultural Indebtedness, 1937 by S.M. Barucha (Hyderabad, Government Central Press)

Report of the Reforms Committee 1938. 1347F [Aiyangar Committee] and *Appendix No. 1. Statistics* (Hyderabad Government Central Press, 1938)
New Hyderabad (fortnightly, 1947)
Hyderabad Government Bulletin on Economic Affairs [monthly], (1947–1952)
Agricultural Statistics, 1949 by Mazhar Husain (Hyderabad, Government Press)
Hyderabad Reborn. First Six Months of Freedom, 1949 (18 September 1948–17 March 1949) (Hyderabad, Director of Information, June)
Communist Crimes in Hyderabad, 1950 (Hyderabad, Government Press)
Rural Economic Enquiries in the Hyderabad State, 1949–51, 1951 by S.K. Iyengar (Hyderabad, Government Press)
A Review of Hyderabad Finance, 1951 introduced by C.V.S. Rao (Hyderabad, Government Press)
Our Legislators. Who's Who in the Hyderabad Legislative Assembly and Hyderabad Representatives in Parliament, 1952 (Hyderabad, Government Press)
History and Legend in Hyderabad, 1953 (Hyderabad, Department of Information and Public Relations, December)
Report of the Anti-Corruption Enquiry Commission, 1954 (Hyderabad, Government Press)

Government of India

1. *Published Records*

Census of India 1901, Hyderabad State (Vol. XXII)
" 1911, " (Vol. XIX)
" 1921, " (Vol. XXI)
" 1931, " (Vol. XXIII)
" 1931, Mysore (Vol. XXV)
" 1931, Travancore (Vol. XXVIII)
" 1931, Baroda (Vol. XIX)
" 1941, Hyderabad State (Vol. XXI) [Part I]
" 1951, " (Vol. IX)

2. *Government Publications*

Imperial Gazetteer of India. Provincial Series, Hyderabad State, 1909 (Calcutta, Superintendent of Government Printing)
India in 1920, 1921 L.F. Rushbrook Williams (Calcutta, Superintendent of Government Printing)
India in 1922–23, 1923 by L.F. Rushbrook Williams (Calcutta, Superintendent of Government Printing)
India in 1925–26, 1926 by J. Coatman (Calcutta, Government of India, Central Publication Branch)
Proceedings of the Conference of Ruling Princes held at Delhi on the 30 October 1916, 5 November 1917, 20 January 1919 and 3 November 1919 (Confidential), 1929 (Delhi, Government of India Press)
A Collection of Treaties, Engagements and Sanads relating to India and Neighbouring Countries (Vol. IX), 1929 by C.V. Aitchison (Calcutta, Government Central Press)
White Paper on Hyderabad, 1948 (Delhi, Manager of Publications)
White Paper on Indian States, 1950 (Delhi, Ministry of States Publication)

Report of the States Reorganisation Commission, 1965 (Delhi, Government of India Press)

Report of the Economy Committee, 1950 (Delhi, Government of India Central Press)

Report of the Linguistic Provinces Commission, 1947–48 (or *Dhar Commission Report*)

Government of Great Britain Publications

Indian Statutory Commission. Interim Report, 1929 (London, HMSO)

Report of the Indian States Committee 1928–29, 1929 (London, HMSO)

Andhra Pradesh Government Publications

The Freedom Struggle in Hyderabad, Vol. I (1800–1857), 1966 (Hyderabad, Andhra Pradesh State Committee)

The Freedom Struggle in Hyderabad State (A Connected Account) Vol. III (1885–1920), 1957 (Hyderabad, published by the Hyderabad State Committee appointed for the Compilation of a History of the Freedom Movement in Hyderabad)

The Freedom Struggle in Hyderabad State, Vol. IV (1921–1947), 1966, N. Ramesan (ed.) (Hyderabad, the Andhra Pradesh State Committee appointed for the Compilation of a History of the Freedom Struggle in Andhra Pradesh)

Brief History of Andhra Pradesh, 1972, Mohd. A. Waheed Khan (Hyderabad, Tarnaka State Archives, Government of Andhra Pradesh)

Highlights of the Freedom Movement in Andhra Pradesh, 1972, S. Regani (Hyderabad, Government of Andhra Pradesh)

History of Medieval Deccan (1295–1724), 1973, 2 Vols (Hyderabad, Published under the authority of the Government of Andhra Pradesh)

Finances and Fiscal Policies of Hyderabad State (1900–1956), 1973, B.K. Narayan (Hyderabad, Government of Andhra Pradesh)

Mysore Government Publications

History of Freedom Movement in Karnataka, 1962–64, 2 Vols, M.V. Krishna Rao and G.S. Halappa (eds.) (Bangalore, Government of Mysore)

Karnataka through the Ages, 1968 (Government of Mysore Publication)

United Nations Security Council. Official Records, 1948.

II. Miscellaneous Publications

Hyderabad Directory and Diary 1936 (Secunderabad, West End Craft)

A Peep into Hyderabad, 1938 (Bombay, AISPC, 25 September)

What Are the Indian States? 1949 (Allahabad, AISPC)

The Hyderabad Problem: The Next Step, 1948 (Hyderabad, Socialist Party Publication)

Land Reforms in India, 1954 (New Delhi, AICC)

The Telengana Movement. An Investigative Focus, 1969 (Hyderabad, University and College Teachers' Convention, May 20)

III. Collected Documents

Banerjee, A.C. (ed.), 1961 and 1965, *Indian Constitutional Documents 1757–1947*, Vol. III (1917–1935) and Vol. IV (1935–1947) (Calcutta, A. Mukherjee & Co.)

Lele, P.R., V. Alva, and B.R. Dhurandhar (eds.), 1945, *March of Events (Being the Case of the Indian National Congress) 1942–1945* (Bombay, Bombay Provincial Congress Committee)

Pandey, B.N. (ed.), 1979, *The Indian Nationalist Movement, 1885–1947. Select Documents* (London, Macmillan)

Poplai, S.L. (ed.), 1959, *India 1947–50. Volume I, Internal Affairs* (London, OUP)

Rao, M.B. (ed.), 1976, *Documents of the History of the Communist Party of India, Volume VII, 1943–1950* (New Delhi, People's Publishing House)

Sharma, J.S. (ed.), 1965, *India's Struggle for Freedom. Select Documents and Sources, Volume III* (Delhi, S. Chand & Co.)

Zaidi, A.M. (ed.), 1978, *Evolution of Muslim Political Thought in India, Volume V* (New Delhi, S. Chand & Co.)

IV. Speeches and Correspondence

Gandhi, M.K., 1965, *The Collected Works of Mahatma Gandhi, Volume XVIII* (Delhi, Government of India Publications Division)

Mountbatten, L. (Earl), 1949, *Time Only to Look Forward. Speeches of Rear Admiral the Earl Mountbatten of Burma as Viceroy of India and Governor-General of the Dominion of India, 1947–48* (London, Nicholas Kaye)

Nehru, J., 1958, *Jawaharlal Nehru's Speeches*, Vol. I (September 1946 to May 1949) and Vol. II (1949–1953), (New Delhi, Government of India Publications Division)

Patel, V.J., 1949, *On Indian Problems* (New Delhi, Government of India, Ministry of Information and Broadcasting)

———, 1967, *For a United India. Speeches of Sardar Patel, 1947–1950*, D. Das (ed.) (New Delhi, Government of India, Ministry of Information and Broadcasting)

———, 1973, *Sardar Patel's Correspondence, 1945–1950*, Vols III, VI, VII, D. Das (ed.) (Ahmedabad, Navajivan Publishing House)

V. Newspapers, Periodicals

Asiatic Review (Asian Review)

Bombay Chronicle 7 July 1939

Dawn (Karachi) 1944–1948

Deccan Times (Madras) 1 February 1942

Economic and Political Weekly

Express (Bihar) 8 February 1923

Journal of Asian Studies

Keesing's Contemporary Archives

Kisan Mitra (Patna) No. 7, 1923

Madras Mail (13 May 1939)

Quarterly Review

The Hindu (Madras) 2 October 1940, 9 February 1942

The Indian Annual Register (Calcutta) 1919–1947

The New Statesman and Nation

The States' People's Magazine (Bombay) 17 October 1940

The Times (London), Cuttings, 1938–1956

The Times of India (Bombay) 1938–1948

SECONDARY SOURCES

A. General Works

Abbasayulu, Y. B., 1978, *Scheduled Caste Elite: A Study of Scheduled Caste Elite in Andhra Pradesh* (Hyderabad, Department of Sociology, Osmania University)

Aggarwala, R.N., 1965, *National Movement and Constitutional Development of India* (Delhi, Metropolitan Book Co. (P) Ltd.)

Alam, M.S., 1965, *Hyderabad–Secunderabad (Twin Cities): A Study in Urban Geography* (Bombay, Allied Publishers Private Ltd.)

Ali, C.M., 1967, *The Emergence of Pakistan* (New York, Columbia University Press)

Allana, G., 1969, *Our Freedom Fighters (1562–1947) Twenty-one Great Lives* (Karachi, Paradise Subscription Agency)

Ashton, S.R., 1982, *British Policy Towards the Indian States 1905–1939* (London, Curzon Press)

Aziz, K.K., 1972, *The Khilafat Movement 1915–1933. A Documentary Record* (Karachi, Pak Publishers Ltd.)

Baker, D.E.U., 1979, *Changing Political Leadership in an Indian Province: The Central Provinces and Berar 1919–1939* (Delhi, OUP)

Barrier, N.G. (ed.), 1976, *Roots of Communal Politics* (INC Cawnpore Riots Enquiry Committee) (New Delhi, Arnold-Heinemann)

Bawa, V.K. (ed.), 1975, *Aspects of Deccan History* (Hyderabad, Institute of Asian Studies)

Berlin, Isaiah, 1954, *Historical Inevitability* (London, OUP)

Birkenhead, F.W. F-S. (Earl), 1969, *Walter Monckton: The Life of Viscount Monckton of Brenchley* (London, Weidenfeld & Nicolson)

Bolton, G., 1937, *Peasant and Prince* (London, George Routledge & Sons Ltd.)

Bondurant, J.V., 1958, *Regionalism versus Provincialism: A Study in Problems of Indian Nationality* (Berkeley, University of California, Indian Press Digests Monograph Series. Number 4. December)

Brass, P.R. and M.F. Franda, (eds), 1973, *Radical Politics in South Asia* (Cambridge, Mass., MIT Press)

Brecher, M., 1959, *Nehru. A Political Biography* (London, OUP)

Campbell, C.A., 1898, *Glimpses of the Nizam's Dominions* (Philadelphia, Historical Publishing Co.)

Campbell-Johnson, A., 1951, *Mission with Mountbatten* (Bombay, Jaico Publishing House)

Chaturvedi, B.N., 1956, *Hyderabad State. A Regional and Economic Survey* (Hyderabad, Hyderabad Geography Association)

Chintamani, L., 1973, *Caste Dynamics in Village India* (Bombay, Nachiketa Publications Ltd.)

Chopra, P.N. (ed.), 1976, *Quit India Movement*. British Secret Report (Faridabad, Thomson Press (India) Ltd.)

Chopra, P.N., T.K. Ravindran and N. Subrahmanian, 1979, *History of South India. Vol. III. Modern Period* (New Delhi, S. Chand & Co. Ltd.)

Chudgar, P.L., 1929, *Indian Princes under British Protection* (London, Williams & Norgate Ltd.)

Communist Crimes in Hyderabad, 1950 (Hyderabad)
Copland, I.F.S., 1982, *The British Raj and the Indian Princes 1857–1930* (Bombay, Orient Longman)
Corfield, C. (Sir), 1975, *The Princely India I Knew. From Reading to Mountbatten* (Madras, Indo-British Historical Society)
Coupland, R., 1942, *The Indian Problem, 1833–1935* (London, OUP)
———, 1943, *Indian Politics, 1936–1942* (London, OUP)
———, 1943, *The Future of India* (London, OUP)
Darda, R.S., 1971, *From Feudalism to Democracy* (New Delhi, S. Chand & Co.)
Das, M.N., 1982, *Partition and Independence of India. Inside Story of the Mountbatten Days* (New Delhi, Vision Books Pvt. Ltd.)
Dass, D.J., 1969, *Maharaja. Lives and Loves and Intrigues of Indian Princes* (Bombay, Allied Publishers)
Davies, C., 1959, *An Historical Atlas of the Indian Peninsula* (Madras, OUP)
de Montmorency, G. (Sir), 1942, *The Indian States and Federation* (Cambridge, CUP)
Desai, A.R. (ed.), 1979, *Peasant Struggle in India* (Bombay, OUP)
Dhanagare, D.N., 1983, *Peasant Movements in India 1920–1950* (Delhi, OUP)
Dixit, P., 1974, *Communalism - A Struggle for Power* (New Delhi, Orient Longman)
Edwardes, M., 1963, *The Last Years of British India* (London, Cassell & Co. Ltd.)
Fatesinhrao, G., 1970, *The Role and Responsibilities of the Princes in Republican India* (Ahmedabad, Harold Laski Institute of Political Science)
Fitze, K., 1956, *Twilight of the Maharajas* (London, John Murray)
Forbes, R., 1939, *India of the Princes* (London, The Right Book Club)
Fraser, A.H.L. (Sir), 1911, *Among Indian Rajahs and Ryots* (London, Seeley)
Fraser, H. (Captain), 1865, *Our Faithful Ally, the Nizam: Being an Historical Sketch of Events ...* (London, Smith, Elder & Co.)
Frykenberg, R.E. (ed.), 1969, *Land Control and Social Structure in Indian History* (Madison, The University of Wisconsin Press)
Furneaux, R., 1963, *Massacre at Amritsar* (London, George Allen & Unwin)
Ghose, S., 1973, *Socialism, Democracy and Nationalism in India* (Bombay, Allied Publishers)
Gopal, R., 1959, *Indian Muslims. A Political History (1858–1947)* (Bombay, Asia Publishing House)
Gour, R.V., C. Chaudhary, G. Hyder, and B.S. Paranjpe, 1973, *Glorious Telangana Armed Struggle* (New Delhi, Communist Party Publication)
Gribble, J.D.B., 1896, *A History of the Deccan*, Vol I (London, Luzac & Co.)
———, 1924, *A History of the Deccan*, Vol II (London, Luzac & Co.)
Griffiths, P. (Sir), 1965, *Modern India* (London, Ernst Benn Ltd.)
Hakim, K.A., 1951, *Islam and Communism* (Lahore, Institute of Islamic Culture)
Hale, H.W., 1974, *Political Trouble in India 1917–1937* (Allahabad, Chugh Publications)
Handa, R.L., 1968, *History of Freedom Struggle in Princely States* (New Delhi, Central News Agency)
Hardy, P., 1971, *Partners in Freedom—and True Muslims: The Political Thought of Some Muslim Scholars in British India 1912–1947* (Lund, Student Litteratur)
———, 1972, *The Muslims of British India* (Cambridge, University Press)
Harrison, S.S., 1960, *India: The Most Dangerous Decades* (Princeton, Princeton University Press)
Hasan, S.A., 1935, *Whither Hyderabad?* (Madras, B.N. Press)

Hendre, S.L., 1975, *Undeclared Civil War in India* (Bombay, Supraja Prakashan)
Hodson, H.V., 1969, *The Great Divide. Britain–India–Pakistan* (London, Hutchinson of London)
Hughes, T.P., 1973, *A Dictionary of Islam* (Delhi, Oriental Publishers)
Husain, Y., 1963, *The First Nizam. The Life and Times of Nizamu 'l-Mulk Asaf Jah I* (London, Asia Publishing House)
Hutchins, F.G., 1973, *India's Revolution. Gandhi and the Quit India Movement* (Cambridge, Harvard University Press)
Ikram, S.M., 1964, *Muslim Civilization in India* (New York, Columbia University Press)
Ismail, M. (Sir), 1954, *My Public Life. Recollections and Reflections* (London, George Allen & Unwin Ltd.)
Jeffrey, R. (ed.), 1978, *People, Princes and Paramount Power* (Delhi, OUP)
Kabadi, W.P., 1935, *Indian Who's Who* (Bombay, Popular Printing Press)
Karaka, D.F., 1955, *Fabulous Mogul. Nizam VII of Hyderabad* (London, Derek Verschoyle)
Kautsky, J.H., 1956, *Moscow and the Communist Party of India* (New York, Wiley)
Khan, A.A., 1942, *The Founder of Pakistan. Through Trial to Triumph* (Published by the author. Printed Cambridge, W. Heffer & Sons Ltd. Preface dated 15 September)
Khan, M.F., 1935, *A History of Administrative Reforms in Hyderabad State* (Secunderabad, New Hyderabad Press)
Khan, S.A., 1959, *Brief Thanksgiving* (Bombay, Asia Publishing House)
Khusro, A.M., 1958, *Economic and Social Effects of Jagirdari Abolition and Land Reforms in Hyderabad* (Hyderabad, Department of Publications and University Press, Osmania University)
Kishen, S.C., 1952, *Forty Five Years a Rebel* (Hyderabad, Deccan Printing Press Ltd.)
Kistaiah, M., 1977, *Sub-Regionalism in India. A Study of Elite Reaction Towards the Six Point Formula for Andhra Pradesh* (Hyderabad, Book Links Corporation)
Kothari, R. (ed.), 1970, *Caste in Indian Politics* (Hyderabad, Orient Longman)
Kulkarni, V., 1944, *The Future of Indian States* (Bombay, Thacker & Co Ltd.)
Kumar, D. (ed.), 1983, *The Cambridge Economic History of India, Vol. 2: c. 1757 – c. 1970* (Cambridge, University Press)
Kumar, R. (ed.), 1971, *Essays on Gandhian Politics. The Rowlatt Satyagraha of 1919* (Oxford, Clarendon Press)
Laik, A. (Mir), 1962, *Tragedy of Hyderabad* (Karachi, Pakistan Co-operative Book Society Ltd.)
Leach, E. and S.N. Mukherjee (eds), 1970, *Elites in South Asia* (Cambridge, CUP)
Lee-Warner, W. (Sir), 1910, *The Native States of India* (London, Macmillan & Co. Ltd.)
Leonard, K., 1978b, *Social History of an Indian Caste: The Kayasths of Hyderabad* (Berkeley, University of California Press)
Limaye, M., 1951, *Communist Party. Facts and Fiction* (Hyderabad, Chetana Prakashan Ltd.)
Lord, J., 1973, *The Maharajahs* (London, Hutchinson of London)
Lothian, A. (Sir), 1951, *Kingdoms of Yesterday* (London, John Murray)
Low, D.A. (ed.), 1977, *Congress and the Raj: Facets of the Indian Struggle 1917–47* (London, Heinemann)

———, 1968, *Soundings in Modern South Asian History* (London, Weidenfeld & Nicolson)

Lynton, H.R. and M. Rajan, 1974, *The Days of the Beloved* (Berkeley, University of California Press)

Macmunn, G., 1936, *The Indian States and Princes* (London, Jarrolds Ltd.)

Majumdar, R.C. (ed.), 1969, *The History and Culture of the Indian People, Vol. XI: Struggle for Freedom* (Bombay, Bharatiya Vidya Bhavan)

Malleson, G.B., 1875, *An Historical Sketch of the Native States of India* (London, Longman, Green & Co.)

Manor, J., *Political Identity in South Asia* (London, SOAS Publication)

———, 1977, *Political Change in an Indian State, Mysore 1917–1955* (New Delhi, Manohar Book Service)

Masani, M.R., 1954, *The Communist Party of India. A Short History* (London, Derek Verschoyle)

Mathur, Y.B., 1972, *Muslims and Changing India* (New Delhi, Trimurti Publications Private Ltd.)

———, 1979, *Quit India Movement* (Delhi, Pragati Publications)

Mehrota, N.C., 1978, *Lohia, A Study* (Delhi, Atma Ram & Sons)

Menon, K.P.S., 1965, *Many Worlds* (London, OUP)

Menon, V.P., 1957, *The Transfer of Power in India* (Calcutta, Orient Longman)

———, 1961, *The Story of the Integration of the Indian States* (Calcutta, Orient Longman)

Minault, G., 1982, *The Khilafat Movement. Religious Symbolism and Political Mobilization in India* (Delhi, OUP)

Mirza, F., 1976, *Pre and Post Police Action Days in the Erstwhile Hyderabad State, What I Saw, Felt and Did* (Saifabad, Hyderabad, Paramount Press)

Mohanty, M., 1977, *Revolutionary Violence. A Study of the Maoist Movement in India* (New Delhi, Sterling Publishers Pvt. Ltd.)

Montagu, E.S., 1930, *An Indian Diary* (London, Heinemann)

Moore, B., 1969, *The Social Origins of Dictatorship and Democracy* (Harmondsworth, Middlesex, Penguin Books Ltd.)

Moore, R.J., 1979, *Churchill, Cripps and India 1939–45* (Oxford, Clarendon Press)

Mosley, L., 1961, *The Last Days of the British Raj* (London, Weidenfeld & Nicolson)

Muhammad, S., 1973, *Khaksar Movement in India* (Meerut, Meenakshi Prakashan)

Mukherjee, H. and U. Mukherjee, 1958, *India's Fight for Freedom or the Swadeshi Movement* (Calcutta, Firma K.L. Mukhopadyay)

Munshi, K.M., 1940, *I Follow the Mahatma* (Bombay, Allied Publishers)

———, 1957, *The End of An Era. Hyderabad Memories* (Bombay, Bharatiya Vidya Bhavan)

Muthanna, I.M., 1980, *History of Modern Karnataka* (New Delhi, Sterling Publishers Pvt. Ltd.)

Nanda, B.R., 1958, *Mahatma Gandhi: A Biography* (London, George Allen & Unwin)

Narayan, B.K., 1960, *Agricultural Development in Hyderabad State 1900–1956. A Study in Economic History* (Secunderabad, Keshar Prakashan)

Narayana Rao, K.V., 1973, *The Emergence of Andhra Pradesh* (Bombay, Popular Prakashan)

Narendra, Pt., 1975, *Arya Samaj in Hyderabad* (Arya Samaj Foundation Centenary Publication) (Delhi, Janshakti Mudran Yantrayalaya)

Nehru, J., 1960, *The Discovery of India* (London, Meridian Books Ltd.)

Nevett, A., 1954, *India Going Red?* (Poona, Indian Institute of Social Order)

Nicholson, A.P., 1930, *Scraps of Paper. India's Broken Treaties, Her Princes and the Problem* (London, Ernest Benn Ltd.)

Norman, D., 1965, *Nehru, The First Sixty Years. Vol. II* (London, The Bodley Head Ltd.)

Overstreet, G.D. and M. Windmiller, 1959, *Communism in India* (Berkeley, University of California Press)

Padmasha, Dr., 1980, *Indian National Congress and the Muslims 1928–1947* (New Delhi, Rajesh Publications)

Pal, B.C., 1954, *Swadeshi and Swaraj (The Rise of New Patriotism)* (Calcutta, Yugayatri Prakashak Ltd.)

Panikkar, K.M., 1942, *Indian States* (London, OUP)

Pavier, B., 1981, *The Telangana Movement 1944–51* (New Delhi, Vikas Publications)

Phadnis, U., 1968, *Towards the Integration of Indian States 1919–1947* (London, Asia Publishing House)

Philips, C.H. and M.D. Wainright, 1970, *The Partition of India. Policies and Perspectives 1935–1947* (Cambridge, MIT Press)

Poplai, S.L. (ed.), 1959, *Select Documents on Asian Affairs: India 1947–50, Volume I, Internal Affairs* (London, OUP)

Pradhan, B., 1973, *The Socialist Thought of Jawaharlal Nehru* (Gurgaon, The Academic Press)

Prasad, R., 1984, *The Asif Jahs of Hyderabad. Their Rise and Decline* (New Delhi, Vikas Publishing House)

Pyarelal, 1958, *Mahatma Gandhi. The Last Phase. Vol. II* (Ahmedabad, Navajivan Publishing House)

Qureshi, A.I., 1947, *The Economic Development of Hyderabad State. Vol. I: Rural Economy* (Bombay, Orient Longman)

Qureshi, I.H., 1974, *Ulema in Politics. A Study relating to the Political Activities of the Ulema in the South-Asian Subcontinent for 1556 to 1947* (Karachi, Ma'aref Ltd.)

Raghavendra Rao, D., 1926, *Misrule of the Nizam* (Madras, Swarajya Press)

Rajagopalachari, C., 1944, *The Way Out* (London, OUP)

Rajshekar Shetty, V.T., 1978, *Dalit Movement in Karnataka* (Madras, Christian Literature Society)

Ram, M., 1969, *Indian Communism: Split Within A Split* (New Delhi, Vikas Publications)

Ramesan, N. (ed.), 1966, *The Freedom Struggle in Hyderabad State, Vol. IV (1921–1947)*, (Hyderabad, the Andhra Pradesh State Committee appointed for the Compilation of History of the Freedom Struggle in Andhra Pradesh)

Ramusack, B.N., 1978, *The Princes of India in the Twilight of Empire: Dissolution of a Patron- Client System, 1914–1939* (Columbus, Ohio State University Press)

Ranadive, R.K., 1950, *Legal Rights of Indian States and of their Subjects* (Baroda, Good Companion)

Ranga, N.G., 1949, *Kisans and Communists* (Bombay, Pratibha Publications)

———, 1949, *Revolutionary Peasants* (New Delhi, Amrit Book Co.)

Rangaswami, V., 1981, *The Story of Integration. A New Interpretation* (New Delhi, Manohar Publications)

Rao, C.R., 1972, *The Historic Telangana Struggle* (New Delhi, Communist Party of India)

Rao, G.R.S., 1975, *Regionalism in India. A Case Study of Telangana Issue* (New Delhi, The Institute of Constitutional and Parliamentary Studies, S. Chand & Co. (Pvt) Ltd.)

Rao, K.V.N., 1973, *The Emergence of Andhra Pradesh* (Bombay, Popular Prakashan)

Rao, P.R., 1978, *History of Modern Andhra* (New Delhi, Sterling Publishers Pvt. Ltd.)

Rao, V.V. and V.R. Rao, 1949, *India's Police Action against Hyderabad* (Gadwal, C. Mallikarjuna Rao)

Ray, M.K., 1981, *Princely States and the Paramount Power 1858–1876* (New Delhi, Rajesh Publications)

Ray, S., 1979, *Freedom Movement and Indian Muslims* (New Delhi, People's Publishing House)

Raza Khan, M., 1969, *What Price Freedom* (Madras, Published by the author)

Reddy, R.G. and B.A.V. Sharma (eds.), 1979, *State Government and Politics: Andhra Pradesh* (New Delhi, Sterling Publishers Pvt. Ltd.)

Russell, W., 1951, *Indian Summer* (Bombay, Thacker & Co. Ltd.)

Sadath, A.K., 1959, *Brief Thanksgiving* (Bombay, Asia Publishing House)

Sahai, G., 1947, *'42 Rebellion (An Authentic Review of the Great Upheaval of 1942)* (Delhi, Rajkamal Publications Ltd.)

Salam, A., 1941, *The How, Why and Wherefore of the "Hyderabad Struggle"* (Bombay, Published by the author)

Sardesai, G.S., 1948, *New History of the Marathas*, Vols II and III (Bombay, Phoenix Publications)

Sayeed, K. Bin, 1968, *Pakistan, the Formative Phase: 1857–1948* (London, OUP)

Sen, S.P., 1972–74, *Dictionary of National Biography* 4 vols (Calcutta, Institute of Historical Studies)

Sen, S.P. (ed.), 1977, *Historical Writings on the Nationalist Movement in India* (Calcutta, Institute of Historical Studies)

Shah, M.A., 1965, *Hyderabad–Secunderabad (Twin Cities). A Study in Urban Geography* (Bombay, Allied Publishers)

Shakir, P., 1972, *Muslims in Free India* (New Delhi, Kalamkar Prakashan Pvt. Ltd.)

———, 1973, *Secularisation of Muslim Behaviour* (Calcutta, The Minerva Associates)

———, 1974, *Muslim Attitudes. A Trend Report and Bibliography* (Aurangabad, Parimal Prakashan)

Shan, M., 1973, *Khaksar Movement in India* (Delhi, Meenakshi Prakashan3)

Sharma, B.A.V., 1980, *Political Economy of India. A Study of Land Reforms Policy in Andhra Pradesh* (New Delhi, Light and Life Publishers)

Sharma, H., 1978, *Princes and Paramountcy* (New Delhi, Arnold Heinemann Publishers (India))

Sherwani, H.K., 1974, *History of the Qutb Shahi Dynasty* (New Delhi, Munshiram Manoharlal Publishers)

———, 1973, *History of the Deccan (1295–1724)* (Hyderabad, Government of Andhra Pradesh)

Singh, L., 1970, *Political and Constitutional Developments in the Princely States of Rajasthan* (New Delhi, Jain Brothers)

Singh, R., 1936, *The Indian States Under the Government of India Act 1935* (Bombay, D.B. Taraporewala & Sons)

Sinha, V.B., 1968, *The Red Rebel in India. A Study of Communist Strategy and Tactics* (New Delhi, Associated Publishing House)

Smith, D.E. (ed.), 1966, *South Asian Politics and Religion* (Princeton, Princeton University Press)

Smith, V.A., 1958, *The Oxford History of India* (Oxford, Clarendon Press)

Smith, W.C., 1957, *Islam in Modern History* (New York, Mentor Books)

Spear, P., 1958, *India, Pakistan and the West* (London, OUP)

Sreenivasa Murthy, H.V. and R. Ramakrishnan, 1977, *A History of Karnataka from the Earliest Times to the Present Day* (New Delhi, S. Chand & Co. Ltd.)

Sundarayya, P., 1972, *Telangana People's Struggle and its Lessons* (Calcutta, Desraj Chadha on behalf of the Communist Party of India (Marxist))

Taylor, D. and M. Yapp, 1979, *Political Identity in South Asia. Collected Papers on South Asia No. 2* (London, Curzon Press, Humanities Press)

Tendulkar, D.G., 1957, *Gandhi in Champaran* (Delhi, Government of India, Information and Broadcasting)

Tirtha, R. (Swami), 1967, *Memoirs of Hyderabad Freedom Struggle* (Bombay, Popular Prakashan)

Titus, M.T., 1959, *Islam in India and Pakistan. A Religious History of Islam in India and Pakistan* (Calcutta, YMCA Publishing House)

Vadivelu, A., 1915, *The Ruling Chiefs, Nobles and Zamindars of India* (Madras, G.C. Loganadhan Bros)

Venkat Rao, P., M. Narayana Reddy, P.A. Choudary, and H.N. Kunjru, 1973, *Crisis in Andhra Pradesh. From Safeguards to Separatism* (Hyderabad, Pemmaraju Publications Pvt. Ltd.)

Venkataswamy, P.R., 1955, *Our Struggle for Emancipation*, Vol. II (Secunderabad, Universal Art Printers)

Wakefield, E. (Sir), 1966, *Past Imperative. My Life in India 1927–1947* (London, Chatto & Windus)

Washbrook, D.A., 1976, *The Emergence of Provincial Politics. The Madras Presidency 1870–1920* (Cambridge, CUP)

Yavar Jung, A., 1949, *Hyderabad in Retrospect* (Bombay, Times of India Publications)

Yazdani, Z., 1976, *Hyderabad During the Residency of Henry Russell 1811–1820. A Case Study of the Subsidiary Alliance System* (Oxford, OUP)

Zahir, A., 1945, *Life's Yesterdays. Glimpses of Sir Nizamal Jung and his Times* (Bombay, Thacker & Co. Ltd.)

Zahir, A., 1965, *Dusk and Dawn in Village India* (London, Pall Mall Press)

B. Articles

Arora, S.K., 1956, "The Reorganisation of the Indian States", *Far Eastern Survey*, Feb., Vol. XXV, No. 2, pp. 27–30.

Barr, D. (Sir), 1905, "Hyderabad, Past and Present", *The Imperial and Asiatic Quarterly Review*, Vol. XX (July-Oct.), pp. 225–43

Barton, W.P. (Sir), 1945, "Post-War Development Schemes in the States of Southern India", *Asiatic Review*, 41 (Oct.), pp. 324–27.

———, 1948, "The Deadlock in India and the Indian States", *Quarterly Review*, No. 281 (July), pp. 16–27.

———, 1947, "The Indian Princes and the Cabinet Mission", *Quarterly Review*, No. 571 (Jan.), pp. 126–38.

———, 1947, "Dark Days in India", *Quarterly Review*, No. 573, (July), pp. 366–75.

———, 1956, "Redrawing the Political Map of India", *Quarterly Review*, No. 608 (April), pp. 245–57.

Bawa, V.K., "Administrative Change under Indirect Rule. The Reforms of Salar Jang I in Hyderabad, 1853–83", Unpublished paper.

———, 1965, "Salar Jang and the Nizam's State Railways 1860–1883", *Indian Economic and Social History Review*, Vol. II (Oct.), pp. 307–40.

Bhatt, A., 1963, "Caste and Politics in Akola", *Economic Weekly*, 24 Aug., pp. 1441–46.

Biddulph, T.H.S., 1917, "The Native States of India in Relation to the Paramount Power", *Asiatic Review*, Vol. XI (Jan.–June), pp. 253–95.

Brailsford, H.N., 1931, "Princes and Peasants at the Round Table", *The Political Quarterly* (London), Vol. II, Nos. 1–4, pp. 548–63.

Chailleux, J-Y., 1975, "Les Castes Dominantes du Village de Peravali face a la Modernisation de l'Agriculture", *Purusartha, Recherche de Sciences Sociales sur l'Asie du Sud* (Paris).

Char, S.R., 1939, "Education in Hyderabad", *Modern Review* (Calcutta), 66 (Aug.), pp. 177–81.

Chenevix Trench, R. (Sir), 1937, "The Hyderabad Civil Service", *Asiatic Review*, 33 (Jan.), pp. 93–97.

Corfield, C., 1970, "Some Thoughts on British Policy and Indian States: 1935–1947" in C.H.Philips and M.D. Wainwright (eds) *The Partition of India: Policies and Perspectives 1935–1947* (Cambridge, MIT Press), pp. 527–34

Das, T., 1949, "The Status of Hyderabad During and After British Rule in India", *Modern Review*, Jan., pp. 21–30.

de la Valette, J., 1932, "Administrative Progress in Three Indian States", *Asiatic Review*, 28 (July), pp. 460–69.

Dhanagare, D.N., 1974, "Social Origins of the Peasant Insurrection in Telangana", *Contributions to Indian Sociology* (New Series), 8, pp. 109–34.

Elliott, C.M., 1974, "Decline of a Patrimonial Regime: The Telangana Rebellion in India, 1946–51", *Journal of Asian Studies*, Vol. XXXIV, No. 1 (Nov.), pp. 27–47.

Fells, H.J., 1943, "The Premier Indian State: Many-Sided Progress. An Appreciation", *Asiatic Review*, 39 (April), pp. 200–03.

Forrester, D., 1970, "Subregionalism in India: The Case of Telangana", *Pacific Affairs*, LXIII, pp. 5–21.

Gray, H., 1971, "The Demand for a Separate Telangana", *Asian Survey*, Vol. XI, pp. 465–74.

———, 1974, "The Failure of the Demand for a Separate Andhra State", *Asian Survey* (Berkeley), Vol. XIV (April), No. 4.

Harrison, S.S., 1956, "The Challenge to Indian Nationalism", *Foreign Affairs*, 34 (4) (July), pp. 620–36.

Holdworth, W. (Sir), 1930, "The Indian States and India", *Law Quarterly Review*, Vol. XLVI (Oct.), pp. 417–45.

Horace, A., 1948, "Communal Peace in India", *The New Statesman and Nation*, Vol. 36, p. 136.

Hydari, A. (Sir), 1931, "Hyderabad To-Day", *Asiatic Review*, 27 (Jan.), pp. 81–101.

———, 1963 "The Position of Indian States", *Journal of the Royal Central Asian Society*, Vol. XVIII, (first published 1931), pp. 83–94.

Khan, R., 1971, "Muslim Leadership and Electoral Politics in Hyderabad. A Pattern of Minority Articulation", *Economic and Political Weekly*, Vol. VI, Nos. 15 & 16 (April 10–17), pp. 783–94 and pp. 833–40.

———, 1948, "India's Intervention in Hyderabad", *The New Statesman and Nation*, Vol. 36, p. 229.

Lal, R., 1981, "The Problems of State Autonomy and its Emerging Trends: A Case for State Autonomy and Democratic Decentralisation", *Indian Political Science Review*, 15 (1) (Jan.), pp. 78–91.

Leonard, K., 1971, "The Hyderabad Political System and its Participants", *Journal of Asian Studies*, Vol. XXX, No. 3 (May), pp. 569–82.

———, 1978a, "Hyderabad, the Mulki–Non-Mulki Conflict" in R. Jeffrey (ed.) *People, Princes and Paramount Power* (Delhi, OUP), pp. 65–106.

Lothian, A.C. (Sir), 1952, "The Passing of the Indian States", *Quarterly Review*, No. 591 (Jan.), pp. 1–16.

———, 1952, "The Last Phase of the Indian States", *Quarterly Review*, No. 592 (April), pp. 164–75.

———, Review of V.P. Menon's "The Integration of the Indian States", *Journal of the Royal Central Asian Society*, Vol. XLIV (1957), pp. 58–62.

———, 1962, "A Neglected Aspect of Recent Indian History", *Quarterly Review*, Vol. 300, No. 634 (Oct.), pp. 392–402.

Low, D.A., 1978, "Laissez-faire and the Traditional Rulership", in R. Jeffrey (ed.) *People, Princes and Paramount Power* (Delhi, OUP)

Manor, J., 1975, "Princely Mysore before the Storm: The State-level Political System of India's Model State, 1920–1936", *Modern Asian Studies*, No. 9 (Feb.), pp. 31–58.

———, 1978, "The Demise of the Princely States: A Reassessment" in R. Jeffry (ed.) *People, Princes and Paramount Power* (Delhi, OUP), pp. 306–38.

Martin, K., 1948, "Fascism in Hyderabad", *The New Statesman and Nation* (London), Vol. 35, No. 889, pp. 230–31.

McPherson, K.I. and L. Brennan, 1967, "An Initial Survey of Source Material on India held in Western Australia", *Asia* (Journal of the Asian Studies Association, University of Western Australia), No. 1.

Meade, M.J., 1926, "Hyderabad of the Nizams", *Asiatic Review*, 22 (July), pp. 382–400.

Owen, H.F., 1968, "Towards Nationwide Agitation and Organisation: The Home Rule Leagues 1915–18", in D.A. Low (ed.) *Soundings in Modern South Asian History*. (London, Weidenfeld & Nicolson), pp.159–95.

Patterson, M.L.P., 1954, "Caste and Political Leadership in Maharashtra", *Economic and Political Weekly*, 25 Sept., pp. 1065–67.

Pickthall, M., 1936, "Hyderabad; the Heart of India", *The Geographical Magazine*, Vol. II, No. 6 (April).

Ramusack, B.N., Nov. 1958 – Aug. 1959, "Incident at Nabha. Interaction between Indian States and British Indian Politics", *Journal of Asian Studies*, Vol. XXVIII, pp. 563–77.

Regani, S., 1978, "The Social Background for the Rise of the Andhra Mahasabha Movement in Telangana", *Itihas: Journal of the Andhra Pradesh Archives*, Vol. 1 (January–July)

Reddy, R.G., 1978, "Language, Religion and Political Identity. The Case of the Majlis- Ittihad-ul-Muslimin in Andhra Pradesh, India", SOAS Publication (May).

Rice, S., 1934, "Education in Hyderabad", *Asiatic Review*, 30 (April), pp. 305–12.

Richter, W.L., 1971, "Princes in Indian Politics", *Economic and Political Weekly*, 6 (9) (Feb.), pp. 535–42.

Sayer, M.C.B., 1934, "Recent Developments in Hyderabad", *Asiatic Review*, 30 (Jan.), pp. 146–52.

Seshadri, K., 1970, "The Telengana Agitation and the Politics of Andhra Pradesh", *Indian Journal of Political Science*, XXXI, pp. 60–81.

Singh, B., 1981, "Federalism and State Autonomy in India", *Indian Journal of Political Science* (July) pp. 68–77.

Smith, W.C., 1944, "The Mughal Empire and the Middle Class: A Hypothesis", *Islamic Studies*, Vol. 18, No. 4 (Oct.)

———, 1950, "Hyderabad: Muslim Tragedy", *Middle East Journal* (Washington D.C.), No. 4 (Jan.), pp. 27–51.

Tharamangalam, J., 1981, "The Communist Movement and the Theory and Practice of Peasant Mobilization in South Asia", *Journal of Contemporary Asia*, Vol. 11, No. 4.

Townroe, B.S., 1937, "The Modernisation of Hyderabad", *Asiatic Review*, 33 (July), pp. 615–26.

———, 1938, "Cultural Development in Hyderabad", *Asiatic Review*, 34 (April), pp. 331–39.

———, 1941, "Britain's Faithful Ally in the War", *Asiatic Review*, 37 (April), pp. 271–80.

Windmiller, M., 1954, "Linguistic Regionalism in India", *Pacific Affairs*, Vol. 27, No. 4 (Dec.), pp. 291–318.

———, 1956, "The Politics of States Reorganisation in India: The Case of Bombay", *Far Eastern Survey*, Vol. XXV, No. 9 (September), pp. 129–43.

Woodruff, P., 1948, "The Wrong Kind of Hat", *The Spectator*, July 9.

Wright, T., 1963, "Revival of the Majlis Ittihad-ul-Muslimin of Hyderabad", *The Muslim World*, Vol. LIII, No. 3 (July), pp. 234–43.

C. Unpublished Theses

Bedford, I., "The Telangana Insurrection: A Study in the Cases and Development of a Communist Insurrection in Rural India, 1946–51" (Ph.D. Thesis, ANU, 1967)

Copland, I.F.S., "Imperial Authority and the Indian Princes, 1858–1921" (M.A. Thesis, University of Western Australia, 1966)

Khan, M.A., "Muslim Politics in Hyderabad" (Ph.D. Thesis, Osmania University, Hyderabad, Political Science Department, 1980)

Shukwal, B.L., "Political Geography of the Indian Republic. An Evaluation of Changing Patterns" (Ph.D. Thesis, University of Oklahoma, Political Science Department, 1969)

Tirtha, R., "Geographical Reorganisation of Indian States 1947–1960" (Ph.D. Thesis, University of North Carolina, 1961)

Wood, H.D., "The Relationship between the Indian Princely States and the Indian Central Government, 1921–1933" (Ph.D. Thesis, University of Chicago, 1951)

INTERVIEWS

(Hyderabad, January to April and October to November 1980)

Mr Jam V. Bhajjan	Mr P.V. Rama Rao
Mr Mahbub Latif	Professor Sarojini Regani
Pandit Krishna Dutt	Professor Rasheeduddin Khan
Mr (former Justice) Ekbote	Professor N.G. Ranga
Mir Akbar Ali Khan	Dr Muneer Ahmed Khan
Mr Zahir Ahmed	Dr Mohd. Ziauddin Ahmad Shikeb

Index